"Mars."

"Yes, Mars."

Frank poised the tip of his tongue between his teeth, and bit lightly. He could feel himself on the threshold of pain, and that was the closest he ever got these days to feeling anything. But to feel pride again? Achievement? To think that his son would be able to look up into the night sky and say, "There he is. That's where my father is."

Were those good enough reasons? He wouldn't be coming back: then again, he wasn't really here either. It'd be a second chance for him, too.

"Where do I sign?"

ONE WAY

S.J. MORDEN

orbit

www.orbitbooks.net

Author photograph by Simon Morden
Cover design by Lisa Marie Pompilio
Cover art by Shutterstock
Cover copyright © 2018 by Hachette Book Group, Inc.

Orbit
Hachette Book Group
1290 Avenue of the Americas
New York, NY 10104
orbitbooks.net

Simultaneously published in 2018 by Orbit in the U.S. and Gollancz in Great Britain
First U.S. Edition: April 2018

Orbit is an imprint of Hachette Book Group.
The Orbit name and logo are trademarks of Little, Brown Book Group Limited.

The publisher is not responsible for websites (or their content) that are not owned by the publisher.

The Hachette Speakers Bureau provides a wide range of authors for speaking events. To find out more, go to www.hachettespeakersbureau.com or call (866) 376-6591.

Library of Congress Control Number: 2018932592

ISBNs: 978-0-316-52218-2 (trade paperback), 978-0-316-52215-1 (ebook)

Printed in the United States of America

LSC-C

10 9 8 7 6 5 4 3 2 1

In grateful memory of Dr David W Collinson
(1927–2007)

[Internal memo: Gerardo Avila, Panopticon, to Data Resources, Panopticon, 10/2/2046]

We are seeking inmates who fit the following profile:

- serving either an indeterminate life sentence(s) or a fixed-term sentence(s) that extend beyond the inmate's natural life-span.
- has had a prolonged period (5 years +) of no contact with anyone on the outside: this includes, but is not exclusive to, family, friends, previous employers and/or employees, lawyers, journalists and authors, advocacy groups, external law enforcement, FBI, CIA, other federal organizations including immigration services.
- has professional qualifications, previous employment, or transferable skills in one of the following areas: transportation, construction (all trades), computer science/information technology, applied science, medicine, horticulture.
- is not suffering from a degenerative or chronic physical or mental condition that would cause death or debilitation in the immediate (5 years +) future.
- is currently in reasonable physical and mental health, between the ages of 21 and 60.

Please compile a list of potential candidates and send them to me by Friday.

Gerardo Avila,
Special Projects Coordinator, Panopticon

"Put your hands on the table."

Frank's hands were already cuffed together, joined by three steel links. His feet were also shackled. The seat he sat on was bolted to the ground, and the table in front of him was the same. The room was all wipe-clean surfaces. The smell of bleach was an alkaline sting in the back of his throat and on the lids of his eyes. It wasn't as if he could go anywhere or do anything, but he still complied with the order. Slowly, he raised his hands from his lap, feeling the drag of the metal biting into his skin, and lowered them onto the black vinyl covering of the table. There was a large hole drilled in it. Another length of chain was run through the circle made by his cuffed arms and into the hole. His guard put a padlock on it, and went to stand by the door they'd both entered through.

Frank pulled up to see how much slack he'd been given. The chain rattled and tightened. Ten, maybe eleven inches. Not enough to reach across the table. The chair didn't move. The table didn't move. He was stuck where he was for however long they wanted.

It was a change, though. Something different. To his left was a frosted window, bars on the outside, a grille on the inside. He looked up: a light, a length of fluorescent tube, humming slightly and pulsing in its wire cage. He could see the guard out of the corner of his right eye.

He waited, listening to the nearby hum and the more distant echoing sounds of doors slamming, buzzers rasping, voices shouting. These were the sounds that were most familiar to him. His own breathing. The soft scratch of his blue shirt. The creak of stress as he shifted his weight from leaning forward to sitting back.

He waited because that was all he could do, all he was allowed to do. Time passed. He became uncomfortable. He could only rest his hands on the table, and he couldn't get up and walk around. Eventually he grunted. "So why am I here?"

The guard didn't move, didn't smile. Frank didn't know him,

and wasn't sure if he was one of the regular staff anyway. The uniform was the same, but the face was unfamiliar. Frank eased forward, twisted his arms so he could put his elbows on the table, and put his weight on them. His head drooped forward. He was perpetually tired, from lights on to lights out. It wasn't an earned tiredness, a good tiredness. Having so little to do was exhausting.

Then there was the scrabble of a key at a lock, and the other door, the one facing him, that led to the free world, opened. A man in a suit came through, and without acknowledging Frank or the guard, put his briefcase on the table and pushed at the catches. The lid sprang open, and he lifted it to its fullest extent so that it formed a screen between Frank and the contents of the case.

The briefcase smelled of leather, earthy, rich in aromatic oils. The clasps and the corners were bright golden brass, polished and unscratched. They shone in the artificial light. The man pulled out a cardboard folder with Frank's name on it, shut the briefcase and transferred it to the floor. He sat down—his chair could move—and sorted through his papers. "You can go now. Thank you."

Frank wasn't going anywhere, and the guard was the only other person in the room. The guard left, locking the door behind him. It was just the two of them now. Frank leaned back again—the other man was close, too close—and tried to guess what all this was about. He hadn't had a visitor in years, hadn't wanted one, and certainly hadn't asked for this one, this man in a suit, with his tie and undone top button, his smooth, tanned skin and well-shaved cheeks, his cologne, his short, gel-spiked hair. This free man.

"Mr Franklin Kittridge?" He still hadn't looked up, hadn't looked Frank in the eye yet. He leafed through the file with Frank's name on the cover and *California Department of Corrections and Rehabilitation* stamped on it, turning the translucently thin pages covered with typeface. Paper and board. Everybody else would have used a tablet, but not the cash-starved CDCR.

"Well, if I'm not, both of us have had a wasted journey."

It wasn't much of a joke, but it seemed to break the ice, just a little, just enough for the man to raise his chin and steal a glance at Frank before looking down at the contents of the folder again.

Of course, no one had called him "Mr" Kittridge for years. Frank felt a long-dormant curiosity stir deep inside, where he'd shut it away in case it sent him mad.

"Can I get you anything?" the man asked. "Something to eat, drink?"

Frank cocked his head over his shoulder at the locked door behind him. Definitely no guard. He turned back. "You could start by telling me your name."

The man considered the request. "You can call me Mark," he said. His tell—a slight blink of his left eye—told Frank that he wasn't really a Mark.

"If we're on first-name terms, Mark, why don't you call me Frank?"

"OK, Frank." The man not called Mark closed the folder, opened it again, turned some pages. "So what are you in for, Frank?"

"I'm assuming you're not carrying that file in front of you because you're short of reading matter. I know you know what's in it. You know that I know. So while this is a pleasant change of scenery, I'm still going to ask you why you're here."

Mark finally looked up, perhaps surprised by the directness aimed at him. "You know you're going to die in here, right?" he said.

"I'm eligible for parole in eighty-five years. What do you think, Mark?" Frank twitched the corner of his mouth. That was his smile these days. "Do you reckon I'll make old bones?"

"You'd be—" Pause. "—one hundred and thirty-six. So, no. I don't think so."

"Well, dang. I was so looking forward to getting out."

"You killed a man."

"I know what I did. I know why I did it. But if you're looking

4

for contrition, maybe you should have asked for someone else."

Mark put both his hands on the file. His fingers were long, with buffed, tapered nails. They glowed as brightly as the brass furnishings on his briefcase. "I want to know what you think about the prospect of dying in jail, Frank."

After a moment's reflection, Frank concluded: "I'm not a fan. But I factored the possibility in when I pulled the trigger, and now? I don't see I have much of a choice."

Mark took one of his elegant fingers and circled it around the seven-pointed star on the cardboard file's cover. "I might be able to help you," he said. "I might be able to give you a choice."

"And how would you do that?" Frank raised his hands, and eased them down again, slowly enough for every link of the chain that bound him to the table to catch against the edge of the hole, then fall. "*Why* would you do that?"

"A private company owns this prison, and runs it on behalf of the state."

"There's a logo on everything I'm wearing. Few years back, the logo changed, but it was the same old prison walls. You're telling me a lot of things I already know, Mark. I'm still waiting for you to tell me things I don't."

"You don't want to hear me out?" said Mark. "That's OK. That's your right. But what if it's something you might be interested in?" He sat back in his chair, and examined his pampered hands.

Frank put on his compliant face again. Inside, he was mildly irritated, but no more than that. "You asked for me, remember? Not the other way around. So, this company, this Panopticon? You work for them?"

"Technically, no. But I've been authorized by their parent company to see if you'd be interested in an offer. And before I tell you what it is, I want to tell you what it isn't." He left a gap to see if Frank said anything, but that wasn't Frank's style. "This isn't a pardon. You'll remain guilty of second-degree

5

murder. This isn't commuting your sentence. You'll serve the rest of your hundred and twenty years. This isn't parole. You'll be at all times under a prison regime. Neither will you get time off for good behavior."

Frank considered what he'd heard so far. "Go on," he said. "You're really selling it to me."

"We can't give you any of those things because we're not allowed to. The State of California—the law—wouldn't permit us to cut such a deal with you. What we can offer you is a transfer."

"Panopticon have another jail somewhere else?"

Mark pursed his lips. It was the first emotional response he'd really shown. Frank thought him, despite the expensive suit, the leather briefcase and the manicured hands, or perhaps because of them, a cold fish. A dead fish, even. "In a manner of speaking."

"So why don't you just transfer me? You don't need my permission to do that."

"No, that's true enough. We need your co-operation, though."

"Do you? I'm not really getting this whole thing, and you seem a straight-up kind of guy, so why not just lay it out?"

Mark doodled with his finger on the cover of Frank's file again. "Given everything I've said, are you still in?"

"In for what? All you've told me is that I'm still going to die in jail. Does it really matter where the jail is?"

"You weren't just chosen at random, Frank. You have skills. A lot more than many—most—of the inmates incarcerated here. Skills that are going to waste. Would you like to use them again?"

"You want me to build you the prison that I'm going to die in?"

"In a manner of speaking," Mark said again.

Frank tried to sit more comfortably in his chair, but his chained hands wouldn't let him. He frowned at the pristine Mark opposite him. "And this is to save you money?"

"To save the parent company money," Mark corrected him. "Yes, that'll happen."

"Mark, I have to say I'm struggling to understand what's in this for me."

"The benefits will be: better food, better accommodation, a small team to work with, a challenging, stimulating environment, an utterly unique project, and considerable personal autonomy. It won't feel like jail. It certainly won't feel like the regime you're under now, that I can guarantee you."

"But I still wouldn't be able to leave, would I?"

"No. This would be a transaction where you'd have to remain on the site in order to help maintain it," said Mark. "That doesn't mean there wouldn't be free time for you to, how do I put it, enjoy the surrounding countryside. You'd always have to return, though. It's in a somewhat isolated position, and there's literally nowhere else to go."

"Where is this, then? The desert?"

"Initially, yes. You'll need to undergo some specialist training at a privately owned facility. Medical tests, too. If you refuse to co-operate in or fail to complete any of the tasks the company set, you'll be bounced straight back here. No appeal. No hesitation, either. Likewise, if you fail on medical grounds." Mark put his hands back flat on the folder. "Are you still interested?"

"Without committing myself, yes, sure. I'm still waiting for the sucker punch, though. Tell me there's a sucker punch."

"If you accept the conditions I've already stipulated, then I'll outline the project more explicitly."

"You're starting to sound like a lawyer."

Mark gave his tell again, and said nothing other than: "Do you accept the conditions?"

"OK."

"Yes?" He was playing games with the language, and it seemed Frank had to play along too. This was legal boilerplate, and it had suddenly become obvious that this whole conversation was being recorded.

"Yes. I accept the conditions," he intoned.

Mark took a deeper breath, and Frank felt like he'd crossed some sort of threshold, an invisible line in his life. A faint wash of sweat broke out across his face, and his hands grew slick.

"Your training will take almost a year. There's a specific deadline we can't go beyond, and either you're ready, or you're not. The training facility is, yes, in the desert. There's some very specialized equipment you'll need to be totally familiar with, and your background in construction and project management will hopefully mean you won't have a problem with that. You'll be introduced to the rest of your team, and you'll learn to work together, learn to trust each other, learn to rely on each other."

"How many?"

"Eight altogether."

"And are they in the same position I am?"

"Seven of them, yes. One company employee will be on site to oversee the project."

"Will the others be ex-prisoners too?"

"Serving prisoners."

"And they have to stick around after we've finished this building work, too?"

"Yes."

Frank looked over to the bright window, then back. "I'd better like them, then."

"That's not the company's concern. Merely whether you can work with them."

"So where is this place, that you want to send seven cons to, to build you a prison and then stay there for the rest of their lives?"

"Mars."

Frank turned to the window again, and stared at the blurred parallel lines of the bars that divided the outside from the inside. There were seven of them, maybe six inches apart. They'd be iron, swollen with rust, peeling and flaking paint pushing off their surfaces like sloughing skin. "You did say Mars, right? As in the planet?"

"Yes. The planet Mars."

Frank thought about it a little longer. "You have got to be fucking kidding me."

"I assure you the offer is most genuine."

"You want a bunch of cons to go to Mars? And build a prison? And then stay there?"

Mark wiped his hands on his suit trousers, a luxury that Frank didn't have. "It's not designated as a prison, but as a federal scientific facility. Let me explain, in order. A convict crew will be sent to Mars. Once there, they will construct a base from prefabricated parts and make it habitable. When the facility is finished, the crew will continue to live on Mars and serve out the rest of their sentences, helping to maintain the facility, expanding it as and when required, and assisting visiting civilian scientists in their work. That the facility will also be your prison is, I suppose, a somewhat technical detail. But as I've already explained, there'll be nowhere to escape to."

Frank nodded slowly to himself as he digested the information.

"You haven't rejected the idea out of hand," said Mark.

"Just give me a minute. I'm thinking."

Once the insanity had been stripped away, it was actually a straightforward offer: die in prison or live on Mars. He was never getting out of this penitentiary alive: he'd been sentenced to a hundred and twenty years for shooting a man in the face, in broad daylight, in front of a crowd of witnesses. Only the fact that he could prove that the dead man was his son's dealer saved him from going down for murder in the first, and onto death row.

He hadn't contested the charges. He hadn't spoken in his own defense. He'd taken what was coming, and he was still taking it. By mutual consent, his wife and his son had disappeared after the trial and they'd both moved a very long way away. Bad people, like the associates of the man he'd killed, had long memories, and longer reaches. No one had ever contacted him subsequently, and he'd never tried to contact anyone either. No, tell a lie: he'd had one message, maybe a year into his sentence. Divorce papers, served out of a New Hampshire attorney's office. He'd signed them without hesitation and handed them back to the notary.

There was literally nothing for him here on Earth but to die, unremembered and unremarked on.

But Mars?

He'd heard the news about the plans for a permanent Mars base, back when he was a free man, but he couldn't honestly say he'd paid much attention to it: he'd been in the middle of hell by then, trying to do the best thing for his family, and failing. And afterwards? Well, it hadn't really mattered, had it? Someone was putting a base on Mars. Good for them.

He hadn't thought for the smallest fraction of a moment of a second that it might include him.

Now, that would be a legacy worth leaving. Somewhere, his son was grown up, hopefully living his life, hopefully doing whatever he was doing well. He'd been given a second chance by Frank, who had loved him more than life itself, even if he'd had a strange way of showing it.

Did the boy think about his father? At all? What would it be like for him to suddenly discover that his old man was an astronaut, and not a jailbird? "This is the big Mars base, right?" Frank asked. "The one they announced a few years back?"

"Mars Base One. Yes."

"That's … interesting. But why would you pick cons? Why wouldn't you pick the brightest and the best and let them be the goddamn heroes? Or did you already throw this open to the outside world, and there weren't enough young, fit, intelligent people with college educations and no rap sheet beating down your doors for an opportunity like this. Is that it? You're desperate?"

Mark stroked his top lip. "It's because, while the company wants to minimize the risks involved, it can't completely eliminate them. And when a young, fit, intelligent person with a college degree dies, the publicity is terrible. Which is why they've offered you this opportunity instead. There's also the need to prove that this isn't just for the very brightest. Antarctic bases need plumbers and electricians and cooks. Mars bases will too. The company wants to show the world that, with the right training, anyone can go."

Frank hunched forward. "But couldn't you just hire the right people?"

"Frank, I'm going to level with you. Arranging a big spaceship, that costs a lot of money and time to build, which will take people out there, and will also bring them home? That isn't a priority right now. As it stands, the company get something out of this, and you get something out of this. They get their base built, quickly and yes, cheaply. You get to spend the rest of your life doing something worthwhile that'll benefit the whole human race, rather than rotting to death in here. Quid pro quo. A fair exchange."

Frank nodded again. It made some sort of sense. "OK, I get that you don't want the pretty people dying up there, but just how dangerous is this going to be?"

"Space is a dangerous place," said Mark. "People have died in the past. People will die in the future. Accidents happen. Space can, so I'm told, kill you in a very great number of different ways. We don't know what your life expectancy on Mars will be. We've no data. It may well be attenuated by a combination of environmental factors, which you'll learn about in your training. But you'll be able to minimize the risks and increase your chances of survival greatly by following some fairly straightforward rules. Whereas the average life expectancy behind bars is fifty-eight. You're currently fifty-one. You can do the math."

"Mars."

"Yes, Mars."

Frank poised the tip of his tongue between his teeth, and bit lightly. He could feel himself on the threshold of pain, and that was the closest he ever got these days to feeling anything. But to feel pride again? Achievement? To think that his son would be able to look up into the night sky and say, "There he is. That's where my father is."

Were those good enough reasons? He wouldn't be coming back: then again, he wasn't really here either. It'd be a second chance for him, too.

"Where do I sign?"

2

From: Bruno Tiller <bruno.tiller@xo.com>
To: Xavier Hildestrom <x.hildestrom@xo.com>
Date: Fri, April 29 2039 15:35:02 +1000
Subject: Big news

Xavier,

Just a note to say how much of a pleasure it was to meet you and the rest of the gang down at Gold Hill. You've got some fantastic facilities to play with down there, and the views are incredible! You're so lucky to be there, and while I realize that you've been plenty busy, I know how much of a wrench it must be for you to be away from Maria.

As you know, Paul's now put me personally in charge of all aspects of the project, and we're moving on to the next exciting phase. You've excelled at everything you've done so far, and I think it's high time you got your reward. There's a position back here in Denver I need someone of your caliber to fill—no one else will do. What's more, I want you to bring your whole senior team with you.

That's right: you're all coming back to the Mile High City! I'm going to oversee your replacements at Gold Hill, and we can have a smooth transition in, say, end of July? I can't tell you how jazzed I am at the prospect of having you back here at XO HQ. And you are going to love your new project. Trust me. It's a doozy.

Bruno

It had taken all day. Ten hours in an unadapted minivan, with him sitting in the back seat, handcuffed but otherwise free to move around, just one man in with him to nominally drive— once out of the prison gates, the autopilot had dealt with most of that—and frequent stops for him to use the restroom or just stretch his legs, and be asked what he wanted to eat.

Tosh, the driver, wasn't even armed. He was just a guy who punched buttons on the dash and sat behind the wheel in case something happened that the car couldn't cope with. Most states had done away with that requirement. Not California.

The men in the other two cars were armed, though. The black SUVs went in front and behind in a linked convoy, always pulling in and driving off in a synchronized ballet of speed and direction. Tosh had warned him that if Frank had it in mind to jump him and try to redirect the car, he'd be rammed off the road, dragged out, and unceremoniously shot in a ditch. Other-wise, Tosh was good enough company. He knew when to speak, and he knew when to shut up.

Once they'd left the prison behind and crossed the bay on the snaking, uppy-downy Richmond Bridge, they'd headed east, into the mountains, where there was still snow piled up by the sides of the roads from plowing. The blue sky of the coast, with its salt smell and warm breezes, was exchanged for low cloud and a gaspy, blustering wind.

Frank watched the landscape slip by. The cars, the houses, the side-roads—especially those, because he was left perpetually wondering what lay along them. He'd never know. This was the free world, just outside the tinted windows of the minivan. He could reach up and open the door and throw himself out into it. Or, if the van had central locking, his window was electric and he had the controls; he could probably squeeze through it, though he'd end up head first over the roadway. If he'd wanted to kill himself, there'd been opportunities before, and he hadn't taken them. No reason to get fixated on it now. Plus, assuming he survived the fall, he'd be shot for his efforts.

14

And it was the built environment that held his attention, not the rolls and folds of the land. He was disappointed that not much had changed since he'd gone inside. He supposed it hadn't been that long, objectively. It had just felt like it: prison had started as a novel experience, then had blurred into an endless rhythm of incarceration. Next to him on the seat was a brown cardboard box, containing the few items he'd salvaged from his former life that time, other prisoners and vindictive guards hadn't whittled away. He didn't open it on the journey, not once; he knew everything that was inside it. But he did touch it every so often to make sure it was still there.

The road had started to rise at Roseville, flattened out briefly at Reno, then wound its way along cold, high river beds between the ridges. The sky cleared once more, and long ribbons of cloud tore themselves out above the gray-brown earth. At some point, trees made a comeback, and the road tilted gently downwards.

The I-80 was bounded by extraordinary areas of just nothing, punctuated by places that appeared to have little reason to exist, except to serve the travelers along the road and the few people who lived in the hinterland.

And he was going—hoped to go, intended to go—to a place that, even with his presence, would be essentially uninhabited.

They stopped for the last time at a tiny rest area placed at the highest point on a pass. It was late in the afternoon, but the air was cold. Frank's shirt wasn't enough, and Tosh had simply draped his own coat over Frank's shoulders before he escorted him to the john. The other two cars in their convoy had pulled over together, a little way away. A man stood by one of them, mirror shades glinting, watching them make their way towards the neat wooden building where the stalls were.

As before, Tosh didn't go in with him, didn't harass him to hurry or denigrate him in any way. While Frank went in and did his business, he just sat down on a white concrete wall outside and took in the scenery. There wasn't much to look at: the road and its sparse traffic, the communications tower on one of the adjacent peaks. A narrow glimpse into the valley beyond and the valley behind. Drifts of shrinking white snow.

It wasn't a taste of freedom. What Mark had told Frank all still held: no reprieve, no parole, no license. His cuffed wrists were an honest reminder of that. But he could get used to being treated like a human being once again. That wouldn't grow old.

He washed his hands in the cold water, and splashed some on his face. His skin felt waxy, preserved, like he'd been dipped in chemicals. He scrubbed harder, using his nails, and it took effort to stop before he clawed himself raw. There were a lot of feelings hanging in the air around him. He'd better keep them in check, or he'd find himself heading back this way.

He dried his hands as best he could, and unlocked the door to the outside. Two of the men from the convoy were talking with Tosh, but the moment he emerged, they separated from him and stood well back.

Frank walked straight back to the minivan and leaned against it. Tosh, approaching, used his key fob to unlock the doors.

"Your friends seem to think I'm contagious," said Frank.

"It's SOP," said Tosh. "Nothing personal. They figure if they're far enough away, they can draw, aim and shoot in the time it takes for you to rush them."

"You could just chain me, or fit me with a shock collar. That'd work too."

"It's also a lot more work for us. You're a straight-up kind of guy. I trust you, at least as far as this is concerned anyway." He opened the door for Frank, and lifted his coat off Frank's back as he got in. He waited for him to be seated. "Less than an hour now."

"Thanks, Tosh."

"My pleasure."

They started off again, the three vehicles falling into line, still on the I-80, but angling south-east. They crossed the flat land, and just as they were approaching the Utah state line, they left the freeway.

Then it was south, bordering the luminous salt flats, and up into yet another line of hills, going deeper into the wilderness.

Frank watched the scrubland slide past. The only indication that they were going somewhere was that the road was broad and smooth, freshly tarmacked and well maintained. This wasn't some dirt track in the wilds, marked out by two tire tracks.

There was nothing outside but bleakness. That, it had by the spadeful. And just when it didn't look like anyone but the damn fool roadlayers had ever headed that way before, they rounded a corner on a small town. Identikit prefab housing was stacked up in neat, ordered rows, and there were people out on the slush-colored concrete, walking between buildings. Lights were on in the small, square windows.

"Is this it?" asked Frank.

Tosh consulted the satnav. "Zero point two miles to go. So it looks that way. This is where I leave you. Where you end up is a different thing."

The convoy drove into the town, and flawlessly came to a halt in front of an anonymous impermanent structure. No one got out.

Just as the journey had started with a single phone call— Tosh had it on speaker, so that Frank could just hear the word "acknowledged"—so it ended with a repeat. The driver dialed a number, and told the soft breathing at the other end they were at their destination. "Acknowledged," was all that was said again in response.

Both SUVs stopped so close they effectively blocked the minivan in. People walked by, close enough to touch, men and women. Frank hadn't seen that much of women the last few years. It was difficult for him to tell if his perception of them had been recalibrated, but rather than finding them all clichédly beautiful, he discovered from the few minutes he was waiting there that the more feminine they looked, the more alien they were to him.

Nothing stirred. Not even his emotions. He frowned at

himself, and looked out of the other window, across the street. The population could be roughly divided in three: the suits, the casuals and the overalls. Assuming this was a company town, then the casuals would be off-shift. The overalls would, depending on the nature of the work, do one of as many as three shifts. And the suits? They'd have it easy, as those in suits usually did. Get up, go to work, come home, kick back.

So where did a bunch of astronauts fit into all that?

Frank was blue collar. Proudly, unashamedly blue collar. He guessed he'd be with the overalls. They were going to work him like a dog, getting him up to speed on all the stuff he needed to know. And all the other things they had to do in order to get that prison pallor off him. Food with actual nutrients in. Sunlight. Exercise other than lifting weights or doing circuits.

How long did it take to train an astronaut? A year, Mark had said. He didn't know if that would be enough, even though he wouldn't be doing any of the flying-the-spaceship heroics. For him, the actual astronaut bit would be, what? Zero gravity? Maintaining the electrical systems and the pipework? A spaceship was just a complicated, compact building, with a big motor at one end, right? Spacesuit wearing, too. Mars had an atmosphere, though the guys he'd seen on the prison television kicking up the red dust were all wearing spacesuits.

They wanted him for the skills he already possessed. Using machinery to build buildings. Frank told himself not to over-think it. See what the job was, work out a schedule, assign the team, get the work done. Pretty much what he'd done his entire adult life.

There was a knock on the window, right next to his head. He didn't jump, just looked round to see a couple of men standing there, one in a suit, one in overalls.

"Have a nice life, Frank," said Tosh. "Don't do anything I wouldn't." He got out and walked to the car in front.

He left the door open, and all the warm air stole out. Tosh was replaced in the driver's seat by the suit, and the other man threw the side door open and joined Frank in the second row. The car in front pulled forward, and driving-suit twisted the wheel so they drove around it and on down the road, fully manual.

Frank looked sideways at the man sitting next to him. The cardboard box was between them, but suddenly that didn't seem quite enough distance or quite enough of a barrier. He pushed with his feet so that his back was against the door. This man seemed to trigger all Frank's fight—flight responses, and he didn't understand why. He strove to remain calm, despite his skin itching like it was about to slough. The man continued to stare at him.

"Making you uncomfortable?" he finally said. His accent placed him to the south and east. Texas, maybe.

Frank was struggling with his comeback. The other cons had mostly left him alone: old guy, nothing to prove. When he had been threatened, he'd usually blown them off and walked away. In the back of a car, he could do neither.

He had to rethink, work out a strategy. He wasn't used to that. "Is that what you want?"

The man blinked. Perhaps he couldn't work out what that meant. He shifted his position, from ramrod straight to a just-as-threatening lean against the upholstery. "Get used to it. I'm here to make your life hell from now on."

Frank swallowed. This guy was going for his ribs: in prison, he'd have had to respond somehow, let the other guy know he wasn't going to be a pushover. But this wasn't a fight he could settle with his fists and his feet.

Instead, he said: "Does that mean you're my new cellie? You taking the top or the lower tray?"

The man was again confused by Frank's reply. "I don't think you quite get it, Kittridge. I'm in charge of you. Everything you say or do from now on, you say it in response to something I've said, you do it because I've ordered you to do it. I tell you when to get up and when to go to bed. I tell you when to start and when to stop. You understand me, Kittridge? I own you."

"I thought the company owned me. And unless you own the company, maybe they own you too."

The man clenched his fists and his jaw, working it as if he was chewing gum. "You giving me sass? You?"

Frank's hands were cuffed, but if it came to a fight, he could still use them. The chain between them might even be useful as an improvised garrote.

He needed to calm that right down. That was prison Frank talking. He hadn't always been prison Frank: he'd been someone else before, and he could go back to being that, if only he could remember how. The man was attempting to intimidate him, make him afraid, assert his authority, and the only entry in Frank's ledger on the credit side was that they'd recruited him. They needed him. It had to mean he wasn't going to get beaten, because who beats up an astronaut, right?

"Hey." Frank raised his arms, bumped his wrists together with a clink. "You're the boss."

"And don't you forget it." The man unclenched his fists again, and continued to stare at Frank. "You want to go back to prison?"

Frank said nothing. It seemed like one of those questions that, whatever he answered, the response was already prepared, and designed to humiliate him.

The man leaned forward and straightened his finger like a gun at Frank's head. "OK. Time for some truth, let you know what'll happen if you crap out here, for any reason. Supermax. Pelican Bay. Security Housing Unit. You know what that is, don't you, boy? For the rest of your sentence, you'll never get to speak to another human being again. You'll be buried. Do you understand?"

It took a moment for it to sink in. He wouldn't be returning to his cell, to spend his life turning gray and desiccating like dust. He'd be in the SHU, the Hole, locked away out of sight and out of mind. The Hole sent men mad.

Frank stiffened in his seat. "That's not the deal I signed." He didn't want to let his fury and terror slip out in his voice, but it did. There was nothing he could do to stop it. He'd been played and he was burning.

"That's changed your tune, hasn't it, Kittridge? That's made you afraid of me. You remember that, now. When I tell you to jump, what do you say?"

His silence was all he had left. That and the Hole. The goddamn Hole.

"I asked you a question, Kittridge. When I ask you a question I require an answer, an instant answer, because I'm not asking twice."

"How high?" said Frank, reluctantly, almost tearfully. Apparently, his decision to go to Mars, freely made, now left him on the precipice of a lifetime of solitary confinement. He wondered what would have happened if he'd turned Mark down in the first instance. Would he already be there, in a tiny, windowless cell, a ball of rage and regret knotting his insides?

He'd dodged that bullet. He had no way of knowing, no way of finding out, how many others they'd asked before him. Perhaps he was the last on the list. He might have been the first. Any feelings of being special, and somehow too valuable to kick to the curb, were gone.

His position was precarious. Yes, he'd remember that. And resent it. Always resent it.

His expression had slipped to briefly unmask his true horror. He tried to drag his impassivity back into place, but the damage had been done. The man had seen it all, and knew him now.

"Tell me you understand," said the man.

Frank understood all too well. "Yeah. I got that."

The man gave a giggle, and only belatedly tried to hide his smirk behind his hand. It was an act, nothing more, nothing less, even if the threat was real. Frank, who'd never really had much cause to hate anyone, even the man he'd shot, realized that he genuinely, viscerally hated this grinning malevolent idiot already.

"At least you won't go forgetting."

Frank was still churning inside. He'd never not be scared now, at least until he got on that rocket and was on his way to Mars. Then, and only then, would he be free of that particular threat.

He turned his head away, so he didn't have to look at the man for a while. They drove around the side of the mountain peak. As the sun slipped westwards, the color leached away, and left a cold monochrome landscape.

The road went on, now turning southwards.

In the middle of precisely nowhere, a double fence barred their way. There were signs with dire warnings about dogs patrolling, of deadly force being used against trespassers, how secret the area was and how many violations an unauthorized person might clock up. But the fence was all that was needed, really. Fifteen, maybe twenty feet tall, topped with a coil of razor wire, and inside that, across a bare kill zone, another identical barrier. If anyone was looking for a hint, it was right there. This was where the world ended. Beyond was … there was nothing. No buildings, no people, just the single track.

They could do literally anything to Frank here, and there was nothing he could do about it.

The car rolled to a stop. "Out," said the man.

He left the car without looking to see whether Frank would follow, presumably because he knew he would. Frank opened the door on his side, picked up his box, and stepped out. It was cool, rather than cold, but the air was dry and strangely thin and it tasted of salt and stone. The wind tugged at his shirt, swirling and directionless.

He pushed the door shut with his foot, and the moment it had closed, the car just reversed back up the road before executing a turn. As if it was afraid. The tail lights receded, and the head-lights soon faded. They were left alone with the wire gate that rattled, singing and shivering in the desert breeze. A camera mounted on top of a pole, halfway across no-man's-land, angled up, and whirred.

The first gate clacked and drew aside.

The man walked forward, and Frank trailed after him, looking backwards, clutching his box tight against his tightening chest. The gate behind them closed before the second gate opened in front. The wirework rattled.

This hadn't been what he'd expected when he'd left Cali. Not welcomed with open arms, maybe. But not this. He'd been … he didn't even know what the word was that described what had happened to him. Kidnapped didn't cover it. Disappeared didn't either.

Another vehicle was coming down the road, from the inside, to collect them. Dust rose from the tires and hung out the back like a silver cloud. It pulled up, and he was goaded in. They were driven away, further in, deeper and down.

Enslaved. That was it. He was their slave. They owned him, body and soul.

Frank clutched his small box of belongings. In the distance was the bright airglow of floodlights, growing closer.

3

[NASA briefing to Xenosystems Operations 2/23/2035: NASA Headquarters Room D64, Washington, DC. In the public domain.]

1. Facility located in environmentally and geologically stable region.
2. Facility located in resource-rich location.
3. Facility in well-mapped location.
4. Facility in area of diverse morphological and geological features.
5. Facility must be self-sustaining.
6. Initial facility must be expandable to include workshop facilities, manufacturing and fabrication using local materials.

Frank was getting used to the taste of acid bile in his mouth, the burning in his chest and the deeper agony of feeling like he was running on knives. He was even beginning to enjoy it, after years of being numb. It was sharp and hard and relentless, a world away from the stultifying atmosphere of prison.

Even the air was different: it was needle-thin and austere, and it hurt to haul it in by the lungful. He'd never been a runner. He'd always thought himself too big and too heavy for that. What he thought, what he wanted, was no longer a consideration. He did as he was told, and right now he was being told to run up a big-ass mountain, as fast as he could. He could run down it again at a slower pace, but up was for speed-work, and his achievement was marked in splashes of vomit by the side of the trail.

He was unfit. He was a fifty-one-year-old man who'd done

24

pretty much nothing for eight years, and eaten some pretty crappy food while doing it. Just how unfit came as a surprise: as it did, he supposed, to most.

The implant they'd inserted under the skin over his sternum talked to a computer, while the earpiece he wore told him to run to the limit of his ability. They—the medical team—wanted to know those limits. They wanted to push him right to the edge, without killing him. And sometimes, times like now, he wondered if they'd really mind if his heart burst and he dropped down right there, down among the mine tailings. For a bunch of doctors, they didn't seem to care that much about his physical well-being, more about how best to manipulate him, puppet-like, to get more work from him.

The sky above was a deep dark blue, fading to a pale ribbon round the horizon, where the land was gray and rough-edged. His feet, encased in some surprisingly light running shoes, seemed to move of their own volition up the dusty path. A beep coincided with every second footfall, and he unconsciously fell into that rhythm. It was faster than he wanted to go, and with his position tracked by GPS, it wasn't just his pace he needed to watch, but also his stride length. A certain speed was required. Every stride was a stretch.

He climbed. His toes dug in to the cushioning, as if trying to grip the cinder-rock trail. Sweat washed down his face, into his eyes, making them sting, into the corners of his mouth, where he tasted salt. His breathing was one-in, one-out, a pant, timed to his cadence, but never quite enough.

His calves ached like they were being flayed. And still he ran.

He ran to avoid the Hole. He ran because Mars was just over the next hill. If he could just get off the planet, then it'd be OK. He wasn't going to crap out. He wasn't going to fail. He'd run up and down the mountain. He'd show them what he was made of. He wasn't going to be broken.

There came a point where all of those thoughts just faded into the background. All that was left was the road to the top,

25

and him. It was pure and clean, and also terrible in its purity and cleanliness. Nothing existed but pain and path. The beeps were just noise, the voices in his head just static. One hundred yards. Fifty. Ten. Five. One.

He stopped, loose-limbed, leaning over. He spat on the ground. Hardly anything came out, he was so parched. He put his hands on his knees and watched the sweat drip down his nose and onto the ground. The beeping had stopped. He coughed and spat, used his already damp shirt to wipe his face, and hauled air, in a controlled, deliberate way that stopped him from hyperventilating.

He had an uninterrupted view to the east, over the salt pan in the valley and into the far distance. There was no habitation visible, and the only indications that people existed there were the contrails of planes far above him. Even the double line of fencing was invisible to his fatigue-etched sight. He was alone.

He straightened up, his hands on his hips, and lifted his chin towards the sun. There was heat in it, despite the chill wind. He had tried to forget. But the moment had gone. He'd dragged all his problems up the mountain with him, and now he had to drag them all back down.

The beep started again, and he knew better than to ignore it. The Hole beckoned. He dreamed of it most nights. The door locking behind him. The close silence. The four windowless walls.

He turned around and pointed himself down the track. Trying to get his legs to work again, trying to remember how to breathe. Beep. Beep.

Going down was a different discipline to up. He had to use his heels on the loose-surfaced path. Too fast, and he'd career head-first down across the rocky slopes, certainly injuring himself, possibly killing himself, but crapping out one way or another. Too slow, and he'd be made to do it again. And he didn't want that either.

He ran, each foot-strike jarring his toes against the front of his trainers. Several of his toenails had already turned black. One had bled so profusely he'd had to soak the sock off, and the nail had come with it. The medical team hadn't cared. Just as long as he could carry on with the battery of tests and exercises they threw at him.

He hadn't met any of the other astronauts yet, so he had no way of comparing experiences. He had to assume there were others. There was no good reason for him to be first and only. They'd promised him a team. All it meant was that they were keeping them separate, for whatever purpose, and they'd bring them together at some point. Perhaps it was just until they'd completed their medical tests—no point in integrating someone into a group only for them to crap out on health grounds.

And maybe there were more than seven of them. Maybe they were competing against each other, unseen, as to who filled the crew slots. Those that didn't make it would end up in the Hole. That wasn't a happy thought. He was a middle-aged man, up against potentially younger and fitter specimens from Panopticon's jails. He could lose out through no fault of his own.

He concentrated on running for a while, feeling the solid impact of each footfall, the way his body adjusted to the changes in contour and surface. Simply winning this race could mean he was condemning someone else to life in solitary. He wasn't comfortable with that, either.

Yes, he'd shot a man. Yes, he'd done it deliberately, in a planned act of violence. He'd put him in the ground, and he'd had no qualms about it. Someone else might have continued looking for ways to solve the problem of his son's addiction and his slow and inevitable enmeshment with dealing and criminality, but there'd been other things they'd both tried over the years, and none of them had worked.

Frank's decision to put a bullet in the brain of his boy's dealer had been coolly calculated and carefully weighed. They were all someone's son, but he'd decided that his own was the one

27

who mattered most. There'd been no innocent parties. Not the perp, not the victim. That, he'd come to terms with.

Sending someone to the Hole, though, just for being beaten to the punch by a determined, driven fifty-one-year-old? That wasn't on the level. Another black mark in Panopticon's ledger, making them fight each other for the limited spaces available. Were they running a sweepstake on it? Did bears shit in the wood? Someone, somewhere, was betting on him blowing up and failing.

The path started to flatten out. His feet hurt. His throat was raw. His shoulders ached. Why would they ache so much? Then he caught himself throwing his hands forwards and backwards, forwards and backwards, as a counterweight to balance his body. Every step, he swung. Could he do that more efficiently? Probably. As if there weren't enough things to concentrate on already, there was now his form. He couldn't afford to waste energy in exaggerated movements, because he had less of it. He had to be wise, and conserve it.

He couldn't do anything about the others, he decided. They couldn't do anything about him, either. He wasn't going to slow down, stop, give up. So sorry, unknown person, even though they weren't Frank's enemy, and he wasn't theirs. It was Panopticon, and this other company, this Xenosystems Operations, who owned them. It was the man who'd intimidated him on that first day here. Brack. He'd overheard that name. At least, that was what he thought he'd heard. Brack, the shaven-headed smirker who delighted in Frank's struggles and went thin-lipped when he jumped another hurdle.

Frank wouldn't try and take him on. He had excellent impulse control. Certainly compared to the average con. Someone else would try, though, even if it meant disappearing into the Hole.

He was on the flat. The beeps slowed slightly, but that just meant he had to take longer strides, go a little faster. Just not as punishing as the climb. They'd really pushed him on the ascent today. And still he'd made it, through willpower alone.

That wasn't going to show up on any medical chart, was it? Courage, fortitude, grit. He'd deliberately shot a man to save his son, knowing that he'd have to endure whatever sentence they handed down. He had courage by the bucketful. It was his aging body he was worried about.

He carried on, down the path, listening for the beeps, pre-empting them, and then into the long slow descent into the valley where the training base was. Squat concrete slabs as yet unbuilt on. Stainless steel pipework extruding from pressure vessels. Long, low hangars, large enough to swallow a jet. Blocks of identikit offices. Electric carts going from one to another, hauling trailers or people. Caverns in the side of the valley, with wide trackways leading to them. Some of the structures he'd been in. Most of them he hadn't. Given that his every hour was dictated, there hadn't been the opportunity to look around, let alone explore. Doors were locked, and opened only on a fingerprint. His finger worked only for the doors he was supposed to use, and no others.

His waking and sleeping, his resting and his activity, what he ate and drank and when, were all strictly timetabled. When he wasn't tossing his cookies out on the trail, he was on the treadmill with a mask over his face, or making simple models out of building blocks from pictures on a screen, or watching yet another instructional video on Mars. The medics had spent longer than his wife—ex-wife—had staring into his eyes, and X-rayed him top to bottom.

And speaking of bottoms, they'd gone in with cameras: but at least they'd had the decency to lube up first.

Mental tests. Physical tests. Everything they could throw at him, they did. He had no idea if he'd passed or failed, but he was still there, so that had to count for something.

He reached the post. It was just that, a metal post in the ground, at the corner of two concrete paths, but it marked his beginning and end points. He knew better than to slow down for it. He slapped his hand on it as he passed—that did nothing, he just did it because he could—and then eased off. He felt a deep and abiding weariness steal over him as he stopped, and he wondered how long he could keep it up for. Long enough to get to Mars, for certain. There wasn't an alternative.

The beeps ended, and a voice spoke. He had no idea if it was a computer-generated voice, or someone with such precise diction that it sounded like a computer. Either way, it never seemed to respond to his replies. "*Report to Building Six, Room Two-zero-five. Acknowledge.*"

"Acknowledged," said Frank. That was mostly all he ever said. It was mostly all he was required to say. Brack needed more, but encounters with him were usually only once every few days, which was more than enough.

Frank wiped his face with his top again, pressing the cloth against his skin, drawing it roughly down to his neck and letting go. Building Six was that one, over there. He wasn't expected to run, but he wasn't to dawdle, either. The staff used carts to get around, but they were print-activated too, and he didn't have the authorization.

He'd named things, in the absence of being told their official names. He was currently stood in the Valley. The decaying, mine-ridden mountain was the Mountain. There was also the Wire, which confined him, and the Bunker, where he slept in Building Three. The medical center was officially Building Two, but he called it the Blood Bank, on account of what they did to him there.

He walked up the ramp to Building Six, pressed his finger to the glass plaque and waited for the door. There were people walking backwards and forwards inside the foyer, but he knew better than to engage with them, or tap on the frame to get them to let him in. It wasn't going to happen.

The door's lock clicked. He pushed against it, went through, and waited for it to shut behind him. He'd get a ticket if he didn't. If he collected too many tickets? He didn't know: he couldn't ask anyone to find out. Not the medics. Not the other staff. Especially not Brack. But he could guess.

30

Room Two-zero-five was on the second floor. He pressed his finger against the lock, waited for it to cycle, and went in. He'd been expecting another training video—but not a roomful of cons as well.

That was what they all were, clearly. They'd arranged themselves in the room in a way that was instantly familiar to anyone from prison: the stronger, more confident ones asserting themselves by taking space, the weaker going to the corners. Six of them. They looked at him, stained with sweat, out of breath. The older, gray-haired woman with the cheekbones and the eyebrows, who'd taken center-stage on one side of the boardroom-length table, wrinkled her nose at him. The thin black kid and the curly-headed white boy—and he was just a boy—were down the far end. Opposite Grandma was another woman, coffee skin and spiral hair. A moon-faced man was right by the door, and the last member was ... vast.

Huge arms, huge legs, neck like a tire. Blond stubble on his scalp. And the tattoos. It took a moment for Frank to scan them all. 1488 on his forehead. HATE on the knuckles of the one visible hand. Swastika on his neck. Aryan Brotherhood.

Frank looked a little too long, and the man caught his stare. He gave a slight nod—I see you—then returned his attention to the short wall at the end of the room, which was one big screen.

"They made me run up the Mountain," said Frank. "Sorry I'm late. And a bit funky."

The moon-faced man kicked out a chair next to him at the same moment that Frank's earpiece told him he needed to sit down. They were all wearing earpieces. They were all wearing identical uniforms. Frank realized with a start that this was his team, his crew of seven.

He slid into the proffered chair, and the moment his backside hit the plastic, the screen flickered and lit up. A commentary started to play in Frank's ear, and judging by the expression of everyone else, in theirs, too. "This is a Xenosystems Operations training video. You will find the following orientation

31

information vital for the successful outcome of your mission. Please pay close attention throughout."

They all started like that.

"Congratulations. You have been selected as trainee crew for Mars Base One, mankind's first permanent presence on the Martian surface. This prestigious project will be built and staffed by Xenosystems Operations on behalf of NASA, for the good of our nation, and all mankind. You have been recruited to help XO to fulfill that contract. You will leave Earth in six months' time—"

Six months. Among those who realized just how short a time that was, there was a murmur of consternation.

"—and travel to Mars. You will be placed in suspended animation for the duration of the journey, which will take in the region of eight calendar months—"

More murmurings.

"—and on arrival, Phase one will begin immediately with assembly of the prefabricated module units. Establishing early self-sufficiency of the base is an absolute priority. Synthesizing enough oxygen and water to provide yourself with life support, growing your own food, and generating your own electricity will be critical milestones on this path. Your complete co-operation is needed in order to complete the base within the time allotted.

"NASA astronauts will already be in flight on your arrival. There is no facility to allow for, nor is there expectation of, a delay in the base's readiness. After the base has been constructed, you will spend time rigorously testing the structure and infrastructure, and then enter Phase two, a maintenance mode which requires you to maintain your particular aspect of the base's systems. If necessary, the delivery of extra materials to extend and re-equip the base will require you to resume your original Phase one functions.

"Visiting scientist astronauts and other NASA staff will have priority over your time. You will treat them with the utmost respect and assist them when and where required, remembering that you will remain serving prisoners and subject to the Californian penal code for the whole length of your sentences."

The graphics playing on the screen showed the landing ship touching gently down on a brick-red plain, already scattered with supply canisters. People—it could only be Frank and the others—emerged and went to the nearest canister and constructed a towing vehicle. While that drove off and corralled the other supplies, the rest of the white-spacesuited crew set to and built the first module. In a slightly improbable time, they connected it to a second, and pressurized it.

Almost as if by magic, solar panels appeared, and a satellite dish. More modules popped up, with parts coming from the recovered and neatly laid-out rows of canisters. The landing craft was off to one side, and nearby there were three parallel lines of modules nestled together on the Martian surface.

Frank turned his head sideways. The base was bigger than he'd thought. Fifteen separate sections, with another couple of independent units close by. Big set of panels, dish, antennae. Other machinery he didn't yet know the function of.

Six months to learn how to do all that? They needed to all train on how to fit the airlocks, and the structural flooring of the modules. There'd be more specialized work inside: bedrooms and a sick bay and maintenance bays and the greenhouse, and they needed power and water and air before they could grow so much as a single potato.

He glanced at the others. The black woman opposite was staring at the screen, one eyebrow arched and the muscles at the side of her jaw flexing. Down his end of the table, they all appeared to be either stunned or frowning. Being exposed to the enormity of the task had put their meager training so far into grim perspective. Frank had been there since ... when? The end of February? It was, was— Did he even know? April? May? Three months, tops. They'd told him pretty much jack, and he guessed that went for the others too.

The graphics continued. Once the base was mostly complete,

another ship arrived in the vicinity. Buggies went out—though Frank couldn't see where the additional buggy had come from—and collected the crew.

The film finished. That was it. That was all they were going to get for now. Frank leaned back in his seat so far that it creaked.

"Well, that was a crock of shit," said the gray-haired woman.

"Six months?"

"A year asleep in a spaceship? Is that even legal?"

"We can't learn to do all that. The regular astronauts are like, trained for years."

Frank tilted his head until he was staring up at the ceiling. "We've got a choice," he said. "We can either do it, or we spend the rest of our lives in the Hole."

"The way I'm looking at it," said the moon-faced man next to him, "that might be more certain."

"How many teams do you think they got doing this?" Frank slowly winched his body back until he could rest his elbows on the tabletop. "How many other groups like us do you think they have?"

"What do you mean?" asked the thin black kid, and Gray-hair rolled her eyes.

"God's sake, it's obvious what he means. You think we're the only ones? You think that if we get our panties in a bunch here, it'll have any impact on them at all? They'll pick another team of people who might actually want to go."

"You all heard what I've just heard: selected as trainee crew. Trainee. We can still flunk this," said Frank. "But let me tell you now: every one of us in this room is going to Mars. It doesn't matter if none of us likes anyone else. If the only way I get to Mars is by you getting to Mars, that's how it's going to happen. Works both ways: you're relying on me to get you there, too. That's pretty much the bottom line."

"So you," and Gray-hair gestured at Moon-face, "whatever your name is: I'm not going in the Hole for you, and neither is anyone else. You get your shit together right now."

"Or what, lady?"

"Or Adolf over there will rip your head off and stick your tongue up your ass."

Everyone looked at the neo-Nazi man-mountain. He shrugged. "I don't do that any more. But neither do I want the Hole."

Moon-face tapped his fingers on the table. "You got a potty mouth, lady."

"Doctor, or Alice."

"You don't even know my name."

"But you'll remember mine." She stared around the table. "No one craps out. Everyone got that?"

"Who said anything about crapping out?" said the black kid. "I'm going to goddamn Mars."

"We've got six months to get this right," said Adolf. "I'm not going to let anyone down."

"Yeah. I guess so." The black woman held up her hands. "It's not like we've anything left to lose, right?"

The white boy squirmed in his seat when he realized people were looking at him. "It's, it's, it's … fine, it's fine. OK. It'll be fine."

Moon-face nodded slowly. "OK. If that's what everyone wants. Just don't blame me when you hate it up there."

Frank steepled his fingers. "We've been bought and sold. Xenosystems owns Panopticon. Panopticon owns us. But we all said yes when they asked us to go to Mars. It's going to be as good as we want to make it. It's going to be our home from now on. You want to shit the bed? You know where the airlock is."

"That," said Doctor Alice, "sounds like a threat."

"No. Just the truth. It goes for me as much as it does everyone else. We do our jobs, we take care of ourselves, respect each other as human beings. You wanted more out of life than that? Maybe we should have all thought just a little bit harder about our life choices."

"He's not wrong," said Adolf, into the silence that followed.

His voice was like a truck passing too close. "Now, I got the little voice in my ear telling me I got to be somewhere else. Play nice."

He slowly got to his feet, seemingly filling the room as he did so, and then ducked out of the room with one more word: "Acknowledged."

The black woman pushed herself away from the table. "Me too. Acknowledged."

Then the kid. "I'm going to fucking Mars. Don't forget that now." Followed by, "Acknowledged, already. Acknowledged."

One by one, they left, until it was just Frank and Alice. He waited for the door to close before speaking. "I remember you," he said. "I know what you did."

"No one else seems to," she said. She looked at Frank, held his gaze. "We can keep it that way if you want."

"Sure. Maybe they didn't read the same news sites I did."

"You can read? That sets you apart from the rest of the lumber they've swept up." Her stare, her contempt, was unflinching.

"Filed my own taxes too. Didn't need some fancy-ass accountant to do it for me."

"I've got some cookies you can have as a reward."

"You don't have any cookies. None that I'd dare eat, anyway."

"We all have a past. We all have a future."

"*Report to Building Four, Room Seventeen. Acknowledge.*"

"Acknowledged," he said, his eyes still on the doctor. "I'm Frank, by the way. And you're still dangerous, Dr Alice Shepherd."

"I'm glad you think so, Frank. Perhaps a little bit of danger will make this trip of ours more exciting."

He left, and walked down the corridor to the stairs. He'd finally put it together at the very end of the presentation, looking past her at the screen and seeing her catch a loose hair out of her tightly wound bun. Then she'd turned her head and in that freeze-frame, he'd recognized her. The State allowed assisted suicide, but not for a doctor to take matters into their own hands. She'd had something like thirty counts of undocumented and unregistered mercy killings against her, and the reports he'd seen alleged many more.

Should he warn the others? That was a difficult choice. It wasn't his business who Xenosystems chose. He had no influence over that. Presumably, she was going to be their doctor, and be treating the crew, so Xenosystems had decided that she wasn't going to euthanize them against their will. So why was he worried?

Maybe he should just keep quiet, and not get sick any time soon.

4

[Private diary of Bruno Tiller, entry under 11/26/2038, transcribed from paper-only copy]

If I hear of yet another robot failure, I swear to God I am going to send the engineers in their place.

Frank had been out on another run. It had hurt, and he was determined to show that it hadn't. In the shower, he'd cramped, and he'd struggled not to cry out in pain, in fear, in desperation. He'd bitten down on the fleshy lump on the back of his hand between thumb and forefinger, and he'd left marks.

And he'd barely turned off the flow of tepid water before he'd got his next instructions. He showered with his earpiece, he ate with his earpiece, he pissed with his earpiece. He was ragged, and felt every one of his fifty-one years. Apart from that one time at the training video, he was as isolated as he'd always been. Brack's intermittent appearances—and really, fuck that shit—didn't count. He could turn from someone who was disdainful and condescending into a mean, vicious weasel in a second. Perhaps he thought it was motivating.

Instead, Frank felt like throwing in the towel. He could just call it quits and make it stop. He could break up his crew, and maybe throw them all in the Hole too.

Maybe he couldn't. He was still on the program. If Alice Shepherd could stay the course, then maybe so could he.

As told, he went to the room they watched their training

videos in. And there was another person there—the black woman.

She was seated at one end—the far end, below the screen—of a long table, in the shadow cast by the dark-tinted windows dialed to almost opaque. Her hands, previously resting on the tabletop, withdrew like the tide and retreated to her lap.

Frank, with deliberate slowness, walked around the far side, and, with the windows at his back, sat down near—but not next—to her, on the diagonal. He made a fist, and held it out, thumb-side up. She looked at it, and him, then at his fist again. She curled her own right hand and lightly tapped it on Frank's.

"Hey," she said.

"Frank."

"Marcy."

"Everything's being recorded, right?"

"Yeah."

"OK." Frank leaned heavily on the desk. He blinked and realized that there was a bottle of water on the desk in front of him. He'd missed it in the gloom. He reached over and snagged it, twisted the top off, and offered it to Marcy first.

"Knock yourself out," she said.

He drank it all, the plastic bottle flexing and snapping as he sucked the last from its neck.

"I seem to be permanently thirsty these days." He hoped it wasn't a sign of some underlying medical problem that was going to get him canned.

"Dry air, I guess. Coming off the flats."

"Sure. That'll be it."

They risked a glance at each other.

"You doing OK?" asked Frank.

"Well enough. Enough to avoid the Hole for now."

"Me too."

"Son of a bitch never told me that when I signed," she said.

"Yeah. That. So let's not crap out."

"Why are we here? You and me. This room. Is this another test?"

Frank wiped his lips with his thumb. "Got to talk to each other sometime, right? And of course it's another test. If we show we can work together, then we're more likely to get on that ship."

"Guess so. What did you do outside?"

"Build shit. You?"

"Drive shit."

"OK. They need people on Mars who can build and can drive."

"But do they need us?"

Frank shrugged. "We're here. We just need to make them think it's easier to take us than can us."

"Like they've left us a choice."

He pushed the empty water bottle away from him, to stop himself from playing with it. "So what do we do now?"

"I don't know. Are we supposed to get to know each other, tell each other our life stories?" Marcy looked down into her lap. "I'm not comfortable with that."

"I don't think they care about that. But while I'm in here, I'm not running up that Mountain and the medics aren't draining my blood. I'm good with that."

"They cut you open?" She gestured to the deeper shadow between her breasts. Frank glanced up long enough to know what she was talking about, and not so long as to make it embarrassing.

"I still feel it, sometimes. At night, mainly. Just a tightness. It's not so bad."

They lapsed into silence, broken eventually by Frank.

"Look. I'm not good at this. I never was. Much rather do something with my hands than say something with my mouth. But we're not going to hurt each other, right? You seem like a nice lady, however it was you got here. That's done. We're astronauts now."

"I killed twenty-six people," she said. "You?"

"Just the one."

Twenty-six seemed a lot. Perhaps his expression gave that away.

"It was an accident. I fucked up." She clicked her tongue. "Seems so long ago now."

"Which is what I'm saying. No one's going to look out for us but us. These jokers don't much care if we stay or crap out: some greener will be along to replace us soon enough. But we have to care, right?"

She pursed her lips and nodded. "Right."

His earpiece buzzed. Hers too, by her quizzical look.

"*Every crew member is required to teach their task to another,*" he heard. "*Marcy Cole is lead driver. You will be her second. Acknowledge.*"

"So who's my second?" he asked.

"*Acknowledge,*" repeated the voice. No change of inflection, no emotion at all. Just cold.

Marcy said into the space, "Acknowledged." She sighed. Her earpiece had been talking to her too.

Frank knew he had to follow suit. "Acknowledged."

They looked at each other, properly, for the first time. She had a fine face, brown skin with a sowing of darker freckles across her cheekbones and nose. Her hair, like his, had been shaved short. His was a flattened mop of black, but hers was growing out in cotton-wool twists. Age? She had at least a couple of decades on him. And she was strong, otherwise she wouldn't have got this far.

"We can do this," he said. "I can learn."

"Depends whether I can teach." She looked up at the ceiling, addressing it directly. "So when do we start?"

"*Report outside immediately.*"

Both of them were so used to obeying, they stood up.

"Remember those times you could just lie in your tray, listen to some music, read a magazine?" Frank put his hands into the small of his back and pushed, waiting for the click before he stopped.

"No. I don't remember that at all."

"Me neither."

Outside, opposite Building Four, was a concrete pad the size of a football field. Probably some structure was going to go on it at some point, but, for now, there was a weird-ass looking vehicle sitting on it, and a stack of orange traffic cones.

And Brack.

"Ah, crap," muttered Marcy.

"Let's get this over with," said Frank, and picked his way over the loose cinders towards the platform. He climbed up, and took a closer look at the thing they were presumably meant to drive around Mars on.

"You break it, you pay for it, Kittridge," said Brack.

The chassis was rectangular, an open, almost lacy latticework of struts and crossbracing. The wheels were huge balloons, and the seat a simple plastic bucket bolted to the top of the frame. There was a roll bar over the top, which didn't look particularly sturdy, and a set of controls mounted in front of the seat.

Frank had seen more sophisticated Radio Flyers.

"And this is what we're taking to Mars?"

"You think you know better? 'cause it's not bright yellow and there's no backhoe? You want a ticket? You refusing an order? You want to get canned?" Brack cupped his hand around his ear. "What's that? Kittridge is on his way to the Hole?" Frank bit down on his lip until he knew he wasn't going to say anything.

"Don't care if you don't love me, Kittridge, as long you stay afraid of me. This is your Mars Rover, boy. You and it need to become intimately acquainted, and yes, if that means you have to take it up the tailpipe, you'll do just that and hold it close afterwards. You got your fuel cell slung underneath, you got your four-wheel-drive electric motors on the hubs, you got your rear-facing cameras and your one-fifty-foot winch and tow on the trunk. That two-wheeled caboose is your trailer. Lights on the front that'll turn night into day. Top speed of a mighty twenty miles an hour." Brack kicked the nearest tire. "Only difference between here and there is that there you'll be using adaptive metal wheels rather than pneumatics, as I am reliably informed they have the habit of exploding in a vacuum."

Marcy shook the frame, and crawled underneath to inspect the connections between the fuel cell and the hubs. "What's the range?"

"Well, that depends. You got one cell, and everything works off that. But under normal conditions, your suits will fail before this runs out of juice. So you'd better get it back to base before then." He giggled, but it wasn't funny. "You got your orders. You make this thing dance by the end of the week. By the week after, it'd better be turning backflips. The pair of you got that?"

"I got that," said Marcy from behind one of the tires.

"Kittridge?"

"Acknowledged," said Frank. He didn't mean anything by it, just the bland acceptance of an instruction, but of course Brack had to take it the wrong way.

"You think I'm some kind of computer, boy? Hell, I'll be the voice in your dreams, not just in your head." He leaned forward and drilled his finger into Frank's temple, and there was nothing that Frank could do but take it.

Brack stalked off, and Marcy pulled herself out from under the rover.

"What d'you think?"

"What do I think?" Frank scuffed the ground. "That the world would be a better place without him."

"Forget about him. I meant the buggy."

Frank dragged his attention back to the job in hand. "You're the professional. What do you think?"

"Strong, lightweight. Center of gravity is low enough to add stability, but it's got a decent enough ground clearance. Let's take it for a spin and see."

She climbed up. There wasn't a ladder, so she just grabbed

43

the lowest strut and hauled herself up. Frank could do that too. They were all now so lean and strong that it was barely an effort. Marcy settled into the seat and for the want of anywhere else to put her feet, braced them on the struts either side of the controls. Almost exactly like a Radio Flyer.

"It's like a video game. Little steering wheel, gas on-off using triggers. Couple of buttons and a screen for stuff." She grinned down at him. "Seriously, come on up. We don't get many moments like this."

She drove it slowly and conservatively around the pan, finding the buttons that'd put it in reverse, work the lights and the winches. Frank hung off the roll bars behind the seat, mildly disconcerted at the concrete scudding by under his feet.

They swapped over, and Frank drove it forwards, then in reverse. It looked like a toy. It felt like a toy. Somehow far less than something they'd be driving around on another planet.

Then the lessons began. Marcy hopped off, set out some traffic cones around the rear of the buggy, and watched Frank drive forward out of the cordon.

"It came out of that space," she said. "All you have to do is back it in again."

Frank crushed three cones. He didn't hear them crumple, and Marcy let him keep on going until he thought he was back in the starting position. He climbed down and stood next to her to examine the debacle.

"Do I get to say it's not bad for a first attempt?"

"I've seen worse." She had her hands on her hips, judging him. "But I'm guessing if we're on Mars, running over a cone probably means we're all dead. What did you do, when you weren't killing people, that is?"

"I ran a construction company," said Frank. He tapped the big balloon wheel with the toe of his reinforced boot. "I hired people to do this for me."

"Not any more. It's me and you, now. Drive it out again, and I'll set it back up." Marcy picked up one of the cones and used her fist to take out some of the dings. "Now you know how difficult it is, you might just listen to me when I tell you how to do it."

"I would have listened to you anyway." Frank climbed up into the cab and swung himself into the seat. "I'm not going to be that guy, OK?"

Marcy dropped the cone back on the ground. It was more or less straight again. "In my experience, all the guys are that guy. Take it forward, thirty feet, and stop. We'll keep doing it until you can slot it in blindfold. Then I get to make it difficult for you."

He knew the basics. He could get it almost in the right place, almost every time. Almost, when he was a million miles away, wasn't going to cut it. The cameras helped when he was some way away. Less so when he was closer, as the cones had the tendency to disappear from view at exactly the wrong moment. Sure, Marcy could spot for him, but there'd be times when he'd just have to do it on his own: him taking ten attempts to get something into place when one should have done was a sure-fire way of burning off the better part of a shift. And he'd be in a spacesuit.

So this wasn't anything like the same conditions he'd be working under. But if he couldn't get it right here and now, he wouldn't be able to get it right then, when it mattered. A mistake could get them all killed, or stranded, or something else bad. He put his hand on the wheel and dabbed his finger on the gas pedal. Shouldn't call it the gas pedal if there was no gas, or a pedal.

He drove it forward a couple of lengths, and let go. There was a brake, but he didn't have to use it, because the motor provided enough resistance to bring the buggy to a stop.

He looked behind him at the space outlined by the cones. He imagined listening to the sound of his own breath loud in his ears, turning his head against the pull of a bulky, padded suit, inflated so that it was like wearing a tire. Marcy was right. He was going to have to be able to do this blind to stand any chance of doing this on Mars. He needed to look at the screens instead. Work out what he should be seeing if it was going right.

She climbed on up and hung off the back of his seat. "OK?"

He nodded.

"You look nervous."

"There's a lot riding on this."

"This is practice, OK? Don't you go freaking out on me. Slow. Dead slow. Barely moving slow. Faster you go, the less time you got to correct. Even if you got someone shouting at you, you play it cool, you keep it clean. They're not driving. You are. You get to decide. If you're not happy, you stop. This rig, this load, whatever it is, is your responsibility. It's up to you to put it in the right place, not anyone else. You got that?"

"I got that."

"You sure you got that? Because folk like us are used to following orders, and someone yelling at you to hurry it up, right in your ear, and you can't turn them off, that's somewhere between a distraction and a compulsion. You want to make them shut up. You want to show them you can do it faster. Don't you?"

Frank took another look behind him, past Marcy, at the corral of cones. Then he looked up at her. "No. I do this at my own pace, or not at all."

She punched her fist into his shoulder. "So let's show these assholes some skills."

Physical contact. It was a little more than he could cope with at that moment, and he had to take a breath. She didn't seem to notice, which was just fine.

"OK," he said. "Dead slow. Tell me what I'm supposed to be watching."

There was a knack to it, a counter-intuitive way of turning the wheel and easing the gas that would put the back end right where it was needed. He wasn't a master at it—Marcy didn't take the controls once so as not to embarrass him—but with care, he became competent. He could throw the buggy around in loops and turns and still park it up in one maneuver.

By the time their earpieces told them to break it up, he was confident he could back the buggy up without driving through a building.

"I don't know when the next time is," said Marcy. "But when it is, we'll do it with a trailer. That's a thing."

"A difficult thing?"

"Enough to make grown men weep." She put her hand to her ear. "Acknowledged. Got to go." She kicked at the ground, looked as if she was going to say something more, then decided against it. She glanced once at the buggy and its guard of orange cones, then walked away towards the buildings just down the slope.

Frank waited for his next instruction, which didn't come. Marcy's dusty tracks settled, and left him alone, standing in the dry, cold dirt. He looked up at the mountain, at the bright blue sky, at the expanse of glittering salt pan to the east and the next, distant ridge quivering in the haze. That was the free world.

He narrowed his eyes. He had a machine strong enough to break through the double fence and rugged enough to get him over the crystalline desert. And almost subconsciously he brushed his fingers against his sternum, where the scar had nearly healed and the hard lump of the implant lodged against his bone.

They weren't stupid. Neither was he. The only way out was up.

"*Report to Building Two. Acknowledge.*"

"Acknowledged."

5

[Transcript of private phone call between (unidentified XO employee 1) and (unidentified XO employee 2) 4/2/2047 0935MT. Note: one side of conversation redacted.]

XO1: Meyer failed his medical. Something about a hormone imbalance.

XO2: ...

XO1: Yeah, I get that.

XO2: ...

XO1: Just send him straight to the Hole, no need for him to interact further with anyone else at Gold Hill. I'll send some guys around to pick him up and take him to Pelican Bay.

XO2: ...

XO1: No, they know better than to tell him. What's he going to do anyway? The chimps don't really exist, so if one goes missing, it's no big deal. I'll bump a replacement up and hope he doesn't flunk it.

XO2: ...

XO1: Sure, later.

[transcript ends]

In his never-ending stream of instructions, he didn't think he'd ever had one for Building Five. Two, Four, Six, Three, and back again, sure. Five was new, and he wondered what they kept in there. Certainly, the foyer area appeared different—this was no suite of offices and conference rooms: it was clean, almost sterile, like a hospital ward, except that was more a Building Two thing.

White coats. He was in scientist country. Room Fourteen was somewhere on the ground floor, and he looked up at the signage to tell him which way to go. There were big double doors. He pressed his finger to the lock, and pushed with his other hand as the lock snicked back.

Bright. Very bright. There was something in the middle of the room that looked like a suspended, crucified, oversized mannequin which, on first sight, didn't fill him with confidence. The detail of the rest of the room—straps and tubes and fixing points and harnesses and taps—made him stop, half in, half out the doorway.

His ear told him to strip. Slowly, shapes resolved in white, full clean-suits with head coverings and face masks. They were carrying bulky bags of equipment towards him. "*Strip*," repeated the voice. "*Acknowledge*."

"Acknowledged." The door clicked shut behind him and he shucked his clothes. He'd been through this drill often enough in the Blood Bank, and it wasn't like cavity searches weren't a thing in the penitentiary. What embarrassment or shame he'd felt had long since dissipated.

He was handed a pair of gray long johns, top and bottom. They were a tight fit. Not too tight, because they knew exactly how big he was from all the previous measurements they'd taken from him. But tight enough that he had to sit on the cold floor and smooth the material up his legs until he could say he was wearing them, rather than the other way around.

He put on the thin, almost sheer, socks and gloves. He put on the bathing-cap beanie. They walked him over to the hanging sculpture. There was a hole in the back, a doorway, complete with a door, and it was open, and there was nothing but darkness inside.

He hesitated, and felt the firm pressure of a hand in the small of his back, pushing him on. Someone had placed a low step at

49

the base of the mannequin, though now he could see that it was no mannequin.

He climbed up on the step, and peered over the top of the thing's shoulder. He was looking down at a clear perspex bubble, and when he looked along the arm, he saw it terminated in a complex glove. It was a spacesuit.

He pointed at the hole in the back of the suit. "In here?"

The technician's eyes—that was all Frank could see—moved in that direction.

Frank used the hard rim of the hatch to steady himself, and he eased his feet into the interior. He had to point his toes and push hard to get his feet into the boots. Left arm, right arm, then duck down and put his head through the neck ring.

He worked his fingers into the outer gloves. Behind him, the technician hooked something heavy to his back. He could feel the weight settle on him.

"*Breathe normally*," said his ear. He hadn't realized that he wasn't. He took a breath, held it, and took another. The faceplate inches from his nose misted. It was like wearing a goldfish bowl.

"*Look down.*"

He could see the broad curve of his suit's front. But not his feet.

"*There's a control unit on your chest. Open it.*"

He found that his arms could move against the complex system of pulleys suspending him from the ceiling. He didn't have to hold them rigidly in the outstretched position he'd first put them in. He reached down to the box hung just below his ribs. It was attached to a flap of material by the top, so that when he lifted it up, he could prop it in position with one hand. With the other, he flipped open the cover. His gloves were surprisingly dexterous, better than his usual rigger's gloves.

Inside was a small screen, with a series of read-outs. The numbers didn't mean anything to him, but all the telltales were green. That was a good sign. The three buttons let him scroll through each menu: up, down, select.

"Go to the top menu."

He navigated to it, tapping the buttons with the very tip of his gloved finger. There were two options: Open, and Close.

"Select Close."

A motor whirred, and the weight on his back shifted position. Something made a substantial, positive click behind him, and outside sounds became muffled and indistinct.

A faint breeze passed his face, blowing against the faceplate, clearing it.

He was in a spacesuit. An actual goddamn spacesuit.

"Close the controls, and walk slowly to the end of the room."

He stood upright, testing his center of gravity, working out where his balance now was, and when he thought he was ready, he tentatively put his foot out. He felt his weight shift in unfamiliar ways, and he staggered slightly, locking his leg to brace himself. His upper body was enclosed in what was essentially inflexible armor, a breastplate and a backplate, with his helmet integrated into it as part of a seamless whole. If he wanted to look at something off to one side, he'd have to either turn at his hips, or just point his feet in that direction. That was going to take getting used to.

He walked slowly as instructed, and the pulleys and their cables followed him across the room. The fabric of his suit was stiff, despite the loose outer layer. It was OK, but going any distance would be tiring. Suddenly, running up and down the Mountain made a whole lot more sense.

He reached the wall.

"Turn around. Touch your head, your shoulders, your waist, your knees, your toes."

He faced the white, bright room of technicians and equipment and lifted his arms. He tapped the top of his helmet, the shoulder joints, his armored waist, and then started to bend forward to touch his knees. The weight shifted again. It was high up on his back, and he realized he could easily tip over and face-plant on the floor. He couldn't even be certain of getting his hands out in time to break his fall. As to whether he could get up again without help, that was unknown.

He bent from his knees instead, squatting down. He dabbed his kneecaps, then reached below his coiled legs and poked the toes of his boots. He straightened up, slowly, with difficulty, but he didn't topple.

"Return to your starting position."

Again, he took measured paces across the floor. There were cameras on stands around the room. He thought he was performing well, and he glanced at the nearest lens. He caught his reflection, and saw a strange, hunchbacked creature, more monster than human, staring eyelessly back.

He stopped and looked more closely, fascinated and repelled.

"Return to your starting position."

The spell broke, and he remembered how to walk again. He parked himself once more with his heels against the short step.

"Open your control unit and select Open."

He checked his chest-screen, and dabbed the lit-up command. The rear hatch opened, and the heavy thing behind him was taken away. He could feel the air in the lab as a different quality to that in the suit.

"Climb out and get dressed. That concludes the test."

He complied. He stripped off the long johns and the gloves and the beanie and the socks. A technician bagged them in a labeled sack and shelved them, while Frank climbed back into his day clothes and knelt on the floor to lace up his boots. He was otherwise ignored. Not that the techs weren't talking, they just weren't talking to him, as if he was merely incidental to the rest of their work.

But this event, surely, was significant. They'd have had to have made the spacesuit to fit him, more or less exactly, unless they had a wide array of off-the-peg solutions, and he'd not seen these types of suits before, either in the movies or on the small screen. This was bespoke. That meant they were spending serious money on him.

It also meant that if he screwed up now, they'd be seriously pissed at him.

"Report to Building Ten."

Goddammit, couldn't they leave him alone, just for five minutes?

"Report to Building Ten. Acknowledge."

Where the hell was Building Ten? If he asked nicely enough, he'd get the instructions in his ear. Don't screw up. Say it. Say it now.

"Acknowledged."

He navigated the paths around the mountain, and was directed to what looked like an aircraft hangar. Deep. Tall. Broad. Certainly as big as the area he was practicing driving on, and probably bigger. Xenosystems didn't lack for green.

The usual trail of electric carts rattled along on the road behind him, but he ignored them. There was a little door set in the big doors, and the usual print lock glowing with one red light next to the handle. He walked across the concrete apron and fell into the cold shadow of the overhanging roof.

His thumb cracked the door, and he pushed the handle down and away. It was dark inside, and it smelled strange. Almost a new car smell. There was sand underfoot, deep enough and dry enough to sink into. The door snicked shut behind him, and the little daylight that had crept in with him was snuffed out.

He stood there and waited. Absolutely nothing happened.

"You have to walk around, so that the lights come on," said a voice to his left.

Frank's medical monitors would have noticed the spike in his heart rate, but not necessarily known the cause.

"Yeah, well. Fuck you for not doing that."

Frank took a careful, sliding step forwards, didn't bump into anything, and took another. The lights were very far away, up in the roof, and they came on in bands starting nearest the door. They ended a long way back.

"Big space," said the voice.

"That's what they tell me," said Frank.

White cylinders, lying on their side like spilled Pringles tubes, took up the middle part of the broad sandy floor. Frank found it difficult to appreciate their scale, but with a squint and turn of the head they could easily have each been twenty or so feet in diameter, thirty-odd feet in length.

The sand scrunched next to him. Close. Too close. "Declan," said the man. "I'm your second."

Frank stepped away and looked this Declan up and down. He hadn't seen him before, and he certainly hadn't been at the group meeting. He didn't have much hair on top. Nor much height or weight underneath it. Damp. Everything about him was just a little ... moist. His eyes were red-rimmed, he sniffed, when he spoke he gurgled in his throat. He wiped the palms of his hands against his sides.

He could already tell the man wasn't a Marcy. But neither of them were in charge of hiring, so they both had to make the best of it.

"You supposed to be part of our team now?"

"I guess," said Declan. "They must have bumped one of your guys. I suppose I should be grateful but, sucks to be him."

"Could be any one of us. Still could." Frank nodded his head at the tubes. "You taken a look yet?" he asked.

"I was told to wait." Declan tapped his ear. "I'm not getting into trouble. More trouble than I'm already in."

"OK. Let's see what they got." Frank set out across the hangar, aiming for the nearest structure.

Declan scurried beside him. "So you build things like this?"

"Like this? No. But I do build things, and I'm guessing Xenosystems think that's good enough. You in construction?"

"Kind of. Commercial electrician. Big power circuits. Wiring up whole buildings. That kind of thing."

"We can work with that."

Now they were closer, Frank could see that the cylinder sides were made of a stretched plastic, but that there was a metal ring at the end of each section, providing the skeleton to support it. Vertical external pylons with feet stopped it from rolling away.

Prefab. This was why they needed him. He was going to have to literally build a Mars base from a kit. The parts would get shipped to the site, and he—and Declan—would have to bolt it all together. Make the frames, get the plastic over it. Actually no: there were two rings, one inside and one outside that fitted together, forming an airtight seal.

He reached out to one of the pylons and gave it a shake. It was fixed to the ground with a screw-in rock anchor. The structure didn't move. It was more solid than it looked. He walked around it, pushing and pulling at parts of it. He guessed that on Mars the plastic would be a lot more rigid, pressurized on the inside. That would help.

The far end was open, and they could walk in. Frank inspected the internal ring, and how it all fitted together. There was a cross beam, stretching horizontally from side to side. He reached up, and hung off it, lifting his boots clear of the floor with a grunt of effort. Yes, there was some flex, but barely any. Put one at the other end, and he could suspend joists between them. Two levels, then. Double the working space.

"You don't say much," said Declan.

"I have my moments." Frank walked to the far end. The plastic membrane that was going to have to stand between them and actual Mars seemed thick and resilient. There was an additional rubber mat between the plastic and the ground, but the sand underneath was going to have to be graded for sharper rocks anyway.

So, in order. Prepare the foundation—whatever vehicle they had, just to drag a scoop in a line, then a manual clearing of the larger debris. Use the same machine to drag the base mat around until it was in position. Internal or external rings next? Probably easier to make one internal, then one external, and get it screwed together. They had wind on Mars, and they weren't going to gain any kudos chasing their shelter across the red desert like it was a stray plastic bag.

Then the next ring. Working on the ground was so much easier than working at height. Would there be, at some point, a need for access to the higher points of the structure? A cherry picker or scaffolding would be preferable, ladders at a push.

They'd need ropes to haul with. Even with a lightweight metal, and this looked like aluminum, the weight wouldn't be insignificant. They could still fix the outriggers while it was on the ground, and drag them into place, screw or fire in the rock bolts. There'd need to be an airlock to get in and out of. Maybe one of the other modules had one he could examine.

He walked back out onto the sand. "This'll work," he said.

Despite the dryness and cold, Declan still felt the need to wipe his hands again. "You reckon? Not going to be so easy doing it wearing a spacesuit."

"Then we practice while wearing a spacesuit. They've color-coded the components. Inner ring's green, outer ring's yellow, bolts are all the same size so we never get to lose the one we need. A trained monkey could put one of these together."

"They're not sending monkeys. They're sending us." Declan didn't sound thrilled at the idea.

"I'm saying that someone's actually bothered to put some effort into the design, with the idea that none of us are exactly the Right Stuff. I don't mind. The easier they make it for us not to screw up, the better."

Frank toured the remaining modules, which were in various states of completion. He got it now: it was a physical version of one of those pictographic manuals from Legos, or flat-pack furniture. No words, just a stage-by-stage walkthrough.

At the far end of the hangar was a finished module. Open metalwork steps led up to the central airlock door, set in a pop-out standing proud from the end section. His footsteps rang as he climbed up. He was expecting an electronic lock, but this was determinedly low tech, just a lever on a bulkhead door.

He pushed it down and put his shoulder to it. The rubber seals were stiff, and broke with a sigh. There was a five-, maybe six-foot-long chamber before the inner door, and though he supposed that it would open even with the outer one also cracked, it might be an idea to get used to keeping one closed at all times.

Then he looked again. Both doors would only open inwards; positive pressure where it was supposed to be—inside—would prevent an accidental breach. He smiled to himself. OK, so this was well done. Someone had seen the problems they'd be facing, years ago, and had done their job. One professional to another, he silently saluted them.

He opened the inner door. The only illumination was that which filtered through the plastic walls; it was gloomy, almost dark. The ceiling was lower than he'd like, around seven and a half, eight feet, when suspended ceiling and sub-floor voids were taken into account. The curve of the roof made the available head-space less than it otherwise would have been. If the neo-Nazi man-mountain was coming with them, he'd find it difficult.

The floor—tiles made from hard honeycomb sheet with a continuous top layer, like corrugated packing—was pierced by a ladder, which led down to the lower level. To complete the tour, he lay on the tiles and looked through the hole at the floor below. He was guessing that level was mainly for storage. It wasn't supposed to be a hotel, but there was a damn sight more room than a prison. Which it both was, and wasn't. He'd need to spend some time poring over the plans, but his confidence to both do the job and win a place on the mission had grown.

He turned to look behind him, and Declan was standing there, poking around, sizing up the space, seeming to be working out where to put the cable runs and string up the internal lighting, but he was also watching Frank.

Frank raised himself up, and Declan made a show of concentrating on the floor, lifting out the square tiles and running his finger along the length of the floor trusses.

"We're going to be working together, you and me," said Frank. "Working together a lot. We need to make sure we can do that, right?" He didn't know how much Xenosystems could see or hear of what he and the other cons did, but it was safer to assume that it was everything.

"I can do ... that," said Declan. "I don't have a problem with you, if that's what you're asking. Do you have a problem with me?"

Given who else might be listening, he took a moment to come up with a reply. "We're good here. Let's see if they've left us some tools and we can try and take one of these things apart. Surprising how much you learn when you do that."

6

[transcript of audio file #14855 5/21/2038 2354MT Xenosystems Operations boardroom, 65th floor, Tower of Light, Denver CO]

BT: No. Just no. This isn't working. No matter how many times you say it will work, it's not working now. We have seven years left. And we need an alternative plan.

AC: You said it right there. Seven years. We can fix all the problems in two, and have five years to practice. I don't think you appreciate just how far we've come. Paul said that himself.

BT: Paul is an ideas man. I have to deal with implementation. Look. Let me take you back to this part ... just ... here. OK. Now you say that your hydraulic mechanisms will automatically deploy the hab. And they do. On Earth. As soon as we tested them under Mars conditions, they failed.

AC: But those components aren't rated for space. This was just a prototype. We didn't need vacuum-rated pistons for it, just off-the-shelf parts we're going to swap out later. I didn't authorize those extra tests, and I don't know who did or how they found their way to your desk. They're meaningless. Just meaningless. I don't know how else to say that.

BT: We have to face the facts. The fully automatic system you want? It's just not practical.

AC: But that's the bid. That's the specifications we've all agreed on.

BT: Look out of the window. Look at the city. Something goes

59

wrong, and people will come out and fix it. How long do you think it would take for all of this to break down? One set of lights? Two, maybe? Followed by gridlock.

AC: You can't be serious. The whole mission is designed around the premise that the base builds itself. We put it on the Martian surface, and it does the rest.

BT: There are too many critical failure modes, Avram. And one is one too many. If we don't deliver the base, we don't get paid. Putting a dozen cargo landers on Mars would be a success in anyone's book, a real achievement. But unless we can guarantee—guarantee—that the base will be habitable by the time NASA need it, XO is history. You appreciate that, yes?

AC: Yes, but …

BT: I'm sorry. I've been asked by the board to seek alternative opinions. You'll receive your full severance payment, and you've already signed the non-disclosure agreement. I've no doubt that your expertise will be invaluable to the right company.

AC: You're firing me?

BT: Don't make this any more difficult than it has to be, Avram. The contents of your desk are already at reception, and these gentlemen will escort you out.

AC: I don't believe this. I just don't believe this. Ten years. Ten years I gave you.

[Anonymous—call him Security 1]: Dr Castor? If you could follow me.

AC: Get your damn hands off me. I know the way. My work won you this project. Don't think this is the last you've heard from me.

BT: I think it is the last I've heard from you. You might not have read the NDA, but I have. You'll want to consider what we can take away from you if you try and breach it. Now, please. You're trespassing.

[Sounds of a brief fight? Difficult to make out]

[Door closes. Pause.]

BT: Paul? It's Bruno. Sorry to disturb you, sir, but you wanted to know. It's done. No. Everything went smoothly. No trouble at all. I'll start bringing in new people tomorrow.

[End of transcript]

Frank was still thinking about assembling the base while he was supposed to be doing driving practice, about how different it was going to be to anything he'd previously experienced.

He knew from the training videos that the equipment that he was familiar with on-site wasn't going to work on Mars. Anything pneumatic or hydraulic, for a start. Not that hydraulics had the best reliability on this or any other world: hoses invariably leaked or came loose. But fluid that needed to come from a supplier ten miles away could be replaced. Not so easy where he was going. Oil designed for lubricating something on Earth would boil away on Mars. Water-cooled cutting machines were right out, along with anything he'd normally rely on a two-stroke to power.

That left him with electrical, and purely mechanical. It was down to battery power and brute force—or finesse—to do the job. His biggest concern was the aluminum bolts, which were notoriously easy to strip. Using a standard nut runner with torque control would work just fine, but there were a lot of nuts. And given that building the base had to happen before anything else could, to rely on two men in cumbersome spacesuits with a couple of torque wrenches, while the rest of the crew kicked their heels? It wasn't the way forward.

Everyone was going to have to be involved in construction, and the only way of telling whoever was in charge was to talk to Brack, which was becoming his least favorite job of all. He'd rather run up and down the mountain, twice.

There wasn't a mechanism for him to set up a meeting, either. Brack would simply appear, denigrate his efforts and whoever else was around, threaten to give him a ticket for looking at him funny, then disappear again. But he was Frank's only point of contact with the decision-makers. The medics in the Blood Bank seemed entirely unconnected with any of the practical aspects of the mission, and utterly uninterested in anything he had to say.

He was trying to concentrate on maneuvering the single-axle trailer around a tight corner, when Brack decided to stand behind him. Frank momentarily contemplated the consequences of just keeping on going, but instinct cut in and he stopped abruptly, hard enough to shake his bones and rattle the chassis.

Marcy, who'd been stood watching, started forward, arms out wide in annoyance, ready to tear the interloper a new one, but then slowed when she saw who it was, letting her hands fall. Brack gave his idiot grin at her, then turned it on Frank.

Frank got down out of the buggy and walked to the back of the trailer. There was a buzz in his ear, asking why he'd broken his training. For once, he ignored it. If they knew he'd done that, they also knew why.

"What do you think you're doing, Kittridge?"

"I need to talk to you."

"You don't get that privilege. All you get to do is say yessir and nosir and threebagsfullsir."

Frank contemplated his boots for a moment, before looking up again. "I need everyone trained on construction. All of us. Otherwise, we're screwed from the start."

Brack reached out and patted Frank's chest, almost friendly, until his fingers curled into the cloth and he tightened his fist around it. "You're a prisoner, Kittridge." He spoke calmly at first, but then his voice started to rise. "You do not disrespect *me*." On that final, shouted word Brack started shaking Frank violently, backwards and forwards.

Frank planted his feet and refused to move.

"It is my opinion—my expert opinion—that we need to train the whole crew on building those shelters, to get them up and running as quickly as possible. *Sir*."

Brack let him go, and smoothed the front of his overalls down. "That wasn't too bad, was it, Kittridge?" He stared at the palms of his own hands, almost as if he'd never seen them before. "I'll pass it on."

And he just walked away.

"What does he do here?" asked Marcy. "He's not coming with us, is he? Oh, God, don't say he's coming with us."

Frank took a deep breath, trying to regain his composure. "I don't know. But I know for certain they already bumped someone."

"I'm second to Zero. The small black kid. Farming. Except he calls it hydroponics. And he's second to Zeus. Who's the AB guy. They're both still in. And us two."

"They've put an Aryan with the blackest kid on the team? It's like they want us to fail." Frank screwed his face up. "Goddammit, what were they thinking?"

"It's not as bad as all that," said Marcy. "Before you came in that first time, Building Six, he stood up and apologized. For his tats, for his behavior. Said he was sorry."

"If he ever bothers you—"

"He'd snap you in half, Frank." She shook her head. "He seemed sincere enough."

Both of them had simultaneous messages in their ears, telling them to get on with their allotted tasks: Frank, learning, and Marcy, teaching.

"We're in charge of jack," said Marcy, retaking her spotting position behind the cones. "We don't get a choice who we work with, right? You said that yourself."

Frank climbed to the bucket seat. "Hope he thinks the same about us."

He wiped the sweat from his hand before settling it at the six o'clock position on the wheel. Trying to forget about everything else but which way he wanted the back end of the trailer to go. He twisted in his seat and looked over his shoulder. How long did they have before Xenosystems had no choice but to put

63

them on a rocket? The longer he lasted, the less opportunity they had to can him. Where did the tipping point come, when he was more useful to them on Mars than he was in the Hole?

Had he just passed it, or had he blown his one chance?

"Whoa whoa whoa," called Marcy. "Where d'you think you're going?"

He stopped and shook his head free of the distractions. "It's OK. I got this."

But it was still in the back of his mind as he went through his paces, pushing and pulling various trailers, loaded and unloaded, backwards and forwards for the rest of the morning. If they tried to can him, what would he do? Would he have the mental strength to force them to kill him, suicide by cop style? Brack didn't carry a gun, but Frank was certain that the guards down at the perimeter did. Perhaps his thought about crashing the fence and haring out across the flats wasn't such a bad way to go after all.

He couldn't get the idea out of his head. He got as far as lunch, after which he was summoned to Building Ten again. What would his monitor say about his heart rate, his blood pressure, his breathing? Did they know? Could they read his mind after all?

Opening the door into the darkness, he walked out across the sand. The lights came on. It was just him: no Declan. That wasn't a good omen, and it felt like a long way to the first module. Maybe he should have run already, because if they came for him now, then he couldn't stop them from taking him down with tasers, binding him and hooding him and carting him away. He might be able to beat his own brains out with a wrench, but that'd be hard.

When he reached the module, he found a flight case, a big one, the size of a packing chest. He glanced around. There were tire tracks in the sand, leading towards the still-dark back of the hangar. He'd never explored down that end. He'd get to it. He flipped the lid of the case open, and pulled out one of six nut runners.

He pulled the trigger, and listened to the spindle turn. They had plenty of spare batteries, too. Did this mean what he hoped it did? That he'd been listened to, and he wasn't going to have to do anything so drastic as try and kill himself?

The door opened. A silhouette appeared briefly before the rectangle of daylight was cut off. A single figure started towards him. What relief Frank felt that it wasn't an XO snatch squad was tempered by his realization that it was the neo-Nazi giant.

This could be interesting.

"Hey, man," said the giant. He clenched his fist and held it out.

"Hey. I'm thinking you're Zeus." Frank had to reach up to tap his own fist against the other's. In comparison, his was tiny. "I'm Frank."

"Good to meet you, Frank." Zeus took in the modules with a slow sweep of his head. "Is this where we're going to be living?"

"I'm guessing they're going in kit form and we have to build them once we're there. It'd be nice to be told, but seems like they're holding back on us."

"And you do this?"

"I do now. You?"

"Pipes," said Zeus. "Plumbing. Used to work on oil rigs, so this is smaller-scale than I'm used to." He reached into the case for one of the tools, spun it up and set it down again. "I can help you with this."

"That's what I hoped." Frank kicked at the sand, and made up his mind. "I'm going to have to ask."

"Thought you might. You know how it is: blood in, blood out."

"I know."

"They've been looking to shank me for a while. Been on the PC for six months. Still not safe there. So when the suit came to me and told me he could get me somewhere else, where I wasn't going to have to watch my back for however long I had? I took it. You can call it a coward's choice: call it that myself sometimes. But seems God hasn't finished with me yet."

"You left the Brotherhood because you got religion?" Frank blinked. "I guess that would do it."

From what he could see of it, Zeus had a Nazi eagle splayed right across his chest, as well as ink on his head. The letters he had on one hand were matched on the other. HATE/HATE. This man had been in deep.

"The kid, Zero. I bet you scare the crap out of him, don't you?"

"I've explained to him like I've explained to you. I've asked for his forgiveness."

"His ... forgiveness? How did he take that?"

"It went well enough." Zeus flexed his fingers and looked away. He shrugged one shoulder and gave a snort of laughter. "I suppose I shouldn't expect miracles, should I?"

"That's your turf now. It's not mine."

The distant door clicked open again, and two more shapes occluded the outside.

"Getting busy in here," said Zeus.

It was the older woman, Alice, along with the curly-headed boy. She walked with all the assumed confidence of someone who knew that nothing and no one was going to hurt her, whereas he was just a child, pale and weak: his steps were jagged and hesitant, like he was terrified of his own shadow.

She rolled up. "Alice," she said to Zeus. "If you hadn't already guessed, I'm your doctor."

The boy stood a little way away. He couldn't take his eyes off Zeus.

"Dee-dee," he said.

"Demetrius," said Alice. "His name is Demetrius."

"He can call himself whatever he wants," said Frank.

Alice tutted. "He has a stammer. When he's nervous." She made it plain that she didn't have time for a stammer, or nerves. Her bedside manner was going to be something to watch out for.

"Don't mind Zeus. He's—" Frank almost said harmless,

which was self-evidently not the case. "—one of us. What's your job here?"

"He does the computers," said Alice, speaking for him again.

Frank felt irritation prickle across his skin, but he batted the feeling aside. It had been a long time since he'd had to instruct a team, and as long as they did the work, it didn't matter.

The door opened again, and they all looked round. Frank picked out Marcy straight away, and the thin shape beside her had to be Zero. They waited for them.

"Marcy," said Marcy. "Transport."

"Call me Zero," said Zero. "They put me in charge of your greens."

"So what did they put you in charge of?" asked Alice of Frank. She tilted her head back so that she could look down her nose at him. "Us?"

He had to work with her, he had no choice. "When we hit the surface of Mars," he said, "I'm guessing we'll have nothing. Getting these oversized baggies up will be the first thing we have to do, before Zero can start growing, or Zeus put in the cans, or Declan—wherever he is—string up the lights. The quicker we put these together, the faster we can get out of each other's faces. We get better food and somewhere to shit. That sound like a plan?"

No one responded.

"I'm not just saying this for my own health," said Frank. "I'm in charge of exactly squat. You want to sit in a spacesuit for a week and watch a couple of guys bolt one of these together? Be my guest. I'm thinking that it might be more comfortable for us all, in the long run, if we at least pretend to pull together. Now, again: is this a plan or am I just wasting my breath?"

"It's a plan," said Marcy. "What do you need me to do?"

"I'm not sitting around, watching other people work." Zeus hefted one of the nut runners. "I don't think anyone will."

"Their choice, big man," said Alice. But after a few moments' silence, she relented. "I don't see I can help much, but why not?"

67

Assent from Demetrius and Zero came in the form of a single nod. Still no sign of Declan, but it was his job to assist Frank. Hell, it was his job to replace Frank if anything happened to him. His co-operation was a given.

"OK? Marcy, we need to work out what we've got. Pretty sure there's a buggy somewhere at the back of this hangar: there are tire tracks heading that way. Could you take a look?"

"Sure," she said, and started out across the sand.

"The rest of you, grab one of these, and I'll show you how to use one. Safely."

Once he was sure they weren't going to hold on to the moving parts of the nut runners, he let them loose on one of the completed rings lying on the floor. They unbolted it so that the sections were separated out, exploded like an engineering diagram, then they started bolting it all back together again.

"You're going to be living in something you've helped put together," he said. "You'll be relying on it not to leak or fall apart. Chances are, if you cut corners, someone dies."

A couple of them resented his advice. Zero, and Alice. He'd have to watch their work, give it a proper assessment. Zeus, on the other hand, just got on with the job. He was probably more used to the labor and the setting—an ocean rig was going to have similarities to a spaceship or a Mars base—but the man's skills were going to be an asset. And a spacesuit was going to hide the swastika on the back of Zeus's neck.

Frank had never meant his life to be like this. All he'd ever wanted was a quiet existence, unremarkable and uneventful, getting up, going to work, having his family around him. Now he was going to spend the rest of his life on Mars with an ex neo-Nazi for company, not to mention whatever it was the others had done. Murderers, some of them. Murderers like him. As if this world didn't have enough crazy, they were now exporting it to other planets.

Marcy drove back across the hangar. She'd found a buggy, and was towing a long cylinder on a trailer.

"We've got this," she said. "I'm guessing we have to do something with it."

Between them, Marcy and Frank got the cylinder off the trailer and onto the ground. She glanced around and pulled him close. "How are they doing?"

"Getting on like a pressure cooker. Zeus is the least of my worries. Least of yours, too. Hell, we've all got some corners we can afford to have knocked off."

The cylinder was closed by releasable bolts recessed into the outer shell and protected by pull-up hatches. Frank pressed on the back of the first hatch so that it lifted proud of the surface, and wedged his fingertips under the leading edge. He pulled, and the spring-loaded mechanism snapped it into the upright position.

Zeus was there, doing the same thing on the next, and Zero beyond him.

The restraining bolts were screw-thread, big wings on the heads, released with a twist and pull. The cavity they extended into was just about large enough to get a hand in. Not Zeus's hand, but he could help open the other hatches while someone smaller—Marcy, in this case—worked the bolt. A tool for this would be useful, but they didn't appear to have one; Frank made a mental note to mention it later. To someone. Maybe even Brack.

Beneath the shadow of the cylinder, the cargo bay door popped, under pressure from inside. Zeus and Frank and Marcy heaved at the door, and it opened up fully. The cargo inside was neatly packed into drums. Zeus was already reaching in for the first, and Frank grabbed one of his own, rolling it across the sandy floor and parking it on open ground.

Each drum was a standard size to fit into the standard cylinder, seven feet across, six feet tall. They were big, and heavy. On Mars, gravity was one third of Earth's. Something that weighed three tons here would weigh just one there.

When all the drums were lined up, Frank went down the

row, reading the labels on the outsides to locate the things they'd need first: the end rings and outriggers, and, critically, the airlock, which came in one complete piece and had its own procedure. "OK. This one first."

The drum opened with simple latches around the circumference of its lid, but it took two crew members to pull the lid off and carry it away. Everything needed to build one section of habitat appeared to be present. It was time to go to work.

"OK," said Frank. "From the top."

He laid out what was required for the inner ring, and let the rest of them put it together.

Wrestling the plastic sheeting to the ground was incredibly hard work. The end panel was a flat disc. That was fine. The tube was terrible. He burned a dozen cable ties making sure it didn't just unfold again before he got it in position. Maybe it'd be easier with no air.

"Don't walk on the plastic. Don't cut the plastic," he warned them. They bolted the outer ring, one section at a time, to the inner ring. Then, awkwardly, trying to make certain that every part of the plastic was caught safely and firmly between the seals.

Zero was lining up the bolts and spinning the nuts onto the thread, accurate and quick with his fingers. Demetrius was less so, and the banter between them had tipped quickly from good-natured to cruel. These were going to be the only people on the planet, at least until NASA turned up, and it wasn't his job to discipline them. He couldn't fault Zero's work, though.

"Demetrius, give me a hand with this," said Frank, and started to drag out the base mat for the finished module. The kid was good with computers, that was why he was here. They needed him as much as he needed them. It wasn't his fault he wasn't good at building things. He was young, though: and he acted young. What the hell had he done to have ended up getting drafted into this mission?

The boy took the other side of the roll from Frank and together they dumped it on the floor.

"Check for rocks."

"There's no rocks," said Demetrius.

"On Mars, there will be. You walk along the route, and you pick up all the rocks that might work their way through the mat and you kick them to one side. Or you hammer the sharp edges off if they're part of the bedrock. Go on. Look, I know there aren't any rocks, because this is graded sand. But this is training. Every time we put out a new module, this is going to be your job. Walk the route, check it's clear. Got that?"

He was malleable enough that he took the instruction without complaint. He trod over the sand, scuffing it up as he went, turned round at the end and scuffed it back.

"It's clear."

"Good work. Now let's roll the mat out." They did, and Frank noticed that there was a nozzle that would take air. Or any other pressurized gas. Or water, even.

When the rings at both ends had been completed, the outriggers assembled, and the airlock bolted on, they tied ropes to the structure and walked it into position. It was—aluminum and plastic—straightforward. The module still needed to be anchored down, but it was up, in something under the two-hour mark. It'd take longer in a spacesuit, of course. He should get them all practicing in the gloves at least, and see how cocky they were then.

That wasn't right. He didn't want them to fail. He wanted them to succeed. He just wanted them to be realistic about what could be accomplished and how long it would take them. If they could get a couple of sections up, join them together, and pressurize them in a day, that'd be a start.

No obvious friendships had formed. Alice seemed to hate everyone. Zero had taken his chance to bully Demetrius. Zeus's ink made it all but impossible for him to get close to anyone. Declan—still no sign of him. Marcy. Him and Marcy. They got on well enough. So not fucking up there would be good.

While he toured the completed module, checking the rings at

71

each end and the attached legs, the hangar door opened up. The crack of light flashed on and off. A shadow was briefly visible in the glare. Declan. Frank met him halfway.

"I was expecting you here already," said Frank.

"I wasn't told until now. They had me running up and down that hill." Declan was wetter than usual. Dark stains mottled his T-shirt, and he rubbed his hands over and over again. He looked past Frank at the five others standing around the newly minted habitat. "This your team?" he asked.

Frank turned to look, and goddammit, yes. In the presence of a newcomer, they'd instinctively moved closer together.

"That's right," said Frank. "This is the rest of my team. Come on over. I'll do the introductions."

7

From: Bruno Tiller <bruno.tiller@gmail.com>
To: Michelangelo Alvarez <m.t.alvarez@gmail.com>
Date: Sun, Sep 14 2036 00:03:29 +1000
Subject: Re: the Project

I've just filed the official documentation on the server, ready for
Monday morning's meeting. It gives an outline of everything we've
done so far: I've included the specs for the vacuum chamber at
Gold Hill, but not the full tech report. I wanted to talk to you about
this over the back-channel.

You know my concerns: we've promised this vast open space,
some five times larger than the SPF, and it's as expensive as
fuck. The tech report says we can build it, but I don't think we
need it. Something with twice the footprint of the SPF—in the
region of 150–200 ft—will do, and it means we've got more in the
war chest when we inevitably run down to Launch Day and have
to throw money at problems to make them go away.

I want to emphasize to you that we cannot, must not, go over
budget on this. The shareholders will crucify us, and all the stock
we hold won't be enough to buy a pot to piss in.

I want you to come to the meeting with proposals for a smaller
vacuum chamber, and the justification for it. There'll be some
kickback, most likely from Castor on the Hab team, but I'll take

the heat and come down on your side. Hab will just have to suck it up.

Don't let me down.

◻

Building Fifteen was bigger on the inside. The back wall, which abutted the side of the mountain, was hollowed out and tunneled through. The electric carts they were in—sitting on rear-facing seats, wearing their spacesuits—drove all the way, then stopped. The voice in their ears told them to get out, and prepare for a live test.

When they turned round, they were confronted by a door that looked like it belonged in one of those apocalyptic movies, behind which the generals and the president shut themselves to escape the oncoming disaster.

"Well, damn," said Marcy. It was almost too difficult to look up to the top. "What the hell do they do here?"

A klaxon sounded and the door ground open, slowly and inexorably. It was huge, and very thick. It opened inwards, powered by massive hydraulic rams that glistened and growled. Inside, across a threshold that was high enough to need steps to get over it, was a gray empty space. Something rattled against the lip of the door, and two white-covered technicians slowly appeared in the doorway as they climbed up. They came down on the outside, and stood at the base of the steps.

Then Brack pushed through them all and mounted the steps, facing them as if he was some kind of general, addressing his troops.

Frank could hear the others groan through the open circuit.

Brack was wearing a headset: they couldn't block him out. "Get moving. We're on the clock."

One by one, they filed past Brack and into the dead area

beyond. Concrete floor, curved concrete walls, louvered open-
ings high up in the ceiling. On the floor, several items drew
Frank's eye. One was a long white cargo cylinder, like they'd
been playing with in Building Ten. The other things were two
igloo-like structures. They had the domed shape, but instead of
an entrance tunnel there were hatches that looked like airlocks.

"Listen up, you retards. This is different. This is for real.
You can die in here, and there's jack anyone can do about it.
In that tube is everything you need to build and pressurize one
module. Against my advice, you have been provided with a
couple of lifeboats. Use them for anything other than a medical
emergency and you will be canned. Use them at all and I'll get
you canned anyway.

"When I step out of this facility, the door will close and the
air will be sucked out. It takes half an hour to pump down,
twenty minutes to refill so you don't explode. After that first
thirty minutes is up, you will get to work. You will be working
in total vacuum, and you are on your own. There are cameras.
Don't interfere with them. But there will be no help except
what you can provide for yourselves."

He stood on the thick concrete sill and kicked the stairs away.
They rolled across the smooth floor and eventually stopped.

"You're the most useless bunch of fuck-ups I have ever had
the displeasure of working with. I'm kind of hoping that when
they open this door again, you'll all be dead or mad. You get
out of this coffin when you've done. Not before. You got that?"

Those who weren't already looking at him shuffled round so
that they could.

"I asked you a question."

"We got it," said Frank. "We know what to do."

The klaxon sounded and the door began to creep shut again.

"And do not start until you are told. Or I'll can you."

The huge door obscured his body, but they could still hear
him.

"I got fifty bucks on you fucking up."

75

The reverberation when the door finally closed was profound. The echo seemed to go on and on. Then distant fans in the ceiling started to take the air away. Frank walked over to the discarded steps and locked the wheels using the brake. He sat down on the third flat, like they were bleachers, ready to wait out the half-hour.

Zeus lumbered over, climbed past Frank and perched on the very top step.

"We going to go early?"

"Tempting, but cameras. We know what we have to do. We know we can do it." Frank felt his suit begin to stiffen. "We've done this before. We've got suit time. Just another day at the office."

"Any idea how long we got to do this?"

"That's probably something Brack should have said. It'll take less time than we have air for. We'll be fine."

The others drifted over. Alice took the seat next to Frank, effectively blocking the rest of the structure to those still standing.

"Anyone feeling light-headed, got cold spots, feel like they're struggling for breath?"

"I'm good," said Zero. "You good, Marcy?"

"Chill. That is, I'm fine. Dee?"

Demetrius nodded inside his suit, and unless anyone was watching, he didn't look like he was moving.

"You got to speak to us, Demetrius," said Frank. "Let everyone know you're OK."

"I'm good," he blurted, too abruptly for the compression to cut out the initial volume. "Sorry. I'm good. This ..."

"Feels like the real deal?" said Declan. "Marcy's right. We should chill. It's nothing we haven't done before."

Frank flipped out his control box and peered down at it. He had solid green lights, all the way. The situation was novel enough that he'd rather trust them than his own impressions. "I'm doing OK. Zeus?"

"Don't worry about me. Just enjoying the view."

Frank closed his controls. He knew it had just clicked shut, but he hadn't heard it. He raised his boot and tapped at the steps. He could feel the vibrations, but other than that, it was silent. Sound simply wasn't traveling. He thought about the consequences of that, being on a building site. If he was driving around in a buggy, no one would hear him coming. If he was reversing, he could run someone over. In fact, he could run them over lots of times, and unless they were on the same frequency, he wouldn't know until he actually checked.

He could be standing right behind someone, and they wouldn't know. And they could be right behind him ...

The suits had decent enough vision out of the front, but didn't allow more than maybe ten o'clock to two o'clock to the sides. He could stand beside someone, and unless they turned towards him, he'd still be in their blind spot.

Which was all pretty bad news.

"I want to change the rules some," he said.

"Oh, God. Here we go."

"Shut up, Alice." Frank paused, but she'd finished lodging her objection. "We've got limited vision, and limited hearing. All the usual things that keep us out of trouble aren't there, and we have to do this differently. So one of us—we'll take it in turns—stands to one side and watches out for the things that no one has spotted. Things that might drop or fall or crush or impale. People about to get in each other's way. That sort of shit. They just have to call it before it happens."

"And you're taking first watch, right?"

"I won't be taking any watches. Declan? You're up first, if that's OK. Just sit up here and keep an eye out. We'll swap it around every fifteen minutes or so, so we stay fresh."

"W-will we really explode?" asked Demetrius.

"No," said Alice. She sounded bored. Bored with even having to think about nursing any of them, now or in the future. "You'll be unconscious within ten seconds, less when you inevitably panic. You'll have a double pneumothorax and you'll go into cardiac arrest within a minute. There's a window of about thirty seconds where, if you're repressurized, you'll live. Probably."

"No one's dying today," said Frank.

"Accidents happen," she said.

Frank exchanged a look with her. "Preventable accidents happen. So let's prevent them."

They waited, and after what seemed an age, the voice told them to start.

Stirring himself, Frank got to his feet, feeling the drag of the life-support system on his back as he stood. The steps wobbled, but didn't rattle. Strange how things that he'd taken for granted were so important in building up the environment around him. All he had was the sound of his breathing.

"OK," he said, and started walking towards the cylinder. He had no idea if anyone else was following him, because he couldn't see them. It was just him, the few inches to his faceplate, and on the other side of that, pretty much instant death.

He was going to a planet where that was the rule, not the exception.

They cracked open the cylinder—the air trapped inside made the hatches pop out—and they started dragging the drums out, lining them up, ready for Frank to give them the once-over.

Declan made what sounded like a yawn, and Frank wasn't having that. "Stay frosty, man," he said, belatedly remembering that everyone would hear him equally loudly. "Declan. We need you alert."

"I am alert. No one's done anything stupid yet, that's all."

The first drum he opened contained the nut runners, and spare batteries. He counted them out, checked them all, and handed them round. He tapped three drums. "This, this, and this. Let's do it."

The mat went down first, rolled out with what should have been a loud slap and a gust of wind, but instead done in total silence. Then the airlock was carried into position—it took four of them—and placed face down on the concrete. Frank checked it, and got Marcy to check it as well: he didn't want the thing going on backwards.

He swapped Marcy out for Declan. They unrolled the plastic from the airlock surround, and started building the inner ring. All in absolute, uncanny silence.

"This is weird as fuck," said Declan.

"Makes it difficult to concentrate. You expect the tool to make a noise. It doesn't. You wonder if it's working, when it obviously is. That's OK. It's a test. We're supposed to find things out so it doesn't freak us when we're up there."

Up there. Mars was no more up than the Sun was down, but soon it would be Earth that was up there, just a pale dot in a pink sunset.

The first inner ring was done. They tied the airlock to it with tensioned cables. They lifted over the main plastic tube and positioned it. They started work on the first outer ring.

And Frank was tired. He was tired in a way that he shouldn't have been. Every move, deliberate and precise, needed additional effort: not much, just a little, but all those added up. His timer told him they'd been working forty-six minutes.

They could go to the hour, and everyone then take ten minutes. They couldn't eat anything, but there was water in the suit, supplied by a little sippy straw.

Frank swapped out Zeus for Alice, because she was as old as he was, and likely to be feeling the strain as much as him. Not that she would ever admit to it. So he cycled her to be on watch.

And people were starting to drop things, misthread and misalign bolts, and get on each other's nerves. Without suits, they'd be halfway done by now, but they were barely a quarter of the way through.

The last section of the outer ring went into place. Zero secured it in position, and stood slowly, wearily. He was almost reeling. Frank had had enough. It was starting to get dangerous.

"OK. Let's take a break."

No one complained. They were that exhausted. They put their tools down—and there was no way they could do that on the Martian surface, so Frank had them all pick them up again and stow them on the belts that went around their waists, and only then could they rest.

Except finding a position to rest in was awkward. Lying on his back wasn't an option, due to the hump of the life support. On his front, there was the bulge of the faceplate. On his side was possible, but sitting, slumped forward, forearms on thighs, head bowed, was about the best any of them could get. Four of them could fit on the steps. Small folding stools would be a bonus, but there weren't any. The remaining three—Frank, Zeus, Marcy—stacked the drum lids up until they reached a respectable height, and sat down.

The cooling air blowing around Frank's face was drying him out even while it cleared his faceplate of fog. His eyes felt scratchy and his skin was tight. He couldn't even rub some life back into his features, so he pulled faces for a while and drank some water.

How bad would this have been if they hadn't forced him up and down the Mountain every day, or made him spin on the static bike until he couldn't feel his legs? He could grudgingly admit to the point of it, while still disliking the actual effort. No, it wouldn't be this bad on Mars. It'd still be grueling, but the suits were designed to work there, not here.

They sat, mostly in silence, or exchanged one or two words that required little in the way of reply. The clock ticked on, numbers on his console that slowly accumulated like falling dust. He could feel the ache in his muscles slowly dissipate, to be replaced by a general fatigue.

He let the timer run past the ten-minute mark, then decided that they should start again.

"You heard what the man said: we don't get out of here until we're done, so let's get it finished."

No one moved until he did. He took his nut runner back off

his belt, and while three of them built the next ring, the others assembled the outriggers.

It was still surreal, as if everything that was happening outside of his suit was being played on a screen with the sound turned off. Disassociative. Mute images of people working. A silent film.

Music. That was what they needed. Anything, maybe without words, but something other than their breathing to measure time by. When they were on Mars, that was what he was going to do. Get Demetrius to load up some music, if they had any, and play it out over the headphones. It was what the chain gangs used to do. Sing. And what were they but a high-tech chain gang? They might be wearing spacesuits rather than shackles, but that didn't fundamentally alter what the relationship was.

He wasn't the only one to think that. He heard someone humming. There was a threshold of volume below which speech wouldn't be broadcast. It often clipped the first word of their conversations if they didn't precede it with an opening sound. That made it difficult now to pick out the tune, but after a few bars it became clear:

"Swing low, sweet chariot."

Frank looked to see who it was. It sounded odd over the speakers. Higher pitched. But everybody was bent over their work, faces down. He couldn't tell.

"I'm sometimes up, and I'm sometimes down, comin' for to carry me home."

"*Keep this channel clear. No unnecessary traffic.*"

It stopped. It hurt when it stopped. Frank spoke into the quiet. "It's OK. We just need to keep going. Stay alert and we can get the job done."

Alice broke in. "Everyone check their suits, make sure you're all the right temperature and breathing the right mix."

They did that, and reported they were all well within the green bands.

Except Demetrius, who said: "I'm losing pressure."

81

Frank put his tools down, then picked them up again and hung them from the clip at his waist. He located Demetrius, who was staring at his chest-screen, tapping at it as if he could make the numbers change.

"That's what this says, right?" He tilted the screen so that Frank could see it. "That I'm losing air."

Frank, reading it upside down, watched as the digits fluctuated up and down. The green indicator was turning amber, then back to green again, as the suit detected the lower pressure and dispensed more air to make up. "Why didn't your alarm go off?"

"I don't know. I don't know why. F-Frank? What do I do?"

"You don't panic. You keep breathing easily. It's a slow leak. We just have to find it and plug it."

"I've got a leak? Do I bail? Do I get canned if I do? Frank, I don't want to go in the Hole."

"No one's going in the Hole, Demetrius. I need to check your suit."

Marcy was there. "It's going to be fine, Dee. Just stand with your arms out."

Frank took one side, Marcy the other. Everyone else was watching. Frank checked the seams, the seals, the outer fabric layer.

"Do you feel cold anywhere?" asked Marcy.

"I don't know: my arm, maybe."

"Left or right?"

"Right. I just thought …"

Marcy was on the right, and she rechecked. "I've got it. There's a tear just above the elbow."

Demetrius immediately tried to turn his arm so he could see, but couldn't because it was his elbow. "What do I do? What do I do? What if I run out of air?"

Frank grabbed Demetrius's arm and held it tight. "Stop moving around. Let me see." Quite why this was his job was anyone's guess, but there he was. He held the cloth taut, and yes, there was a rent, an inch long, just behind the elbow joint, on the upper arm. "How the hell did you do this?"

"I just got caught on a latch. I pulled, and … it came free. I didn't know."

"You got to be more careful."

"What do we do? We've got something to fix this with, right?"

They hadn't been given anything. Help was the other side of a six-foot-thick concrete wall.

"You're going to use one of the lifeboats."

"He'll can me. Brack'll can me."

"He might can everyone," said Alice. "I wouldn't put it past him. We know there are others in training, and we've already had one replacement." She looked pointedly at Declan. "I'm not going to risk that. So we improvise."

She pushed Marcy out of the way and inspected the tear in the cloth. She dug her fingers into the hole and pulled it apart. There was no tearing sound. She pinched and pulled at the inner suit, and stepped back. "God only knows what you thought you were doing. You caught the seam at the elbow pad, yanked it hard enough that you've torn a flap in the pressure garment. Mostly seals when you bend your arm, but when you straighten it, the inner suit relaxes and it opens up more."

"Have we got something to fix it with?" asked Marcy.

"We could use a ratchet strap as a tourniquet," said Frank. "What's the long-term effect of vacuum on just an arm?"

"Swelling, bruising. Possible embolism. If we tourniquet it too long, he'll end up losing his arm. I wouldn't recommend it." Alice looked at the hole again. "Get me the strap anyway: I'll need it. Find me something with a blade, or that can be sharpened to a edge. I can seal a hole that size."

"Shouldn't I just put my hand on it, or something?" Demetrius tried to put his free hand over the tear, and Alice batted him away.

"You're losing air, you little punk. You'll continue to lose air until that hole is sealed. I am not, repeat not, getting canned because you did something monumentally stupid. Do you hear me?"

Demetrius nodded inside his helmet.

"Now I need a blade."

"We don't have a knife," said Frank, "or anything like that."

"He made that hole with something, didn't he? We're cons. If we can't make a shiv, what the hell are we doing here?"

"I can get one of the latches," said Zeus. "Five minutes rubbing it down on the floor will give it a rough edge."

"It'll do." She held Demetrius's arm bent. "Don't move."

Zeus broke off the latch with part of the unfinished ring, and started stropping it on the floor. They were all just standing around watching him, and there wasn't really any need for that.

"OK, this is Alice's thing," Frank told them. "We can get some work done: the sooner we're out of here, the better."

They left Demetrius with Alice, and went back to work. Declan took up spotting for them again, and with Zeus making the blade, it was just Frank, Marcy and Zero.

"We got to work fast, man," said Zero.

"No we don't. Just steady. That's all. We can't afford any more mistakes."

"But Dee's air?"

"Which is why we need to carry on. We're getting there. Ring's almost done. We just need the outriggers fixed on, and the module set out. Then we can inflate it, and we're finished."

"This wouldn't happen on Mars, right? We'd get him inside straight away and that'd be that. We wouldn't have to do any of this. So why didn't they give us anything to fix the suits with?"

"I don't know. Perhaps we should ask for stuff. Sticky patches and the like."

"You going to ask, Frank?"

"OK. I'll ask."

Zeus finished sharpening up the flat piece of metal, and he carried it over to Alice. Frank let the other two carry on working, and went to see what she was going to do. Zeus was Alice's second, but there wasn't any medical stuff going on here. This was suit repair.

"It's sharp," warned Zeus. "Don't get that anywhere near *your* suit."

"Loop the strap around his arm, around the biceps." She used the blade to saw away some of the loose outer layer, and wadded it up, folding it in half, and half again. She gave that to Frank. "Don't just stand there: make yourself useful. Zeus, straighten his arm, hold him tight."

"What're you going to do?" Demetrius's voice was tight and high. "What?"

"Shut up," said Alice, and stabbed his elbow through the tear.

"Fuck," said Frank.

"Pad," she said. Then she just snatched it from Frank and pressed it hard against the sudden bloom of frothing blood. "Strap."

Zeus pushed the fabric strap down one-handed and tightened it in place. He held Demetrius fast with the other.

"Not too tight. We're trying to hold the pad in place, not stop his circulation."

"You cut me," Demetrius protested. "She cut me."

"The blood will soak into the cloth, and when it coagulates it'll form an airtight seal. Any more questions from anyone?"

"You could have told us," said Frank. "You could have told him."

"Because that would've kept his breathing rate down, wouldn't it? He can still spot for us, and now he's not leaking out."

It was true. Demetrius's suit's internal pressure had stabilized.

"Go sit down," Frank told him. "You'll be fine."

The boy's face was ashen, but he nodded. He went over to the steps, and Declan rejoined them down at the ring.

He grinned. "I don't think much of her bedside manner, but she gets the job done."

Yes, she'd got the job done. But she was dangerous. Frank wondered what XO made of that little show. "Go and get the ropes," he said. "Let's get this upright."

8

[Press release from Xenosystems Operations to coincide with the second anniversary of the Mars Base contract, embargoed until 2/5/2037]

We dream of space. We dream of new worlds. We dream of possibilities and futures. We dream of open skies and wide horizons, of sights that no human eye has ever seen. We dream, and then we build. Xenosystems Operations has, since its birth, always been reaching for the unobtainable, the impossible, the unimaginable, and making it real.

We are the world leaders in spacefaring technology, trusted by governments and corporations to deliver on our promises, and admired by people everywhere for our far-sighted vision of the destiny of the human race. As we enter a new era of exploration, of colonization, of adaptation and exploitation, XO is simply in a class of its own.

No wonder that, two years ago, the historic partnership between XO and NASA was announced, to create a permanent presence on the surface of Mars. Mars Base One will combine innovative engineering solutions with tried and tested techniques to provide a unique living space on the red planet. Brave men and women will follow in the footsteps of Gagarin, Glenn, Tereshkova and Ride, Armstrong and Lou, pioneers breaking new ground on a hostile planet, taming it and turning it into a place of refuge and peace.

Two years in, and our research facilities are already producing amazing results. Technology that will enhance the lives of every man, woman and child on this, and other planets. Compact, automatic machines to aid us in our daily chores. Medical advances that will save countless numbers of our loved ones. Monitoring systems that can safeguard our communities, and protect us from our enemies. There has never been a better time to be alive, thanks to the advances XO is making every single day.

Our dream is to provide an environment in which astronauts can live and work, and one day may even call 'home'. Our task is to make that dream a reality. Xenosystems Operations. We are worlds apart.

"We're not ready," said Frank.

"You don't have a say." Brack slapped his hands on the table. "Time's up, Kittridge."

It was just Frank and Brack, in a room, sitting opposite each other.

"Give me some credit for knowing how ready we are. We know a few things well. We know other things less well. Some things we know jack about. We're undertrained. You can send us like that: you're right, we don't have much choice. But we know how good we are, and your," Frank circled his finger towards the ceiling, "controllers have to know that too."

"They don't give a shit what you think. Your past six months has been so closely watched they know how much wind you've passed. If they think you bunch of fuck-ups are ready, then you salute the company flag and shout 'yessir' until your lungs bleed."

Frank ran his tongue over his teeth and grimaced. "Like I said, none of us can stop this. We were yours—Panopticon's, XO's—from the moment we knew where we were headed. Doesn't stop us from having an opinion."

Brack leaned back so far in his seat that Frank thought he might fall out of it backwards. He was staring up at the ceiling, where the lights and the cameras and the microphones were. "You know, Kittridge. I don't like any of you. You're a mix of killers and perverts and the just-too-stupid-not-to-get-caught. No one is going to miss you here on Earth. That's why you were chosen. You're the things we forgot we had."

"I get that."

"Now, here's the deal. You get to Mars. You know what you got to do, because you know if you don't, you won't survive longer than five minutes. But XO are getting edgy over whether you can keep it together up there: that the only reason you're working together down here is because you want to avoid the Hole. You want to stay out the Hole, Kittridge?"

"I'm not a fan," said Frank.

"Once you're on Mars, there's no Hole. No discipline. No one to keep you in line. You'll fall apart, and with it, the project. You know how much Uncle Sam is ponying up for this?"

"I read about it somewhere."

"Trillions. All that money's been spent getting us to this point. And you, and your fine fellows, are now the only people standing between Mars Base One and an expensive failure. Which is why I'm going with you."

After a while, he looked across the curve of his chest.

"You took that calmly enough."

"I was expecting it. I can, after all, count as far as eight. So I'm guessing this decision was made a while back, and you're not telling me anything I don't know."

"And perhaps, you're just saying that." Brack shifted his legs and swung back towards the table. "I'm going to level with you here, man to man. I'm going to be one lawgiver in a town of outlaws. That's a tough beat to walk. Now, there's you. Out of all of you, you're the one I trust most. That's not saying much, but there you are. And if this sheriff is going to keep order, he's going to need a deputy."

Frank steepled his fingers. "You treat me like something you trod in for months, and suddenly I'm good enough to be your right-hand man? That's such a quick turnabout, I'm getting whiplash."

"I'm not saying you got to dress up and act like some trusty. You'll still be a lifer, still be one of them. But I got to sleep sometime, Kittridge. I need someone to watch my back, tell me of any loose talk. I need you to help keep me alive. Just in case."

Brack stared at Frank, who stared coolly back. "You want me to be a snitch."

"We can make it worth your while."

"The last time someone made me an offer, I got sent to Mars. So this had better be good."

"You know what's supposed to happen. You go, you build a base, you stay until you finish your sentence, which is sometime in the twenty-second century, right?" Brack smirked at him, and how Frank hated that. And now he knew he was going to see it every day, just when he could have been rid of it for ever.

He wasn't going to show how much he loathed the man. How much time he spent imagining ways in which he'd die. "You were talking about how you were going to make it worth my while."

"I'm going with you. But you've got to understand that I'm not staying, because I'm not like you. I got me a ticket home. Not straight away. But when we're done. You understand?"

Frank nodded slowly. "I get that."

"So XO have hired me to keep you all in line. They want to know their investment is secure. When we've hosted that first NASA mission, and it's gone well, it'll be safe for me to hand over to someone else. I'll take up their seat on the ship back to Earth, because for me this isn't a sentence, it's a job. You could be coming back with me."

Frank scratched at his chin. Time seemed to be moving very slowly. He could hear the rasp of his fingertips on his stubble over the wash of the air con. "And what's going to be waiting for me when I step out of the lander?"

"An open door. There'll be some restrictions on your

movement. You'll be tagged. But you'll be free." Brack smiled at him. "Look at you. You didn't expect this, did you? I love this bit, watching your little brain turn somersaults, trying to process it all."

"And the only thing I have to do is make sure that you stay alive?"

"Wouldn't be much point in it otherwise. You scratch my back, XO will scratch yours. Leave the other deadbeats up there and come home. How does that sound, Kittridge? Hell, we've got all your psych scores: we know you're going to say yes."

"The others aren't going to be happy with the arrangement. They're going to be pissed. Really pissed."

"They're never going to know. And if they find out, the deal is off. Finito. Finished. Total secrecy is the only way this goes down."

"And," asked Frank, "what happens when you and me get to skip off into the sunset together? They'll probably realize something's going down at that point."

"Leave them to me. I just need you to tell me I have your co-operation." Brack leaned across the table. "You want to go home, right? Everybody does. Fuck that shit about being pioneers and colonists and stuff. That's for the hardcore nerds. You and me, we want to do a job, finish it up and go home. Kick back in the La-Z-Boy. Have a beer or two. Watch the game. Without the air outside trying to kill us."

And to be free. Free to find his son again. It was a hell of a long way round to go. Prison. Mars. Back.

So what about the others? What about their hopes and fears for the future? Leave them to me, Brack had said. Just how was he going to handle that? Did Frank care, if the prize at the end of it all was worth it? Oh, that was cold. But it wasn't like he hadn't had to make that kind of calculation before and live with the consequences.

"Can I ask you a question?"

"Hell, boy. You can ask. Doesn't mean I'll give you an answer worth jack."

Frank leaned over the tabletop on his forearms. "What are they saying about us, outside?"

"You think you're all some kind of big damn heroes because you're going to Mars? Let me disabuse you of that straight away. To the outside, you're just Prisoners A through G."

"They don't even know our names?"

"XO didn't want all your victims' relatives kicking up a stink. It's got public relations disaster written all over it." Brack waved his hand at Frank. "Like you fuck-ups actually matter."

Nothing was going the way Frank had planned it. He'd assumed—he'd hoped—that his son would be proud of him just for going to Mars. That wasn't going to happen now, until XO dropped the embargo on their names, or ever. What should he do now? What else could he do, but agree to this last chance of creating something good out of the void that was his existence?

"OK," said Frank. "I'll do it."

"That wasn't so bad, was it?"

"I'll have to keep up appearances. Make sure that everyone thinks I still hate your guts."

Brack gave his silly little grin. "You'll put on a good show, Kittridge. But you'll remember, won't you?"

"I'll remember," said Frank, and wondered if Brack knew that sometimes words had two different, opposite meanings.

"Go and get your things. Transport leaves in half an hour."

Frank went back to his room. It was bigger than his old cell, and technically en suite, which meant there was a door between the bathroom and the bed. It had never felt different, though. He knew he'd swapped one cage for another, and had simply shifted his brown cardboard box between prisons.

Sure, he was leaner, fitter, more purposeful. He didn't resent any of that. He had a use, rather than just rotting away out of sight. That was good. But it was all he'd thought he'd ever have. Now ... he rested his forehead against the cool of the wall.

Totally unexpected. Yes, he'd always known they'd send a supervisor with them, but Brack? Goddammit. Did they deserve that? Not that they weren't terrible people: they were. But despite everything, despite their natural instincts to go to the extremes, or blame others for mistakes they'd made, or a lack of any kind of internal warning voice, they'd sort of made up a team. They were all qualified to be there, and as long as they all did their jobs and as long as they didn't deliberately push each other's buttons, they got on well enough. The base would be large enough when it was finished that they could have their own space. Bumping along like that was no different from being on a cell-block landing.

Whether they could do it indefinitely was another matter, but there were going to be people coming and going, and the base was supposed to expand as time went on. They'd be diluted, and eventually become just the crew—which wasn't too bad, all things considered.

He'd prepared himself for all of that. Prepared himself for being a remote role model, an example of how a man could do something awful, and turn himself around. Now the twin revelations that no one outside knew his name, and that this might not be the end after all meant …

The son he knew he had and thought of all the time wouldn't have to spend all his days wondering what had become of his father. They could sit out in the yard together and watch that small red dot appear over the horizon, and maybe the grandkids would want to hear of the time Gramps went to Mars. He just had to stay strong, and survive, and make sure nothing happened to Brack. A year traveling. A year or two or three working. A year on the way back. That wasn't such a bad exchange for something passing for freedom.

He lifted the lid of the box and went through all the things he knew were there. His few books. His few letters from his ex-wife. He sat on the edge of his bed and read through all the letters he could, starting at the beginning, when there was consternation and confusion, and working his way through, watching it slowly drain away, until there was nothing but cool, defensive detachment.

She'd divorced him. Of course she had. He'd told her unequivocally that she should, and she'd agreed faster than he thought she might. But he'd betrayed her, by not telling her what he'd been planning. And if he'd loved her more, he might not have done it.

Rereading the letters gave him comfort, though. He had been loved. He had had the capacity to love. He might even love again, at some point. He had known once upon a time how to do that and what it had felt like.

"Report to Building Two. Acknowledge."

"Acknowledged." It might be the last time he heard that voice in his ear. "It's been real."

He picked up his box and headed down towards Building Two, where there was a line of minivans waiting. The evening air was cool, and coming off the desert, so it tasted of salt.

The others were there, congregating at the steps up into the medical center, each of them was holding a California Department of Corrections cardboard box. Marcy's was tied up with string. There were also suits, but they were waiting on the other side of the road. Apart from their earpieces, the cons were alone.

Zeus, sitting on the steps of the Blood Bank, moved across to give Frank some room. "Good?"

"Good enough."

"I have a bad feeling about this." Zeus's thick fingers dug into the board of his box, perched across his knees. "This is too quick."

"I've registered my objections already. It made no difference. We just have to suck it up, big man." The wind tugged at Frank's ankles. "We're on our way. We've been on our way since we left the pen, but someone, somewhere, had one of those big clocks and it's counted down."

"That's always bugged me. The countdown business. If everything's ready, why not just press a button and launch?"

"I guess it's more complicated than that," said Frank. "You wouldn't turn on a pump until it had liquid inside it, so people have to know the order in which to do stuff."

"I suppose so. If there was someone we could have asked, that would have been cool, you know? It's like we're being kept in the dark on purpose." Zeus glanced behind him at Building Two. "Do you know how they're going to do this?"

"We get in the cars and they take us to wherever, where they do whatever it is they do to us. Then we wake up on Mars." Frank saw he had an audience. "That's what they're going to do."

Alice jerked her head at one of the vans. "Go and take a look in the back."

"Which one?"

"Any one."

Frank put his box down and walked slowly over. He shielded his eyes against the reflections around him and peered in through the tinted side windows. He frowned, and hunkered down for another, better look.

Inside was like the back of an ambulance. There were machines and straps and wires and tanks, and things he couldn't even recognize.

"They're going to put us under here," she called. "We won't even get to see the rocket. We're the cargo. We're not important."

Frank realized that he should have expected this. That every time his jailers had the opportunity to behave like decent human beings, they disappointed him. They were determined to let him down at every turn. All he'd wanted to do was step up to the rocket like a regular astronaut, so that he felt as if he was actually going on a journey. Brack had said "transport", but they were just going to freight them all as frozen corpses. It would explain why they were waiting outside the Blood Bank.

"Well," he said. "Goddamn." He walked back to the steps, picked up his box again and cradled it against his chest.

The door to Building Two swung open, and the suits shifted their stances, in exactly the same way that prison guards did when they thought something was about to kick off. Rather than a message over the earpiece, it was one of the medics, holding a tablet, calling them inside.

Frank looked around at the others. Did any of them seem more agitated than usual? Were they going to make a futile run for it? There was nowhere to go, and no one going to help them. Demetrius was almost shaking with fear, and Marcy put her hand between his shoulders. She whispered something to him, and the boy nodded hesitantly.

"We're not quitters," said Zeus. He got to his feet and started up the steps. "We might be a lot of things, but not that."

Then he started to sing.

"Oh mourner, let's go down, let's go down, let's go down. Oh mourner, let's go down, down in the valley to pray."

"No singing," said his ear.

Not this time. Frank couldn't sing. Couldn't so much as hold a note from one word to the next. He'd never really tried out of childhood. But damned if he wasn't going to try now. The words weren't familiar to him. He was more West Coast than he was gospel, and maybe he'd heard the tune once before, with different lyrics.

"Go on, Zeus. Sing it for us."

Zeus glanced behind him, and gained strength from what he saw. "As I went down in the valley to pray, studying about that good old way." His voice was high and clear and clean. For a big man, he sounded more like a choirboy. "When you shall wear the starry crown, good Lord, show me the way."

The medic wordlessly stood aside for the line of them, Zeus in front, Marcy propelling Demetrius ahead of her at the rear. When it came to the chorus, Frank joined in, hesitantly and very inexpertly.

"Oh sinner, let's go down, let's go down, let's go down. Oh sinner, let's go down, down in the valley and pray."

"*No singing*," said his ear again. Presumably in Zeus's too, but he wasn't going to be put off either. Not this time.

"I think I hear the sinner say, come, let's go in the valley to pray. You shall wear the starry crown, good Lord, show me the way."

They were walking down the corridor, down to the very far end, where Frank had never gone before.

"Oh mourner, let's go down, let's go down, let's go down. Oh mourner, let's go down, down in the valley and pray." Was it everyone now? It was difficult to tell without stopping to check. It sounded like most of them. Perhaps not Alice, but then again, why not? If an ex-white supremacist could sing a spiritual, then there was no good reason for a doctor guilty of murdering her patients not to do so.

It was an act of defiance, for certain. There was nothing that their jailers could do to them. Not now. It was also an act of contrition. Zeus was singing the songs of the people he'd tattooed his hate for across his body.

The double doors at the far end of the corridor opened up, revealing a bright, white space beyond, and Zeus strode into it, carrying the rest of them along in his wake.

Seven tables. Seven coffins. Screens between them. Two medics in each bay.

Zeus's voice faltered, just for a beat, before he resumed. "I think I hear the mourner say, come, let's go in the valley to pray. You shall wear the starry crown, good Lord, show me the way."

One of each pair of medics came forward to claim their victim, and led them to their separate areas, where it was just them, the three of them together.

"*Get undressed*," Frank was told, and he got undressed, like he had done a hundred times. He put his box on the floor in front of his white, plastic coffin, and purposefully took his clothes off, trying to record for posterity what it felt like.

"Oh sinner, let's go down, let's go down, let's go down."

The roughness of the fabric, the weight of it as it fell away. The cold, antiseptic air giving him gooseflesh. This might be the last thing he ever remembered. The slickness of the rubberized floor. The strange envelope of the stretchy one-piece he had to put on, that went right over his head and left only his face exposed.

"Oh sinner, let's go down, down in the valley and pray."

Rockets blew up sometimes. Even those carrying people. And if they were going to Mars, sometimes they didn't get there. Or if they did, they plowed into the ground and left a new crater.

"I think I hear the sinner say, come, let's go in the valley to pray."

He used the steps to climb up into the coffin. It was even colder inside. Water-cooled cold. There were pipes going in and out of the shell.

"You shall wear the starry crown, good Lord, show me the way."

He laid himself down. He didn't know what to do with his hands. They were going to be in the same position for a year, so he ought to be told whether to put them by his sides, or cross them at his waist, or fold them against his chest.

"Oh mourner, let's go down, let's go down, let's go down."

His teeth were starting to chatter. He was utterly at their mercy, and he always had been. He might not be going to Mars at all. He could wake up anywhere. He might not wake up at all, and be used for spare parts. That was stupid. Why all the training, otherwise?

"Oh mourner, let's go down, down in the valley and pray."

One by one, their voices were being stopped up. He couldn't see what was being done to them, but his own team of medics was holding out a mask over his face. He could hear the hiss of gas, and caught a whiff of magic marker pens.

"I think I hear the mourner say, Come, let's go in the valley to pray."

The mask came down, and he needed to breathe the gas in, and didn't want to breathe it in at the same time. Keep singing. Keep singing. He was the only one left.

"You shall wear the starry crown, good Lord, show me the way."

9

[Redacted report from Gold Hill Assessment Center Building Two (2) to Project Sparta 5/20/2047]

Kittridge, Franklin Michael.
DOB 1/20/1996.
POB Modesto, CA.
Married: Scott, Jacqueline Christina 6/11/2022. Divorced 7/5/2040.
Children: 1, Scott, Michael Clay 12/5/2023.
Arrested: 7/4/2038 Murder One.
Sentenced: 3/20/2039 Murder Two 120 years detention without
    parole.

Dominance 38
Emotional stability 78
Openness to change 35
Perfectionism 82
Privateness 92
Rule consciousness 86
Self-reliance 87
Social boldness 25

Overall Utility 83

The pain woke him up.

He felt as if he was on fire, and for a moment he saw the white phosphorous flames that were engulfing him. But that initial wash passed by, and all he was was cold.

Something was trying to push through his lips, and he couldn't turn his head to get away from it, but he could clamp his jaw shut to prevent its entry.

His cheek stung with the slap, and when he gasped, a lukewarm, moist mass was pushed into his mouth.

"Chew it, and don't swallow. It's a sponge."

That was ... Alice?

The inside of his mouth was as dry as a sepulcher. The water-soaked sponge slowly loosened his tongue, while she ripped the tape—faster than was strictly necessary—from his eyelids.

The glare was too much to start with and, what with that and the eyedrops that more or less went in the right place, he was still functionally blind. He chewed at the sponge, and when he'd drained it completely of moisture, he pushed it to the front of his mouth and let it roll out.

"Mars?" he croaked.

"It's either that or a particularly shitty version of the afterlife."

He tried blinking, and it was scratchy, but doable. The lights over him started to resolve out of the white mist into individual sources. A tube replaced the sponge, and a jet of cold water splashed over his tongue.

"Swallow."

He did so, and it was like taking down a stone. He was gasping with the effort.

"Again."

He didn't want to, but knew he had to. Unless she was poisoning him. But there was no way he could have stopped her from doing that, so he wrapped his tongue around the bolus of liquid and choked it down.

"We don't have much of this: what's in here is yours. But it turns out that we don't have much of much."

He heard her shuffle around out of his eyeline, which was forcibly directed to the ceiling by his head restraints. He tried to twitch his fingers, and was surprised when they responded first time. His toes, too.

"Meaning?"

"It means we're critically short on supplies. We can afford to go hungry, but we can't go thirsty."

He was lying in some sort of form-fitting soft rubber, cut so that it held him in place. He lifted one arm, and it came free with a distinct sucking noise.

"But Mars?"

"There's a window downstairs you can look through, and there are cameras on the hull. It certainly looks like it. But the kicker is the reduced gravity: can't fake that. Be careful how you move, because it's a bitch." She held out her hand, and he failed to grasp it at the first attempt. "Just stay still. Let me do the work."

She gripped his wrist and pulled. Everything felt wrong and nothing felt right. He was weak, stupid and dizzy, and had to hold on to the sides of his coffin while his world, whichever one it was, stopped spinning.

"You won't feel up to much for a while. But the sooner you get moving, the better. You won't be the only patient I have."

Frank didn't recognize where he was. He'd never seen the inside of the capsule before. He squinted, looked at the two tiers of four coffins arranged against the circle of the wall, and the hole in the center of the open grid floor. There didn't appear to be anything above them—so they were near the top of the lander, then.

Alice threw a set of overalls at him. He didn't try to catch it, just allowed it to wrap around his face and then slide down onto his legs. The way that it had flown through the air, on a flat arc, looked odd. Alien.

"Crap. Can't hit jack," she said. "Come on, up. Marcy's next, and I guarantee you she's going to whine like a baby."

"Who else is up and running?"

"Brack. Me. You. And seriously, we haven't got all day."

A day which now lasted forty minutes longer.

"You're not special. I'm doing this in order of priority, and currently you and Marcy are the priority. Now get out of my way."

Her face looked puffy, and florid. Perhaps his did too. They were living under reduced air pressure and reduced gravity. He'd been told to expect fluid to pool in places it shouldn't, at least until his body had got used to it all. And even though he'd been asleep for … however long it was … he'd been in zero g almost all the time.

He picked up his legs, right then left, and dangled them over the side of his coffin, and laboriously struggled into his one-piece overalls. There was an embroidered patch on his pocket. Not his name, nor one of those fancy mission patches either. Just a number. Two. He was number two.

He managed to focus on Alice, and saw she was wearing the same blue as him. She had her back to him, taking read-outs from one of the other coffins: Marcy's, presumably.

"What?" she grunted.

"What number are you?"

"One," she said, without looking round. "Because I'm better than you, I guess. Jeez, I don't know. It's not my prison number, so they probably just assigned them at random."

"And how are you?"

She paused, and glanced over her shoulder at him. Her pony-tail moved with unnatural slowness. "I'm doing OK. Maybe women's physiology is better at coping with this crap, I don't know. XO will want to know how we all are. There are tests I have to do on you all." She turned back. "Brack's down below. If it's any comfort, he's not in any better state than you are. But thanks for asking. He didn't."

Frank got his arms down his sleeves and zipped himself up. He sat there for a moment, thinking that it should be more momentous than this. He was on another planet, joining a very short list of people who'd been there before him. Yet, it was utterly anticlimactic. Like getting up in the morning, hunting down the first coffee of the day, feeling ill and still knowing he had to go to work.

He tried standing up. A lifetime's worth of learned experience hadn't prepared him for the sensation of both falling and flying. His hand shot out—thankfully at normal speed—to hang on to the curved top of the ladder. At least he hadn't pitched himself to the floor or slithered down the hole.

Alice wasn't making any big moves. Her actions were small and precise, and when she needed to get across the cabin she shuffled, dragging her feet over the gratings. He had to move like Alice, because he was certain he didn't want to spend the next six weeks wearing a jury-rigged cast on a broken ankle.

He put his water bottle in a long pocket in his overalls, and placed one foot on the top rung. Slowly, purposefully, he made his way down, one step at a time. It felt wrong, and he was going to have to get used to it.

The floor below was full of panels of switches and screens. He had no idea what any of them did, so he didn't touch them. The ladder kept on going down. He was about to continue with his descent when the image on one of the screens flipped from being an interior shot to exterior.

Pale pink stones in dark red sand. A mountain in the distance, rising up in a dusty haze. The image changed to one of Brack moving from console to console. Frank could hear him, too, below his feet.

"Get your lazy ass down here, Kittridge. We got ourselves a situation and I need to apprise you of it."

Frank climbed down and found Brack staring at a computer screen with several windows open on it. He couldn't see any seats. Brack was hunched over, his elbows pressed against the edges of the fold-out keyboard.

"Is there anything to eat?" asked Frank.

"About that," said Brack. "Shepherd told you we have limited supplies? You scarf it down now, we've got nothing for later, and we might need it." He relented and held out a foil-wrapped rectangle containing something that, when he bit into it, had the consistency of a chewy brick. Frank could only nibble on the corner. What he really wanted was coffee, but he settled for some lukewarm water.

"Is there a problem?"

"It's your problem, Kittridge. Or should I call you 'number two'? Kind of suits you." Brack tapped at the screen, and brought one of the maps to the fore. "We're here, a couple of miles off target, but still in Rahe crater."

Frank hunkered down next to Brack, aware of a strange antiseptic smell coming from him. He probably smelled like that himself. He looked at the screen. The map was familiar to him: an irregularly shaped crater, some twenty miles by ten, carved out by an impact that had left a hole the shape of a football stadium, at the foot of a big-ass dead volcano.

"This is where we're supposed to be building the base." Brack tapped another window to the front. "And this is where all our materiel is."

Frank tilted his head, trying to make sense of the screen. He knew what it should all look like. That oval was the crater, Rahe, where they were. To the south, there was something that looked like a giant bullet wound. The volcano. There was the arc of another smaller one to the north. A sprinkling of craters dotted the landscape.

Across the plain, to the east of the crater, were scattered points of light, like someone had taken a handful of gravel and tossed it to the ground.

"Are those our cylinders?"

"Bet your ass they are."

"Crap."

"For once, Kittridge, I agree wholeheartedly with your assessment. This furthest one, here, is eighty miles out. The closest one is fifteen. I'm making a list to collect them, in order of priority. And when I say priority, I mean which is most important for our survival."

"You need your drivers. That's why I'm up, and why Alice is getting Marcy up." Frank sipped water, gnawed more off the bar. "What's going to happen to the others?"

"The others are staying on ice. They can contribute precisely nothing to this part of the mission, will consume valuable resources, and I'm not having them yapping in my ear while you and the Highway Killer sort out our little local difficulty."

Frank chewed and swallowed, and concentrated on staying upright as Brack shuffled the open windows around. But he had caught Marcy's nickname: Highway Killer. He stored that away for later.

"OK," said Brack. "We caught ourselves a break. The closest cylinder is the one containing the buggies."

"Wait, what?" Frank coughed up sticky crumbs. "We don't have the buggies?"

"Sure we do." He tapped the screen. "Fifteen miles out."

"No, on this …" Frank didn't quite know what to call it, or whether it had an official name like *Eagle* or *Endeavor* "… ship."

"It wouldn't be so much of an emergency if we did, would it?" Brack brought up the map. "It's fifteen miles. You can walk that in, say, four hours. Gravity is a third of what it is back home, so you'll expend less energy and use less air and water than you would do on Earth. You've got nine hours' supply of air, so a couple of hours to build two buggies, and another hour driving them back. That will still leave you two hours for any fuck-ups."

"Four hours to cover fifteen miles in a spacesuit?"

"It's a Surface Exploration Suit now. You telling me you can't cover fifteen miles in four hours? What kind of pussy are you?" He was interrupted by the sound of Marcy gagging two floors up. They both glanced up, then slowly looked back at each other.

Any idea that Frank had that Brack might be different on Mars, more co-operative, less confrontational, slipped away in the rarefied atmosphere.

"You're ordering me to do it."

105

"Nothing has changed, Kittridge. Nothing at all. You do what I tell you, when I tell you to do it. Every breath you take, you're using my air. You have to pay me for that. So I'm done explaining your shit to you. You're both going. Now, I got a whole pile of other things to check, so I'll let you break the news to Cole yourself." Brack turned back to his screens, and after a moment murmured, "Why are you still here?"

Frank pocketed the food and water and pulled himself back up the ladder. It wasn't like floating, but neither was it like climbing. He went hand over hand nevertheless, through the compartment with the monitoring equipment, again catching sight of the barren pink desert that lay just outside, and up into the top chamber.

Marcy was hunched over clutching at her knees. She was naked apart from her thin bodysuit, and wrapped in what for once was appropriately called a space blanket. She was shivering and gasping—using up Brack's air—and her fingers were digging deep into her skin as each fresh wave of pain took her.

"Tell me it stops," she said through chattering teeth.

He hadn't experienced what she was going through, and he almost said so before he realized that Alice was glaring at him.

"It stops," he said. "You'll be fine."

The doctor refocused her concentration on filling a syringe with a clear liquid. "Side effect of the tank. This will sort it out." She wasn't wearing gloves, Frank noticed, and neither did she bother to swab Marcy's upper arm. "Hold her still. I can't get the needle in otherwise."

Frank hesitated, which earned him a growled, "Do it."

He hadn't done more than knock fists with another human being—the personnel at the Blood Bank didn't count—for years. And he suddenly realized that he was scared to break that taboo. Touching someone in prison meant harm, one way or another.

"Now." Alice brandished the syringe in a way that indicated she'd stick it in him if he didn't do as he was told.

He took a deep breath and snaked his arms around Marcy,

taking in as much of the blanket as he could. The bodysuit was so thin it was barely there, and her skin was cool to the touch. She jerked away from him, but that could have just been her uncontrolled shaking. He held her quaking body tight, his head against hers, and could see Alice line up her shot.

"OK. Let go now."

Frank released his grip and backed away, as much as the small compartment would allow him. Marcy shuddered for a few seconds more, then quietened. She pulled the rustling blanket tighter and looked about her.

"What was that?"

"Atropine. Should have had an auto-injector, but no." Alice looked down at her computer tablet, dabbing her fingers rapidly across the screen. "You are … stable."

"You can tell, just like that?"

"I've got your vital signs right here, in real time. So yes. Just like that. If you want a second opinion, be my guest. Nearest other doctor is a hundred million miles that way." She pointed out the top of the capsule, back up into space.

Frank reached for his food bar and managed to work it in two. He held out one half to Marcy. "This is what passes as something to eat. Alice'll find you some water. Then we need to talk. Things haven't quite gone to plan."

"This is not what I thought it'd be like." Marcy lifted the bar to her mouth and dabbed at it with her tongue. "I've had worse. And at least it's not ramen."

Alice closed up her screen. "Brack's told me jack so far. So if it's not some stupid security thing, I'd like to know why I'm not waking the whole crew up."

"We should give Marcy a moment," said Frank.

"I'm not made of glass. I won't break." Marcy took the water Alice proffered her and coughed each time she took a sip. "Tell us."

Frank shrugged. He looked down at the metal grille floor. He could just about make Brack out between the gaps. "The supply cylinders aren't where they're supposed to be. Some are eighty miles out from where we are. Which isn't so bad, if you consider how far they've come, but we don't have any transport. So we—you and me, Marcy—have to walk fifteen miles and hope that the manifest is right and that's the one with the buggies in."

"And if it's not, or they're broken?"

"We'll probably have enough left in the suits to make it back."

"There's nothing we can use that we might have, you know, brought with us?"

"Brack says not. Everything we need to make the base is scattered across the desert. Everything we need to live is out there too. All the machines that make air, water, power, food. I don't know who's to blame for this, but that doesn't really matter now. We're here, and we have to fix it."

"When do we have to go?" she asked.

"As soon as we can," said Frank. "I don't even know what the time is now, but I guess this is a daylight thing."

"You're going nowhere today," said Alice. "You're my patients until I discharge you as fit for duty." She raised her voice. "You hear that, Brack? Tomorrow will be soon enough."

They all listened for a reply. None came.

"Can you do that? Can you overrule him?" asked Frank.

"I don't give a shit what he thinks. What's important is what you do," she said. "If he tells you to do something stupid or dangerous, you can just say no. Just because we've got less gravity doesn't mean you can do without your backbone."

10

[transcript of audio file #10206 12/19/2036 2147MT Xeno-systems Operations, Room 62B, Tower of Light, Denver CO]

DV: We can, with current technology, routinely achieve Mars surface landing at eighty-five (85) per cent success.

BT: So you're saying we need to budget for fifteen (15) per cent wastage.

DV: At least. There are other factors, including that we cannot predict which elements of the cargo are going to be lost. We can probably afford to lose a couple of hab sections, simply by sending more than we need. A single RTG costs half a billion (500,000,000) US. We lose that, the mission is over. If we send two, then we're spending twice what we need to to ensure one makes it to the surface. And you'd need to order it five years before launch in order for it to be ready on time.

BT: What are our options?

DV: We can drive our success rate upwards with existing technologies at a cost, and with new technologies which may be initially expensive in R and D, but eventually lower unit cost. Something might come along in the next few years that turns out to be a game-changer. But we can't bank on that, and integrating whatever it is into our existing program will inevitably introduce delays. Landing on Mars will never be easy, but with inflatable heat-shields and retro-rockets, we can get to the eighty-five per cent mark reliably. What we would normally not do is put all our eggs in one basket: by dividing the mission-critical loads across several separate

109

containers, we ensure that at least some of all of them survive the E/D/L phase.

BT: But that won't sit well with the automatic building program.

DV: It complicates it. Simply put, whatever we send, however we send it, we might not be able to use it. If we plan for total redundancy, we increase our costs by around half. If we send just enough, not enough will survive to complete the contract. Somewhere between the two is probably where you want to draw the line. Too far or too little along that line will bankrupt XO. It's your call.

BT: Merry fucking Christmas. Come on, Deepak, what can you offer me?

DV: Well, if you're coming at it from the left field, we've some non-mission-rated landers that are as dumb as rocks, but they get the job done. They more or less get to the surface in one piece, at the expense of accuracy, which is why they're not mission-rated. If I was in charge, I'd look into bringing those back on line. Once your cargo's down, getting it into position is an easier problem to solve than replacing whole cargoes.

BT: My desk, tomorrow. Got that?

[transcript ends]

The ship airlock was only large enough for just one person at a time. Frank volunteered to go first, and Marcy had argued with him. They settled the matter with rock-paper-scissors, and he'd lost in a two-out-of-three.

His spacesuit—he'd keep calling it that, rather than an SES, because it was a goddamn spacesuit—was either identical to the one he'd trained in, or it was the actual suit. It fitted around him a little too well: the lower pressure was bloating his whole body, though Alice assured him that would sort itself out in a few days.

He waited at the inner door, looking through the small pane of double-glazed plastic into the airlock beyond. Marcy's back unit, containing both her life support and her entry hatch, swayed as she moved, resting on one leg then the other as the air was pumped out around her.

"I still got green lights," she said in Frank's ear. He heard the echo of it in the cabin behind him. Alice was looking at a screen of vital signs, and Brack? Brack was just standing there, that same faint smirk on his face.

Frank didn't know why. The situation, assuming that Brack was telling him the truth, and there was no good reason to disbelieve him, was immediately serious and long-term catastrophic. Everything they needed to live was spread miles away across the Martian desert and unless they could recover a substantial portion of it—there being very little built-in redundancy—they were all going to die.

They'd die without air, they'd die without food, they'd die without water. The amount of power they'd use would eventually defeat their generation capacity, deplete the batteries and they'd freeze to death. The solar panels they needed to connect up were somewhere out there, as was the thermoelectric generator that was going to provide their base load. Even going out of the airlock was wasting air: the pumps could only recover so much, and the rest had to be vented into the emptiness of Mars. Replacing that ate into the reserves.

Frank could find precious little to smile about. Alice wasn't even certain that they'd been sent enough supplies to cover their asses in the best of circumstances. There were going to be difficult choices ahead, and Frank didn't have to wonder as to who the person making those choices would be. Quite how Brack was supposed to handle that was anyone's guess.

But for the rest of them, if he and Marcy failed to get the buggies up and running, there was only going to be one result. The two of them were their first and best shot at saving the mission. Anyone else that Alice would defrost wouldn't have the right knowledge. They'd be less likely to succeed. They'd make more mistakes.

111

Marcy used the button in the airlock to tell the outer door to open. The whole structure twitched as the last of the air blew out. It was something that Frank could feel through his feet, but the only thing he could hear was the sound of his own breathing. He peered through the window, and watched Marcy shuffle forward towards the widening gap of rose-red light.

"Oh my God," she said.

"Control your breathing," said Alice, "or I'll do it for you."

"But it's so ... big."

"And you have to walk across it, so contain your excitement, child."

Brack adjusted his headset. "When you've stopped playing the tourist, feel free to leave the airlock. Number two is using up what's in his tank."

Marcy turned round to face the airlock, gave Frank two thumbs up through the tiny window, and slowly walked backwards down the external ladder, using the integral handrails to guide her. The outer door slid shut, and pumps repressurized the tiny chamber.

"OK, Kittridge. Let's not hang around. You got your tools, and you know how long you have."

"Aren't you going to wish us luck?"

"Let's just say, 'failure is not an option'."

"Failure is always an option," said Alice. "I've treated enough people to know that."

The inner door hissed open; there was nothing left but for Frank to waddle into the airlock. The door closed behind him, and he flipped open his controls, looking at the green lights and willing them to stay green.

The acoustics of the room changed, the reverberations leaking away with the air. He felt his suit expand around him, the pressure inside fighting the elastic material. Standing there, in a space barely bigger than a cupboard, knowing that on the other side of the metal door was a whole new world just waiting for him to screw up so that it could kill him.

But in a moment of clarity he realized he'd already screwed up to get himself here in the first place. At least on Mars, the rules were clear and the penalties obvious. That door would open onto a simpler, more honest environment. Was he going to die here? Possibly. But not necessarily.

The door mechanism flashed green, and Frank pressed the button to pull it aside. The sudden outrush of the remaining air dragged at the loose outer cover of his suit. Then there was Mars. First a crack, then a sliver, then a widening rectangle of brown-pink. The door pulled back to its stops, and he shuffled forward.

He was on the threshold of the airlock, holding on to the jambs, looking out at an utterly barren wasteland, where fine red dust had drifted around angular blocks of toffee-colored rocks. As his eyes became adjusted to the light, he could see the pale, distant disc of the sun rising into a rosewater pink band of sky over the crater wall. Over to the north was the black line of the horizon, and off to the west, much closer, were a series of raggedly stepped scarps.

It resembled Utah, in some respects. In others, it was completely alien. There was, of course, no sound. This desert was silent, empty and dead.

He turned round on the small platform as Marcy had done, and climbed down to the ground. The last step was a jump of a couple of feet, and he landed squarely into the bootprints that were already there.

Looking up in the suit was difficult. He had to lean back slightly, which unbalanced him. But he wanted to get his first look at the spaceship that had brought them here. It was an unremarkable cylinder, bullet-topped, with four extendable legs sprouting from the sides. Right underneath, where the rocket had lowered them to the ground on a pillar of flame, was nothing but bare rock and scorch marks. The white surface of the ship was already tinged pink, and the XO logo prominently displayed was around a year older than at lift-off.

It looked tiny. It *was* tiny, compared to the living area they were supposed to create. It was nothing but a fragile can, strangely unimpressive, and it was never going to sustain their existence, let alone allow anything approaching real living.

He couldn't think about what came later, nor what Brack had said to him about going home. He had to stay alive now, to earn that reward. That they were the only people on Mars was beside the point: they were the only people who they could rely on to do the job.

"It's empty," said Marcy. "It's just nothing. Everything outside of the ship is …" She tried to shrug, but the suit wouldn't let her. "You know."

"Not quite everything." He turned round again and carefully took his first steps on Martian soil. The ground was a hard rock substrate, covered by a thin layer of fine dust that compacted under his weight. It felt solid enough to build on, at least the structures they were contemplating, and it had the advantage of being mostly flat, too. The loose pieces that littered the surface would need to be cleared, and there were more of those than they'd trained for. That part of construction would just have to take longer. No short cuts.

He crouched down—easier said than done—and picked up a fist-sized rock. It seemed too light for its volume, but he realized that was just down to the gravity. It was solid enough, a gritty sandstone. What was more interesting was the little patch of pale frost that was hiding underneath. He watched it smoke away until it was all gone.

He dropped the rock back down, and it fell slowly and silently. His suit was telling him it was minus four Fahrenheit outside. Cold. Freezing cold.

"We'd better get moving," he said, carefully straightening up.

"The clock is still ticking, boys and girls," said Brack. His voice was inescapable, and anything they wanted to say to each other would be immediately overheard. "It's now oh-seven-oh-eight local mean solar time. Your life support will keep you going until sometime before sixteen hundred, but your suits will give you much more of an accurate measurement. Pay attention to them, because otherwise whoever goes out next will be walking past your corpse to complete your mission. Cole, you have the map, and you're in charge. Over and out."

Her tablet was in a pouch, carabinered to the belt at her waist. She brought it up to her helmet and pressed at the screen with her fat fingers through the protecting plastic.

"It's this way," she said, and started to pick her way across the rock field, placing her feet between the scattered debris. Frank fell in beside her, and faced into the pale sun. The dome of the sky was slowly changing color, from the deep red of dawn to the paler pink of morning.

There were clouds. He hadn't anticipated clouds, high tails of pearl-white against the blush of the sky. They were running away behind him, fleeing the sun, stretched ragged and vanishing like the frost had in its pale light.

"So," he said, watching his feet. "Mars."

"What do you think?"

He looked up, momentarily, but the only way either of them was going to make any progress was if they concentrated on the ground. The rising sun wore a bright crown of light that diffused into the rest of the sky. The distant crater walls were slowly resolving into detail. It was as dim as a winter's morning.

"It's pristine. Everything we do, everywhere we go, we'll be first. Yes, we're a bunch of convicts, out here on a chain gang: but we're a chain gang on Mars. That has to count for something."

The external temperature was rising with the sun, to a balmy five degrees. The ground appeared to be smoking, and a knee-high fog formed.

"Dew," he said. He bent down and swirled it away with his hand. His glove remained stubbornly dry.

"We've a long way to go," said Marcy. She turned her tablet towards him and showed him the red line they had to traverse. The ship was barely any smaller behind them. "We'll have to do the sightseeing later."

It was all novel at first. The mere fact of being on another planet, the knowing that they were the only people—the rest of their crew excepted—for a hundred million miles, the situation where people were relying on them for their survival. And then, surprisingly quickly, it grew boring.

The terrain remained initially exactly the same. Even though the white tower of the ship grew tiny and indistinct, the ground around them was still the rock-strewn hard surface that lay directly outside the airlock. And their destination—invisible in the distance—showed no sign of getting closer.

Picking their way over the rocks was still easier than kicking them aside, but it was inevitable that they ended up hitting some as they walked. Eventually, one that Frank knocked rolled away, and kept on rolling. He was surprised enough to stop and watch it go, only then realizing that it was heading downhill, and the nature of the ground was changing.

It wasn't a steep slope, but it did steepen further down before leveling off onto the main crater floor below. And the difference in height was some two hundred feet. The edge of the slope looked as if it had collapsed several times before, as if bites had been taken out of the plateau, the bitten-off material collecting below. The line they were following led straight down the incline.

"Does that look safe to you?" asked Marcy.

"If you wouldn't walk up it, don't walk down it." Her proximity to the potentially unstable edge was making him uneasy. "I'd be happier if you took a couple of steps back."

She looked at her feet, and hopped away.

"It doesn't look as stony at the bottom," she said. "But maybe there's a better route." She opened her map and expanded the part they were on. "If we follow the edge, we can go down here, where these ridges are."

It was a less direct route, but held less potential danger. Less obvious potential danger, that was. Neither of them really knew what they were doing or heading into.

"When we bring the buggies back, we'll have to make sure we avoid this area. Can you mark it on that?"

"I don't know." She poked at the screen, but the red line stayed resolutely straight. "Brack? Brack?"

"Didn't you have training on proper comms discipline?"

"There's only us here, Brack. Who the hell did you think I was calling?"

"Discipline, Cole."

"Oh, Jesus."

"What was that, Cole? You're breaking up."

She turned and looked back in the direction of the ship, now finally vanished from view. "I can't believe you're making me do this. Cole to Brack, Cole to Brack, over."

"Brack to Cole. That wasn't that difficult, was it? Do you have a problem, or are you just missing me? Over."

Her hand hit her helmet. Frank didn't know which gesture she was going for, facepalm or fingers down her throat. She could do neither.

"We've hit the edge of a slope, and it looks loose, so we're taking a detour, but I can't mark it on the tablet. Can you do that?" She waited for a response, and when she realized none was coming, finally, grudgingly, added, "Over."

"You've gone three miles in an hour and a half, and you want to take a detour? At this rate, you're barely going to get to the cargo before your air runs out. Taking detours isn't part of the plan, Cole. Not unless you want to die out there. You have one job. Jump to it. Over and out."

"Three miles? Three? That can't be right." She looked at the map, bringing it so that she could judge the whole length of the route against their current position. "We've gone three miles in an hour and a half."

"It looks easier going from now on," said Frank. "But we're going to have to pick up the pace."

"And no detours."

He looked at the slope. Walking poles? Something to test

the stability of the slope before risking their necks on it? Just a little bit late now. He took two steps to the edge and over with a little jump. He rose, and fell, and his feet landed on the ocher sand, one foot up slope and taking most of his weight. Grains slid and slipped, carrying him slightly further before the slope stabilized and his boots dug in. He bent his knees and jumped again, bounding lower, balancing for the impact. More sand slipped down, but it didn't seem like he was going to bring anything substantial down on top of him.

"I guess that's safe enough," he said. "Follow me."

It took a fair few jumps to reach the foot of the slope. Marcy bounced down after him, causing only as much sand-fall as he had. Their boot-marks were deep dents in the loose material, and after the initial infill, seemed to freeze in place.

They were now both pink up to their waists. Frank drew on his leg with his fingertip, and just ended up pressing the dust into the silvered skin of the outer covering.

"Three miles out of fifteen," said Marcy. She took up the map again and orientated them with the landscape. "That's too slow, Frank."

"But we're still going to pace ourselves. Our turn-back point is four hours."

"By which time we would have gone eight miles. That's not enough. At that rate we'll be getting to the cylinder at seven hours plus. That gives us just two hours. One to put the rover together, one to get it back before everything stops working."

"Then we turn back now, and try again tomorrow."

"And tomorrow will be exactly the same as today." She looked into the distance, fixed on a point, and started walking. "Same problems. Same distance. Same kit. Come on, Frank. Up and down the mountain. They made us do that for a reason, right? This reason."

The ground was reasonably flat, and while it was dusty and loose on the surface, it packed hard enough when walked on. Going faster, though. That was hard. On Earth, gravity brought his feet down with a slap, ready to push off again. On Mars, he flew. He had to wait to make each stride, even though each pace was longer. And lean forward more, to force his foot against the loose Martian sand.

And though his two hundred pounds registered as less than seventy in the reduced gravity, making forward progress was technically hard. His legs started to ache, and his shoulders—swinging his arms was one of the ways he could work his body to do what he needed it to do—began to burn.

When they stopped an hour later, they'd covered nearly three and a half more miles. They drank water. They chewed some of the energy bar that was fixed in a holder inside their helmets. They looked at each other. Six and a half miles in two and a half hours.

The same again would see them within sniffing distance of the cylinder, but they'd have used over half their air to get there. If that cylinder didn't contain the buggies, then they'd never make it back to the ship in time.

"Brack?"

The airwaves hissed.

"Kittridge calling Brack. Over."

"That's how you do it. Your progress isn't good enough, Kittridge. What are you going to do about that? Over."

"We've upped the pace, but we're not going to make it to the cylinder by the start of the third quarter. Over."

"Well, I guess you and Cole are just going to have to make the call. You're not going to be stealing any of my bases though. I want a home run from you. Nothing else will do. Over."

"Can you tell me for sure that the cylinder we're heading for has the buggies in it?"

"That's what the manifest says it is. The only way to check is to open it up and take a look."

"If it's wrong, we're dead and this base never gets built."

"Then you'd better pray the manifest is right. Shame you were never the praying type, Kittridge. Over and out."

119

11

[Transcript of private phone call between Bruno Tiller and Project Sparta 8/5/2040 1430MT.]

BT: We've crunched the numbers and we're still coming in high. Not over-budget high, but I'm convinced there are more savings here. Make me look good.

PS: How far are you willing to dig down, Mr Tiller?

BT: All the way. Give me my options.

PS: You misunderstand me. Personally, how far are you prepared to go? Our analysts have some new scenarios for you to consider, but whether I show them to you is dependent on the content of your character. If you're at all, shall we say, squeamish, then we've probably gone as far as we can go.

BT: The content of my character? This is Bruno Tiller you're talking to. You know what kind of man I am.

PS: I need you to spell it out for me. We've already made significant departures from the contract, which NASA have reluctantly agreed to. Any further deviations will necessarily have to involve you being economical with the truth. Certainly to NASA. And perhaps to the XO board to provide them with plausible deniability. The current scheme will come in on time and within the agreed budget. It'll provide the contractors with what they've asked for, and XO will be paid handsomely for it. At this stage, no further alteration is necessary.

BT: All the way. You hear me? All the way. Everything. Down
   to the last cent.
PS: I'll be in touch, Mr Tiller.
[transcript ends]

Frank and Marcy were four hours out. They'd walked eleven
and a half miles. If they carried on, they were into their safety
margin, and either it worked out or they suffocated. One of the
two. No one was going to come and rescue them, because there
was no one to come and rescue them. Even if Brack had decided, inexplicably, that he might help them, there was nothing
he could do anyway.

A line of long, low hills ran down the center of the crater,
with rubble-strewn sandy slopes. Further out, the terrain was
less broken and the sand was deeper, though there were still
craters, difficult to cross and easier to go around. They'd navigated all those: now they were back out on the crater floor,
approaching the main wall.

They were close. Three and a half miles away. Their target
lay somewhere near the rim, on an eroded part of the wall,
which looked almost like a bay between two cliffs.

Frank put his helmet against Marcy's. "What do you want to
do?"

"Why's this my call?" she asked.

"Because Brack put you in charge. And I don't want to have
to make a decision that might kill you."

"But you're good with me killing you?"

"Something like that."

"Thanks." She turned to look at the distance they'd already
covered, and back at the distance yet to go. "What would you
do?"

"Land the ship closer to the buggies. But that doesn't really
help, does it?"

"We have to work with what we got. If we turn back now,

121

where does that leave us? We just have to do all this again tomorrow, and we're not going to be any faster, and we're not going to be any further on."

"We could have brought spare gas. Although, since we have to change out the old tanks in an atmosphere, unless they've swapped out the open buggies for some closed-cab ones we're never going to get the chance."

"So we go on. We can't really do anything else."

"Except if we do, and things aren't right at the far end, all we can look forward to is a couple more hours in each other's company. You want to risk that?"

"We're on Mars, Frank. You're going to worry now about risk?"

"Before, I was worried about getting canned and put in the Hole. Now I get to worry about staying alive."

Marcy took a step forward. "I'm going on. Are you coming?"

All or nothing, then. As he watched her walk away, he thought about what someone might have to do to earn the nickname "the Highway Killer". He was guessing it had something to do with not knowing when to stop. "I'm coming."

He followed her across the plain, his tool belt shifting with every one of his own strides. His life was measured in breaths: the harder he worked, the fewer he had left.

It was better if they traveled side by side, avoiding each other's kicked-up dust, and even then, a thin film of pink covered their helmets. It made the already dull day darker. The sun was almost overhead, and the external temperature was a solid plus twenty-three: nothing the Bay Area ever suffered, but almost reasonable. The shadows had shifted so that the color of the land was more brown, and the sky was ... not blue, but as blue as it was going to get.

That's when he saw it, the smudge of other against the different shades of red, a smear of black and white, twisted into a candle and melted against the ground.

He slowed. The suits' lack of peripheral vision meant that

Marcy didn't see him, and the distance between them widened.

"Marcy? Marcy, hold up."

When she eventually stopped, it took a while for her to find him. He pointed at the object, at the base of the slope. It was obvious, once pointed out, and it was roughly in the direction they'd been heading anyway—it wasn't as if they'd been likely to miss it.

"What is that?"

"I think it's a parachute. That's the only thing it can be."

She opened up her map and held it out in front of her. "The cylinder has to be close by."

Frank took the opportunity to check both the clock and his suit's reserves. They'd kicked over the five-and-a-half-hour mark, and his tanks were reading just under forty per cent. That was right, wasn't it? He tried to do the math, and it sounded reasonable. They could actually do this.

They covered the last mile more slowly, not knowing how accurate the map was. It didn't take long to see the cylinder, though, lying on its side in a slight depression at the base of the slope. Further up, there was a blackened area, and signs that the supplies had touched down there, then rolled. The canopy, patterned with concentric black and white rings, had caught in the wind, dragging its hugely long shrouds behind it before entangling with a boulder.

The cylinder looked intact. The contents weren't spilled across the crater floor, and neither were they burnt up.

"OK," said Marcy. "That's our cargo."

It was just like they'd trained for. The big white cylinder, the near-vacuum around them, the dust and the sand. The only things that were different were the rocket unit bolted to one end, and the parachute attached by impossibly long lines to the other. Somewhere, miles away, would be a discarded heat shield. They had no way of finding that, even if it was now littering the surface of an otherwise unspoiled planet.

The parachute material, and even the empty cylinder, might

123

be something they could recycle into useful things. The fuel that remained in the rocket motor, too. It had made it all this way, just as they'd done. It'd be stupid to throw it away.

Frank selected the tool from his belt that would open up the hatches, and tried, pointlessly, to blow the settled dust away from the mechanism.

"Did you just do what I thought you did?" asked Marcy.

"Hush. Kittridge to Brack, Kittridge to Brack. We're at the target. Over."

"Copy that. Don't waste your breath on talking to me. Get to it. Over and out."

Frank flipped the cover of the bolt, and slipped the crank over the head of the wingnut, moving along the closure, one bolt at a time. If it wasn't the buggies inside, then ... it was over before they'd started. No, he wasn't the praying kind. Maybe they should have woken Zeus after all to intercede for them.

He put the tool back in its loop and tugged at the manual release. A puff of air—actual air, or just an inert gas?—came out, and helped the door open. It rose up partly, and Frank had to lean into it to lock it fully in place. All he could see was packaging that had grown enormously plump.

"What have we got?" Marcy was suddenly beside him, peering in.

"Can't see yet. Let's get the other door open." He pulled the lever and the door swung towards them. He still expected a heavy sound of movement, not the silence with which it shuddered into place.

Marcy immediately reached forward and dug her fingers into the protective material, trying to pull it apart as if it was Christmas morning.

"We need to save this too. As much as we can."

"Why? It's just stuff. What would we ever need it for?"

"I don't know. Just that if we don't have it, we can't use it." Frank pulled out a box-cutter knife that had a spring-loaded retractable cover. He needed both hands to work it, but that was the point: to keep any part of him away from the blade.

He cut through the layers, the air pockets in the insulation wilting as he sliced. He took it slowly, making sure he didn't hit anything underneath. Each unheard pop reminded him of the air he was breathing and would never get back.

"OK, now."

Marcy peeled back the insulated covering. "I can see a chassis. It's the right container. Thank fuck for that."

"Kittridge to Brack. We've hit that home run. Over."

The reply came back, choppy and indistinct. "Copy. Over." That was all. Frank thought Brack might be just a bit more enthusiastic about their discovery, and the fact that they might not die after all.

He checked his air. Thirty-five per cent.

"We build one, drive it back, and come and get the other one tomorrow," he said.

"Not both? Why not both?"

"Because we don't have time to do that." He used the knife to cut the latticework chassis free of its ties, and together they lifted it out of the container. Picking a patch of open, not too rocky ground a little way away to work on, they set it down. It was lightweight titanium tubing, and on Mars it weighed even less.

The sealed drums contained a lot of the other important kit. The wheels, great big springy things that doubled as shocks and had a motor in each wheel. The control board, which fixed on to the chassis in front of the driver. The seat, which bolted on to the deck of the frame. And the power pack, the most complicated and critical part of the whole set-up. If that didn't work, all they had was a giant shopping trolley.

The fuel cell was a black box—literally a black box—with plug-in terminals on the outside. No user-serviceable parts inside, it proclaimed, though it was inevitable that they were going to have to open it up and fix it at some point. It wasn't as if anyone else was going to do it.

They'd practiced this, though. Frank and Marcy weren't exactly a well-oiled team, but they had worked well enough together, listening to each other's grunts and curses, watching each other's expressions of exasperation or concentration.

Frank did the heavy lifting, holding the chassis up while Marcy rolled a wheel into place. Neither of the pair of nut runners that came with the cargo was charged up: either they'd gone flat over the year in storage, or they'd been shipped in that state. The wheels were going to have to be tightened by hand, and they had one adjustable wrench between them.

That was going to slow them down. A lot.

He checked his air. Twenty per cent. That gave him nominally ... OK, that wasn't a good sign. He should have been able to just come up with the number. He was good with numbers, calculating quantities and part-loads in his head and getting it right. An hour and forty-five.

They were going to be cutting it fine.

"Anything we can leave till next time, we leave," he said. "Let's just get this working."

"I thought I was the one in charge, Frank." Marcy cranked the last nut on the hub, and handed him the wrench, while she went to collect the second wheel. It was as tall as she was, yet she managed to effortlessly bounce and roll it across the Martian surface. Puffs of dust rose and fell around her. It coated everything.

Frank wiped his faceplate with his free hand. "You are. I'm just keeping you straight."

"Don't need keeping straight. Just do the job. I still think we've got time to make both buggies."

"Why don't we see how long one takes first?"

"Why don't you lift the chassis and let me get this wheel on?" She turned the tire and held it in position while Frank batted his gloves together—the dust plumed out, and almost immediately dropped to the ground—and pushed at the open strutwork.

"Higher," she said, and he complied. "Hold it."

From the satisfyingly solid vibration in his hands, the wheel had slipped into place.

"Wrench."

He handed it back, and kicked his heels while he watched her work. So that was part of the problem: he didn't have as much to do as she did, nor enough distraction.

He could test the electrics. The fuel cell assembly was genuinely heavy, and back on Earth it took two of them to lift it. Here, not so much, but it was an awkward length, and difficult to carry. But he could test it where it was, still in its drum, by carrying the control board to it.

The board had read-outs, and a fat, insulated cable running from its back, terminating in a plug that slotted home and locked in place on top of the fuel cell's black casing. He held the board, minus its steering column, under one arm, and leaned in over the edge of the drum to fix the connector into place.

His suit's hard torso stopped him from bending over that far. He stood on the drum lid, and tried again, this time just getting the degree of movement he needed to push the plug in and twist the locking ring.

He put the board on the rim of the drum and lifted the cover from the on-switch. His finger hovered over it, and then he wondered what he was waiting for. Either it would power up, or it wouldn't. If it didn't work, it wouldn't be a disaster.

Not yet, anyway. There was still another one in the cylinder, meant for the second buggy.

He pressed down, and the board waited for a heart-stopping second before lighting up and going through its boot-up sequence.

"We're good," he said. What he wanted to do was wipe the sweat off his face, and he could only let the fans slowly clear that. He drank some water, and watched the read-outs. "We have one hundred per cent capacity. System pressure is stable. Full power. It works."

"I'm ready for the next wheel."

Frank put the control board down inside the drum, so it didn't even remotely run the risk of falling off, and hefted the chassis again. She did that thing of getting the wheel on first time, which was good, because if the usual speed of the buggy was ten miles per hour, it was going to take them an hour and a half to get back. Frank had almost exactly that amount of air left.

If they were driving, they wouldn't be walking, nor expending that extra energy and using up that oxygen. There was some slack. But they were getting down to the wire. They certainly weren't going to build another buggy. Not today.

He started dragging everything into place, so that they wouldn't need to keep going back to the cylinder for components. Power cables for the wheel motors. The bucket seat. The steering column for the control board he could fix in right now, and given that the third wheel was on already, he could at least put it on hand-tight to the frame. The winch and the towbar assemblies would just have to wait. And the lights. And the roll cage. And the cameras.

If they didn't start back in ten minutes, they weren't going to make it. Fifteen, maybe. Those weren't numbers he wanted to bet against.

Fourth wheel.

"You know, if you can do this a bit quicker, that'd be really excellent."

"You want a wheel to fall off as we go? We do it right, first time, or not at all."

"We're running out of options, Marcy. Good enough is good enough."

"Then start plugging things in, get the cables secure, and put on the seat. The fuel cell can go in last."

He wrestled the cables out. They were stiff and inflexible due to the cold—as were the cable ties he was supposed to fix them to the tubing with. The connectors were necessarily now behind the wheels. Reaching them was straightforward enough, but pushing them home and securing the lock was harder than it needed to be. Haste simply made it more difficult.

And every time he needed to take a breath and steady himself, it was one breath fewer he had to take.

Marcy was done. She leaped up on the chassis and worked the bolts on the control panel. "Give me the seat."

He half-passed, half-threw it at her. She slotted it home and laboriously began to tighten the nuts at each corner.

"I'm down to fourteen per cent," said Frank. "Leave that. Help me with the power pack."

She reluctantly put down the wrench and jumped down. Even that took too much time.

They heaved the fuel cell out of its drum. Packaging spilled out across the rust-colored sand.

"Seriously. Leave it."

There was a cage at the front of the chassis, into which the fuel cell slotted, the idea being that there'd be preferential weight on the front wheels, making it easier to drive. It had a solid base, to protect the casing, and open sides for the connectors. There was even an arrow in red, telling them which way needed to point up and forward.

They manhandled it into position, and got the bottom edge inside.

"Slide it home. Nice and straight."

Marcy fastened the cage opening with a cable tie and Frank plugged in the other ends of the power cables, one, two, three, four. Lock them in place. She finished securing the seat while he connected the controls. Push. Twist. Pull.

She pressed the on-switch, and lit up the console. The steering column looked like a video gamer's steering wheel. It was only minimally attached. Things like the gas pedal and the brakes were controlled by grips inside the wheel.

Marcy flexed her fingers and took the wheel.

"If you're coming, climb on. We'll see if we can do better than ten miles an hour."

Frank scrambled up behind her, and remembered to pick up the wrench from where she'd left it, balanced across two spars, and put it back in his belt. He threaded his feet through the open frame and leaned forward to grab tight hold of the seat back.

"Any time now would be good," he said.

She squeezed the accelerator, and the buggy rolled ever so slowly forward. "I got this," she said.

Marcy drove around in a circle, the wheels spinning up or down dependent on the direction of the turn. When she was pointing back down the crater towards the distant, low mound of the volcano, below which was their ship and their survival, she tightened her hold and they sped away, dust trailing in their wake.

12

[Project Sparta report, dated January 11 2039—recovered document headings, section 7]

7. Crew functionality
  7.1. Comparison of robots vs human crew
    7.1.1. Robots are task-specific
      7.1.1.1. Human crew are multifunctional
    7.1.2. Robots do not learn
      7.2.1.1. Human crew will complete tasks faster and better with repetition
    7.1.3. Robots are not resourceful
      7.1.3.1. Human crew will become adept at doing more with less
    7.1.4. Robots are unreliable
      7.1.4.1. Human crew are self-healing or responsive to medical intervention
    7.1.5. Robots are not reactive
      7.1.5.1. Human crew will respond instantly to problems
    7.1.6. Robots require significant electrical power
      7.1.6.1. Human crew will require significantly less
    7.1.7. Robots can be reprogrammed instantly
      7.1.7.1. Human crew can be taught new tasks only over time
    7.1.8. Robots do not consume resources
      7.1.8.1. Human crew will require significant ongoing resource inputs in order for them to operate for the duration of the build phase

7.9.1. Robots do not require protected environments
   7.1.9.1. Human crew will require significant front-loaded
   infrastructure commitment
7.1.10. Robots do not complain
   7.1.10.1. Human crew will require psychological
   management
7.1.11. Robots do not tire
   7.1.11.1. Human crew will require rest periods
7.1.12. Robots are emotionally expendable
   7.1.12.1. Human crew will react emotionally to losses

The shadows had changed. Unregarded, the sun had risen high and started sinking again, back towards the horizon. They were driving towards it, and it was still only as bright as a dull winter's day. The rocks on the surface were deepening in color, and the sky was turning from pink to red. The airborne dust seemed to hang close to the horizon, like a soft-edged blanket. As the sun dipped, the more shadow the dust cast.

Frank was coated with it. It was inexplicably sticky, a film that he could push about but not actually dislodge. He didn't know how he was supposed to get rid of it.

And now he was worried about the build-up of dust on any machinery they might use. His sites had always kept the plant clean, because then it was easier to keep it in good working order and spot any faults, as well as being a good neighbor. He grunted as Marcy found the edge of a small, half-buried ridge of rock that sent a jolt through the frame and into Frank's bones. She had the seat. He was hanging on behind her, hoping she hadn't forgotten that he was there.

It felt like they were doing a damn sight more than ten miles an hour, though Frank couldn't see the speedometer to tell, only the ground between his feet. Neither could he let go to find out just how much time in the suit he had left, because if he let go, he might be bounced off. At that speed, it seemed that the wheels couldn't deform fast enough to absorb the shock of obstacles—even the smaller rocks were jarring. Slower would be more comfortable. Right now, his comfort wasn't his chief concern. Just as long as Marcy could get them back before … before they ran out of air.

What would it be like? Would he even notice? There'd been an accident once, with fatalities, early on in his career and before he had his own company. They were demolishing an old gas station, clearing it for the developers to come in and slap some identikit housing on it. A couple of guys had gone into the old underground tanks, and that's where he'd found them, just slumped at the bottom of the ladder. Heavy gas had settled in the tanks and pushed all the air out, and they'd lowered themselves right into the middle of it. He might have joined them, if older, wiser hands hadn't restrained him.

They hadn't suffered. Just gone to sleep.

He wasn't going to do that. He had a base to build. And he had a promise that he'd make it back home again. But first he had to make it back to the ship, that was still invisible in the distance.

Was Marcy going as fast as she dared? Probably. And faster than that, even. It hurt, and he had to hang on. If he fell off, would she come back for him? Would she even notice? It wasn't like she could turn her head and look behind her. If he called out, what would she do? She'd probably stop, pick him up again, even if it killed both of them.

He did and didn't want to know how much margin of error they had left. Ignorance was both bliss and terrifying.

Despite only having been this way once, and from the other direction, he was starting to recognize the terrain. The low, ragged hills down the middle of the crater. The rise of the walls a thousand feet up, completely enclosing the low land. The bulk of the volcano, felt rather than seen, on the southern edge. And the steep rise that was looming ahead of them that they'd had to navigate on the way out.

The one that had loose granular sand all the way up to the top.

Marcy throttled back, and let the buggy roll to a halt. She took a moment to check her suit controls, and after closing it back up, shook her arms out.

"You OK back there?"

"Still here."

"There's a trick to getting up dunes. I know it's not a dune, but it's like a dune, so I'll treat it the same. The run-off is pretty smooth, and the slope not too steep, but it's long and tall. If it looks like I'm going to flip it over or I start going sideways— you're going to have to jump clear. If you're still on, you're going to break your neck."

"And what about you?"

"I'll be bailing out too, so don't sweat about that." She flexed her fingers and put her hands back on the steering column.

"I'm on five per cent," said Frank. "You?"

"Same."

"That's enough to get us back. Just." If the suit read-out was accurate. Anything greater than the margin of error would be fine.

He climbed out of the frame and knelt down on top of it, wedging his feet against the crossbars and bracing himself with his hands. It wasn't the best position, but at least he could try and leap free if he had to.

The buggy sank a little as Marcy dialed down the stiffness of the tires—the ridged plates flexed apart and presented a wider face to the ground—then they were off again, smooth acceleration all the way to the base of the slope.

The wheels kept turning, clawing their way up. They didn't seem to slow down at all, at least initially. The slope sharpened halfway up, and the sand deepened. The surface started to cut up and spill away. But Marcy had judged it right. She kept them pointing straight up the slope and let the momentum she'd built up carry them over the hump and to the shallower upper reaches.

And he could hear it, a low bass rumble throbbing around

him. It had been all but silent for the whole day, and he thought he was imagining it at first, or feeling it through the metal frame he was clinging to. What he was hearing was the four motors straining and the impact of the wheels against the shifting sand.

When the sound began to die away, they were almost at the top: there was just the lip of the rise to breach, a soft edge. Marcy clenched the steering controls and leaned slightly forward, and they chewed their way through. The buggy rocked forwards, then back again, and slowed.

"Do we have to do that every time?" he asked.

She didn't answer straight away. "Yes," she said eventually. "There'll be easier ways up and down. Need to map them out."

"That was good going." Frank patted her shoulder, or the hard carapace covering it at least. He felt her shudder, and he took his hand away quickly. He heard her grunt, and suck at her straw. He drew back, settling himself into position again, and waited for her to restiffen the tires and pull away across the rock-strewn plateau.

She didn't.

"Marcy?"

"Some." She coughed. "Things. Wrong."

"OK, hold on. Alice? Alice, Marcy's got a problem."

There was a moment of dead air. "Shut the fuck up, Brack. No one cares whether I'm Shepherd or Alice. Is it with her or the suit?"

"Don't know yet." He clambered over the top of the buggy's frame until he was the other side of the controls, facing Marcy. "She's very dark."

He reached out and wiped her faceplate. He could see her eyes, red and moist. "Marcy? Marcy."

She stared at him, uncomprehending. Her mouth was open, and she seemed to be panting.

"I've got her diagnostics up. Blood oxygen is good. High breathing rate. High heart rate. Raised blood pressure. Hold on, I need to see an ECG."

135

"Marcy?" Frank took hold of her helmet and drummed against it. "You in there? I'm talking to Alice right now."

"Heart rhythm is ectopic."

"What?"

"She's skipping beats. What does her suit say about the amount of CO_2? I can find it here, but you'll be quicker."

Frank flipped her suit console down, and looked at the upside-down screen. He started to press the buttons to scroll through the menus, when Marcy knocked his hands away.

"What doing?" she slurred.

"I'm trying to help." He went back for another go, and she pushed him away again. "She's not letting me."

"Give me a minute."

"We haven't got a minute, Alice."

"Best guess. Her CO_2 scrubber's failed. She's breathing too much of it in. Can you take over the driving and get her back here?"

"I'm doing it now."

He stepped around the console and punched the buckle release. As the crossing straps fell away, he took her arm, one hand under the armpit and the other under the bulge of the life-support system.

"Get up, Marcy. I'm driving the rest of the way."

She fought him, and the violence of her attack caught him unawares and off-balance. His foot slipped, and he fell backwards. Slowly. But still holding on to her, so that she was dragged out of the bucket seat.

He had time to work out what to do, whether to let go or keep his grip, before he hit the ground. He didn't want to land on his back, and he didn't want to land on his face. Shoulder, then, and keep his hands in. He pulled Marcy to him, to try and protect the vital parts of her suit.

They landed, Frank with his arms around her. There were rocks, but nothing punctured. Dust plumed up, and settled down on them. Marcy started spasming. Her eyes rolled up, and vomit splashed against the inside of her helmet.

"She's ... having a fit. Alice, what do I do?"

"Get her on to her face. Open up the hatch on her back. Hard reset her life support."

"Turn it off?"

"And turn it on again. Do it."

Marcy wasn't resisting now. Frank turned her over, his blunt fingers scrabbling at the opening mechanism. He got his fingers in, and pulled. The lid flipped open. He'd been trained to know what he was looking for: the recessed buttons on the top right.

He hit the red one. The lights faded.

"How long?" he asked.

"Ten? Ten seconds?"

"Don't you know?"

"No. I'm doing my best here."

He waited until eight and couldn't stand it any longer. He pressed the green, and watched the suit power up again.

"Frank?"

"Alice."

"Her heart's arrhythmic."

"Is there anything I can do?"

"No. Pick her up. Put her on the buggy and get here as quick as you can."

"She's been sick again."

"Then keep her face down."

"I'll need to tie her down. I can't drive holding on to her."

"Then do it. Jesus, Frank. Just do it."

He picked Marcy up, and she was like a rag doll, light and loose-limbed, but still awkward to carry. Her legs dragged and her arms flopped, and though the upper part of her body was held in the rigid shell of the suit, it added bulk. There was no way he could get her gently up on top of the buggy, so he threw her up in the air in an imitation of a clean-and-jerk, and then bounced her across the frame.

He had some cable ties left over. He wrapped one around her wrist, tightened it, and threaded another through it to attach her to a strut. He did the same with her ankle. He looked at her face through the mess of the inside of her helmet. Her eyes were closed. She was completely unresponsive.

He didn't have time to wallow. He needed to get her back, and for Alice to work some kind of magic. Even climbing into the seat took seconds that he didn't have. He certainly wasn't going to bother with the driver's harness. He gripped the steering wheel and squeezed the accelerator. The motors rumbled through the latticework and the tires clawed at the dirt. The buggy rolled forward.

He could see the ship. He could see it, getting larger and more detailed ahead of him. He was bare minutes away. He couldn't turn to see Marcy. Or even tell if Marcy was still attached. There were rear-facing cameras, but they'd put them in the pile of parts to do later.

There was a familiar feeling rising in his guts. The feeling of powerlessness, of the inability to do anything to change the situation, of being condemned to watch while …

… while someone he'd come to care about, someone he was responsible for, died.

And he couldn't even fix it by shooting anyone.

The buggy was responding differently than it had done on Earth. It floated over the surface, getting airtime whenever he hit a rise, and each hit on a big rock made that tire lose contact for a moment. Maybe it'd be different if he wasn't driving so fast. He had to wrestle with the steering, continually adjusting the direction as if he was rally-car racing.

He gritted his teeth and concentrated.

"Alice? I'm close. I'm almost there."

"As soon as you get here, you get yourself inside. You understand? I'll deal with Marcy."

"I can carry her."

"You have no air left, Frank. And I don't want two patients

and have to decide which I'm going to treat first. I'm the medical officer, and that's an order."

"I don't have to do what you say."

"You do if you want to live."

Thirty seconds away. Twenty. Ten.

He parked right outside, and realized that the noises filling his ears were his suit alarms sounding urgent and constant. The airlock was already open, and someone was standing there on the top step, waiting for him.

"Alice? That you?"

"Come on, Frank. Come on in."

He climbed out of the seat. His hands were numb, and his forearms ached with the vibrations from the uneven terrain. He couldn't hold on to anything. It was almost impossible to navigate the open latticework of the buggy, and he half-slid, half-fell to the ground.

Alice picked him up, put him on his feet, and with a hand in his back, pushed him up the steps.

"What about Marcy?"

"I said I'd deal with her." Alice put him in the entrance to the airlock and shoved him hard. He flew, staggering against the far door, and she reached in behind him to press the button. The outer door started to close.

"Marcy?"

She pushed him all the way in again, and stood on the threshold while the door was still wide enough for him to try and leave. When it wasn't, she stepped back onto the outer platform, and the door closed Frank inside.

"What are you doing?"

"I'm saving your life, you little idiot."

"But Marcy."

"She's dead, Frank. She's been dead for five minutes. Nothing's bringing her back."

"But."

"There are no buts. I, of all people, should know what dead

139

looks like. She went asystole and stopped breathing. It'll take me another five minutes to get her back inside, five minutes plus to get her suit off, clear her airways, inject her with adrenaline and start CPR."

His own suit was still clanging at him, but the quality of the noise changed as the air filled the space around him.

"And you, you're going anoxic. You're not thinking straight, so as soon as the pressure equalizes, you're going to have to open your suit. Got that?"

The inner airlock door slid aside, and Frank stumbled to the floor, at Brack's feet.

"You heard the doctor. Open your suit."

Frank, still on all fours, flipped his controls. His vision blurred. He couldn't see.

"I ..."

"Geez, Kittridge. You can't even do the simplest things."

Frank blinked. One of the choices was lit. The other wasn't. He stabbed down with his finger and hoped.

A click, a whirr. The first hint of cold, thin air filtering around his sweat-drenched back and his stinging eyes.

The airlock cycled again, and Alice came in. She hauled Frank to sitting, then stood in front of Brack, an obvious, immediate challenge.

Brack turned away and looked at his screens.

"Patch him up. Get him ready to go out again tomorrow. And defrost another," he said. "We need to stay on track."

13

[Internal memo: Project Sparta team to Bruno Tiller 3/7/2039 (transcribed from paper-only copy)]

We suggest that you don't treat this as a colonization project. More of a practice run. If we consider that everything that you will learn on this mission will be the first time you learn it, we predict crew attrition to be moderate. Mistakes will be made. Equipment will not function. Not everyone will survive. You will therefore be expecting perhaps up to two crew members (twenty-five (25) per cent) to meet with a fatal or incapacitating accident—odds which, were they known, would limit the pool of potential recruits.

Given that we would be losing XO employees in good standing, with friends within the company and families without, and given that the cost of litigation and compensation that would have to be factored in would erode the savings we've made—savings which would almost pay for another Mars base—I'm going to suggest a radical solution.

XO bought a security company called Panopticon eighteen (18) months ago. Part of Panopticon's portfolio includes a contract with the California Department of Corrections to run four of the State's prison facilities. This presents us with the opportunity to transport— legally and literally—convicts to Mars and use them as labor. I am advised that this is permissible, if we designate the Mars base a correctional facility.

You probably have many questions regarding this proposition. My team have already been working on finding out those answers. I'm going to suggest we meet next week so that I can present you with our full findings.

Frank didn't know if Dee had ever seen a dead body before, but once Frank had cut through the cable ties, there wasn't any other option but for them both to lift Marcy down from the back of the buggy. Perhaps it was something in Frank's body language that managed to translate itself through the bulky suit, but Dee didn't so much as murmur a complaint or objection. It was something that Frank was grateful for. Neither was strong on conversation, so they worked mostly in silence.

Alice said she'd make good on her promise to "deal" with Marcy. He didn't know what that meant. Presumably, there was some sort of protocol for burying the dead: if there was, he didn't know about it. He didn't even know if they had shovels. And that was as far as he wanted to think on the subject.

He had the head end, by unspoken agreement, but he kept his eyes elsewhere and they laid her on the ground face-down. Her suit was still plump and pressurized, still as heavy as it was before. Whatever the human soul weighed, it wasn't so much as to make a difference. He unclipped her tablet from her waist, powered it up to make sure it still worked and had sufficient battery life, and fixed it to his own belt.

"You ready, Dee?"

Dee nodded, his young face slack with awe as his gaze skittered across Frank to the ship and the volcano and the crater wall and the pink sky.

"You have to talk to me, Dee. Tell me you're OK. You've got to stay in touch, let me know if you feel hot or cold or breathless or sleepy or sick or you've a headache or one of your alarms has gone off. Got that?"

Dee nodded again before getting a grip on himself and saying: "OK, Frank. Sure."

"Climb up, thread your legs through the struts and hold on to the back of the seat. I'll take it easy, stop to check on you—so we can check on each other—and no stupid risks. Got that, Dee?"

"Got it, Frank."

They had two jobs today: build the second buggy and fit out the trailers, then drive up out of the crater and retrieve the solar panel array. Because if they didn't, they had no way to recharge the fuel cells. The ship's own generators and batteries were at full stretch, keeping the ship's systems going. If the buggies ran out of power then they wouldn't move. If the ship ran low on power, they were going to have to sit there and freeze, or suffocate, whichever was first.

It struck Frank as another flaw in the mission plan. There were others, most intractable of which was the one supply cylinder that had dropped eighty miles away. That was pretty much out of range, and it might as well have been halfway around the planet for all that it mattered.

Many of the problems would have been solved by simply putting their ship closer to the eastern end of the crater, and actually parking up in the middle of the drop zone. Granted, none of them were pilots—at least, he didn't think Brack was a pilot, but he didn't really know anything about him—and they'd all been asleep. But someone back at Mission Control had known where the cylinders had come down, and still put the ship nearly at the original target.

He wasn't in charge. If there was a reason for it all, he wasn't party to it. He and the others just had to put up with the nonsense and try and sort order from chaos.

Frank sat in the seat, wiped his visor clear and set the buggy off at a steady ten miles an hour towards the drop-off. He'd seen on the map—Marcy had shown him, only yesterday—that the slope was least where it butted up against the edge of the crater. It added a little extra distance, but it was safer, and that was what they needed right now. Not to add to the danger that was all around them, just the other side of their faceplates.

The lower speed made travel much smoother. The tire plates deformed when rolling over a rock, and sprang back when they had passed over. Even the downslope onto the crater floor was nothing more than a gentle ride, only requiring Frank to keep the buggy wheels pointing in the same direction

"Any of these places got names yet?" asked Dee.

"Aside from the volcano and the crater? I don't know."

"Maybe we should start doing that."

"Maybe." He'd not thought of naming things here, even though he'd done it at the XO facility on Earth. It seemed like something someone who was going to stay for ever was going to do. He was only on his third day awake, and perhaps the unreality of yesterday had affected him. He felt like he was dreaming still, and to give this slope, that line of hills, a sharp-edged crater, or a big blocky boulder a name, a permanent name, would solidify his presence. If he named things, he took ownership of them.

Once down on the crater floor, he found the tire tracks they'd made the previous day, still sharp and obvious in the dust. He could put the map away now, and just follow them east.

Just over an hour later, they were at the cylinder, and Frank made them check their suits over, looking at the contents of the air tanks, the water tanks, the pressure, the composition of the gases inside. There'd be no real exertion from either of them. Both were still at ninety per cent. How very different from yesterday.

Dee had to be talked through everything, but that wasn't so much of a problem: "stand there and hold that" was good enough for most of the tasks. When it came to the few that required some expertise, Frank went through them step by step beforehand.

With both buggies out and fully fitted with their lights, cameras, roll cages, towbars and winches, they turned their attention to the trailers. These required some assembly—the lengths were fixed by through-bolts and the wheels went on two thirds of the way along.

When they were done, and had clamped the trailers to the buggies, Frank clambered into the empty cylinder and checked that they'd not left anything behind. Dee gathered up all the packaging and passed it to him in drums, which he stowed alternately left and right, until all that was left was to pack away the huge canopy of the parachute.

It should have been difficult, but it wasn't, even though the size was monstrous. There was so little air to get trapped in the folds that the canopy could be bundled up and carried by the two men. Frank closed the doors on the supply ship and checked his tool belt.

"That was OK," said Dee.

"It was OK because we know we're not running out of air. Everything's easier knowing that."

"Sorry, Frank. She was … she was nice."

Alice had told him how Marcy had killed twenty-six people, by jacking her truck's autodrive to beat traffic control, and hitting a queue of stationary vehicles on the freeway. But she'd been nice, all the same.

"Yeah." He chewed at his lip. He really didn't want to have to discuss it. The wound was raw and open. She'd died at some point between him tying her to the back of the buggy and arriving at the ship, and most likely Alice would never tell him exactly when. He felt he could have done better, except then he'd have probably died too.

Dee pressed his gloved finger onto the side of the cylinder and made a mark in the dust. No, not a mark, a letter. He spelled out BRACK?

Frank wrote underneath RADIO ALWAYS ON. CAN HEAR ALL.

Dee took a step to one side, to write more. CAN FIX THAT. WILL SAY WHEN DONE.

He then smeared the whole conversation out with quick wipes of his palm, and batted his hands together, as if getting rid of the evidence.

145

Frank nodded. "We have to get to the next drop, and you're going to have to drive. Did you get your license?"

"I got it. Not that it means much up here. But I played computer games, too. Controls are even the same as on the handsets."

"This isn't the same as some shoot-'em-up. Take it easy and follow me."

"I got it, Frank." Dee climbed up onto the second buggy and settled into the seat. "How do I turn this thing on again?"

"Button, right-hand side," said Frank. "Tell me if you start to lose traction or you get warning lights. At any point: don't wait until it becomes a problem."

Frank mounted up and consulted the map. The crater wall was, for most of its circumference, a rampart: not quite a vertical wall of stone, but high steps of layered, fractured rock piled on top of each other, and totally impassable to anyone but the most serious mountain climber. At the eastern end, where they were, the wall had collapsed along a mile-and-a-half stretch. The rock had tumbled down, and the sand from the high plain had blown in and covered it, making a much shallower slope. A ten per cent gradient, against a hundred per cent elsewhere. He saw it as the first stroke of luck they'd had.

He still dialed down his suspension, and told Dee how to do the same. It was impossible to tell how deep the sand layer was. Those same rock ledges which dominated the crater wall elsewhere might lurk just below the surface.

How fast to take it? Marcy would have known, but Frank realized he was going to have to guess. Medium-quick, build up the momentum at the bottom and hope that it'd be enough to carry him up to the top. The crater floor was some fifteen hundred feet lower than the rim. They were climbing a mountain, no matter what their eyes told them.

He relayed his instructions and swung his buggy around to get the best run-up. He checked his suit again. Seventy-five per cent. Very different from yesterday. They should have been more prepared, with some kind of contingency plan. Marcy'd still be around, and he wouldn't be having to nursemaid both Dee and his grief.

He used his rear camera to check where Dee was, and squeezed the throttle to slowly build up a head of speed. The wheels turned and bit down and he felt the land rise up underneath him, forcing him against the back of his seat. There was a jolt, followed a moment later by another as the rear wheel hit the same unseen obstacle, but he was moving smoothly enough. He squeezed down harder. Fifteen seemed like fast enough for the lower slopes.

The image on his screen showed Dee was already losing ground. "Give it some gas. You're pulling, so don't be scared."

The empty trailer was bouncing hard without any weight on it. It didn't have adjustable wheels in the same way that the front end did, just regular dumb ones, no motor, no active control. And in the lower gravity, it was slewing and fishtailing away, and now he was worried about damage to the linkage. He felt he had no choice but to ease off slightly, go slower and run the risk of stalling.

No, not stall, since the motors gave him maximum torque at zero revs, but that brought its own problems with overheating and burnout.

He kept going, and felt like his face was pointed towards the sky. The top of the slope was all he could see in front of him, and the curtain of the crater wall extending either side. Time dragged out. He was climbing, he knew that, but without a clear view behind him—the rear-facing camera couldn't resolve the crater floor properly—he was unable to tell just how far he'd gone.

He found himself wondering what it would look like from above, from space. These two tiny insects crawling across the vast red brick wall of the planet. Their huge journey just a tick on the whole monumental edifice that was Mars, insignificant and meaningless.

The top of the slope seemed to be growing closer. Or was that an illusion? Steeper, certainly. He could hear as well as feel the motors growling around him: loose sand and rock crackled underneath. His speed was falling, and he tightened his grip around the throttle. Lots of loose material. He had to increase the traction. Lean forward slightly. Even though that last part wouldn't do anything in itself.

He watched the odometer tick round in tenths of miles. Surely he had to be at the top by now? But the slope was inexorably upwards, and the ground swelled to meet him.

The motors changed note. For a moment, he thought he'd blown something, but his seat shifted under him and the nose of the buggy nudged downwards. The sudden expanse of emptiness, vast and uncaring and frigid, brought him abruptly to a halt.

The haze in the distance meant he couldn't see forever, but it felt like it. Emerging from the narrow confines of the crater to be exposed to the full force of the Martian view was like getting punched in the guts. He was actually winded.

"Frank?"

"Alice."

"You OK? Heart rate up, blood pressure up, breathing rate up. You're hyperventilating."

"At the top of the crater wall. You need to see this."

"Describe it to me instead."

"I guess. OK. There are three huge volcanoes, like blisters, one directly in front, one to the left, and ..." He made sure the brakes were on and climbed out of his seat. Dee was coming up behind, slowly, laboriously, in his own time. "One behind, over Rahe. The ground doesn't really rise or fall. It's like the Midwest. Flat. Huge sky. Blue, almost black overhead. Pink haze down to the horizon, and I can't even tell how far that is away. It's huge. And there's nothing. Just rocks and sand and craters of all sizes, different shades of red and brown."

"Your breathing's under control now, so you can shut up.

Seriously, I can't nursemaid you—any of you—and you have to look after yourselves. You faint, fall, cut yourself, whatever, while you're out there, you have to deal with it. I can sit here and watch over your vital signs like Mother Hen, but I got to go and defrost Declan and he's a whiny little shit at the best of times. Go and get the solar panels and bring them back here so I don't have to spend too much time cooped up with him. Got that?"

"Ma'am."

"Just do it. And try and bring your companion back alive this time."

That was acidic enough to burn. Even when it had started to heal over, he was going to go back to that scab and pick at it.

"Loud and clear, One. Out."

Marcy, veteran of the open road, would have loved this view.

Frank held up his hand to Dee and the other buggy slowed and stopped a few yards away from his.

"Let's check our suits and our vehicles. Take a look around and orient ourselves, then we can head off to the target." He walked around the buggy, taking his time to inspect the wheels and the underside of the fuel cell: there were a few scratches, and some of the tire plates were dinged, but nothing serious. The hitch was robust, with no sign of cracking on the metal welds.

Dee probably didn't know what to look for, so Frank took him around, shaking the wheels and making sure all the bolts were still tight.

"You OK?" asked Dee.

"Fine."

"Because—"

"I'm fine."

Dee had enough sense to desist at that point.

Frank took out the tablet with the map and scrolled across it. The little white crosses of where the supplies had fallen looked uncomfortably like an old cemetery. When he put his finger on

149

each cross the screen detailed the manifest: solar farm, hydroponics equipment, air plant, water maker, habitat module, communications, internal fixtures. Somewhere out there were their personal effects, too. Frank's little brown box, and his letters, and his books. He guessed that wasn't a priority, but if he was passing, he might be tempted to swing by.

"Five point six miles north of here. If you're ready?"

"Ready."

The landscape was novel. For a while. But after the first few miles, it became a repeat of yesterday. Nothing changed. The volcanoes were no closer, and one expanse of sandy ocher ground littered with fist-sized rocks was very much the same as the next. Half an hour of monotony. Frank kept on telling himself that this was Mars, a completely different planet, a whole new experience. But it didn't feel real. There was a disconnect between his experience and his body.

Perhaps it was something to do with the thickness of perspex between him and outside, and that most of the sound was deadened to the point of non-existence. Like watching a screen on mute. He'd have to watch out for that.

He navigated his way over to where the map told him the cylinder was lying, and again, he saw the parachute before he spotted the—

"Ah, crap."

The cylinder was crumpled, and the Mars surface strewn with debris. There was a trail of spilled packing material that extended away into the distance, snagged around rocks and half-buried by blown dust. The top of the container, where the transponder hid, was intact, but clearly the rockets that were supposed to lower it to the ground had failed in some way: fired too soon, too late, or cut out before landing. The bottom end was crushed like a soda can, and the impact had caused one of the two door-hatches to fail completely.

Frank kicked the cylinder as he stalked past it. Things were broken. Of the drums in the container, the lowest two had disintegrated completely, and the next one up had burst around its circumference. There might be something salvageable inside it, but until they could wrest it out, they wouldn't know.

"It doesn't look good," said Dee. He lifted a flat shard and shook it free of dust. It was part of a solar panel, black and shiny. "We probably needed this, right?"

As much as he didn't want to talk to anyone in the ship, Frank felt he had no other choice.

"Alice. Is Declan awake enough to answer some questions?"

"Just about. Hold on."

He heard some scratching and scraping, then: "Yeah. OK. I've been asleep for a year, so don't expect much sense."

"The supply ship containing our solar farm managed to smash itself into the ground. Not crater-hard, but we've probably lost, I don't know, a third of it, maybe more."

Frank could hear Declan's breathing. "Which third?"

"It's a crap shoot. Do you want me to bring it in anyway and you see what you can do with it?"

"I'll get a feed off your suit camera. Give me a second."

"Hey," said Dee. "We've got cameras?"

"Jesus, Dee. Pay some fucking attention once in a while, will you?" Declan sighed, and fell silent as he assessed the grainy pictures. "OK. Fuck my life. That's not what I wanted to see."

"Sorry about that."

"We need to get some sort of power generating system set up. Those glorified golf carts you're riding around on aren't magic, and they're going to run out of juice soon enough. Let's have a look at the map."

The airwaves went dead for several seconds, during which Dee started picking up random crap off the ground, shaking it and dropping it again. Frank scowled at him.

"Dee. Sharp edges. What happened last time?"

"OK," said Declan, "I've found it. It's another eight miles, east of where you are now. It's the RTG we were going to use as the base load, when we'd got everything set up. But we can use it now while we see what's left of the solar array."

"What do you want us to do with this stuff?"

"Load what you can. Especially cables, regulators, switch boards, everything except the obviously trashed gear. Then get the RTG and bring it straight back. And ... if that happens to have plowed a hole in Mars, remember it's basically a big bucket of radioactive metal and you're going to die if the casing is ruptured. Got that?"

"Sure. We copy that."

Frank checked his suit readings, and made sure Dee did the same.

"You heard the man. Let's load it up."

14

[Internal memo: Mars Base One (Logistics) to Mars Base Knowledge Bank 5/12/2042]

Notes regarding the ongoing supply of the Mars base

It would be more cost effective to wait and find out what the requirements are, and then send that, than guess what might be required and oversupply. Each pound of payload costs in the region of eighty thousand (80,000) dollars to get to Mars. One ton of supplies will therefore cost in the region of one hundred and sixty million (160,000,000) dollars.

It takes a rocket on a standard transfer orbit on average two hundred and sixty days to get there, with shorter or longer journeys possible on specific launch windows and delta V requirements. We now envisage a two-staged launch, with the initial base and infrastructure cargo leaving Earth between the months of December 2045 and April 2046, and the NASA specific equipment leaving early in 2048.

We will know by the second round of launches what has failed to arrive on the surface. Transponder/orbital photography data will clarify the position by November 2046: early enough, in the event of mission-critical failures, to advise the NASA mission at that point. We will resupply as necessary at our cost.

They had power. The RTG sat on the sand outside the ship, as far away from it as the fat electrical cable snaking from its mid-section would allow. It looked like a squat Angel of Death, its wings radiating so much heat that the air above it—what there was of it—shimmered.

Declan was outside, trying to piece together what he could of the solar array that was supposed to provide them with the rest of their energy. The greatest damage had been done to the panels themselves, and there weren't many workarounds for that. New ones would have to be sent from Earth.

What power they had was going to have to be rationed, at least to start with. They had only enough to work a domestic water heater, but a lot of the systems were designed for low energy consumption. The ship had its own generator that was nowhere near as powerful, but still potentially useful, if everything was combined.

Brack had nixed that idea almost as soon as the words had left Declan's mouth. The ship stayed intact. End of.

The next priority was air. The air plant would need electricity, which they didn't have enough of, to produce oxygen, which they didn't have enough of either. With five of them now awake, they were getting through the stores faster, and it seemed that XO had neglected to pack any spare in case of emergency.

The buggies needed a full half-day plugged in to strip the water back down into its component gases, ready for the next mission, but the air plant also had to refill the oxygen tanks in their suits' life-support systems.

Frank didn't like the sums either, especially when other necessities like water and heating and light were factored in. They were always going to be short, having to choose which things to turn off if they needed more elsewhere.

"That's over your pay grade, Kittridge," said Brack. "You need to concentrate on getting everything back here and working."

He debated whether saying anything more would help, and eventually decided, almost solely because of the expression on

154

Dee's face, to speak up. "And what if we can't? What if we don't have enough kit to make a viable base out of what's reached the surface in one piece?"

"Have we not got an atmosphere in here? Are you struggling to make out my words?"

"What's our contingency? What's the fallback position?"

Alice reached out to put her hand on Frank's shoulder, and he shrugged it off, almost instantaneously. There was no space on the lowest level to escape from anyone. They were face to face, whether they liked it or not.

"You have one job here," said Brack. "One job. To get the base up and working. If you don't like it, there's the airlock. Go find someone to complain to."

Frank could feel uncharacteristic heat rise inside him. All he had to do was hit Brack first, a good solid punch to the head so that he smacked him against the ladder as well. What did the man actually do but just breathe and eat and drink, without contributing anything?

But there was the promise: if they lived—if they both lived— they'd both go home.

"No one's explained to us why we don't have enough food. No one's explained to us what happens when we run out of that, or water, or air. Maybe if we knew what was going on ..." He crushed his emotions. "What else can we get while we're out there?"

"Better. We can't keep on drinking our own piss indefinitely, but we can manage for a while. We're going to run out of food before we run out of water. Get a hab module. Next run out after this will be the hydroponics." Brack stood there, hands on hips. "So what are you waiting for? You and Stutter-boy need to suit up and head for the hills."

Alice retreated to the place they'd all started calling the ice-box, even though the crew in storage were only cool, not freezing. Frank checked over his suit, and encouraged Dee to do the same—the boy had a strangely lax attitude over something that

155

was only going to preserve his life if it worked perfectly, each and every time.

He checked his tanks, his scrubber, filled up his water supply and put a fresh energy bar into the holder, and watched while Dee happily played with the chest console, tapping buttons and scrolling through the menus.

Frank synced the tablet to the main computer, getting updated map information and details. Now that, Dee was interested in. He waved for Frank to hand him the device, and he poked around on it while Frank started climbing into his suit.

"Dee, put it down and get ready. We've got work to do."

"Just checking what I'll be working with, when it's all up and running." He handed Frank the tablet and looked to see where Brack was. The man was standing at the main terminal, his back to the pair, and Dee gave Frank an exaggerated wink. Frank had no idea what that meant. Brack was working the controls almost absent-mindedly, concentrating on something on his screen, and saw nothing.

Frank clipped the tablet onto his waist belt, along with one of the now-charged nut runners, before easing the top half of his body into his suit. His head pushed through the neck ring and into the helmet. He was getting used to the muffled, close sound it surrounded him with. He closed up his suit, checked all his numbers and the flow of air around his face, before giving Dee the thumbs up.

Dee finished climbing into his own suit, and closed and sealed his back-hatch. Frank went first into the airlock.

He felt the now familiar filling out around him as the air was pumped away, and was ready for the sudden suck as the outer door opened. He stepped out onto the platform, and looked at his surroundings. There were the buggies. There was the ship. There was the crater wall. There was the hazy sky, pink and blue. The addition of the black RTG—as tall as Frank and as wide as his arm span—didn't make much of an impact.

Declan and his jigsaw puzzle of solar panels was more obvious.

His suit moved among the components, testing and connecting and disassembling. The frames for the circular panels littered the near distance, but none were yet complete.

"Declan. How is it?"

"It could be better. It could be worse. This is supposed to be a fifteen-kilowatt array, for an average load of ten kilowatts. The good news is, both battery packs are intact. The casing's cracked on one of them, but that's just cosmetic. The bad news," he said, gesturing around him, "is that we've seven kilowatts of generating power at best. Add it to the three we get as baseload, and that makes about ten. Which is fine for between mid-morning and mid-afternoon. All other times, we get less, and only the three at night if we don't use some of the daytime juice to charge the batteries."

"We need more power."

"Another couple of kilowatts would mean we could heat the habs at night. If," he added pointedly, "we can't use the ship's generator, we're going to have to try and think of something else."

"Like?"

"It's not as if we can go down the wholesaler's for parts, is it? I'll have to see what I can come up with. And Demetrius is supposed to be my second. He should be helping me sort out this god-awful mess."

"Brack decided. You can have him back when someone else volunteers to drive the other buggy."

With Demetrius out of the airlock, they were now wasting air-time. They unplugged the buggies, checked the fuel cells, and Frank felt the need to tighten the frame and wheel nuts with the nut runner. Most were on tight enough. One or two were worryingly loose, and he didn't know if that was because they'd been shaken free, or whether they'd not been done up properly in the first place.

"We're losing daylight," said Dee.

"I'm saving your life. Again." Frank went round the trailers too, pressing the bit onto the top of the nuts and giving the trigger a squeeze. "One of these comes off, we're in trouble that we didn't have to be in."

They drove to the drop-off, and because no one was going to stop him, Demetrius called it the Heights, and the crater floor the Valley. The raised ridge that ran the length of the center of the crater became, inevitably, Beverly Hills, and the route they took to the south of them, Sunset Boulevard.

They passed three craters on the way that were too small to have official names, but were large enough to have to drive around. The first was Compton, the second, Vermont, and the third Hollywood. Frank was a San Franciscan native, but Dee had grown up—until he'd got locked up—in LA. Frank didn't know if the labels were ironic or descriptive: probably both. And none of them had any weight, save what they gave them themselves. Either they'd catch on, or they wouldn't.

But when they stopped at the bottom of the crater wall, at the point where they'd driven up the day before, Demetrius took the tablet from Frank and somehow entered the names onto the map itself. He named the upslope they were about to tackle Long Beach.

Dee beckoned Frank closer, and opened the suit controls on his chest. He pressed buttons, as he had done on the ship, then did the same for Frank. He leaned their helmets together.

"Can you hear me?"

And Frank could: just not through the speakers inside his suit. Dee's voice had carried through the touching perspex.

"What did you do?"

"Turned the microphones off. The transmitters are still working, so they won't flag as a fault, but no one else can overhear."

"Neat trick. How do I turn it back on?"

"From this menu here: down, down, right, right, down, select. That's on and off. Pretty certain it's not supposed to be there, but it is."

"Privacy. As long as we stand like this."

"D-did I do good, Frank?"

"You've done fine, Dee."

"We might need it. Maybe. At some point."

"You never know. We'd better turn them back on, though, in case they notice the drop out." Frank tried to remember the sequence, and Dee talked him through it again. They separated, and Frank said: "Ready to tackle the wall again?"

"Sure." Dee went back to his buggy, and climbed on. Frank took the lead, but didn't know whether driving up the same path was a good thing or a bad thing. The tracks he'd left were smudged but still prominent. At least he knew that there were no terrible surprises on that route, no sudden collapses or sandtraps or impossible gradients, so it was worth trying again. It might not always be that way, and complacency might see him break down or turn the buggy over.

They ought to schedule a visual inspection of what was so far the only way up out of the crater, but that might only become an important factor if they had reason to leave Rahe after they'd collected all the supply drops. Otherwise, it became something for someone else to do.

They reached the top, and were confronted by the same wide open vista, Mars in all its naked, frigid, terrifying glory. Frank pulled over and showed Dee the map.

"The air plant cylinder is twelve miles north-east. The nearest hab unit to that is three miles further on, due east. That gives us a total round trip of about sixty miles. If there are any problems, we abandon one or both cylinders, and the trailers if we have to, and make our priority to get back to the ship."

"Frank, it'll be fine. Sixty miles is nothing."

"It's two thirds of your air. No one's going to be calling triple-A for us. Do you remember what it was like when you split your suit, and Alice had to stab you to seal it? Do you remember how scared you were?"

"Sure, but they really weren't going to let me die, were they?"

Frank jabbed the tablet against Dee's hard torso. "We'd have got a new guy the same way we got Declan. They didn't give a shit about you. We didn't even have suit patches."

"We've got them now, though."

"We've only got them because it'll cost them a fortune to ship another con to Mars. To them, we're a resource. To us, we should be more than that." Frank walked back to his buggy. "No one is going to keep us safe but us. You need to start thinking that way."

And while Demetrius thought about that, Frank got to consider how they were going to recover the cylinder that was eighty miles away. At that distance, plus the time it took to load the cylinder onto the trailer, it was out of range. They needed a pressurized environment to change out their life-support systems, and unless they built one, say at the top of Long Beach, there was no way they could collect all the parts.

So that was the obvious solution. Erect one of the habs with an airlock out on the plain, pressurize it, and use it as a staging post for as long as they needed it. Then, when they didn't, take it down again. The only problem he could see would be taking the air to the hab once it was up. It only needed five psi of pure oxygen to work, but whether the scheme would work was dependent on whether they could find enough tanks to fill.

Even better, just take the airlock. He'd have to practice changing the life support in such a confined space. But that would be quicker and easier to arrange: he could just tow one to the right spot and dump it until he needed it, rather than truck everyone out to the edge of the crater and have them build a full hab. He'd need to pressurize it, but once they got the air plant running, they could use one of the scuba tanks to do that.

It would put everything in range. And it would provide anyone out on the plain with a lifeboat.

Would Brack say no? If he wanted the base actually built, then he'd say yes. He'd be forced to say yes in the end: XO would surely tell him that he had to.

All they had to do now was solve the energy crisis. He had no idea how that was going to pan out. Perhaps XO would demand that Declan took the power from the ship. Perhaps it was XO's decision not to allow it, and Brack was simply following orders. But surely, if there was spare capacity, then eventually they'd have to use it, allowed or not.

They traveled on. The wheels rattled and bounced over the rocks on the surface, making their hands numb and their teeth ache. And after an hour, the cylinder containing the air plant should have been dead ahead on the wide, open landscape, but Frank couldn't see the telltale parachute. The canopy was almost thirty yards across which, considering the transponder was giving him a distance of a couple of hundred yards, should have been visible.

He slowed down and edged forward. If the air plant had hard-impacted, then it was pretty much game over. And there was a crater, right in front of him. But it didn't look sharp-edged and fresh; the rim had eroded down to the same level as the surrounding plain.

He parked up and waved at Dee to do the same. He jumped down, and walked as his map indicated. There was the parachute, and there was the cylinder, some hundred feet down in the bottom of a depression that was a thousand feet across.

"Well, that's not helping."

"At least it's not broken." Dee stamped his foot on the ground. It seemed firm enough. "Drive down?"

"I'll walk it, and you can follow. If we leave one buggy at the top, at least we don't get stuck if something happens."

"What if we need both to drag it out?"

"We've a hundred and fifty feet of cable on each winch. If we can get the trailer to within that distance, we can use both. But the slope's not so bad, less than ten per cent. Long Beach is steeper."

Frank stepped down into the crater. The sides were packed-down gravel: the base, a cracked rock pavement. He had thought it might have more dust and sand blown into it, filling it up, but

161

the reverse seemed to have happened. The whole basin seemed scoured, like a pot.

He waved Dee down behind him, and crunched his way to the cylinder. The scorch marks from the rockets had faded to gray, and the painted XO logo was, along with the rest of the white pigment, worn thin. He opened up the cargo hatches and saw that everything was still packed in tightly.

No need to disturb anything yet. Wait until they could get the thing home.

Dee couldn't back the trailer up, so Frank had to, and it took even him three goes to line it up correctly. They decoupled the motor unit from the bottom end of the cylinder—the fuel remnants were toxic, explosive, and best left where they couldn't do any harm—and attached the winch cable to the rest, winding it slowly on to the open framework until the balance of the trailer had shifted enough for the weight to tip forward. The rear end came up, and the buggy shuddered as it found a new equilibrium.

"OK. Fast across the flat and let your momentum carry you up. If you start to slip, keep it straight and stop only if you have to." Frank looked up at the pale sun and checked his timer. Nearly four hours in. "Go. I'll see you at the top."

Dee pulled away and headed up towards the lip of the crater, leaving Frank to trudge along behind. The walking was fine, though: a steady gradient and none of those fist-sized loose surface rocks that seemed to predominate out on the plain.

He was halfway out when his earphones suddenly squawked, overloading with signal. He winced, and instinctively his hands went to the sides of his head, where they encountered only his helmet.

"Who the hell was that?"

"Frank? Frank? It's me. D-Dee. What's happening, Frank? What's going on?"

The back end of the trailer had already vanished over the crater rim. Dee and the buggy were invisible. The only choice Frank had was how fast he dared run.

162

It was more skipping than running, faster than the low, loping pace he'd managed with Marcy, but slower than a full sprint on Earth. He still spent too long in the air, and not long enough pushing himself forward on the ground. And the suit restricted his full movement, too. He felt strangely incapable of speed, almost as if he was dreaming and fighting to wake up.

He scrabbled up the last few steps.

"Hang on, Dee. Hang on. Don't panic. I'm co—"

The sight struck him dumb. Tornadoes. A dozen, maybe more, it was difficult to tell, were spinning and snaking towards them. The tubes were almost ghost-like, pale and fading high into the sky, where they maintained sinuous curves. But at their bases, they were white with spinning dust.

"What do we do, Frank?"

Frank was mesmerized. The bright funnels tracked briskly across the ground, and then they were among them. One passed over Frank's trailer, then right past him. He could hear the patter of dust against his helmet, but rather than pelting him with debris, it seemed to strip off what he'd accumulated, and carried it away.

The twister descended into the crater, obliterating his footprints. The others took their own paths, all roughly in the same direction. The air cleared, and the tornadoes moved away, becoming indistinct in the horizon's haze.

He was aware of another voice in his ear. Alice.

"Frank. Report."

"It's OK. It's OK. Just ... surprised, that's all. Bunch of Martian twisters ambushed us. I'll check over the suits and the buggies, but we're OK. We've got the air plant."

She seemed satisfied. Frank walked over to Dee's buggy and stared up at him.

"Next time, you tell me what the actual problem is." He was still breathing heavily after his exertions. "Or, goddammit, I'll kick your ass all the way back to the ship. Got that?"

It took a moment, but he managed to wring an apology out of Dee.

"I … sorry. Sorry."

"Damn right you're sorry. You're not a child. You're an astronaut. Try and behave like one." Frank turned round and stalked back to his own buggy. "Let's find the hab and go home."

He was angry. Angry with Demetrius, but mostly angry with himself. He knew he should have reacted sooner, and got out of the twisters' way, rather than just standing there like an idiot. He'd had no idea what might have happened, and it could all have ended very differently.

He was going to take a few minutes, on his own, to calm down. Because otherwise he'd end up doing something even more stupid, and he didn't want that. Not now.

15

[Internal memo: Project Sparta team to Bruno Tiller 7/6/2040 (transcribed from paper-only copy)]

Minimum crew requirements

On the assumption that we send zero (0) robots and use zero (0) automatic systems, and using a working estimate of between one hundred and twenty (120) and one hundred and fifty (150) man-hours to build a single (1) hab section, pressurize it, fit it out and make it habitable, from scratch:

(We require an accurate figure as to the number of man-hours required.)

However, based on the above figures, we are currently recommending that the crew during the build phase is no less than six, and no more than eight. This assumes a minimum input per crew member of eight (8) man-hours per sol, rising to twelve (12) man-hours per sol after initial hab erection.

The build phase is therefore expected to last something longer than a month, but no more than two.

Following completion of the base modules and infrastructure, there will be a testing phase to ensure all components function as predicted and any potential faults are identified and rectified: it is expected that the labor requirements will fall to between four (4) and six (6) man-hours per sol per crew.

The testing phase is expected to last no more than a month.

Thereafter the base moves into maintenance mode. It is estimated at that point that the labor requirements fall to essentially zero (0).

It is therefore anticipated that the active phase of construction will last no longer than three (3) months.

It was the first time that all of them had been awake. All, except Marcy. It chewed at him. Yes, it had been an accident. Her air scrubber had worked perfectly for eight and three quarter hours and then failed. He wasn't to blame. No one was to blame. They'd both been at the very ends of their life-support systems. It could have been her leaving him to die.

And still it grumbled in his guts, like a bad meal, refusing to quieten down and let him be.

If Frank had thought there might be a change of plan due to where they'd landed, and that they'd be building the base around the ship, he was wrong. Brack asserted that everything had to be constructed on the original site, nearly a mile and a half away, at the bottom end of the valley that had deposited the shelf of material—the Heights—that they'd landed on. That there was a valley, and that it had been formed by running water, enough to wash down the debris from the top of the volcano to the bottom, was strange enough to think about, but the valley itself went all the way to the top of the volcano, some thirty miles continuously uphill, and a climb of nearly fifteen thousand feet.

There'd been a river on Mars, and Dee called it the Santa Clara.

They grumbled about the site, because it was a forty-minute walk away, but it wasn't anything they could alter. That's where

NASA wanted their base, and apparently that was where it had to be built.

"Can't we, you know, move the ship closer?" asked Zeus.

Brack made his lips go thin. "You a spaceship pilot?"

"I guess that's a no. I thought perhaps you might be."

"Suit up, Number Seven. You got work to do."

Declan cleared his throat. The dry, reduced atmosphere seemed to have stopped him sweating, but he still habitually rubbed his hands together. A nervous thing, maybe.

"About that," he said. "I've been thinking."

"You've been thinking?" crowed Brack, but uncharacteristically Declan cut him off.

"Someone has to fix the fact that XO plowed our solar farm into the ground and broke it, leaving us terminally short of power. And when I say terminal, I mean we could die if we don't fix it. So if you'll do me the kindness of shutting the fuck up and listening, I'll tell you how we're going to do just that."

No one said anything, waiting on Brack's reaction to the challenge inherent in Declan's voice. The lowest floor, with seven of them crushed in together, was closer than any of them were comfortable with.

It didn't come, and some of the tension ebbed away.

"We get three kilowatts of power from the RTG, but that thing is belching out heat like a high school furnace. A hundred kilowatts, according to the specifications. Do I need to explain to anyone what a hundred kilowatts looks like? No? Good. We lose all that because it's a by-product: it goes straight up the chimney. What I'm proposing is that we use that waste energy to heat the habs."

"Go on," said Zeus. He was thinking, too, the tattoos on his forehead crowding together.

"It's a big-ass lump of fissile material, so let's treat it as a nuclear pile. We run pipes with cold water around the cooling fins, heat the water, port it around the habs, then back out when it's cold again. Closed system. No losses. If we're smart

167

we can make it entirely passive, no moving parts, everything gravity-fed."

"So we'd heat the habs," said Zero, "but what about the electrics? What about my lights?"

"A substantial part of the energy budget is earmarked for heating at night, because it gets cold enough to freeze the air. If we can get that energy from another source, we can use what's left to do the other things we want. It's not perfect, but it'll work. There's only two problems."

"Pipes," said Zeus.

"And water," added Frank, "assuming you mean regular water."

"We could run it on pressurized liquid CO_2. But water's better. There are degrees of sophistication, but the more surface area we get in contact with the fins, the hotter the water gets. In an ideal world, we'd submerge the whole damn thing in a tank of water and boil it and make steam and run turbines off it. We'd have so much electricity and hot water it'd be like the swankiest condo ever."

"This water's not going to be radioactive, is it?" asked Zero.

"No. Sealed unit."

"And how long is this going to last us?"

"We'll all be dead long before it gives out. The specs say eighty years before there's a noticeable drop in performance. Once the water maker's up and running, we can get as much of that as we want. Now, it might be all we have to do is stick a big pan of it on top of the RTG. But we need the pipework. Preferably insulated pipework, but we can bury the pipes to whack out most of the diurnal range."

"The what?"

"Geez, Zero. Difference in the daytime and night-time temperatures."

"I knew that."

Declan coughed, wiped his hands. "Pipes, people. Can we take anything from here?"

"No. You cannot," said Brack.

"First it's the power, now it's the pipes. This ship is going nowhere, right? We should be cannibalizing it for parts." Declan was standing opposite Brack, flanked by Zeus and Zero. Reason dictated that in a fight between the cons and their jailer, there was going to be only one outcome, and Frank really didn't want to have to stand between them, though he would for his ticket home. But it was Declan who backed down. "Fine. Anyone else?"

"The r-rocket motors," said Dee. "On the supplies."

"That's ... not a bad idea. That'll be good quality shit right there. What do the rockets burn?" When no one offered an answer Declan shrugged. "We can look it up, or talk to Earth. But there'll be pressure vessels and pumps and valves in all of them. Flush out the fuel, and we're good to go."

"How much time is this going to take?" asked Brack. "And what are you going to have to put holes in to make it?"

"I don't know, and I'm guessing a couple, if we have to. We're working at five psi, and we've got what we need to seal that. If we've enough pipework to make a secondary system then we won't even have to do that. This is going to make the difference between dying and not dying, so we're just going to have to wear the extra work. There's going to be some maintenance: if the water freezes, it'll block the pipes, and we'll need to build in a pressure valve to the hot-water tank."

"I can do that. It's not difficult," said Zeus. "We'll draw up some plans, depending on what we've got to work with."

Brack relented. "As long as it doesn't interfere with the base-building."

"It's your ass too," said Zero.

"My ass comes before all your asses. Don't forget it, you little punk."

Frank stepped in. Brack had conceded what they'd needed him to concede. There was no point in riling him.

"We need power to the air plant to inflate the hab. We'll take what's left of the solar panels out with the first hab and set it running. It can store the air while we build. We can transport everyone over, but at some point, I'm going to have to go with Dee and get another couple of cylinders. That leaves four of you to put everything together."

"It could be five if—" started Zero.

"Brack's got his own work. We're building the base. That's our job. If you want to be kicking your heels around here tomorrow, getting in each other's faces for a full day, then OK. Otherwise, we split up."

"Airlock order is three, two, seven, five, four, one," said Brack. "Get to it. Day's not getting any longer."

Frank was out second. Declan was already loading the panels into a drum to put onto the trailer.

"This is going to work, right?" asked Frank.

"It's the best I can do. In the circumstances." Declan hefted the drum. "Look at that. No longer a ninety pound weakling." He carried it to the buggy and set it down again. "The circumstances are less than ideal—you get that, right? It's not going to be perfect."

"But it's the best we can hope for."

"Something like that."

"I don't fancy freezing my ass off, and I'm betting the NASA guys won't either." Frank tilted back to look at the sky. A bright object, shaped like a peanut, was moving perceptibly in an arc above them, from west to east. One of the moons. He couldn't quite remember the name of it. "I don't get," he continued, then stopped. Like Declan, he wondered why Brack wasn't more amenable to them using the ship, but the threat and the promise of an eventual trip home was making him hold his tongue. "Doesn't matter. We'll bring a rocket motor back with us."

"Whoa, there, cowboy," sounded loud in his ears. Brack. "Those motors are a big old can of boom. I'm going to need clearance from Earth, and a copper-bottomed way of making them safe before anyone thinks about moving them around. Tell me you've got that, Kittridge."

"OK. Copy that."

"Take pictures, then," said Declan. "Good quality close-ups. Whatever you can."

Zeus joined them and helped load up. The cylinder containing the hab was still on the back of the other trailer, and Frank gave the job of driving that buggy to Dee, while he took the more sensitive solar panels for a ride. Declan and Zeus sat on the back of his buggy, while Zero and Alice climbed up beside Dee.

Zero tried to persuade Dee to relinquish the driver's seat.

"You've even less experience than he has," said Frank. "There's going to be time later for all of us to get some wheel time, under supervision." He almost added, 'now that Marcy's gone', but he didn't.

Frank led the way at a pedestrian pace. He spent time with his map, trying to get the location exact, eventually parking up right in the dry throat of the Santa Clara.

"Here. Just here."

He dismounted and looked around at what would be his home for … years, at least. To the south was the Santa Clara valley, flat-bottomed and steep-sided, and to the north, the Heights and the descent into the crater. The crater walls left and right merged with the valley's, with sharp-edged scarps marking where the river had burst down from the volcano above and flooded into the deep depression below.

He caught a glimpse of another world, where water rushed in torrents and formed waterfalls and filled low-lying land to form vast circular lakes. But when he blinked, he was left with dusty red soil smeared against his faceplate.

Time to unload the hab. Frank unhooked the hitch, fixed the winch on to the end of the cylinder and dragged it backwards onto the dirt. The soil was similar to that around the ship. There were fewer but bigger rocks, and the land was flatter.

He and Dee walked the path where the hab would sit, pushing the blocky boulders aside and into a pile. It didn't take long before they were stacking the rock into a conical cairn, their first permanent marker on the face of the planet.

The others were lifting the drums out of the cylinder, opening them up, searching through them for the mat. Zeus brought it over, and they rolled it out in a roughly north–south orientation. Ideally, Frank would have a team of surveyors in, with sticks and flags and laser leveling equipment. But as Declan had already said, circumstances were far from ideal. Frank knew enough to get it right, and good enough would do.

He and Dee unloaded the solar farm while the first ring was under construction, and then prepared to head off for another two hab sections. Before they left, though, Alice broke off from the building group and waved Frank down. She opened her suit's controls, and by the way she pressed the buttons, he guessed she'd been talking to Dee.

He muted his own microphone, and in the shadow of the front wheel of his buggy, they touched helmets.

"What's up?"

"We're running out of supplies," she said. "Food, water, air. I ran some figures yesterday and it's not even tight. We're short."

"How short?"

"We've got the air plant, but it can't be in two places at once. If you don't get the water maker this time out, we're going to have to ration water, and even then. With four of us awake, we could have managed, but seven? Even with complete closed-loop recycling, we now have to wait for the machine to filter it for us. And the food: it's like they didn't want us to eat."

"So what are our options?"

"Frank. We don't have enough. Even if we get the greenhouse working in the next couple of days, I'll have to put us on starvation rations. If we all eat regularly, we'll have literally nothing before production kicks in."

"And the air?"

"The ship can make air, but again, with seven of us doing EVAs every day, we can't recharge everyone's life support without eating into the reserves. That's going to cut down into the rate of work, and it just compounds the problems we already have."

Frank thought for a moment. "What did Brack say?"

"'Deal with it', and then he went back to doing whatever it is he does. Breathing, drinking and eating as if it's never going to run out."

"Am I allowed to interpret 'deal with it' as an instruction to, you know, actually deal with it?"

Alice hesitated. "You could do."

"Which is more important? Water, food or air?"

"Food at the bottom. We can stand being hungry. Air at the top: you know how that ends. Water? We should never be in a position to have to choose. The sooner we get all three, the better."

Frank separated for a moment to see what progress the builders had made, then leaned in again. "We've got three hab sections in that can. The greenhouse needs two. So we use this load for that, fill it with air, get the hydroponics kit inside and get it up and running as soon as we can. Talk to Zero about that, maybe without telling him why you're asking. He'll need water, and lots of it. So me and Dee will bring back the seeds and the fish eggs and everything he needs, and the water maker. We can store it in the pressurized hab, and once he gets the plants growing, it'll take the edge off the air issue. That's right, isn't it?"

"The plants will help in the long term, but they're not the solution in the short or medium terms." She looked up at him. "What are you going to do? You're in charge of construction."

"I suppose I am, but the idea that I outrank Brack in any way?"

"It's your call. But I agree that telling anyone else will just lead to panic. None of us are particularly stable under pressure,

173

are we? Someone's likely to do something stupid. So let's not let that happen."

Frank studied Alice's face. It had been a long time since he'd been that close to another person—did Demetrius count? Their conversation was nowhere near as long, or meaningful—and this felt oddly, awkwardly, intimate.

"Fuck it. We'll get the water maker and Zero's plants. Tomorrow, we'll get more habs. We'll have to hammer this hard. We're all going to be pushed close to the edge, and we'll have to rely on you to keep us safe."

"Do it."

She pulled away and restarted her mic. Frank watched her skip back over to where Zeus and Zero were working away with the nut runners, and Declan assembling enough of the solar panels to get the air plant working.

Dee, sitting on top of his buggy, was looking at Frank, narrowing his eyes at him. Frank stared back.

"Problem?"

"No," said Dee. "No problem."

"Good." Frank climbed up next to him, and opened the map. "These are our targets. We have to get them both, and get them back here. Today."

Dee looked sideways at the distances involved. "How far is that?"

"We get to Long Beach and we split up."

"But we're supposed to—"

"I know what we're supposed to do, Dee. We can be in radio contact the whole way, and you do just what you did yesterday, without the freaking out at the sand devil thing, and you'll be fine." Frank tapped Dee's waist, where he wore his own tablet. "Turn it on, take a look, plot a route. I'll meet you back at the crater wall. We'll be apart for an hour and a half. Two hours tops."

"I don't know, Frank. Shouldn't we—"

"He can hear everything we say. If he wanted to object, he would have done so by now."

That silenced him, for a few moments at least.

"What's changed?"

"We're not tourists, Dee, and we've got deadlines."

Frank swung himself down and mounted his own buggy. He checked his air. It'd be enough. Just.

16

[Internal memo: Mars Base One (Logistics) to Mars Base Knowledge Bank 5/16/2044]

Discussion re: food requirements for crew member

The minimum calorific intake for a resting male is approximately nineteen hundred (1900) calories, and for a resting female approximately fourteen hundred (1400) calories.

From arrival to first harvest from the greenhouse, we will need to provide sufficient calories for the crew member to function effectively. Note that the effects of low calorific intake can result in symptoms including irritability, low morale, lethargy, physical weakness, confusion and disorientation, poor decision-making, immuno-suppression, and the inability to maintain body temperature, leading to hypothermia, heat exhaustion, and heat stroke.

We propose that sufficient (daily 3600 men, 2600 women) calories are provided throughout the physically active build phase, and thereafter reducing (2800, 2100) during the test phase. It is expected that the greenhouse will begin to supplement stored food by Week 5 and by Week 12 will begin to supply carbohydrates. Protein (in the form of groundnuts and tilapia) will be available by Week 14. Vitamin supplements will be needed in addition to those derived from food, for the foreseeable future.

By unspoken consent, Alice slept on the third floor of the ship, the rest of the cons on the second, and Brack on the first. The five men in the middle had just about enough room to lie down; they snored, they turned, they talked in their sleep, they—consciously or unconsciously—were concerned about their cellies' close proximity.

Whether anyone could have said they'd slept the whole dark night was debatable. When it had been just him and Dee, and then him and Dee and Declan, Frank had found that he could sleep without fear of accidentally touching someone else. Zeus … he was just on a different scale. He filled a space up without meaning to, and his tattoos were inherently threatening under the dim emergency lighting. And Zero twitched randomly: that was a difficult habit to get used to.

Lying there in the minutes before the alarms sounded and lights brightened, Frank listened to the sounds around him, both human and mechanical. He'd mostly tuned out the perpetual hum of the air scrubbers, and wondered if he'd notice if they ever stopped.

He was staring up at the gridwork over his head, looking at the blank rectangle of Alice's mat. Everything would be better once they'd built the base. They'd have room to avoid each other, and they'd be busy with their own specialties. They wouldn't have the immediate worries of whether there was enough air to breathe or food to eat. There might even be time to, what? Explore? Create? Relax? If they were making more resources than they consumed, why not? Even though they were still prisoners and everything they remembered was a hundred million miles and a rocket ride away.

He wondered what was happening back on Earth. What were they saying about the mission they were on? Mars things were the lead news items for a while, and even when they'd become more routine, they still featured. Mars Base One wasn't routine, and neither was using convict labor to build it.

Would someone, at some point, try and force XO to reveal

the names of the cons? The ACLU, maybe? Some fancy lawyer looking to make their name? What would XO do? Would their anonymity be busted, and Frank's son find out where his father was?

While he lay there, he heard, then saw, Zeus stir. The man scratched himself, and got to his feet.

"Where you going?"

"Can," said Zeus. "Beat the morning rush."

He picked his way through the bodies to the tiny cubicle that served all of them. It had a folding door, but did little to mask what was going on. Zeus could barely fit inside as it was, and whatever it was they were eating didn't make things particularly friendly for anyone else having to share the same atmosphere. Thankfully, the same scrubbers that took out the bad part of the air also took out the smells. On the whole, despite the confined space, it was anodyne, almost hospital antiseptic.

A few moments later, the lights dialed up to maximum, and the chimes sounded. Whether they were meant to be a gentle replacement for the harsh prison buzzers and klaxons, Frank couldn't tell: they had the same purpose, and he couldn't control them. They were therefore just as bad.

They stretched, they complained, they cursed each other for getting in the way, they hammered on the bulkhead next to the toilet to get Zeus to hurry up. Below them, Brack was already illuminated by the bright glow of the screens, and above, Alice hadn't so much as stirred.

"Alice? Time to move."

Nothing.

Frank reached up and smacked the flat of his hand against the underside of the grating. "Alice?"

Something fell past his face. It was tiny and white, like a snowflake. It passed through the floor at his feet without stopping on the way.

"Alice?"

Maybe it was something in the tone of his voice. The

178

bad-tempered ruck around him quietened, and one by one, they looked up. Zeus pulled back the door to the toilet, started to say something, and didn't get any further than breathing in.

"What's going on up there?" called Brack.

"I'll go," said Frank. He scaled the ladder, quickly and fearfully, and stuck his head through the hole to the top floor. "Alice?"

She was curled up on her mat, like a baby in the womb, asleep, still. Her face was towards Frank, her eyes were closed, her mouth slightly open, and her water bottle in the void between her arms and her body. In her hand was a small blister pack of pills, which Frank reached out and gently pulled from her grip.

He read around the burst silver foil: Fentanyl, 600 mcg buccal tablets.

"What's fentanyl?" he asked.

Zero's voice came back: "Man, that's bad shit. China white."

"But what is it?"

"Like heroin. But stronger."

"How much stronger?"

"Pharma-grade. Like a hundred times."

Frank reached out again, and touched her cheek. It was cold, inelastic. Like touching wax. He counted out the missing drugs. Six pills. And she'd died before she took the seventh that fell through the floor.

"Get Brack," he said. "Get him up here."

"What's happened to her?"

"She's ... checked out."

"Fuck, man. She was," Zero paused. "She was our doctor. What the actual fuck?"

"Out of the way. Kittridge? Up or down."

Frank chose up, and Brack coiled himself next to Alice's body. He listened for breathing, felt for heartbeat, held her eyelid open, and then rocked back on his heels.

"If anyone knew how to do it, she did." He grunted as Frank

passed him the blister pack. He flipped it over, then threw it back. "Stupid bitch."

Frank snatched the pills out of the air. He felt the strange, alien rage rising inside again. "Don't call her that."

"What would you call her, Kittridge? She was weak, she took the coward's way out, and she's left you up a narrow water filled defile without an effective propulsion device. How're you going to build the base? Five of you to do seven people's work? Christ almighty, there's no chance of you doing it now."

They squared off across Alice.

"You could help us."

Frank's suggestion met with stone-faced rejection. "I keep the show running back here. I keep the systems of this ship working so you fuck-ups can do your jobs. Anyone else want to kill themselves? We got the means right here. Quick and easy, just like your mothers." Brack stood over Frank. "I'll deal with this. Get a bite, get suited up, and get out there."

"Is it true?" Frank balled his fists, then deliberately unclenched each finger in turn. "We don't have enough supplies."

"And where did you hear that from?"

Frank nodded down at Alice.

"Her. She said we're running out of everything."

"We've got enough. Just as long as you jokers stop treating this like a summer camp." Brack held out his hand for the drugs, and Frank passed them over. "Did everyone hear that? Do I have both your comprehension and your compliance? No more mistakes. No more making free with the medical supplies. Work. That's all I want and need from you."

"Brack. She's dead. Have some respect."

"Maybe we can get our tame, painted Nazi-boy down there to sing us some kumbaya. Light a couple of candles in our hundred per cent oxygen atmosphere. She screwed you, Kittridge. She screwed all of us. Everything she knew, everything she could do, she took with her. That's how much respect she had for you, and I'm giving her the same amount of respect back. Yes,

180

she's dead. And you're still alive. You want to keep it that way? There's no cavalry going to ride over the hill on this one. There's no one else here but you."

From below, Zeus spoke up. "We'll do something later. Tonight. Right now, we have to carry on. Come on, Frank. Come on down."

He felt disgusted with himself, and he couldn't work out why. When he'd been in the pen, he'd not gone out of his way to make life difficult for his guards, but neither had he snitched on his fellow inmates. What he wanted to do was get rid of Brack. What he was, was compromised. So he climbed down the ladder, and went to the stores and got out some of the bland pulp they ate for breakfast and refilled his water bottle and spent a few minutes in the can recycling all that liquid back through and checking his suit and his life support, and spent no time at all talking to anyone or remembering anything about Alice.

He synced his tablet with the main computer—just a question of pushing a button and letting the software do the job—and selected the targets for the day: Zero's hydroponics and the water maker were already on site, which represented more than enough labor. They had, just about, a working module. Frank needed to spend some time checking it over, and fixing in the last pieces of cross-bracing. But they could inflate it with the air plant, using the power from the solar cells, and start installing the floors and racks and tanks and heaters. The pipework that would feed water through the trays and drip down into the aquariums, taking nutrients with it, was prodigious, but Zeus had all that in hand. The lights and heaters were Declan's specialism.

Zeus would do the work of two, work until he dropped, and then get up again and carry on. He worked like he had something to prove. Like it was his penance. It probably was. Maybe a day away from the ship would help, and Frank was in charge of both construction and transport: he could do whatever he wanted. Dee could use spending a day inside a pressurized environment,

181

and Frank could teach Zeus how to handle a buggy, get him to sit down and slow down.

"Dee? I'm taking Zeus out today. You're working with Declan." He kept his eyes on the short-term goal. They needed somewhere to sleep where they weren't going to be falling over each other: there was living accommodation in this drop, seventeen miles north-north-east of Long Beach, and the central connecting module was in a cylinder twenty-two miles northeast. "Anyone got a problem with that?"

He still needed to practice changing his life support midjourney, because there were two supply drops that were at the edge of or beyond range. One was the communications equipment—the ship had its own set-up, but this was high bandwidth kit for the base—and this was the furthest away. The other was a stand-alone hab for doing dangerous things in: making fuel, soldering, anything that required both pressure and air that wasn't going to burn in the presence of the tiniest spark.

Both of those could wait for now. They needed the extra space. Tomorrow, they'd all build, and by nightfall they might have done enough to mean they'd actually made an impact on Mars. A Mars that had already taken two of them.

No one had a problem with his itinerary. He hooked up his life support, clambered into his suit, and closed the back hatch. The airlock was the first place he felt alone, and even then it was only until the outer door opened and there was Mars, pink and red and gold in the weak morning sun.

Mars was a thing. A living, breathing thing.

Even though he couldn't feel it, he could see it and hear it. There was a wind that blew flecks of rust into the air and across the sand, somewhere below knee level, and the low static hiss that ebbed and flowed around him came from outside, not from his earphones. The trampled ground, the tire tracks that crisscrossed the area in front of the ship, the burn marks from the landing rockets, all were blurred and erasing themselves even as he watched.

Weather. They had weather. It was never going to rain, but it was cloudy above, pale streaks like mares' tails stretching out across the sky.

He felt the steps vibrate, and he shuffled round to see Zeus bearing down on him.

"We need to take the air plant over to Santa Clara," said Frank. "Dee can cart the others across, and we'll take it from there."

The device was the size of one of the drums, and solid. Frank unplugged it from the RTG, and removed the hoses that fed oxygen to the ship, and he and Zeus—mainly Zeus—hefted it onto a trailer. They coiled up the power lead and the hoses, put them in an empty drum, and collected the empty reserve tanks: big, black, lightweight cylinders made of carbon fiber. They stacked everything, tied it all down with ratchet straps, and mounted up.

Frank made Zeus sit in the driver's seat and talked him through the controls. They'd not done any of this on Earth, assuming that Marcy and Frank would do what was required. That clearly wasn't going to stand. They needed to all learn something about what everyone else was doing. Just in case.

Zeus took the wheel, and even though it looked like a child's toy in his hands, he drove at a very cautious pace over towards the Santa Clara. Dust streamed away from the wheels like thick smoke, blown horizontally by the wind.

The hab was where they'd left it. Seeing it resolve out of the distant haze, first as a long, gray-white blob, and then with the sharp edges of the rings and the plastic stretched between them, was a relief. It looked very much like a building site, piles of materials waiting to be used, cylinders and drums sitting empty, packing material too heavy to shift, but shuddering and twitching in the wind.

The solar array was already tilting itself towards the sun, the black glossy panels turning like flower heads.

"Bring us to a halt next to the hab," said Frank, and Zeus

slotted the buggy between the containers and eased off on the throttle. The sand around them hummed a low bass note when the wheels came to rest. They started unloading. In the distance, the second buggy's dust trail was growing bigger.

Frank beckoned Zeus over, and they muted their microphones.

"Why'd she do it, Zeus? She didn't have to."

"Maybe after a taste of what it'd be like for her here, she decided it wasn't for her. Maybe she felt like her work was done: she'd got us all up, and that was all she was hanging on for. Maybe she blamed herself over Marcy. Or maybe she couldn't live with the memory of all those people she killed. Maybe she was just lonely. Maybe she'd just had enough. Don't hate on her, Frank. Brack says it's the coward's way out, but I don't know. Alice never struck me as the cowardly type, even if her ghosts did catch up with her in the end."

"Tough being the only woman on Mars. But it would've been fine. Wouldn't it? That wasn't the reason, was it? No one was going to mess with her." Frank grimaced as a thought came to him. "What if she killed herself because of the food situation? One less mouth to feed. Giving the rest of us a fighting chance of making it."

"We're never going to find out. We can ask all the questions we like, but she's gone. Those who are left have to deal with that, best we can."

"This isn't how I imagined it would be."

"How did you imagine it to be?"

"Better. Better than this."

"Frank, I killed someone too. I punched them in the face and they fell down and they died. You? I heard from someone else what you did. And we're not even getting what we deserve. We should have ended up in Hell, and instead we got Purgatory. We can forge our lives anew on the anvil of this planet. We can redeem ourselves. We can work ourselves righteous, Frank. Remember that."

He stepped back and restarted his mic, then single-handed lifted the air plant from the trailer and dumped it in the sand. The other buggy cut through the saltating dust, and Declan and Zero climbed down.

"We need to get the greenhouse materials in the hab," said Zero. "Quicker with people outside handing to people inside. Could do with some steps up to that airlock, too." Wherever the open-frame steps were, they weren't in the same cylinder. The airlock module, in the center of the circular end, was some fifteen feet above the ground.

"I'll check the inventories. See where they are." Frank leaned back. "Park the buggy under it and pass the stuff up. But we have to be careful about putting things inside the hab. Sharp edges, OK?"

He uncoupled the trailer and moved the buggy under the airlock. Zero leaped up and manually cranked the airlock doors open—there was no power to the telltales, and no pressure against the inward-opening doors either—and jumped down inside. The outer skin of the hab was just about translucent, and they could make out his shadow moving around inside.

"Man, it's warm in here. Like a, you know, greenhouse. Suit's reading forty-plus degrees over already. Plants are going to love this."

Frank followed Zero's example, and jumped from the back of the buggy up to the airlock, and they spent the next half-hour passing beams and panels and bolts into the hab. And even in reduced gravity, it was hard.

"How are we supposed to get in and out without you here?" asked Declan. "You know, when you take the trailers away and everything?"

There were enough drums lying around to be useful. They'd make big steps, six feet tall, but easier than trying to jump the distance in one go.

"Fill four of them half full with rocks. Stack them three on the base and one on top. If you clear the site of the central module,

185

which goes about here—" Frank indicated on the ground roughly where the base mat would sit, thinking to himself that what he really needed were flags on sticks he could push into the soil "—and here, where the second hab's going to go, we won't need to do that tomorrow. OK?"

Declan gave it a thumb up. "Sounds like a plan. Demetrius? We need to set the air plant running. And Frank: we're all sorry about Alice, but we need to stay focused, right?"

"Focused. Got it."

He turned away and set his face like the land. Cold. Hard. Unforgiving.

17

[transcript of audio file #8106 (Engineering team briefing) 3/10/2036 0830MT Xenosystems Operations, Room 35E, Tower of Light, Denver CO]

AC: This is the final preliminary design for the hab before we go for a half-scale proof-of-concept mock-up. The engineering is heavily influenced by the early nineties work on a modular assembly reusable structure, or MARS, by A and M. The design has been simplified somewhat—you know what these architects are like for their little flourishes—and there are further changes we may have to make as topology demands.

Essentially, the problem is this: we need to fit a working habitat, two storeys tall and some thirty feet long, inside a volume that is an eighth of the expanded size, and including the hydraulics and pneumatics that drive that expansion. What we've settled on is a system of supporting rings at intervals, with external stanchions, separated by telescoping beams to give the required distance. The rings are made of sections that, in transit, only occupy a fraction of the finished circumference, and the environmental sheath is integrated into the design.

Once deployed on the surface, the hab is inflated in two stages: the first is to drive the rings outwards to their full extent, locking them in place. The second, assisted by the hydraulic rams, is to expand the linear dimension. The whole process is expected to take twenty-four (24) hours, with remote-visual checks by Earth-based personnel taking up a considerable proportion of that time.

Once proof-of-concept has been achieved, we'll move into full-scale production, and adding those topologically difficult pieces like floors and walls. I'm assured by our mathematicians—especially those with an interest in origami—that this is not just possible, but routine for prefabricated buildings here on Earth.

We may never personally get to Mars, but what we do here will. Remember that people's lives are going to depend on these structures and our skill in making them. We owe them to do it well.

[end of transcript]

Frank felt the suit around him relax as the air pressure increased. The airlock lights flicked over from red to green, and he could hear the lock safety click. He opened the door—the equalization was perfect, but the seals always required an extra shove—and stepped through. There were already four other suits hanging from hooks on the wall, like empty shells, and the life-support rack was pumping fresh oxygen into the depleted tanks.

He was dusty. He was always dusty. Everything was covered in a thin film of orange that proved almost impossible to remove. About the only thing that did it was water, and while they had some, they didn't yet have plenty, and it didn't work outside. Frank seemed to spend his life staring out of his helmet around the smears. Zeus told him it was a salt rime, but knowing what it was didn't help much. The only cleaning cloths that they had were parachute material. It was thin and light and incredibly hard-wearing, but it wasn't absorbent.

He opened up the back of his suit, and crawled out backwards. He was lean. Hungry all the time, yes, but wolfen rather than starving, though it was only because they'd lost Marcy and Alice that they'd had enough food to last them this far. He wasn't the only one, and hungry men argued—not about calories, but about everything else that wasn't.

He put on his overalls—dirty, torn in a couple of places, the number on the pocket losing its crisp edges—and put his suit on an empty hanger. He disconnected his life support and slid it into the rack, plugging it in to the power and the air. He needed the can, and at least this was now plumbed in to the water reclamation system. And there was space: he had three doors to choose from. One, another airlock, led into the greenhouse. Left went to what should have been, and what would be, the sick bay. Zeus hadn't started unpacking the supplies yet, as he'd been too busy on the pipework. Right to the rec area—they called it the yard, even though it was inside—and the crew quarters.

Frank padded through the yard and along the corridor to the john. The non-airlock doors didn't close automatically: they were supposed to be left open, to allow air to circulate better than the narrow between-floors ducting nominally allowed. Even shut they were only airtight up to a point, and it was up to the crew to seal them properly in an emergency, using the hard upswing on the door handle.

That something as basic as screens, doors, and curtains would make such a difference to him, to them all, had surprised him. Literally, the first thing they'd done after fitting out the greenhouse was put up the walls for the bedrooms. They slept alone, initially on their foam pads on the floor, and now on a bed base with storage underneath.

Not that they had anything to store. There was still no sign of their personal effects. Frank's books and letters were nowhere to be found, and what little the others had managed to save from their former lives were likewise absent. Brack answered all questions on that with "I don't know". He was the only person in contact with XO. If he'd ever asked Mission Control where their gear was, he never let on.

Frank pulled the screen across the toilet cubicle's opening, squatted down, read again the instructions for use—pull handle A, press button B, release handle A, pull handle C, press button B again—and rested his chin against his chest. He was tired. More tired than any of them.

Zeus still exhibited an endless appetite for physical labor, trying to prove his worthiness to a power even higher than XO. Dee and Zero were young men, and Zero spent all day in the greenhouse, planting seeds and watching them grow. Dee was more active, wiring up the habs with Declan, but the heavy lifting and the long hours outside fell to Frank.

He still hadn't seen Brack do a scrap of actual work. He was their guard, their overseer, but they didn't need guarding or overseeing. They all knew what was at stake, and Brack's role was redundant. It was hardly a free ride, but he knew he wasn't the only one to resent it. At the back of his mind, though, was the deal he'd made: Brack had to survive for long enough for Frank to book the trip home.

Frank pushed and pulled everything in the correct order, and washed his hands and face. Water, sterilized, lukewarm, splashed into his palms. He rubbed them against his cheeks and into his growing hair. His skin felt so very dry, the effect of spending most days in his suit, the blowers pushing air across already parchment-like flesh.

The air in the habs was wetter. They were making water, more every day, and storing it in repurposed drums on the first floor of the greenhouse, but it also got piped to the other habs using click-and-connect pipework that went through bulk-head walls and bypassed airlocks. Some of it evaporated, and made things a bit more pleasant. In the greenhouse, the walls streamed in the mornings. They had enough power to warm the air as it entered, but it was still cold. In all the habs bar the greenhouse, it was breath-condensingly chilly. They'd need to fix that, especially as their power demands were going to go up as they installed more of the lights and equipment. They were already tripping fuses when they turned something on, and one day they'd take out something critical.

Which was dangerous, as Declan told them, loudly and frequently, as he stomped off to find the offending circuit, isolate it, and restore power to the base. It was just one of the things that caused tension, and kept everyone on edge: still not enough of the basics, and always one accident away from disaster.

The plan to route hot water from the RTG and into the habs was still just that, a plan. It had been refined slightly to go in through the greenhouse first, since that hab needed to be kept warm anyway, and using the greenhouse to store the hot water in would free up the heaters to be used elsewhere. The details of the gravity feed loop were coming together, as was the permission to take apart the rocket motors and bleed the remnant hydrazine off.

Tomorrow, they'd move the RTG over to Santa Clara. Today, Frank was spent.

He dried his hands: no towels, so there was more parachute material which didn't really work, and went in search of the others.

They'd eventually have a laundry in the crew quarters—even though the washing machine was designed to be hand-cranked. They'd also have an intercom, and computers, and gym equipment. They'd be able to download entertainment: music, films, books. They'd have chairs. Frank never thought he'd miss chairs, but apart from the drivers' seats on the buggies, there weren't any chairs on Mars.

Eventually. Some of those things were on the surface now. Some of them, he assumed, were in transit. Maybe that included his stuff. Maybe he should stop obsessing about that.

He turned out of the kitchen area and down the corridor to the cross-hab again.

Here was the paradox. The pure oxygen atmosphere, that kept him and everyone else alive, wouldn't support plants. So the air in the greenhouse needed to be buffered with carbon dioxide. Only a little. A tenth of one per cent. Less than that would mean the plants would wither and die. More than that wouldn't help, and increasing amounts would be dangerous to humans.

Hence the airlock between the greenhouse and the rest of the hab. The air needed to be carefully controlled, inside and out. Frank opened the outer door and walked in. The airlock, confused, because it could read the same pressure on both sides, showed green lights anyway, but Frank went through the cycle of closing the door, pumping the air, and waiting for thirty seconds before opening the further door into the greenhouse.

There were racks and racks of warm, dripping matting, already with their first flush of green. Blue-white lights were everywhere, directed downwards and suspended bare inches from the mats. The glare was painful, and left after-images.

The greenhouse was on two levels, with an open grid floor between them. Frank could see Zero below, adjusting the flow rate of precious water onto the capillary matting, and he dropped down one of the ladders to land next to him.

Without turning round, Zero held out a fist, and Frank dapped it with his own.

"'Sup?"

"Checking you've got enough kit to be getting on with."

"I've got my NFT trays running, and the drips more or less online. More growing medium would be good. I can flush the perchlorate out, but it's the texture I need. Granular, like kitty litter, and absorbent. I guess we have to go back to breaking rocks like old-time convicts."

"Crushed rock. OK. Anything else?"

"More lights?"

"Declan's not going to be happy about that."

"Two things I need from him. Light and heat. That's it. The

192

rest I can do myself." Zero spun round. "You want to eat? I can't bring half of my growing space online because he says he can't afford the power. Five hundred watts, man. Five hundred. That's like, not even a hairdryer. We'll have fish, and salads, and roots and beans and peas and groundnuts, Strawberries. We can grow strawberries. I got experimental wheat here, for bread, and that's not going to happen until he gives me more power."

"I'm not in charge of that. You can talk to Brack if you want, ask him to order Declan to give it you. But he can't give you what we don't have."

"Can't he just mend some of those broken panels?"

"Sure. In time, maybe. But for what feels like the hundredth time, we haven't got a workshop, and I don't want him burning the hab down. Goddammit, Zero, it'd be easier if you guys talked to each other instead of expecting me to act like some sort of hostage negotiator. You're both adults. Just do it."

Zero huffed. "He gets on my fucking nerves. Like, why's he even here?"

"Because he did bad shit and got sent down for a Buck Rogers like the rest of us."

"He never says what he did, though. You know?"

"No. Never asked you why you were inside, either." Frank looked at all the tiny plants and the glowing blue-white lights and tried to imagine it on a scale that would get a grower sent down for life. "I've probably guessed. But it doesn't matter. We have to work together. You know this. Just talk to him, OK? I'll get you your rock, but you have to talk to him."

He couldn't tell whether he'd extracted a promise from Zero, or if the kid had just blown him off. Frank clanged his way back up the ladder to the upper deck, and just about caught his parting words before he left through the airlock.

"I could grow some dank weed in here. Just saying."

Frank shook his head, and closed the door.

Zeus was working in the ceiling void under the medical bay, fitting lengths of plastic pipe together with push-fit connectors.

It was cold, and the rubber seals on the joins were stiff. His breath steamed in the thin air, and his bare, black-inked arms were glossy with sweat as he reached up into the space over his head. He could manage without a stepladder. Or standing on a chair, for that matter. He was the only one who could. Frank's fingertips just about touched the ceiling panels.

Zeus stopped humming a hymn for long enough to ask: "What's it doing outside?"

"Sun's setting. You're going to have to leave this soon."

Zeus was holding two ends of pipe to warm them up. "One more length. Can you move the light?"

There was a directional LED lamp on a tripod, down by his feet. Frank picked it up and carried it to Zeus's other side, angling the beam upwards. "That do?"

"Thank you, brother."

"I need some help of my own tomorrow."

Zeus grunted as his fists squeezed the two sections of the pipe together. They resisted even his strength for a few seconds before relenting and pushing home with a hollow click.

"Going for the long one?"

"It's now or never. We need to put up the last habs, and that'll mean fixing the airlocks in place. We need to take an airlock with us to swap out the life support during the trip."

Zeus lowered his arms, and let them hang limply by his sides for a moment, just dangling. Then he pulled his sleeves down and covered his tats.

"We can wait. We haven't got enough power for the habs we've already got."

"Declan needs the workshop in order to fix the panels. And once we've picked up the last of the cylinders we can see what we're missing, and get Brack to radio home for spares."

"Spares?"

"Tell me about it. I just don't understand what XO were thinking." Frank turned off the portable light, even though it consumed less than five watts. They were left with the emergency

194

lighting of point LEDs. The color made it seem even colder. "You'll come with me?"

"There's nothing happening here that can't wait for a day." The big man shivered, but didn't otherwise move. "We could do with the hot water from the RTG."

He turned his head in the direction of the black-finned device, currently stuck on the sand behind the greenhouse. It was working at full capacity, generating electricity, but all the heat it generated was wasted: more than enough to keep the entire base subtropical.

"Shame we can't just bring it inside," he said.

"You've seen the figures," said Frank. "We couldn't vent the excess heat fast enough."

"We need to control it. Tame it. We will do."

"We'll bring the last two cylinders in whole—drain the hydrazine before we do—so we don't have to go out as far again." Frank wrapped his arms around himself. "How can you stand this? It's freezing in here."

"Work. I've been out on rigs in the Arctic Ocean, where the ice was so thick you could hear the rig creak under the weight of it. This? This is mild weather. Come on, brother. Let's heat some food through."

They climbed to the upper deck, where it was fractionally warmer, then through to the crew quarters. Because it was night, they closed the doors behind them, to keep the heat in. The solar panels were offline, and for the next twelve hours they were relying on whatever was stored in the batteries.

The food was in pouches, designed for spaceflight. Dehydrated, and mostly unappetizing. Zero had targeted the herb seeds to grow first, because whatever the freeze-drying process had done to the meals, it had robbed them of any flavor, and rendered them all essentially the same, whatever it said on the outside.

Mixed with hot water—it was technically boiling, but because of the air pressure it only managed hot—the mixture then had

195

to be kneaded for five minutes while it grew even more tepid. It was fuel for the body, nothing more.

"Why didn't you ask Demetrius to do the trip?" asked Zeus. "Or did you?"

"No, I didn't." Frank looked down the corridor from the galley, to see if either Dee or Declan had appeared, but they were still on their own. "The kid's fine. He does what I tell him. But he's flaky. And for a trip like this, where we have to squeeze into an airlock that's not attached to anything, and pressurize it, and get out of our suits and swap life support over? I don't want someone who might freak out. Two deaths is two too many. A third would …"

His voice trailed off.

"You're protecting him."

"From himself. I guess so."

In the absence of chairs, they sat against the end walls of the galley, feet extended in front of them.

"How are you doing, Frank?"

"Why? You going to offer to pray for me?"

Zeus shrugged. "I pray for all of you anyway. Even Brack. Love your enemies, do good to those who hate you. Though I don't think of him as my enemy. He's trapped in the same way we are."

Frank almost said something about that. The words were on the tip of his tongue, and he had to swallow them back inside. Brack wasn't trapped. What were they paying him? Surely whatever it was, wasn't enough.

"People do stuff for all kinds of reasons. Out of love, out of hate, out of greed, out of wanting to just feel alive. I don't know why Brack signed up for this. I'm sure as hell not going to ask him."

"You haven't given me an answer, though." Zeus tore the top of his meal off and inspected the contents. It didn't look anywhere near enough, the portion dwarfed by his huge hands.

"How am I? Does it matter?"

"Matters to me. You're worried about everything. You're worried about the food, the habs, the power, the buggies, the cargo, about how we're all getting on. You're worried about someone else dying, and I'm worried it might be you. Just practically, you know how things work around here, and you keep the peace between Zero and Declan."

"You noticed?"

"You're still not answering the question."

"And I don't have to give you an answer." Frank opened his own food pouch. It didn't smell bad, but it didn't smell of anything. "Don't push it."

"I give up." Zeus squeezed some of the pulp into his mouth, and chewed, even though the consistency meant he didn't have to. "It's not that much different to a rig, this place. Isolated. Hostile environment just looking for ways to kill you. All men. I'm used to this."

Frank thought about Marcy and Alice, and how it was strange that both women had died. He thought about it, but didn't know what to feel about it. He extruded his own meal and realized that he was hungry, just not for what he was eating. He choked it down anyway.

"We've still got a lot to do. And if just one of those things we rely on breaks down, we'll have to retreat back to the ship. There should be two of everything, twice as much as we need. We should have it in plenty." He washed down the pap with some water. "I'm tired because I'm scared all the time. Scared of what can go wrong."

"You ever think about him, Frank? The man you killed? I think about mine all the time. I don't even remember how it happened, I was that far gone. Whether he picked a fight with me, or it was the other way round. We already know what can go wrong."

"I don't think about him at all. Guess that makes me a bad person, right? We both made our choices sober." Frank shook his head a little. "But like I said: don't push it."

"Here's something else you might not have thought about: when the greenhouse is up and running, we're going to produce more oxygen than we need. We'll have to bleed out what we can't store. We've got enough water and food and air for now. We'll make more power: I've a couple of ideas for a steam turbine. And XO are going to send us more panels for the farm, and until then, we'll make do."

"What happens when the NASA guys turn up, and they find we've got a steam engine powering the base?" Frank stretched his feet, heard his ankles crack. Old, was what he was: old.

"They'll know about it long before they get here. None of this is going to be a surprise to them. They're awake the whole journey, not like us."

"You mean, they're valuable, not like us."

"They're valuable to more important people, but that doesn't mean we're worthless. We have to keep this place going before NASA arrives, and after they leave. That makes us the custodians and janitors, and that's OK. It's better than what we had before."

Frank couldn't deny that.

Noises in the corridor—door opening, feet on the floor panels, voices—made him look up. Demetrius, then Declan, came single file towards them, rubbing their numb hands and cupping them in front of their mouths to breathe life back into them.

Frank drew his legs in to make room for them. Days had started to take a predictable rhythm, with them all gathering together in the galley to eat, talk, bicker, swap stories and problems. Brack was still camped out in the ship, and showed no sign of coming over. Declan was convinced that they couldn't be overheard, since they'd put the habs up themselves from scratch. It would have been all but impossible to sneak hidden microphones and cameras past them.

There were going to be cameras, linked to an automated fire-suppression system that could be monitored from what would become the control room. But it was all just a mess of unplugged wires and powerless monitors at the moment. They had freedom, real freedom, but they kept on doing their assigned work anyway because this was their home and no one else was going to do it for them.

The other two selected their meals from the bin and started mashing them with the hot water, grumbling about the cold and the never-ending nature of their task, even though there was clearly an end to it.

Then Zero arrived.

"Hey hey." He was dangling some foil sachets from his lean fingers, shaking them like tambourines. "Who wants to start the party?"

Declan, with unexpected speed, snatched one away, and peered at the tiny writing on the side.

"Coffee. You found some actual coffee."

"I wouldn't say 'found', but we are, after all, criminals."

Zeus looked up. "You stole it?"

"From the ship. What's Brack going to do? Send us down for life? We're doing that already." He threw sachets, one apiece, at each of the men. Frank's landed in his lap.

How long was it since he'd had a decent cup of joe? At least a year, even though he'd slept through most of that. Months, then.

Frank put his sachet to one side, climbed to his feet, and poured the water in his plastic beaker down the sink. He carefully tore the foil packet open, shook the granules out into the beaker, making sure to get every last one, and slowly poured hot water from the little heater until the cup was half-full. He swirled the contents and leaned over to inhale the steam.

"I will personally bury all evidence of this tomorrow morning. In the meantime," he said, raising his coffee and saluting each of them in turn. "To us. The best men on Mars."

18

[Message file #41303 10/7/2048 0053 MBO Mission Control to MBO Rahe Crater]

MC: Completion of Phase one [1] acknowledged.

Frank stood in the lee of the RTG housing, and rattled the repurposed drums to make sure they were secure. Inside, six feet down—and hadn't they had the worst job digging out that hole in the hard-packed, frozen alluvial soil of Santa Clara's run-off?—the reactor belched out heat and, more sparingly, electricity. But the heat: the solution was simple, crude almost, but it worked. A cargo drum, lowered into place over the hole, and filled with water, captured some of the excess energy radiating from the black fins. The hot water rose to the top of the tank, and through a buried pipe—insulated with the material that had been around the cargo—to the unused airlock at the back of the greenhouse. From another tank inside, it was moved around the habs with a simple fifty-watt pump scavenged from a rocket motor.

As the water cooled, it got heavier, and returned to the fish tanks. Filtered water went back outside, returning parallel to the feed, and into the tank halfway up. Zeus had fitted it all up with isolation valves and emergency drains so they could just dump everything if they had to. After a few weeks of running the water maker, they were so good at conserving the resource, they turned it off. If they needed more, they could just turn it on again.

They had hot showers. They had abundance. It had been an extraordinarily hard road. The last, long run out onto the plains to pick up the two most distant cylinders had been the worst, and also inexplicably the best. The mile after relentless mile of red dust was punctuated twice—going out and coming back—by the unique, unsettling experience of climbing into an unattached airlock and swapping out their life support. Frank hadn't freaked out, because Zeus had been right outside, talking to him. What help Frank had been to Zeus was more difficult to ascertain.

They'd done it. All the way out to the lower slopes of Uranius Mons. Loaded up and brought them home. They hadn't killed themselves or each other. It was a triumph. A record-breaking journey, even. Afterwards, they didn't have any reason to do anything like that again, and their lives had shrunk back and now revolved around the base.

But they had food and air and heat and light and water and clean clothes and space to move around in and jobs to do. It almost didn't feel like a prison, even though it still was.

The hot water tank was surrounded by another upturned drum, packed with more insulation to protect it from the weather. It was warm too, but nothing like the fierce heat of the vanes underneath. He checked the ventilation was free of windblown dust, scraping out what had accumulated with the edge of an improvised shovel—an access panel bolted on to a support strut.

The prevailing wind blew from a definite direction, west to east, so they knew where to park the buggies and set up the workshop. The solar farm was on the east side, to best catch the rising sun. It was someone's job—usually Declan's—to manually dust the panels three times during the day in order to maximize the power generation.

They had enough. Just. If they remembered to turn things off they weren't using, and with the heat coming from the RTG, they could run the control panels and safety systems, the cameras and the air compressors. The big antenna outside didn't take much to broadcast, but the tracking motors were two two-fifty watt beasts and powering them up needed advance warning.

They still tripped the circuit breakers from time to time. It wasn't quite the scramble to get everything back on that it had been before.

Zeus was working on his steam engine. It still sounded ridiculous, but he was convinced he could get it to work. He had a big pile of parts, and time on his hands, when he wasn't unblocking drains. Dee had more work, cataloging data and using the uplink to pass details of their ad hoc modifications back to XO. Declan spent his waking hours prowling the corridors, looking for things that consumed power and trying to sync the lights into a day-night cycle without affecting anything that happened in the greenhouse, which was where Zero lived, emerging only to eat, sleep and shit.

Frank's work had settled into a series of tours, inside and outside. His constant companion was the nut runner, because the range of temperatures between midday and just before dawn was so extreme, the bolts they used to hold almost everything together had a tendency to slacken. That problem hadn't been immediately apparent. Fixings that were rock-solid by day were barely finger-tight when the temperatures crept down to minus one hundred and fifty.

He maintained the buggies, too, every day making sure they worked, and using some of that time to go a little further afield than he might normally do. He knew he could be tracked, and he was consuming resources in the form of watts, and wear and tear on the tires. But no one—Brack, mainly—had told him he couldn't.

Their overseer commuted backwards and forwards from the ship. The first time he'd done it, he'd walked the couple of miles to Santa Clara with only the most perfunctory of warnings, carrying only a locked metal case with him. He installed himself, not in the crew quarters, where there was plenty of room, but over in the medical bay, in what was purposed to be a private consulting room.

It had the only lockable door in the whole base. Frank wondered if that was by accident or design. Brack spent most of his time on the base either in the comms room with Dee, or one floor down in Control, doing something or other. Most of the time, the cons could forget about him—Declan assured them the cameras were there for fire detection, not keeping tabs on them. Frank wasn't so sure.

But on occasions when they wanted to let off steam and bitch about Brack, and there was nowhere they could safely do that, they resorted to whispered side-by-side conversations while they were working. It was the best they could do. Otherwise, they'd have to all suit up, step outside and turn their microphones off. Which wouldn't look suspicious at all.

It was why Frank liked driving up the Santa Clara. The sides of the lower valley were steep enough that he couldn't exit onto the broad slopes of the volcano, and he couldn't get those same panoramic views as he had done on the top of Long Beach. But if he climbed uphill for a couple of miles, the space to the south did open up, and he could see beyond the walls of the crater.

The base looked tiny, a small pale collection of rectangles, no bigger than those ranch-style houses he'd built out towards San Fernando, and covering less ground than the boneyard of empty cylinders and drums that they'd stacked, more or less together, the far side of the workshop. The ship was out of sight, across the Heights to the east, but there on the horizon was another volcano, rising from the plain like a pimple. He'd look at it some days, and believe it was further away than the twenty miles it was. Its height was almost the same as the peaks in the Sierras, but there it was, just popping out of the ground without foothills.

And sometimes the sky was almost blue. It made it—only for a moment—almost like home. But the thin, ice-white clouds, the fast-moving moons tearing overhead, the redness all around, soon broke into his daydreaming. He'd remember he was in a spacesuit, on Mars.

Other times, if he was lucky, he'd have a ringside seat on a delivery. Some ship would throw a package at the planet, and he'd catch sight of a bright spark halfway between the sand and the sun.

It would burn and flicker, pulsing like a firework, and soot and smoke would trail out behind, blown ragged by the high winds. There'd be a low booming noise, the sound of distant thunder, rolling across the landscape. Mostly, that would be all he'd hear and see. But twice he'd spotted the dark smudge of a parachute moments before it passed from sight. Still moving almost as fast as an object in freefall, but that was what it was: a huge, extended canopy, very far away.

The first time it had happened, he'd got excited. He'd thought that it had meant a delivery for them. A cargo rocket, either one of XO's, or one of NASA's.

But the times didn't add up. The incoming ships would have left Earth before Frank and his crew had even arrived on Mars.

And on getting back to base, he found that they didn't have a signal from it anyway. Someone else's, then, descending onto the broad Tharsis plain. Brack had nixed space piracy, and eventually they'd just got used to it happening every week or so. Mars was a busy place all of a sudden.

Frank drove back down the valley and resumed his tasks. He parked up near the workshop, and before he plugged the fuel cell into the grid to recharge, he checked with Declan they had enough spare capacity to do that.

"How long does it need?"

Frank interrogated the console. "Couple of hours?"

"We're not up to full batteries yet. I can give you an hour now, and an hour in the morning."

"OK." It wasn't worth arguing about the when, as long as it was done. He climbed down and took the cable end out of the drum it was stored in—it was buried for most of its length, and came out through a hole in the bottom of the container—and slotted the end home. Lights changed on the console, telling him it was accepting charge, and he checked the clock to know what time he had to disconnect it. Not that Declan would let him forget. He recorded everything like that on his tablet, and set an alarm ahead of time.

He walked to the main airlock, now partially obscured from view by the combined Comms/Control hab, and knocked the dust from his feet against the metal steps. He went through the whole suit ritual, noting how dirty the floor of the connecting module was getting, and how the red, on contact with the moist air, turned from a coating of dust to a smeary layer of dirty grease.

Someone was supposed to deal with this, and he couldn't remember who it was. Alice? Did they really have the doctor on cleaning duty? Maybe they did, assuming that doctoring wasn't going to take up too much time. They'd have to rota this unpopular chore between them. Did they even have any specific cleaning materials? They didn't even have toothpaste. Perhaps they needed to root around in the unopened crates that were stacked on the lower level of the medical hab.

He went to use the can, always preferring to sit and think for a minute than use the collector in his suit. Wearing overalls made it more difficult, having to shrug out of the top half before pushing them down to his ankles. The air in the crew quarters was warm now, thanks to the plumbing, though the seat was still chilly on first contact.

"Frank?" It was Declan.

"Goddammit, Declan. A moment, OK?"

"Relax, I'm not coming in or anything. Just wanted to know something."

"Can't this wait? A couple of minutes maybe?" No, of course not. Declan was just being his usual dickish self.

"Straightforward yes or no: did you check the fuel cell level on the buggy before you took it for a drive?"

Frank sighed. "I checked that it had enough juice."

"Did you check the actual gas levels and log them?"

"No."

"Can you do that in future?"

"Seriously?"

"Completely seriously." Then Declan lowered his voice and pressed his head up against the screen. "Someone's been using it other than you."

"Brack comes and goes."

"Outside of that."

"When?" Frank frowned. "At night?"

"Just log it for me, will you?"

"OK."

Declan pulled back and Frank could hear his footsteps recede. There were always tire marks on the ground around the buggy park, but the buggies themselves were always pretty much where he'd left them. Or so he thought. Were there trackers on the buggies? He didn't know. There were on the suits—or was it just the medical implants, working off ... what? Some sort of Martian GPS? He hadn't really given it much thought, and just assumed that it was a standard set-up, just like it was on Earth.

But driving around at night didn't make much sense. Firstly, it was dark, and while the buggies had lights, it was still danger-ous enough in the day with the potential for hitting something sub-surface. And secondly, going solo where no one knew where you were and no one was in Comms to take your emergency call?

Unless they weren't going solo? That would mean two people keeping a secret, and that didn't seem likely. If it wasn't him, and it wasn't Declan, then who? Brack had no need to sneak around. If he wanted a buggy, he'd just say so and take one. That left Dee, Zero or Zeus, and Zero didn't seem to want to leave the greenhouse, let alone the base.

Was it actually a problem? Joyriding a buggy during the freezing night was pretty stupid, but as long as they brought it back in one piece, where was the harm? When he took a buggy up the Santa Clara, wasn't he doing the same thing?

Yes and no. He was authorized. They weren't.

And it was all assuming that Declan was right, and his over-zealous protection of their power consumption hadn't got to him. Frank decided that it wasn't up to him to call this one: he had enough on his plate as it was, doing two people's jobs. He pulled the levers and pressed the buttons, washed up and zipped.

The expansion and contraction of the base's exterior also translated inside. He had hundreds of bolts to check in each section, often, now they'd fitted out the habs with their floors and ceilings, involving accessing hatches and lifting panels. It was long and laborious and done on a strict schedule so that he didn't miss any of them out from one inspection to the next.

No one was pretending it wasn't monotonous work. It was, however, monotonous work on Mars. He worked his way along the top floor of the cross-hab, before climbing down the ladder to the first floor. No one but him went there now. The red dot on the three-sixty camera on the ceiling had been disabled by Declan (less than half a watt, but he wasn't having it), but he could still be seen. He did his rounds: things inside did seem to be settling down now they had a more constant temperature. He could probably even scale his duties back and check less often.

And still his personal effects were nowhere to be found. None of their stuff had turned up. His books, his letters, were gone. He'd been through every inventory himself, and they weren't listed. One possible explanation was that there was a missing cylinder, either burnt up on entry, or still spinning around in space. However, that was difficult to reconcile with the fact that they'd eventually located pretty much everything for the base.

He moved from the cross-hab to the med bay. He pressed his hand for a moment against the skin of the module. The light that seeped through turned his splayed fingers into silhouettes, and the coldness of outside stole in. The base needed better insulation. He could shovel dirt against the sides, building it up over the days and weeks until each section was half-buried. Not completely covered, though, because it was only the rings, not the plastic, that were weight-bearing. Even then he'd have to worry about sharp edges.

Use the cargo cylinders as formers? Something to ramp the soil against? He might suggest it, but to shovel that amount of soil, he'd require something like a bulldozer attachment to the buggy. He had a half-formed memory somewhere at the back of his mind, about turning soil into bricks, like adobe. That would be easier. More permanent, too.

He checked the fixings on the floor joists, lifting the panels and peering into the voids, working his way down through the yard to the far end, then as before, down the ladder to check the first floor. Nothing needed doing. Which was good. He was proud of the way the base had gone up, how they'd struggled and how they'd fixed things.

"Boredom is your enemy, Kittridge."

Frank felt his heart rate spike and he involuntarily raised the nut runner, ready to lash out. Brack was just sitting there, among the unopened boxes that were . . . what? Lab equipment? Medical stuff?

Brack reached out and pushed Frank's arm down. "Easy there, tiger."

"I'm doing my work. I don't want to miss anything off my itinerary."

"I know you don't. I keep an eye on all of you. That's my work. Best you remember that."

If he did, then either he already knew who was taking the buggy out, or he was lying about being able to keep an eye on them all, and he had no idea. Either way, he didn't need Frank to tell him what was going on. The cons could sort this between themselves. This wasn't so important that they needed to rat each other out to Brack.

"I'm not getting bored," said Frank.

"You didn't see me there because you were bored and you stopped paying attention. Let's not go down the rest of that road. Each day's going to throw different stuff at you. You got to be ready for that."

Frank wasn't sure what Brack meant. Unless this was a test? To see if Frank would inform on the others? "I'm ready," he said.

"Well, I'm mighty glad to hear that. Because I don't want to lose you." Brack laughed, just the one little giggle.

Then he was gone, climbing back up the ladder.

Frank gritted his teeth, and waited until he was calm. Brack was right, and wrong. Yes, he hadn't been paying attention, but no, he was certain that if he'd caught sight of something out of the ordinary, he'd have reacted to it. OK, so he was getting maybe a little sloppy with his daydreaming. What was it they said to each other? Stay frosty?

The thought that a stray spark could immolate him and potentially burn the entire base to the ground in a matter of seconds should have kept him frosty enough, but it was easy to forget. This life was now normal. As normal as being ruled by buzzers and bells and the sound of cell doors slamming, and he'd surprised himself how quickly he'd got used to that.

He was about to leave the hab himself, when he got curious about what Brack had been doing there. He looked up at the camera. He could go and check the boxes and try to work out what had been disturbed. But then Brack might be able to observe him while he did. What was he going to do?

Frank left the boxes alone for now and climbed the ladder.

Dee was in the Comms room. Frank looked in and nodded. "Brack?"

Dee gestured below. Control wasn't out of bounds, but that was where Brack spent most of his time. None of the cons wanted to share a space with him, and it was unfamiliar territory to all except Dee, who'd had the job of setting all the consoles up.

209

"I'm pretty much done with the transmissions for today. Data's loaded up. New pictures of Mars. Looks big."

"Because it is big. Can you give me a hand? Need some help shifting things."

Dee pushed back his chair—they had chairs now, formed from one piece of cast plastic, lightweight and disturbingly flexible—and followed him from the room. They crossed through the yard and the galley to the connector, then into the med bay. Frank slid down the ladder, stepped back, and Dee joined him in the gloom, surrounded by boxes.

"What needs doing?"

"Just start moving these around." He gave a box to Dee, and under the cover that gave him, he quickly checked the crates where he'd first spotted Brack. Most were still sealed. Two were not.

"What's going on, Frank?"

"There's some weird shit going down." Frank was going to keep Declan's name out of it for the moment. He casually flipped up the lid of one of the crates and peered inside. "Someone's been taking the buggies for a ride. I need them to stop, because the heat's coming back on me."

He had no idea if it was Dee, but he'd have the exact same conversation with Zeus and Zero, and warn them all off.

"And you think I know something?" Dee glanced at him, then went to pick up another box.

"I don't know. I sleep hard at night. Maybe you don't, and you've woken up because of something." Frank was looking at blister packs of pills, all different shapes and sizes. OK, that was interesting.

"They're doing it at night? Are they nuts?"

"It's possible. It's also the last thing we need, because if someone busts one up, we're half-screwed. Anything you might have seen, heard?" Frank flipped the lid shut again and moved the container over to the opposite rack.

"I ... no. I can't think of anything." Dee put his box down on

210

the shelf and slid it along. "Does you-know-who know?"

Frank shook his head. "Don't know. But we need to sort it first."

"I'll be your crow."

"Thanks for your help," he said, loudly. "I can take it from here."

Dee stopped moving cargo, and Frank got on his hands and knees to shift a newly exposed floor panel. He peered into it, and extended the nut runner into the void.

"I'll go then," said Dee.

"Thanks again."

That was always going to be the problem with a bunch of cons. Trust, that had been difficult to build up, was so easy to destroy. Drugs. Joyriding. Just when everything seemed to have settled into a decent, quiet routine. Whoever was responsible, Frank wasn't going to risk them jeopardizing his ride home.

19

[Internal memo: Mars Base One (Power) to Mars Base Knowledge Bank 10/20/2038]

Power team

Just to confirm the power inputs with everyone.

The base load will be provided by one (1) RTG, producing three kW (3000 W) of continuous power. This value is not expected to fall below two point eight kW (2800 W) for ten (10) years.

Variable load will be provided by three (3) twenty-four kWh (rated at 2,000 W) closed-cycle fuel cells.

The fuel cells will be recharged during the twelve (12) hour Martian day by a solar array capable of operating at fifteen kW (15,000 W).

The total power consumption of the initial base is not to exceed ten kW (10,000 W). Extra solar units and fuel cells can be integrated as the power requirements increase, and aresthermal sources (boreholes/heat pumps) come online.

Note that the RTG will provide power for the minimum LS—base heat and atmospheric CO_2 scrubbing—indefinitely, but will not provide for full functioning of environmental factors. RTG cannot be used to charge fuel cells without degrading LS.

We do have a problem with the build phase, though. The specs on the assembly robots indicate that their daily power expenditure will exceed the initial base power budget by a factor of three. We need to be able to supply some thirty kW (30,000 W) continuous load in order to keep all of the machinery running. This will require an additional sixty kW (60,000 W) of solar array if all applications are to be run simultaneously: the battery packs for each robot are internal, so no additional fuel cells are required.

That someone was using the buggies without telling Frank was such a little thing. The power consumption was low, and Declan had managed to cobble together another couple of panels from the broken pieces, which gave them most of a kilowatt extra. It wasn't really an issue of balancing those needs any more.

He'd discovered that Declan had been right by logging the gas and water volumes in the fuel cell, and they'd shown slight differences more than once, indicating that the distances involved were small. He'd also drawn thin lines in the sand behind each wheel, which were impossible to spot in the utter darkness of the Martian night.

Each morning, the marks had been smudged, and were no longer in position under the buggy. He'd scuff them out, and think back to the night before, trying to work out if any of the noises aside from the creaks and groans of contracting metal could have meant anything. This had gone on for a week now.

The buggies had no keys, no locks. They were company property, just like the crew. No one had any need to sneak around, and yet they were.

He'd had a quiet word with everyone. None of them had felt the need to own up. Or stop, for that matter. There were a limited number of possibilities. Someone suiting up and driving around in their sleep was one he'd considered, and discounted.

Brack was another. And it was the one he kept on coming back to.

Because there was literally only one place to go to. The ship. There was nothing else for miles around, and as the numbers on the dials showed, the mileage wasn't anything extraordinary. A couple of miles across the Heights and a couple of miles back would account for most of the consumption. The cold—he hadn't tried it himself—might account for the rest.

He didn't think there was anything in the ship that any of the cons needed. So, if it was Brack, what was it that he did there, secretly, that he needed most nights to do?

The drugs? That bothered him a whole lot more. There was a whole pharmacy just lying around that any one of them could help themselves to. To the best of his knowledge, no one had inventoried the medical supplies. Alice would have done it, if she hadn't sampled some of the wares. Zeus was Alice's second, but he hadn't had the time, or the inclination, for such a tedious, persnickety task. So the pills had been just left there. And some-one had, at the very least, opened up two of the sealed boxes. If they hadn't then gone on to pocket some of the contents, then Frank would color himself surprised.

And Brack knew about that. He'd been clearly doing his own poking around. Did he know who it was? If he did, why hadn't he done anything about it? Frank was having suspicions that Brack's claim to be all-seeing and all-knowing was just a crock. But then again, Brack refusing to eat anything but shipped-out food was beginning to make more sense.

It made Frank uneasy. He hadn't really considered Brack at all for weeks. He was like a ghost in the background—odd noises, shadows outside, things getting moved, that was just Brack doing stuff. Maybe there was more to it. Frank didn't know what, though.

But on the assumption that it was Brack driving to and from the ship at night, he needed to warn Declan off from poking around further.

Frank arranged things so that both he and Declan were outside at the same time: checking the buggies and tilting the panels.

He motioned to him that he was turning his microphone off, and waited for Declan to finish cleaning the array as it turned towards the midday sun.

They touched helmets.

"It's Brack?"

"It's none of us."

"What is it that he's hiding from us? And why?"

There was dust between them. It grated and crackled against the faceplates.

"We don't need to know. And we probably don't want to know, either."

"Well, I want to know," said Declan.

"You ask him, then. I'm sure as hell not."

"Of course you won't. Why not? Because it's not part of your mindset. He's the boss, the mighty whitey, and you're not to question what he does. You're still a prisoner." He tapped Frank's helmet with his index finger. "Up here. My guess is that he's talking to XO."

"That doesn't make any sense. We've got the Comms center right there at the base."

"So he's talking to XO about stuff he doesn't want us to overhear."

Frank shrugged. "Why would that be unusual?"

"Don't you want to know what it is he's saying to them?"

"No. Not really. Because it hasn't got anything to do with us."

"Jesus, Frank. It's going to be *about* us. Aren't you curious? At all?"

"Maybe, on some level. But this is just causing trouble we can do without. Look, we're doing fine. We're doing what we came here to do. NASA's going to turn up, and we get to hang out with astronauts. Let's not rock the boat."

"Frank, listen to yourself. You're institutionalized. We need to know what Brack's up to, in case it does rock that boat. I'll talk to Dee. See what he can find out."

"You've got to leave the kid out of this."

"We can't hear what Brack's saying to XO, but maybe we can get the other half of the conversation as it's beamed back."

"I'm serious, don't drag Dee into this. He doesn't need it."

"What he does is up to him. He's an adult, Frank. And you're not his father."

That hurt. Hurt like a stab to the heart, even though Declan could have no idea why. Frank pulled back, almost reeling away, and Declan regarded him coolly. The electrician pressed the buttons on his suit control, and the conversation was over. Frank was left to walk away, to the other side of the base where the RTG sat, silently infusing the tank of water above it with life-giving, free, heat. He made a perfunctory pass of it, remembered Brack's words about boredom, and decided to make a better job of checking it, in a minute or two.

He turned his microphone back on and stared out over the Heights, down over the tops of the Beverly Hills, towards the distant crater wall. It was always hazy, to some degree or other. There were days on Earth, just after it had rained, when the air was clear and the horizon pin-sharp. Mars didn't do that: there were just shades of haze, from distant to near. In a dust-storm, visibility would be effectively zero, and they'd get no power from the solar farm at all, for days, possibly weeks.

That would be interesting.

He was still thinking in the long term. But this wouldn't be for ever. Brack would take him home. Eventually.

What was he going to do? Was he going to tell Brack that they'd worked out that he was making nocturnal visits to the ship, and some of them—Declan, mainly—were more interested in that than they ought to be? He still had to live with the man, rely on the man, and work with the man.

What he was going to do was go back and check the water heater properly, all the pipework, and the fixtures into the rear airlock of the greenhouse.

He needed a new project. He'd overseen the building of the

modules, done the majority of the driving: dangerous, difficult work. Now that was over, the constant living on the edge fading into memory, the one thing he missed was the sharp sense of feeling alive. Prison was dull, and he didn't want to slip back into thinking the base was another prison. It wasn't. Not to him.

So he would talk to Brack. Not about whatever the hell he was doing with the buggies, but about more building work. About soil ramparts and adobe bricks.

If Declan wanted to snoop … it was difficult to know how successful he'd be. And what Brack would do about it in return. The atmosphere on the base was OK. They were bumping along, mostly fine, with only the occasional source of friction. Mainly the power. Mainly Declan being Declan.

There was the drug thing—the possibility of the drug thing. There was a lockable room. Why not put them in there? Why hadn't Brack put them in there as soon as he'd found the boxes had been tampered with?

Fuck them. Seriously, fuck them. If everyone was going to go all secret squirrel on him, let them. It wasn't his job to keep anyone in line. Just as long as he kept his own nose clean, right?

He finished up by the RTG and went around the back to the workshop hab. It looked slightly different. Slightly wrong. Deflated.

He quickened his pace, pushed his hand against the end of the hab as soon as he could. There was normally much more resistance.

"Dee?"

"Frank. 'Sup?"

"I'm out by the workshop. You got any alarms from it?"

"I'll check."

Frank tried to peer through the plastic. The sun was overhead, and he couldn't make out anything other than vague diffuse shapes.

"OK, I just remembered there's a problem with the alarm: we turned it off."

217

"And we did that because?"

"Because the telltale measures the amount of oxygen in the air, and the air in the workshop is pressurized regular Mars air, and it was doing nothing but triggering false positives."

"Where's Zeus?"

"Said he was going to the greenhouse to do something or other to the tilapia tanks."

"I think we've got a leak. I'll check it out. Can you dump some patches in the cross-hab airlock for me?"

"Sure."

Frank climbed up the steps to the workshop airlock and cycled it through. He twisted the handle, and pushed, and found the door was stuck. He put his shoulder to it, wedging his hard external carapace against the dusty red of the airlock and bracing himself with his feet. If this didn't work, he'd have to get some tools.

He shoved hard, and the door gave about six inches. Smoke started to peel around the opening, thick streamers of it, twisting away and vanishing in Mars's hungry air.

"Fire," said Frank. "Fire in the workshop."

There was clamor in his ears, alarms sounding and Dee, then other people shouting. After a few seconds' confusion, Brack shouted for everyone to shut the fuck up.

"There's no fire because there's nothing to burn, dipshit."

"Then where the hell is this smoke coming from?" It was still boiling out, up and away, white braids dancing in the wind.

"It's not smoke," said Dee. "It's not smoke, Frank."

"Then what is it?"

"It's Zeus."

"Fuck no." Frank hit the door hard with his shoulder, once, twice, three times. Zeus was a big man, heavy, dense, and he'd fallen behind the hinge. Because Frank was in his bulky suit, no matter how hard he tried, he just couldn't reach the man. He slammed the door shut again. Too late. It was too late. He knew that. But he still had to try.

218

He needed to cut his way through the hab's skin. He didn't have a sharp edge. The plastic was thick and hard and he couldn't tear it and he needed a knife, an actual knife or a saw blade or something and he didn't have one and he couldn't do anything.

He backed away down the steps. There were rocks. He could use rocks. He picked one up and started stabbing at the deflated side of the hab, and succeeded only in scoring the surface rather than cutting through. He kept on going, because Zeus deserved his effort, his perseverance, his sweat.

"Put it down, Kittridge. Put it down."

Frank turned, rock still mashed into his fist. Brack was there, just standing, regarding him.

"We have to get in there."

"It's too late."

"We don't know that."

"We do. He's flatlined. No heartbeat. No resps."

The implant. It didn't lie.

Frank dropped the rock at his feet and looked up at the curved side of the hab.

"Get back inside, Kittridge."

"I need to do … something."

"That's an order. Get back inside."

"No."

"Don't you go sassing me, boy. I gave you an order, and I expect that you obey me instantly and without question. You are currently dangerous. You are out of control. You are not in your right mind and you will do what I tell you when I tell you to do it. Get your ass inside the base. Now."

Frank listened to the sounds of his own breathing. The harshness of it as the air rattled past the knot in his throat. His heart was hammering, as if to make up for the fact that Zeus's was now still.

From somewhere deep inside, a growl became a moan became a scream became a roar. It died the other side of his faceplate, stifled.

219

Brack was still there when Frank had finished.

"Get inside. I'll deal with this."

There wasn't anything else to say. Frank trudged back to the main airlock, and pressed his helmet against the wall while the air cycled through.

Through the inner door, he dragged himself out of the top half of his suit, and just sat, legs splayed on the floor.

How had that happened? What possible sequence of events had led to Zeus being in the airlock, both doors closed, without his suit? What was he even doing there? He should have been with Zero, playing around with the fish. Which is what they all did sometimes, moving their bare arms through the tanks full of wriggling baby fry.

The workshop had sprung a leak. OK, but anyone working there had a tank of oxygen and a scuba mask to strap over their faces, so they wouldn't have drifted off to sleep. There was also going to be their own spacesuit right there by the airlock door, so that even if they didn't have time to put it on, they would have been able to drag it in with them. Close the door, open the valve on the oxygen tank to repressurize, use the suit comms to call for help, climb into the suit and seal it.

He shouldn't have died. He shouldn't have been in the lock without his suit.

Wait. There'd been no sign of Zeus through the little window in the outer door. Of course, Frank would have glanced at it, through it. They all did, unconsciously, as they got to the lock. Checking there was no one in there, or if someone had left the inner door open. He hadn't seen Zeus, because he'd already been crushed up against the outer door, out of sight.

But if he'd still been alive, he might have been savable. Frank could have done something different if only he'd realized.

He looked up. Dee was standing at the hab door.

"What happened?"

"I don't know what happened."

"Is he ..."

"Yes." Frank wanted to throw something, anything, hard. He remembered he was in a pressurized balloon, and though there were lots of objects to hand, he held back. "Yes, he is."

"I was hoping ..."

"Well, don't."

Frank stared at the floor, and eventually Dee got the message and left. He wasn't sure how long he'd sat there. Eventually Zero came out of the greenhouse. They looked at each other for a moment longer than was comfortable, and then both looked away.

"Sorry, man."

Frank acknowledged the comment with a nod.

"You thought he was with me."

Nod.

"He said he wanted to work on a pressure valve. Making it out of plastic pipe, or something. Left an hour ago."

Nod.

"I had a kid brother. He was smart and stuff. Too smart to get caught up in my biz. Got shot. Stray bullet from some drive-by, on his way back from school. Hit him in the neck, right here." Zero touched a place just behind his ear. "That's what they all said: he didn't suffer. Doctors, police, people coming to the house to see my mama: they all said he didn't suffer. I don't know, Frank. Is that a good thing? That he didn't suffer?"

Frank's head came up, and he tapped the back of his skull against one of the racks. "I depressurized him, Zero. I sucked out what was left of his air, and I opened the door to Mars on him. None of us have any idea whether he suffered or not. Stupid fuck would probably have wanted to suffer."

He slammed his head back once, the panel making a boom that startled Zero.

"I thought we were over this."

Zero stayed quiet, and eventually headed for the greenhouse airlock. While the pumps shuffled the air around, he stared at the door.

221

"If he'd been able to, he'd have let you know he was in there. He was already gone."

"Maybe."

"Don't beat yourself up about this. He was gone. Like my brother. You just happened to be there first."

Frank let his head fall forward, chin on his chest.

"Whatever."

Then Zero had gone too. The pumps chugged again, and Frank could hear the greenhouse inner door open. He couldn't just sit there all day. He needed to move.

He pulled off his shoes and shuffled out of the legs of his suit. He stowed the life support, hung up his suit, put on his overalls and ship slippers. Every action was exhausting, like he'd run a race just moments before. He was spent. Dammit, he was so tired.

He just happened to be there first, three times now. Marcy, Alice, and now Zeus. That struck him as being long odds. Though if he'd been born lucky, he would never have been on Mars at all.

He needed to know what had killed Zeus. He needed a shower. Pathetically, the shower won. The other thing was just going to have to wait.

20

[transcript of audio file #10126 8/2/2038 0930MT Xenosystems Operations boardroom, 65th floor, Tower of Light, Denver CO]

BT: I thought I'd get you up to speed, Paul, sir, with the work my team have been doing. With your permission.

PL: Carry on, Bruno. I'm intrigued. And concerned. We've fallen behind where we should be.

BT: I promise you here and now, that this will catch us up, and even put us ahead of schedule. I think you'll be pleased with the progress we've made, and not a little impressed. We can build on the great strides we've already achieved at the Gold Hill facility, and seamlessly integrate that into what I hope you'll endorse as the way forward.

PL: OK, Bruno. This all sounds very hopeful. I'm sure I don't have to tell you how we view failure here at Xenosystems. That's simply a word we don't recognize. So, please. Continue.

[Assume a tablet presentation. Haven't been able to track that down, and believe lost]

BT: The original plan was utterly revolutionary. A fully automated set-up from cargo pods, with only remote intervention required. Proof-of-concept testing showed that it worked perfectly, when it worked. Which was, as you can see here, only sixty-five [65] per cent of the time. There were multiple failure modes. The cost of rectifying each failure increased exponentially, in time, in weight, in failsafes on the failsafes. The obvious solution was to send a human operator to fix the problems in situ, but the contract we bid for uses only non-man-rated cargo vessels.

PL: And a man-rated capsule is so very expensive.

BT: Very, very expensive. And at the time of winning the contract, the only way to get someone to Mars. Two years on, and there's a potential solution on the horizon.

PL: Well, don't keep me in suspense.

BT: That's exactly what we're going to do. Suspended animation. We can literally store a person like cargo, and wake them at the far end. They'll consume no resources, no food, no air, no water, on the journey. They won't have to be entertained, they won't need space to exercise, and they won't go mad. It's the perfect synergy between what we want and what we need.

PL: It'll require a particular sort of person, of strong moral courage and ingenuity.

BT: I forbid you to volunteer, Paul. But seriously, we have time to search for exactly the right candidate. They're going to be on site to fix the robots and any other potential problems we might have. All we require is NASA's confirmation they'll bring our man home again. I can't see there'll be a problem at all.

PL: This suspended animation. It's still experimental, right? The FDA haven't signed off on it.

BT: They will by the time we launch in eight years' time. You have my word on that.

[End of transcript]

Frank went back to the workshop. He knew that Brack had finally forced his way in, and taken Zeus away. He knew where they were heading: a buggy was missing, and there was dust over towards the ship. But he didn't know what Brack was going to do, any more than he knew what he'd done with Marcy and Alice. He should ask, really. He assumed that somewhere out the back of the ship would be a line of graves, shallow scrapes in the ground, covered by rocks. Three cairns. The human conquest of Mars.

The outer airlock door was closed, and he hesitated with his hand on the handle. What was he going to find?

He didn't know that either. He swung the door open, and there were red stains on the floor, spatter marks that crossed the walls.

There was also a black canister of oxygen, and a soft face mask, abandoned in the middle of it all. The mask was coated on the inside with a film of blood, coughed from lungs too weak to draw a breath.

He didn't want to go inside. He'd be standing where Zeus had died. Where Frank had killed him. He looked down at the floor, and eventually took that short step across the threshold. He closed the door, and stooped to pick the gas bottle up. The film in the mask shattered and fell away, crumbling into ever-smaller flakes. Perfectly dry, it was already turning into something indistinguishable from the dust of Mars itself.

He opened the inner door, walked through, closed it.

There was no air but outside air. Zeus's suit was draped over the workbench just the other side of the airlock, the helmet staring blindly at the roof, and the arms and legs limp and lifeless. He placed the cylinder next to it, and draped the hose between the mask and the valve across its chest.

There were bits and pieces from Zeus's DIY activities littered across the two long benches: fragments of pipe and cargo drum and rocket motor scattered in between meters and wires and makeshift drills and vices and clamps. They were never going to get a steam engine now, even if it had been possible. That project had died with Zeus. Frank certainly didn't have the smarts to make one, and he doubted anyone else did either.

The remains from Declan's repairing of the solar cells were further down. Shards of crystalline black glass glittered in a discarded pile.

225

He couldn't see a break in the plastic envelope on the top level—though he might be missing it, it wasn't obvious. He climbed down the ladder to the first floor, and turned on the lights. Empty racking either side of the walkway shivered soundlessly. He slowly walked down to the end, and still couldn't see anything that was wrong.

"Declan? I'm going to start the pump, take it up to maybe six psi, and do a pressure test."

"Roger that."

The pump was against the far wall, taped into its ducting. He flicked the switch and opened up his suit controls, watching the external pressure rise, even as he could feel his suit relax and sag. The walls of the hab slowly stretched out, and sound returned. He could hear the rhythmic putt of the pump now, but no high-pitched whine of air escaping.

He walked the lower level again, peering into all the dark corners and pushing against the plastic, searching for the tear. Nothing. He moved the racking, one tower at a time, and got down on his hands and knees, lifting up floor panels and smoothing his hands across the hab cover where it met the thick rubber mat. Still nothing. No rocks had worked their way through.

He'd spent so long, the hab was up to almost seven psi. He hurried to turn the pump off, and sat there in silence, expecting to see a slow, gradual decrease in the numbers.

After half an hour, there was no change.

He stood up again and climbed to the upper level. He waited for another half hour. Still nothing. If there was a leak, it was almost imperceptible. Yes, there were pressure fluctuations with the changing temperature, but they were trained to check the outside pressure before taking their suits off, even if they thought it was safe.

There wasn't a leak. Yet the hab had definitely been depressurized.

Had Zeus done something stupid, and accidentally opened

the hab to outside? Was there any way for him to do that? Neither airlock door, on manual, would open against the nearly eight tons of air pressure on the inside. Even Zeus couldn't manage that. The pressure either side of the door needed to be almost equal. Had the pumps malfunctioned, or been altered to cycle air from the hab into the chamber, and then again to the outside?

No, because the locks went one way. The pump from the airlock only fed into the hab, pressurized or not.

There were the connecting feeds that they used to run the cables and pipework through from hab to hab. That was the only other weak point. And as he'd proved so far, there was no leak. But he checked them anyway, inside and out, and they were airtight.

He'd done enough. He went back inside the workshop, slung the empty oxygen cylinder over his shoulder, and gathered up Zeus's spacesuit in his arms.

It dragged on the ground on the way back to the main airlock. He looked into the distance. The dust had settled, and he could see the pale finger of the ship rising from the Heights. How long did it take to bury a body? Clearly, longer than the time he'd spent trying to work out why they had a body to bury in the first place.

There should have been a ceremony. The first two deaths had happened when they were at such a breakneck pace there'd been no time to stop. Now, there was space to do something meaningful. And Zeus would probably appreciate that, even though he wasn't around to see it. In the end, anything they did wouldn't be for him, but for the living.

As he climbed the steps to the main hab, Zeus's boots knocked on each riser.

"Goddammit, man."

"Frank, you good?" asked Dee.

"Talking to myself. I'm coming in. I could do with a hand, though."

He punched the button to cycle the lock, squeezed in, and pressurized the chamber. Each action he made, he watched carefully, trying to work out ways he could inadvertently subvert the safeties. He couldn't. He couldn't understand how the workshop had leaked out, when there was no leak.

Dee opened the door, and took Zeus's suit from him. Frank put the oxygen cylinder on the floor, and opened up his suit to the hab's air.

"Did you find it?"

Frank scraped his fingers across his head. "Find what?"

"The leak."

"No." He pushed his suit down to his knees. "No I didn't."

"But ..."

"I don't know. I've left it under pressure. If it goes down, I'll know I've missed something."

"What do you mean, if?"

"Not now, Dee. I've been through the whole hab. I've checked the seals and everything. You want to go out there and do it all again? Knock yourself out. Just get off my case."

"You're responsible for this shit, Frank. Buildings and maintenance. That's your bag."

"Don't you think I know that? And you're responsible for agreeing to turn the fucking alarm off, the one thing that might have saved his life."

Dee was slight. The time spent in hibernation, and then on reduced gravity, hadn't made him any bigger. Frank had been physically active every single day. If they squared up, there was no question as to who was going to win.

Dee was just a kid. Currently, just a scared kid. Beating up on him wasn't going to solve anything, and was only going to make it worse.

"Why don't we stay out of each other's way for a while, Dee? Probably best for both of us." Frank felt the first flush of rage turn into something else. He'd never been one for much introspection. He preferred to keep busy. So why not keep busy doing this, digging into detail of the workshop until he had his answer?

It was in all their best interests, because whatever had happened could happen again, and if Zeus had been caught out, it could be any of them next time. They wanted him to be responsible? OK: the workshop was out of bounds from now on, until he declared it safe.

Dee dropped Zeus's suit where he stood, and left, only to be replaced by Declan.

"What? You going to smack me down too?"

"No. Just that I had an idea, and I wanted to show it to you. I'll be in the medical bay."

Frank was alone again. "Well, fuck. If I'm going to burn bridges, may as well burn them all down at once."

He hung his suit up and plugged his life support in, and picked up the oxygen canister from the floor. That had to be refilled manually from the air plant, and he wasn't going to stand over it while it filled, not now. He saw that Zeus's mask was missing. The hose must have got detached in the workshop. He'd collect it later, when he went back to test the pressure.

And there was Zeus's suit. He hefted it by the shoulders, and stared in through the dust-smeared faceplate for long enough to reach the moment where he could imagine Zeus's broad, tattooed face staring back out at him.

For an ex-neo-Nazi, white supremacist gang member, he'd been OK. Dependable. Reliable. Kind, even, if a little intense.

Frank hung up the suit and racked the life support, and went to see what Declan wanted.

He was sitting on one of the beds—a metal-framed gurney that could be moved higher or lower by a lever—with a box of blue nitrile gloves open by his side.

"You coping?"

"It's pretty shitty, everything considered."

"That it is. However." Declan took one of the gloves, shook it out, and gave it a few preparatory stretches. The white dust

229

coating floated into the air, and danced under the lights. Then he put the sleeve of the glove to his lips and gave a couple of puffs so that the fingers inflated slightly. He pinched the glove at the wrist, twisted it to trap the air, and swiftly knotted it. He tossed the thing that resembled a limp blue octopus at Frank, who caught it and held it up.

"What am I supposed to do with this?"

"Put it in your pocket." Declan started making another. "Go on."

Frank didn't have the energy to argue. He squashed the glove into one of his pockets. "Now what?"

Declan tied off the second glove, hopped off the bed, and walked to the airlock at the end of the hab. They weren't supposed to use it—emergencies only—but it was fully functional. He opened the inner door, tossed the glove on the floor, and closed the door again. He beckoned Frank over, and pointed through the tiny window.

"Watch."

He flipped the switch and the air started pumping out, back into the hab. Frank peered down at the glove, which slowly and inexorably started to plump out. It kept on expanding, bigger and bigger, until the pump stopped and the glove was the size of a party balloon, stretched out to a translucent blue skin with five fat extensions.

Frank patted his pocket, feeling the small, rubbery mass there.

"Do you think you'd notice that?" asked Declan.

"I reckon."

"It's yours to keep." He cycled the lock back up to pressure, and retrieved the now much deflated glove from the floor. "If, for some reason, the alarms didn't go off, or they went off too late, it might just save you."

"It would've saved Zeus." Frank turned away from the airlock. "I don't get it. There's nothing wrong with the hab."

"And yet he died because he couldn't inhale the oxygen that was right in front of his face. Something depressurized the workshop, and by the time he realized—and clearly he did realize, otherwise he wouldn't have made it into the airlock—he was already dying."

"He should have been able to pressurize the airlock with the O_2 can he was carrying."

"If he was unconscious he couldn't. And you know that the airlock is only sealed from the hab when you're pumping it down."

Frank stopped his slow walk to the connecting corridor.

"Even if he opened the valve all the way, the gas would have just blown out back into the hab. He'd have had to manually close the valve by opening up the maintenance panel and isolating it. But as I say, you knew that, right?"

"Maybe I'd forgotten." Frank leaned against the door frame. "Why are you here, Declan? What did you do? I mean, I know what I did. I know what I deserve. And Alice, and Marcy, and Zeus. We all killed people. I know Zero got into the supply chain, and Dee got mixed up in some serious cybercrime. You? You just seem so normal."

"We all have our demons, Frank. Mine are just a bit more specialized, that's all." He blew out a long breath. "You really want to know?"

"Yes. No. Maybe."

"I liked to watch, Frank." Declan let that sink in, then continued. "In my line of work, at my level, it meant I could watch a hell of a lot of people doing all kinds of things. When you get caught, and you run a couple of hundred nickel sentences together, turns out you end up inside for the better part of a millennium. Which wasn't quite what I'd bargained for."

"So you made a deal?"

"Same deal you made. Die in prison, or live on Mars."

"Yeah. About that."

"You weren't getting ground glass or worse in every meal. Sooner or later, someone would have offed me. I think I had even less to lose than you did." He shrugged. "Well, there you

231

go. I've got to check some battery efficiencies, because I've a suspicion that the long-term effect of massive temperature fluctuations between day and night is degrading their ability to hold charge. You need to go and do whatever it is you need to do. For what it's worth, I don't think you killed Zeus, by anything you did or didn't do. It's this fucking planet."

He picked up his tablet and brushed past Frank, leaving him alone in the med bay.

Frank tidied up. He put the gloves back in their box, then back in the packing crate they'd come in. He brushed his hand across the wipe-clean vinyl surface of the bed's foam pad. Then he went back to the boxes. They'd all been opened. There was more than just high-grade pharma lying around now. Surgical packs. Pre-sterilized, sealed, but right there was a scalpel sharp enough to notch bone, with only a plastic guard and a blister pack in the way.

Could the reason that Zeus didn't notice the depressurization be down to narcotics? There were hundreds of foil packets, all stacked up in neat rows. One or two or more missing was going to be difficult to spot.

Zeus was Alice's second. In her absence, it would have been his job to count the drugs. There'd been no evidence that he'd checked them against the manifests, but maybe, informally, he had. Alice had killed herself with fentanyl. Now, possibly, Zeus had been at the tablets.

Perhaps "going to work on the steam engine" was code. The cameras wouldn't have picked anything up. Popping a pill could be done in an instant. Taking a swig of water afterwards wouldn't appear anything special. Who was going to take the time to watch him for hours to see he was actually working?

None of that explained the depressurization. It merely explained why Zeus had been caught out by it. If—a big unanswerable if—he was right.

Frank closed the boxes, and leaned heavily on his knuckles against the racking. It was no good, he was going to have to talk to Brack about all of this. Get him to secure the drugs. Take them back to the ship, maybe, as the lock on the consulting room door was pretty flimsy. None of them were doctors, and while all of them had had basic first aid training, only Zeus had anything more than that. Getting the more dangerous drugs out of the way wasn't going to cause them any problems.

When they were at Gold Hill, "What if one of the crew turns out to be an addict?" hadn't come up. It should have: they were criminals, and of course unfettered access to a whole pharmacy wasn't going to be a good idea. It was bad planning. It was a mistake.

Zero, of course, was the only one with drugs on his rap sheet, unless Alice and her overprescribing counted. If the kid had been helping himself along with Zeus, then he was going to be pissed and develop withdrawal symptoms. Frank knew what that was like. He'd seen it with his own son.

How much of this was his suspicious mind, fine-tuned to the consequences of drug-taking, reacting viscerally against the mere possibility of it? He had no evidence, and unless he was prepared to account for every single pill in all of the boxes, something going on for a year's supply for a busy dispensary, he'd never get any.

And how much of this was deflecting his own guilt, looking for other people to blame? Because that hadn't been a pattern in his life, had it? There was a fault in the workshop hab. He was going to find it, no matter what.

233

21

[transcript of audio file #7893 2/5/2035 0830MT Xenosystems Operations boardroom, 65th floor, Tower of Light, Denver CO]

PL: Ladies, gentlemen. Today marks the beginning of a new and exciting direction for XO. Our direction of travel has always been upwards and outwards. From our first satellite, to our first launcher, to our first human-rated module, we've been at the forefront of innovation, pushing the limits of what can be done because we can imagine doing it. We have slipped the surly bonds of Earth for the vast, majestic reaches of space. But now is the time to start taking our next step among the stars, not just to explore, but to exploit the abundant resources that lie just beyond our reach. To this end, I can confirm this morning, that our proposal for designing and constructing a permanent settlement on the Martian surface was approved by the House SST committee—fully funded.

[applause, some yelling and whooping]

PL: Thank you, thank you. We've worked long and hard for this. Our representatives in Washington have been tireless in their efforts to place XO as the lead contractor, and let me tell you, fighting off the bigger, more established competition hasn't been easy. Or cheap.

[laughs from around the table]

PL: We are where we are because we believe in this. We believe in the commercial opportunities that colonization

234

can bring. We believe that these lights in the sky that our ancestors looked up at, named after gods, and populated with monsters, are rough jewels for us to cut and shape and sell. There are riches there to be had by the brave and the bold, and XO will be in the vanguard. We can talk about science and surveying, but we all know that the only reason for doing something is to turn a profit. Marco Polo knew it. Magellan knew it. Columbus knew it.

BT [? possibly]: Damn right, sir!

PL: We have a ten-year head start on this. A decade to invest and equip and build, all at the federal government's expense. And at the end of that decade, it will be our flag, XO's flag, that'll be planted on Mars. There's much to do between then and now, but if I may be permitted, I hope I can persuade you to join me in a brief moment of celebration.

[doors open, rattling sound of glass on glass. Some speech, but too low/indistinct to be definitive]

[sound of corks popping]

Unidentified: You've seen the budget, right?

TD: I have the biggest hard-on ever, just thinking about it.

PL: If you'd raise your glasses, I'd like to propose a toast. To us. To XO. To the future.

All: To us. To XO. To the future!

BT: To Paul, without whom none of this would have been remotely possible. You, sir, are my guide, my inspiration, my leader, and it's an honor to serve under you.

[Polite applause]

Unidentified: Fucking brown-nose.

PL: Thank you, thank you. Well, drink up, everyone. We deserve this. We've come a long way already, and we've much further to go. We've great works to do. Legendary works. When the history books are being written, we are going to be the ones writing them. We were born to succeed.

[End of transcript]

Frank found himself sitting in the workshop and wondering why it was still fully pressurized some eighteen hours later. He kept his spacesuit on, because he didn't trust his environment, yet it was as they'd built it: an airtight hab.

So now his mind turned to ways of deliberately depressurizing it, just to see if he could replicate the conditions that Zeus might have found himself in.

The construction of the airlock was such that the only way to move air outside was that last tiny puff that remained in the chamber before the outer door opened. Otherwise, air simply cycled backwards and forwards from inside the hab. It was idiot-proof, and that had to be a good thing. So, how to manually override the safety features?

There was a vent that led from the chamber to the hab, that the pump was attached to. There was also another vent that led from the chamber to the outside, in case the pump failed—the inward-opening doors were impossible to use if there was pressure on the inside and none on the outer side. Manually venting the chamber, and letting the air outside, balanced the pressure. The outer door would now open.

He tried that. It worked.

There was also a manual override going the other way. If a hab lost power, someone from outside could vent the airlock chamber, enter it, then open another valve to equalize the pressure with the hab.

Each time this happened, the hab would lose an airlock's worth of air to Mars.

But what if ... what if he could open both valves at the same time? Leak air from the hab into the airlock, and simultaneously vent to the outside? Under normal circumstances, he'd have to be insane to try that.

He did it anyway. The valves were operated by levers. They could be left open, although the hatches that housed them wouldn't close with them in that position, so it'd be obvious what state they were in.

Stuck inside a suit, it was impossible to tell whether it was working or not. He couldn't hear the air moving, so he got a square of parachute canopy and held it up over the grille. It fluttered weakly. He was now venting the hab. And he could do all of this from the airlock. He didn't have to set foot inside the hab. The same valve that opened the hab to the chamber could be accessed either side of the inner door.

He returned the valves to closed. He shut the panels. He cycled the airlock in the normal way, and went back to sitting at the workbench, propping himself up on a high stool.

Was there another way of dumping the air outside, faster than the trickle that passed through the airlock? The only other possibility was the pump on the first floor.

He spent half an hour trying to break it, make it run backwards, push things into it so that the double baffle that sealed itself would stay open. He couldn't do it.

Then he went outside with a long, thin piece of tubing culled from a rocket motor, a piece that Zeus had been using to help prototype his steam engine. He found the shielded vent on the outside of the hab, lifted the cover off, and pushed the rod in. He pressed up against the first baffle, and, with considerable effort, managed to break the seal behind it.

Then he pushed again. A brief plume of mist shivered into the Martian air. He bent down and applied as much force as he could manage without bending the pipe. It went in, and stuck. He picked up a handful of dust and trickled it past the outlet. It fell straight down, and then puffed away in a tiny gale.

Frank started the timer on his suit, re-entered the hab, and watched the external pressure reading. The numbers were already falling. It took fifteen minutes to drop to half pressure, and at that point, anyone would have been struggling to breathe normally. It took another thirty minutes for the air to equalize with outside. Forty-five minutes in total, and all it took was a stick.

He retrieved the pipe, remounted the cover, and repressurized the hab.

So there was no way that the workshop had accidentally decompressed. Someone had done it deliberately. The only question was, had Zeus done it to himself, or had someone done it to him?

The mask was on the floor, next to the airlock. The blood that was left in the crevices had dried hard into them, and Frank spent some time scrubbing it out with a black square of parachute. The mask itself was more or less unmodified firefighter's equipment, working off a pure oxygen tank at the same five psi the habs did. He checked it over without really knowing what he was looking for. Zeus, because of his experience on oil rigs, would have been the expert on this. Frank would have to pull the user manual to check the specifications, but he was pretty certain it wouldn't work as breathing apparatus at Mars pressure.

He'd done all he could. He still had his actual work to do, tightening bolts and shaking things down, and he'd better get on with that, because he was still on the clock.

He wasn't going to concentrate, though. The whole situation worried at him. It was more than not wanting to be responsible—though that was a big part of it. Frank needed to know if it was another suicide, because if it wasn't, they were all in danger.

He picked up the mask, and trudged back to the cross-hab. On his way over, he heard a growl of thunder, and stopped to watch a line of sparks and soot draw itself across the sky. It started in the far east, and arced towards the south. As the incoming object slowed, it grew less obvious to Frank's eye, and when it disappeared altogether, he turned and climbed up the steps to the airlock, his feet heavy but silent on the metalwork.

Brack was waiting for him, casually leaning against the greenhouse entrance as if one of his team hadn't just died.

"So what did you find?" Brack pushed himself off the doorway and scooped up the mask. He peered into it, going as far as to sniff it.

"That the hab's sound. It doesn't leak. But it can be made

238

to leak if you deliberately sabotage the safeties." Frank racked his life support and dragged his suit over to the hangers. He swapped it with his overalls.

Behind him, Brack let the mask dangle on its straps. "So what are you saying, boy?"

"Either Zeus deliberately overrode the safeties, or someone else did. It wasn't accidental." He started to get dressed, facing the wall.

Brack looked over Frank's shoulder. "Shut the fuck up, and come with me."

Frank pulled the overalls up to his waist and gathered the arms around his front.

He walked through to the med hab, and found himself dragged in and slammed against one of the partition walls. The hand at his neck tightened. Brack was right in his face, standing on tiptoe.

"Now you listen here. You better be absolutely one hundred per cent sure about this or so help me God I'm shoving you out that airlock and watching you burn through the little window."

"The hab is airtight. Pressure stayed up all night." Frank didn't struggle, even though he was increasingly uncomfortable. "There's nothing wrong with it."

Brack let go, and wiped his palm against Frank's chest. "So how did you prove that?"

"You can play with the manual valves in the airlock, so that it vents the whole hab outside. It's difficult and it takes a long time to deflate. The other way is at the pump: you can break the seals from the outside and get the hab to a dangerous pressure in a quarter-hour. Just jam something in the vent."

"Could he have done it himself?"

"Sure. Same way I did it. But then he wouldn't have been alive to tidy up afterwards." That was it. That was what had been bothering him all along. "When I got there, the airlock was normal. I didn't go round the back to where the pump inlet is, but I was still able to use it to pressurize the hab the same day."

"Tell me. Tell me straight."

"Someone depressurized the workshop. They might not have known Zeus was in there. They might not have cared. Maybe they did it deliberately, but didn't mean to scare him so much that he climbed into the airlock without his suit. Maybe they did want to kill him. Maybe they thought the scuba gear would be enough so he could save himself. Whatever, whoever, they were smart enough to cover their tracks." Frank's gaze wandered over to the boxes of medical supplies. "Maybe they drugged him first. Or they knew he was taking drugs, and took advantage of that."

"Christ almighty, Kittridge. You bunch of lazy, useless fuck-ups. If it wasn't bad enough to die in an accident, and commit suicide, now you're starting on each other."

"We both know someone's been in the drugs cabinet. But only you know who that is, right?"

"Maybe I do. Maybe I don't. I might have exaggerated a little on how close an eye I can keep on you so as to keep you in line."

"Goddammit, Brack, either you know or you don't."

Brack pressed himself forward again, into Frank's face. "Watch your mouth, Kittridge. Remember I'm the one in a Mars base with four potential murderers."

Frank, half-naked and consciously vulnerable, couldn't escape Brack's closeness. "I know I didn't do it."

"You crossed the line once before. Easier to do the second time around."

"I didn't do it. Zeus was—" Frank stopped.

"What? He was what? Were you going to say 'he was my friend'?" Frank could feel Brack's breath against his skin. "People like you don't have friends. You got the Mark of Cain, boy."

"I didn't kill him."

"So which one of you did?" Brack turned away, stalking along the length of the med bay and back. "Little Demetrius wouldn't say boo to a goose. Nature-boy doesn't leave his Garden of Eden. The pervert? Hell, OK. I'd buy that. He's got cause to be outside, and he's a little bitch about his precious power consumption."

Frank seized the opportunity to feed his arms into his sleeves and jerk his overall up to his shoulders. "The spacesuits have got trackers on, right? Can you use those?"

"When you go out looking for cargo drops, what's your resolution?"

"What's my resolution?" He frowned. "I ... maybe a hundred yards or so?"

"That covers the whole base. You can be anywhere inside or outside, and it just registers as 'here'. You're going to have to try harder than that, Kittridge."

"*I'm* going to have to try harder?"

"I thought we had a deal where you said you'd be my eyes and ears. Don't you go backing out on me now. Not now the shit's getting real."

"Can we at least tell whose suits were used?"

Brack slung Zeus's breathing mask onto the racking. "This isn't a police state. This whole thing, this whole enterprise, it works on trust. There aren't the systems here to keep tabs on everyone all the time, because that's not in the contract. This is supposed to be a working scientific base, not the wing of a Supermax. Trust, Kittridge. Forget what I said about keeping tabs on you all. I have to trust you, God help me. And if this base ain't right by the time NASA gets here, it's my ass on the line, not yours."

"Do you want me to find out who did this or not?"

"Do you want to know what I'll do to the man when we do?" asked Brack. "We ain't got a prison cell up here. You tap someone for murder, there's only one sentence. We're going to have us a spacing."

"I'd better be certain, then."

"Boy, you have to do better than that. Cast-iron, copper-bottomed, one hundred per cent certified proof. I'm not calling home to tell XO I've wasted one of their valuable assets because he looked at you funny." Brack jabbed him in the chest with a rigid finger. "Do this right or don't do it at all."

Then he checked and double-checked that no one else was listening in.

"You want that flight home? You make damn sure they don't got wind of this. Not a word. Not a whisper. Got that?"

"I got it."

"Good. Now get out of here and act normal." Brack grabbed him and pushed him stumbling out of the med bay.

Frank took a moment to compose himself, and then finished zipping up the front of his overalls.

"You OK?" Declan was passing through, staring mostly at his tablet.

"Fine. Mostly."

"Did you find anything?"

"Out at the workshop?" Frank had racked his life support. The oxygen tank he'd placed on top of the recharger earlier had gone. He frowned. "No. Nothing."

"Does that mean we can use the workshop again or not?"

"I've talked to Brack. It's up to him. As far as I'm concerned, the hab's safe." He checked the separate cylinder bay, and there it was, charged up. If there'd been any evidence of tampering, he'd lost the opportunity to find it.

"So ..."

"I don't know, Declan. It's like Marcy, it's like Alice. It's just one of those things."

"OK, OK." He paused and looked down at his screen. "Doesn't seem likely to be just one of those things, though."

"It wasn't the hab that killed him. That's all I know. I didn't screw up."

"So who did?"

Frank slid on his ship slippers, and straightened up. "Maybe Zeus did. Maybe he did something stupid and he died. He's not around to ask now, so all I got is guesswork and spit. If you've

242

got anything, records of things he turned on and off, then that might give us some answers."

"Why not?" Declan nodded. "I'll look into it."

Frank found himself lying easily. It wasn't what he wanted to do, but he'd been told to do it. Any stress in his voice would be understood as something else. He watched Declan as he walked away, wondering if it had been him, wondering about the timings, about everything. He didn't seem that concerned, as if he knew the answers already.

For that matter, Zero could have picked up his suit and life support from the rack, dressed in the greenhouse, and left through the rear of the hab. No one would have seen him creep around the back of the workshop with a length of pipe, temporarily disconnected from the hydroponics.

The cameras, though. They would have spotted something, wouldn't they? Even though they were there to watch for fires, their feeds could still be accessed by someone in the control hab. Were there recordings?

He didn't know. He'd have to go and ask Dee.

22

[transcript of audio file #7907 2/10/2035 1000MT Xenosystems Operations boardroom, 65th floor, Tower of Light, Denver CO]

PL: Come on in, Bruno. Take a seat.

BT: Thank you, sir.

PL: You know to call me Paul by now, Bruno. Drink?

BT: Yes. Just a tonic water for me. I'm sorry, Paul. I respect you more than anyone alive. It's only natural I call you "sir".

PL: Well now. I hope I can somehow repay the level of trust you place in me.

BT: You owe me nothing, Paul, and I owe you everything. I mean that sincerely. I'd be nowhere without you.

PL: I'm sure that's not true. A man of your obvious talents and dedication would have been an asset to any corporation. We were lucky enough to bring you into the Xenosystems fold early on, and your rise through management has been nothing but appropriately meteoric.

BT: The company is my family, sir. I've dedicated myself to its well-being since I joined. I'm one hundred per cent loyal. I'd do anything for you.

PL: You even came in on a Saturday, for which I'm grateful. I have a favor to ask of you. It's a big one, and I want you to consider it carefully.

BT: I'm listening.

PL: I've had my eye on you for a while now, and you have qualities I appreciate. You're not afraid of making difficult decisions, and you get the job done on time and under budget. Do you think you're ready for the challenge of your life? It'll take your best years from you, but I guarantee that when you're done, you'll be able to do literally anything.

BT: I'd like to think I was equal to any challenge you could set me, Paul.

PL: I'm looking to put you in charge of the Mars contract. Oh, there are people who are possibly more experienced and longer serving, and they probably expect that they'll be offered it. I know they expect they'll be offered it. But they're older, and more cautious, and more bureaucratic. I want someone who's quick on their feet and who'll still be around in, say, fifteen years' time, rather than eyeing up a retirement ranch in Oregon or a private island somewhere halfway through. What do you say, Bruno? Can you help me out here?

BT: Sir. Paul. I'd be honored.

PL: Good. I didn't think I'd misjudged you.

[glasses clink]

BT: To Xenosystems Operations.

PL: To Mars.

[End of transcript]

They didn't keep recordings, not from the spacesuits, not from the fire control cameras. They didn't have the computer storage space for it. Brack was right: the base had been designed to be a place for scientific research and planetary exploration. No one had envisaged there'd be a need to watch the crew for a potential saboteur in their midst.

Dee did, however, show him how the fire control worked. The ceiling cameras weren't normal cameras, but infrared ones, tuned to spot for high heat sources that might trigger ignition in the oxygen-rich atmosphere. The background was almost uniformly black, and the crew pale ghosts washing across the screen. The only real contrast was offered in the greenhouse:

the areas under the growing lights and the fish tanks. The hot water storage, held in a drum on the second floor, was insulated enough to appear merely dark gray.

There was no way anyone could be identified through their image.

And to think, Frank had been worried about being spied on.

"Who was your second?"

Dee left the screen on a five-second cycle, even though the camera software continuously monitored everything. "Alice. That didn't work out so well."

Frank watched the black and gray picture on the screen. "Just hope none of us gets sick. We can always radio home, get a doctor to talk to us. And when the NASA guys are here, they'll have a medic with them, right? Someone to look after them on the journey: they don't get frozen like we did."

"There was one guy I read about once. Russian. He was the camp doctor in a base at the South Pole, and he got appendicitis." Dee made a slicing motion on his abdomen. "He had to operate on himself. No anesthetic. He had people hold up mirrors so he could see inside himself and do it that way. That's just extreme."

"That's the kind of thing I could have imagined Alice doing. She was a tough old lady. Still don't know why she did it." Frank reached across Dee and dabbed at the cameras. "Why did we install one in the workshop? There's no risk of a fire in there."

"It was in the specifications. One for every hab section, upper and lower floor."

"So you can tell from here where everyone is, just not who everyone is." Frank looked for the ghosts. Zero was in the greenhouse. There was him and Dee in Control. Declan was in the yard.

"I guess so. But we're just piggybacking the fire-detection software. None of this was designed for us."

"And there are still no cameras outside at all?"

"No." Dee frowned. "Why would there be?"

"I don't know. I'm just used to being watched, and I thought I was."

"If you'd have asked sooner, I would have told you sooner."

"Zero knows?"

"Sure. Told him when I put the cameras in the greenhouse. He said I was working for the Man, and I explained that they weren't watching him, just looking out for fires."

"Well, don't I feel the idiot now?" Frank leaned back and looked around. Control didn't have much hardware, but it did have redundancy. It was one of the few places that had more than what it strictly needed. All the cameras, all the other environmental sensors, fed into a series of black boxes. The radio traffic was logged there, and one station was set aside for video messages, with a camera facing the chair, and a mic and headset combo still in a cellophane pocket on the desk.

There were screens, too, flat ones that were of a new generation to what he remembered from life outside: as thin as a sheet of plastic, just stuck into a frame like a picture. They consumed power, so were currently dead. Dee sat at the only one that was active.

"So what can you do from here?"

"Do? Pretty much everything. I've got read-outs from all the habs: those get logged and transmitted. I've got read-outs from us—"

"Hold up. You've got access to our medical implants?"

Dee tapped through the menus on the screen.

"So this is Zero. This is Declan. This is me. And this, this is you."

Frank placed his hand on his chest as he watched the lines cross the screen. His heart rate. His breathing rate. His body temperature. His blood pressure and something called pO_2.

"How does it collect this stuff?"

"Wireless. Same way the tablets work."

"I mean if we're in our suits."

"Gets picked up by the suit and broadcast back here."

"Well, damn." Then a thought. "Does Brack have one?"

"If he does, it's not on this system. It's just the four of us. For now." Dee tapped a couple more keys. Marcy: no signal. Alice: no signal. Zeus: no signal. He clicked off that screen. "So this is the electrics—this is what Declan looks at for most of the day. Red is higher power consumption, blue is less. The greenhouse takes most, but when we go and heat up food in the kitchen, that goes reddish too, or when we need to turn the satellite dish or recharge the buggies. You know. Total consumption is here, and what we make goes in here. Batteries are on a separate screen. Then we've got the same for water and air."

"But you can't start and stop things from here."

"Sure you can. All the automatic systems. You can reset them, change the levels, turn stuff on and off. It's not difficult, but I mean, why would you want to? I leave all that shit well alone. All I'm doing is bundling up the daily reports and transmitting them to Earth. I keep them all for a rolling seven days in case the files get corrupted and I have to resend, but that's all we can hold. Then I overwrite them with the day eight data. I've written a script to do all that automatically. It's no big deal."

"So you don't actually need to be here."

Dee blew out his cheeks. "If something went wrong, you'd need me. Otherwise, I guess not. I just come in here to goof off. Don't tell Brack. Don't tell anyone."

"So what do you do all day?"

Dee returned the screen to the top of the menu tree, so that the XO logo was staring out at them. "I just ... read. Manuals. Tech stuff. Geological reports. Maps. I like that kind of stuff." He pressed his hands together and looked down at the floor.

"It's OK. It's fine." Frank risked tapping his fist against Dee's shoulder. "You can keep doing that. I'm not in charge of you, or anything."

"I just want to be useful to the NASA guys when they get here. Knowing things that they might not about the base, about the local area, that's going to be good, right? They'll need someone to carry their kit and lend them a hand. I want them to think … good thoughts about me. Include me. Come to rely on me. You know."

Frank knew. "I get that. I know this is going to be a stupid question, but do you need a password to access any of this stuff?"

"Why would you need that? It's not like we're vulnerable to hackers, or unauthorized users. We're all authorized. Everybody who comes to the base is."

"I don't know: I just thought that maybe Brack—"

"Brack always calls home from the ship. It gets routed through the main dish for ease, but it doesn't pass through this computer." Dee tapped some keys. "This is the uplink log for the last seven days. It's just automatically generated reports, like I said."

"Declan told me he was going to ask you to hack XO's responses to Brack. I'm kind of hoping you didn't, because I think that'd be a very bad idea."

"He hasn't. Why would he do that?"

Frank ignored the question. "If he does, turn him down."

"They're encrypted." Dee shrugged. "I can't crack them."

"You tried already?"

"I was just seeing if I could. They're working off of some public-private key thing, so I can get the message block, I just can't tell what the text says. Brack will have the key in the ship, and, well, whatever: I'll just tell Declan what I've told you."

"And there's no way you could crack the code?"

"No," said Dee. "This is a key of twenty or so random characters that work in an algorithm to scramble the data. I could write a script to try every possible combination, and I'd be old a hundred times over before it got even close to working. Unless I have the key, it's not going to happen. Just forget about it."

"Forgotten," said Frank, holding his hands up. "Thanks for showing me around. I feel like I learned something."

"No problem."

Frank turned to leave.

"Why did Zeus die?" asked Dee.

Frank stopped. "I don't know yet," he lied. Mostly lied, at least. Why he died was different from how he died. "If someone comes by and asks you to do something you're not comfortable with, or throws questions at you, or just does something you don't expect, you could let me know."

Dee looked down at the screen, then back up. "Frank, what's going on?"

"I haven't worked it out yet. But stay frosty, OK?" Frank went back to the crew quarters to push the button. He ended up sitting there for longer than he needed to, thinking about things. Water reclamation was below the yard, and was little more than a machine that exposed their waste to vacuum and caught the water as it boiled off. The dry solids were sterilized, turned into bricks, and handed straight over to Zero. All of that had been Zeus's job.

It, along with Dee's comment that the computer system didn't really need him until it really did, got him to wondering just how many people were actually required to run the base? What was their minimum crew?

Marcy had been their driver. But they could all drive now. Alice had been their doctor. But since she'd dragged them from their long hibernations, they hadn't needed her expertise. Zeus was plumbing, but since it had all been put in place and water pulled from Mars's freezing soil, they were a closed loop. If they needed more water, a couple of shovelfuls of fresh dirt in the machine would make it for them. He was construction, and everything had been built, in this phase of building at least. Thermal expansion happened, but after the first few weeks, the bolts pretty much held everything together. Dee had set up Comms and Control so that neither needed intervention from him or anyone. Declan? How much did he do over cleaning the panels by hand and stalking the corridors to find people to shout at? Brack? He didn't do anything related to the upkeep of the base.

Zero: he was the exception to the rule. They wouldn't eat without his efforts. A lot of his work was monitoring the growth of his beloved plants, analyzing the mix of the nutrients being fed into the hydroponic reservoirs, and adjusting the flow rates. He harvested and replanted. How much, or how little, would carry on without him, was something Frank was going to have to look into. But out of all of them, Zero worked the hardest and complained the least.

So to answer his own question: a couple. Zero could probably manage on his own for months, maybe even years, until something broke down that he couldn't fix. For all his smarts, he couldn't know everything and he didn't seem to want to, either. He was content, and Frank had to admit that perhaps he was a little bit jealous of that. But maybe even Zero needed someone else, running around behind the scenes, keeping all the systems fine-tuned.

Given all that, which one of them could have decided that Zeus was surplus to requirements? Was it even that calculating? Did Zeus die simply because someone thought they could get away with killing him?

He didn't want to agree with Brack, but kept circling the same conclusion. If—and there still might be something that he'd missed that made Zeus's death accidental and not deliberate—Zeus had been killed, neither Dee nor Zero seemed at all likely to have done it. Neither of them had had any beef with the man while he'd been in training or on Mars. Zeus's Aryan Brotherhood tats could have unnerved Zero or Dee, as they did Frank, but there'd been no evidence of animosity.

Declan. It came back to Declan every time.

So what was Frank going to do about that? He didn't have proof, and neither did he have any way of getting that proof, save trying to beat a confession out of Declan. Which, if he was right or wrong, wasn't going to make anyone happy at sharing a confined space with him.

How was he supposed to do this without turning himself into

a pariah? Was that even possible? He'd promised to help Brack in exchange for a ride home. With a possible murder on the base, Brack had called that promise in. How much did Frank want to go home?

Frank didn't love Mars that much. He found it fascinating, beautiful, stark, lethal. But it wasn't his home, and it wasn't where his son was. OK, so he wanted to go back to Earth more than anything, in order to see his son. What was he going to do about that?

He was going to make some assumptions. Firstly, that Declan had done one of the two things to the workshop—either fix the airlock valves or open up the pump vent—that had ended up killing Zeus. Maybe he'd incapacitated Zeus beforehand by slipping him something. Or Zeus had done it to himself, and Declan had got pissed with him and wanted to teach him a lesson. Secondly, that having killed one of them and got away with it, he'd be much more likely to try and kill someone else when they pissed him off too.

Zero was too important to lose, at least at this point. So next, it was either Frank, or Dee, or Brack. If Brack died, there'd be no trip home. If he died, he wouldn't need one. Dee? Dee was just a kid who no more deserved to be on Mars than he deserved to be serving life. There were more than enough tech companies in California for one of them to have hired the boy and kept him out of jail.

The best way to off someone and get away with it was to make it look like an accident, and to keep the base intact as much as possible while doing it.

Where was he most vulnerable, then? Outside, in his suit, or driving? His suit was his own suit, identifiable, but the life support was a random pick from the rack. The buggies? Both he and Brack drove, and Declan hardly ever did. Neither did Dee or Zero. Declan spent a long time outside, unsupervised, unwatched. If he wanted to do something to a buggy, then he could.

Frank decided that he'd ask Dee to pull the full manual on the buggies. His training had been almost all practical: how to identify and solve problems. Not included were those catastrophic errors that would have meant he wouldn't be around to solve the problem at all. Was it possible to fix the fuel cell so that it exploded? There were compressed gases and lots of energy stored inside, and the driver sat almost directly over it. Shards of fast-moving fractured casing would slice a spacesuit into shreds.

So much to think about. So much of it depressing. He didn't want to spend his time on Mars doing this—playing detective. Definitely playing. He had no idea where to start.

He pushed the button and pulled the levers, zipped up and washed his hands and face. Part of the training. A stomach bug would pass around the crew like wildfire, and there'd be no hiding place.

There was Zero in the kitchen, and Frank walked up the corridor to see what he was doing.

"So I've never done this before," said Zero, pointing at a fish in the bucket between his feet. "I was told how to defrost the eggs and grow them on in tanks, how big they have to be before we start chowing down on them. Not how to get one ready to cook."

"Last time I saw them they were no bigger than my finger." Frank got down on his hands and knees and peered in. "Look at the size of them. Longer than my hand, some of them."

"They gain weight fast, just chewing algae. I figured we could do with cheering up, so I picked out four of the fattest, but man, I've no idea what to do now."

"You've got to clean them."

"You've lost me."

Frank dipped his hands into the lukewarm water and scooped up one of the tilapia. It was strong, trying to wriggle out of his grasp, and slimy too, its slippery mucus layer making it difficult to hold.

253

"I need a knife. Sharpest we have. And a plastic tray."

Zero picked a knife up from the bench. It didn't have a point, but the blade was keen enough. Frank pinned the fish inside the tray and with one swift slice took its head clean off.

"Jesus, Frank!"

"It's a fish, Zero. They barely have enough brains to register pain." He turned the fish in his palm and sliced down the belly. He put the knife in the tray and scooped out the guts with a pull of his two fingers. "And that's how you clean a fish."

Zero had gone visibly pale, and his eyes were as round as saucers.

"Why don't you go make us a salad?" suggested Frank. "I'll deal with the rest."

"Sure. OK. Whatever you say, man."

Frank dispatched the three remaining fish and tossed the waste down the john. Almost perfect recycling. The plants would feed off the detritus, and the water flow ended up in the fish tanks. He washed his hands and caught sight of loose silvery scales circling the plug as he rinsed, shining like tiny planets.

He watched them spin in ever tighter circles, then vanish into the drain.

How to cook them? They had two options: microwave, or steam. Steam them, then. See what herbs they had, stuff them in the cavity and give them five minutes. Long enough to round everyone up and get them sitting down together. How long was it since they'd done that? Normally they just smashed and grabbed an evening meal when they felt like it. Why not make this an occasion?

Except he was already thinking about turning any conversation to his advantage, whether there were any off-guard comments that he might use to catch someone out. Everything from now on had to be about finding out who killed Zeus, and every opportunity had to be turned to that purpose.

23

Mr Tiller: we will be working through these various scenarios and producing SWOT analyses for each in the next two weeks. If you or other XO board members have comments, then please append.

1. Specifications as agreed. Timescale as agreed
2. Specifications as agreed. Timescale lengthened by 5–10 years
3. Renegotiate specifications. Timescale as agreed
4. Renegotiate specifications. Timescale lengthened by 5–10 years
5. Renegotiate entire contract
6. Cancel contract

It was different without Zeus. It had been different without Marcy and Alice, but they'd died at the beginning of the mission, when everything was new and nothing was routine. The base hadn't been started, let alone completed, and the remaining five cons had spent difficult hours and days helping each other, shouting at each other, deliberately ignoring each other and ultimately deciding they still had to work together, whatever their feelings about each other. That cycle had gone on more times than any of them cared to remember.

Now there was a hole. Zeus was gone, and his duties had to be picked up by Zero, who really didn't want them, but since the state of the plumbing was so intimately tied to that of the

255

greenhouse, he didn't have much choice.

That next morning, Frank went round with him to try and learn how all the pipes moved fresh water from the storage tank to the habs, and the waste back to the recycler. There were manuals for that. Not so for the hot water system which Zeus had more or less single-handedly cobbled together. The few scribbled drawings that he'd left on the computer system were simply inadequate. The notes he'd made for NASA did make more sense, but there were times when the two of them were reduced to chasing tubing through the underfloor panels, trying to work out where it went next.

But Frank still had his own jobs: maintain the fabric of the habs, and keep the buggies running. After a morning with Zero, he had to go outside to carry out his inspections. There was a feeling of unreality to everything. Zeus was dead, murdered. The list of suspects was tiny. And still he had to go round checking something as mundane as nuts and bolts, because someone deliberately spacing him wasn't the only way he could die.

The habs were holding up well. The pressurized skin didn't seem to be degrading at all. It had all the appearance of lasting for years.

The buggies—buggy, since Brack had taken one back to the ship, presumably to talk to XO about how their cheap convict crew had been worth every cent they'd spent on them—had fared less well. The fuel cells, save for a few dings in the bottom of the casing, were still operating at one hundred per cent capacity. The frames were scratched, but the damage was superficial. For ease of construction, the wheels came in a single piece, motor, actuators and tires, and damn but those things were heavy. The drive motors needed dismounting and opening up at some point, to see if the seals were still good or whether there was a build-up of dust.

The tires, though, were the most immediate worry. The metal plates that provided the grip were degrading, whether through the mechanical wear of driving over a surface that was littered with little rocks, or whether the perchlorate in the soil was actively eating away at the material: it didn't much matter which. With less than a thousand miles on the clock, they could already do with a swap-over.

They had no spares. Frank wondered if he could make replacement plates out of drum material, or even cylinder casing, because there was no alternative. One broken tire would mean one buggy completely out of action. They'd start cannibalizing it, and the inevitable end was that they'd eventually run out of parts. Whereas if they could fabricate a good enough replacement, then it might be they'd never run out. Tires were consumables: he couldn't quite believe he'd been reduced to this.

Today, the sky was particularly pink, high dust turning the weak sun even weaker—even a smudged entry trail angling down towards the surface looked pale. Declan was fretting about power regulation yet again. He was outside with Frank, cleaning the black glassy surfaces with a piece of parachute material. Actually, yes: Frank had noticed a build-up of dust on the buggy controls, and perhaps there was a big storm to the south that was pushing dirty air over the equator.

Rahe didn't seem to generate the dust devils that happened out on the plain, but they still had weather all the same. The base didn't have a meteorological station, which seemed odd. Perhaps it was in the same shipment that their personal effects had been in, now circling in deep space or smeared black against the red of Mars.

They didn't get any weather reports either. They didn't get anything at all. No news from Earth. No messages. Nothing. As if it had ceased to exist, and there were just the five of them left, hundreds of millions of miles away in a tiny, ignorant bubble.

But Brack was in communication with XO, and Dee was getting information from somewhere. Earth was still there, and Frank wanted to go back to it.

"What you doing, Frank?" Declan looked up from buffing the panels.

"Looking for the buggy manuals." Frank poked around on his tablet, but his fat, gauntleted fingers kept on making mistakes, despite the software being configured for use with a spacesuit. "If we can't repair the tires somehow, then we're going to have to make some calls home. Our NASA guests won't be happy having to walk everywhere."

"We haven't got the power for making anything. We haven't even got the power to run all their experiments." Declan shook the cloth out, and he gestured at the dust puffing away in ephemeral pink clouds. "We were down fifteen per cent at midday. Stuff's going on standby if it doesn't pick up."

Of course it was. It always was. But somehow they managed the balancing act with watts to spare, and no one took him seriously any more. Declan complained, and the rest of them just got on with it.

"I guess I'll just have to talk to Brack," said Frank, and even though he couldn't see Declan's face clearly, he could tell his expression had soured. He didn't like the idea of being over-ruled. None of them did, because it reminded them that they had responsibility without authority, and that they were still cons who had an overseer. But it really rankled with Declan.

"I'll take a look at the figures. Work out a budget," he said after a moment of dead air.

"Appreciate it."

The Boy who cried Brownout had had his bluff called again.

"Dee, you there?"

"Hi, Frank. What's up?"

"Have we got the buggy manuals on the downlink yet?"

"Probably. I'll take a look. You got a part nu—"

The noise in Frank's ears, before the headphones cut out through overload, made him temporarily deaf. He staggered against the buggy and braced himself on the chassis while he recovered. Declan, over by the panels, reeled away, ineffectually clutching the sides of his helmet.

"Dee? Dee?"

No answer.

Frank started running, skipping, across the rocky Martian surface towards the airlock.

"Zero? Can you hear me?"

If he could, he couldn't make himself heard over the alarm blaring in the background. The fire alarm.

"Zero. Stay where you are." Frank knew full well that Zero's suit was racked in the cross-hab, and with the alarms sounding, the temptation would be to rush to suit up. But the greenhouse had its own airlock, and was pretty well isolated. Frank could be there faster, and already in his suit.

He took the steps three at a time, and punched the airlock cycler. Declan was making his way over too, but Frank wasn't waiting. He pushed the door in, kicked it shut behind him, and cycled the hab air into the chamber. It took only a few seconds, and it seemed like an eternity.

He opened the inner door to the cross-hab, not knowing what he'd find.

It was as he'd left it. No sign of fire. No smoke, no damage. He moved quickly down the corridor to the crew quarters, and it was the same. Normal.

"Dee?"

His voice carried, muffled, into the hab, where it lost its way, battered by the still shouting alarm.

"You found him yet?" asked Zero in his ear.

"No."

"Hurry it up, man."

Frank took the turn to Comms. The door to the module was shut: he threw it open, and there was Dee, slumped on the floor. There were tendrils of white vapor in the air, but no fire, nothing to tell Frank the reason for the alarm.

He crouched down and turned Dee over. The boy flopped like one of the fish, his skin a livid red. He wasn't breathing, and Frank didn't have time to check the computer for his vital signs.

259

"Zero, clear the greenhouse airlock. I'm bringing him in to you."

Declan was suddenly behind him, and startled Frank enough for him to slip to one side. All Declan did was jump over Dee and take hold of his ankles. Frank scooped his hands under Dee's armpits and together they carried him to the greenhouse airlock.

There wouldn't be room for all three of them, so Frank said: "Kill the alarm. I can't hear myself think," then dragged Dee over the threshold of the airlock.

Declan reached in and pulled the door closed, and Frank elbowed the cycler without letting go.

Zero opened the door on his side, and Frank pulled Dee through, laying him out on the gridwork just the other side.

"What happened to him?"

"Gassed with CO_2. Start CPR. I'll get out of the suit." Frank thumbed his control panel.

Zero just looked at Dee, scarlet and unresponsive.

"You've got to do it, Zero."

"Jeez. He's gone, Frank. He's gone."

The suit's rear hatch was opening with glacial slowness. "Do it, Zero. Just fucking do it."

"Hey, OK, OK." Zero knelt down, folded his hands together over Dee's sternum, and started rhythmically pushing.

Frank's suit gave him the green light and he scrambled out backwards. The alarm finally cut off, and the silence—save for Zero's grunts, and the bubbling of flowing water—was profound. Frank leaned over Dee's face, pinched his nose, tilted his head and huffed into his lungs.

They worked for a minute, two minutes, three minutes.

Then Zero rocked back on his haunches. "We need to stop, Frank. We're not doing anything."

Frank carried on, making Dee's chest rise and fall. "We can't give up on him."

"Listen, Frank. If we bring him back, what are we going to do

260

with him? We've no doctor, no idea what to do next, anything. Even if he lives, he's going to be gone. You know what I'm saying, right? We need to just let him go, before we do something worse to him."

Frank breathed into Dee again, then sat back, his hands clenched into fists.

"Goddammit," he said. "How could this happen?"

"There was a fire—"

"There wasn't a fire. There was no fire at all."

"The alarm."

"I was in there, Zero. No fire. None."

"Then ... something went wrong. I don't know." Zero pulled himself upright using some of the staging. "Maybe the fire got put out, and you missed it. Maybe it worked like it was supposed to."

"It wasn't supposed to kill Dee. It should have given him time to get out."

"He fucked up. He forgot his drills. He took a deep breath and he passed out. He kept on breathing that shit in and it killed him."

"It was a couple of minutes, tops. He should still be alive. Why isn't he still alive?"

"I'm sorry, Frank. There was nothing we could do." Zero walked to the end of the greenhouse and stared out at Mars through the tiny windows in the airlock there.

Frank reached out and pushed Dee's eyelids down, one, then the other. His skin was already growing cool. How could this possibly be an accident? No one group of people could possibly be this unlucky.

He left Dee there, scarlet, dead, on the upper floor of the greenhouse. He climbed into his suit again, and thumbed the hatch closed behind him.

"Declan? Where are you?"

"I'm in Control, trying to find the seat of the fire. Did Dee make it?"

"No. No he didn't." Frank cycled through the greenhouse airlock. "Hook up the air plant and get the scrubbers on. We need to reoxygenate the air."

"When I'm done."

"It's going to take hours and we don't have that much daylight left. Either the air plant goes on now, or we'll be sleeping in the greenhouse tonight."

"Who put you in charge?"

"Goddammit, Declan, just do it. Just—do it without picking some pissy argument with me. We can't breathe the air in here and that's kind of a big thing. I'll look for what set the alarm off, because that's supposed to be my goddamn job, not yours." Neither did he want Declan in the hab while Frank wasn't there. If there was evidence—if he was hiding evidence—Frank needed to get him out.

They passed each other in the corridor, and they banged against each other, hard torso against hard torso. Declan was lighter, and maybe not expecting the contact, so he rebounded against the wall of the connector too.

Neither said anything to the other, and neither was going to forget the slight either.

Where the hell was Brack? Back at the ship, yes, but with his comms off? Not that there was anything he could say at that moment: everyone already knew what they had to do to get the base running again. Frank stood in the doorway to Comms/Control and wondered what he was looking for.

Something had caused the fire alarm to trip. Some spark, some incandescent heat source, had caught the eye of the cameras, and had been ruthlessly suppressed by the compressed CO_2 cylinders which instantly diluted and displaced the five psi oxygen atmosphere. The alarm was supposed to sound fractionally before the air was rendered unbreathable. Deep breath, and run. Close the doors behind you.

They'd all trained for this. Dee should still be alive. And he had been, up to the point the alarm went off. He'd been at the console, speaking into the microphone, checking the files for the ones that Frank had wanted.

Frank put himself in Dee's position, literally, standing where he would have sat. His finger touched the screen, and it bloomed into life. There was the last thing that Dee had been looking at, the search screen for the system. He'd been asking Frank for the part number.

Then something had gone wrong. There'd been intense heat in this part of the hab—the two floors had separate fire suppression systems—and somehow, Dee had forgotten everything and breathed in. He would have started to feel faint almost immediately, but he would still have had time to get out of the hab. It was three, four steps to the door. Once that was closed, the CO_2 would have been contained, and the air on the right side of the door would have had enough oxygen in to revive him, even if he'd been near collapse.

What had Dee been doing in the minutes beforehand? Frank went to check in the crew hab, around the cans, in the bedrooms, but there was no evidence he could find that Dee had done something that would mean he couldn't react normally.

Drugs? Again? He should have searched Dee's pockets, because it wasn't like they could do any forensic work, what with their doctor being dead already, months ago. But like Zeus, being under the influence shouldn't have meant a death sentence. And Dee had sounded perfectly normal in the moments before the alarm had gone off.

Where had everyone been? Frank, outside by the buggy. Declan, over by the solar farm. They'd been in sight of each other. Brack was two whole miles away in the ship. That left Zero and Dee as the only ones inside. Could Zero have done something in the time between the alarm going off and Frank reaching the airlock? Twenty, thirty seconds? It took nearly the same length of time again to cycle it through.

His estimate of a couple of minutes had been good. Then turning him over, he and Declan carrying him to the greenhouse, getting him through the airlock and starting CPR.

Four, maybe five minutes. Dee's chances of survival were nosediving by that point. But he should still have been savable. Shouldn't he? Breathing almost pure CO_2 for that length of time? He didn't know enough to say one way or the other.

But none of that would have mattered if Dee had just done what he'd been told to do: hold his breath, run, slam doors. And before then, too: what had set off the fire alarm in the first place?

Frank didn't know, and he couldn't tell. The chair that usually sat in front of the console was halfway across the room, and on its side. He picked it up, and set it down in front of the screen.

Four. Four of them left. It didn't seem fair.

24

[Internal memo: Project Sparta team to Bruno Tiller 6/21/2038 (transcribed from paper-only copy)]

Thank you for your input regarding the earlier memo. We have now exhausted all existing avenues, which leaves us with more choices, but also more problems. It is clear that you see the timescale as unalterable. There are minimum requirements NASA require you to meet in terms of the base: it's possible that we can finesse the delivery of those requirements, in that you will supply everything the contract states, but not in the contracted manner.

I have a proposal to put to you, and I think it would be best done in person. Perhaps you could suggest 'neutral ground' for this conversation.

Brack eventually did his thing of taking the body away. Frank wrapped Dee in parachute cloth, and carried him to the main airlock. What happened to him after that, he didn't want to see.

The body was still wet. The water would boil out of it as it had done out of Zeus. By the time Brack reached the ship, there'd be a dried husk of a man to bury in the cold Martian soil, lined up next to three others.

How Dee had died was as straightforward as how Zeus had died. Zeus should have been able to get his suit into the airlock with him when he realized that the workshop was depressurizing. Dee should have been able to get out of Comms/Control before suffocating on the CO_2 extinguishers. Neither of them had acted in the obvious way that would have saved their lives.

Had they been doped? It was a possibility. Something in the water? Not the communal water, but something individual, like their spacesuits? Not enough to kill, but enough to make someone too weak to escape whatever fatal scenario the killer had constructed. How was he ever going to prove that? He was now at the point of distrusting not just everyone, but everything. Frank was still in his suit. The air in the habs wouldn't be replenished for another few hours, and it was either his suit, or in the greenhouse with Zero. And he wanted to be alone. Frank had made sure that Zero's suit was inside with him, already loaded up with a full life-support pack. Declan was somewhere else in the base.

Frank went back to worrying at the problem. He couldn't sit down in a regular chair, so he leaned against the door of Comms and tried his hardest to look dispassionately around again, walking himself through the last few seconds of Dee's life. Answer the radio, twist in the seat, tab up the search screen.

Absolutely nothing that would have involved a power surge or a flashover. Frank walked around the console and arrived back at the door.

The fire alarm sounds. Jump up so quickly the chair spins away across the floor. Run to the door.

This was where Frank didn't get it. The door, the way out, was right there. Why hadn't Dee taken it? Why had he—

Frank pushed the door shut.

The door had been shut when he'd found it. Goddammit, Zero.

Both he and Declan had been outside. Only Zero had been inside. If he'd tripped the fire alarm—how?—then had held the door shut while Dee had scrabbled at it, only to realize he couldn't get through. Then listened for the thump as Dee hit the floor. If Dee had shouted at Zero to open the door, he'd have been taking lungfuls of CO_2-saturated air. It wouldn't have taken more than a few seconds.

Then run back to the greenhouse and, with the pressure the same both sides, Zero wouldn't even have to worry about cycling the airlock. Just open the door, step in, close it. He was home and dry.

Not Declan, then.

And the greenhouse had two airlocks. One into the hab, and one that led directly outside, to the back of the base, where he could come and go as freely and unwatched as he wanted. All Zero had to do was collect his suit, as Frank had just done for him, and then re-rack it. He could have used any number of tools from the greenhouse to hold open the valves in the pump, and simply walked back to the greenhouse.

He knew his drugs. The black market prescription drugs, not just the street ones. Crap. That was it. That was the missing link. He was the only person who could have killed both Dee and Zeus.

But why? What was the point of it all? Frank knew why he'd killed: love, the best, purest motive of all. But Zero? Jealousy? Rage? It couldn't be money or sex, because there wasn't any money, and as far as he could tell, any sex either. The walls were thin. They could hear each other breathing at night, let alone anything else going on. That left revenge, but Frank couldn't see that either.

In order to save the rest of them, he'd have to tell Brack. What Brack was going to do with the information was up to him, even though Frank knew what would happen.

Brack would have to make a decision: if that ended up with Zero being kicked out of an airlock without his suit, it'd be just Frank and Declan running the base. How was that supposed to work? Neither of them knew how the greenhouse functioned. At this point, Zero was keeping them all alive even while he was killing them off.

Frank opened the door again, and Declan was standing right

there. Startled, Frank raised his hands to ward off an attack that was never going to come, and a moment later, with his arms still up defensively, he felt like a fool.

His shoulders sagged and he stepped aside from the door. Declan edged in, and they stared at each other for a while, saying nothing, only searching each other's expressions for any clue as to what to do next.

Frank turned off his microphone, and waited for Declan to do the same.

"What's going on, Frank?"

"Trying to work out who killed Dee and Zeus."

They didn't need to touch helmets. There was plenty of atmosphere for their voices to carry through. But it was hard to break the habit.

"You think it was Zero," said Declan.

"It couldn't have been you. It couldn't have been me. We don't have a lot of suspects left after that."

"Why would he do that?"

"I don't know. Maybe he just wants to live alone on Mars, grow his crops, and feed his fish. Makes as much sense as anything else."

"A couple of things have been bothering me," said Declan.

"Just a couple?"

"Shut the fuck up, Frank, and listen. Alice."

"Alice killed herself. Most likely because she could see us starving to death."

Declan separated contact, and walked around the console, leaning his hands on the desktop. "Did she?"

"There were pills in her hand."

"Were there any in her mouth?"

"I ... I didn't look. But there were pills, and there was water, and she was dead, Declan. I'm not a cop, but what other answer are you looking for?"

"You found her, right?"

"You were there. I climbed up the ladder in front of you."

268

"I was there. I wasn't there when Marcy died, though."

"What the fuck, Declan? What the actual fuck? What are you trying to say?"

"Marcy died. You were with her. Alice died. You found her. Zeus died. You opened the airlock door on him. Dee died. First on the scene again. Are you not spotting a pattern here? You think no one else has noticed, Frank? Maybe they haven't. Maybe Zero's too stupid, and I'm pretty certain Captain Brack isn't the sharpest knife in the block, otherwise he wouldn't be here with us deadbeats. But I've noticed. I've been watching you for a while now."

"Because that's what you do, right?"

"Nothing wrong with turning a vice into a virtue. You haven't got away with this. Just because we're on Mars doesn't mean you can just kill people and walk away."

Frank looked around. "Walk away? Walk away? There's nowhere to walk to. Look, I've not killed anyone."

"Well, that's not true, is it?" Declan started for the door, and Frank blocked him.

"I've not killed anyone here."

"And that's supposed to be OK, is it?"

"He was dealing drugs to my son."

"Most people would have just called the cops."

"He was the cops. The sheriff's son."

Declan moved closer and touched helmets. "All I see is a whole lot of bad parenting going on. Now get out of my way."

Frank pushed him back. "I'm not a killer."

"Of all the people in this room, hands up who hasn't killed anyone." Declan raised his arm. "Anyone else? Anyone?"

"This is serious, Declan."

"Don't you think I know that? I'm trapped on Mars with a psycho. And at the moment, the only thing that'd make this whole scenario better would be being trapped on Mars without a psycho." He wheeled away, and took up his position behind the console again. "I liked you. I actually liked you. I thought we could get on, at least. You seemed to want to treat me like a human being and not some rapo scum-of-the-earth. And Dee looked up to you. He was just a kid. And Zeus: he was easy in your company. Alice? She was difficult to like, but you could respect her. And Marcy was fun, and she was dead before I even got defrosted. Why, Frank! Why? What possible advantage do you think you're going to get?"

"But I haven't done anything. It was Zero."

"Zero wasn't even out of bed when Marcy died, Frank."

"Marcy died because her scrubber failed. She died in my arms. I did everything I could to save her, and it wasn't enough."

"So you say."

"And Alice took pills. She checked herself out."

"That was what it was made to look like, sure."

They resumed staring at each other across the room.

"Fighting in a spacesuit is a really stupid idea," said Frank.

"That's something we can agree on."

"I didn't kill Marcy, I didn't kill Alice. That's just crazy talk. We know how they died, and it was no one's fault. No one living's fault. But Zeus was murdered. Someone deliberately depressurized the workshop."

"And Dee?"

"They shut him in here. There's no way he couldn't make it out the door in time. But if you hold the door closed, he's got nowhere left to go and nothing else to breathe."

Declan scanned the console, the hab's softly glowing walls, the strings of LEDs he'd put up himself. "Do you know what tripped the alarm?"

"No, I don't know enough about the system. It works off heat, but there's no evidence of a fire. I just don't understand how it could have gone off without an actual flame."

"What is it about you that makes you so incurious?" Declan risked stepping around the desk and used his gloved finger to work his way down through the system's menus until he could access the fire-response mechanisms. "There. See?"

Frank looked over his shoulder. There was a schematic of the hab, and on-off tabs that could work the cameras. Status bars that indicated the fill level of the CO_2 extinguishers. A manual purge button for each.

"It's the backup. You can hit the switch and activate the extinguishers if they don't go off automatically. Probably too late by then—a hab breach will kill a fire stone dead, assuming there's no oxidizer. You can do this through your tablet. No special controls."

"Why the hell didn't XO tell us stuff like this?" Frank stared at the screen.

"Because we're just the monkeys. We're not meant to mess with this; this is for the real astronauts who know what they're doing, and aren't likely to use the deep controls to try and kill each other." Declan shuffled around, and was face to face with Frank. "You know, I want to believe you. We knew it was risky. I want to believe that four people dying in a matter of a couple of months is just one of those things. But we both know that it's not. I'm just going to let Brack handle this. That's his job, right?"

"You've got a problem with that, Declan: I was outside, with you, when Dee died. I couldn't have held the door shut. You're my alibi."

Declan aimed a finger at Frank's chest. "And you're mine."

Frank blinked and turned away, heading out through the door. What if there wasn't one killer, but two, working together? And they were framing him for everything, deliberate and accidental? The base, where he was, was now literally the worst place he could be. He could feel his heart rate spike, and his skin go cold. He had to get out, the only problem being that the base was it, the single place on Mars that he could live. He'd have to come back at some point.

But he could go to the ship. He could go to the ship and find Brack, and tell him he'd found his evidence. It was his last chance. And he had to do it now, before anyone tried to stop him.

271

He grabbed a fresh pack from the life-support rack. Then he hesitated. Unless he wanted to wrestle it all to the ground inside the airlock, the only place he could swap packs would be the greenhouse. Zero was in there.

What kind of accident would Frank die in? Would his suit fail him? Would his air fail him? Or had it gone beyond that pretense now? Was it going to come down to shivs and shanks, or a sock full of rocks?

He could just carry it with him, swap it when he got to the relative safety of the ship. Brack had one buggy. He'd have the other. Even if they wanted to chase him, they'd be the better part of an hour behind.

"Hey," said Zero, a faint disembodied voice. "Who's that in the cross-hab?"

"Frank," said Frank. He turned round and saw Zero's face at the greenhouse airlock window.

"What you doing?"

"Thinking about swapping my life support out."

"You not got enough?"

"I'm not taking the chance. That OK?"

"Whatever, man. You don't need my permission." Zero turned his head so he could peer partway down the connecting corridors. "You going outside?"

"Despite everything, I've still got chores to do."

"Chill. Do it tomorrow. Base isn't going to fall down because you've skipped a day."

"Maybe it will, maybe it won't." Frank started to back towards the airlock that led outside. He had the spare life support cradled in his arms. What else did he have? A nut runner and his tablet hung from his external belt. A pouch of slap-on patches for immediate hab repair. Not anything good in a fight, though the nut runner would make a impromptu blackjack. He needed to tool up. He couldn't head for the kitchen, because Declan was in that direction.

"You're not coming in to swap over? I'll clear the way for

you." Zero's face disappeared, and Frank darted towards the med bay instead. The boxes of drugs and equipment were still sitting on the shelves. He put the bulky life support down, looked at the labels, then opened one particular box, took out a sealed pack of surgical instruments and slipped them into the same pouch as the patches.

He hoisted the life support again, and rather than go back to the main airlock, left the base through the little-used one in the med bay itself. He felt his suit tighten around him as the air pumped down. He ought to be used to the feeling, but now it felt as it had done at the beginning: claustrophobic and constricting. He waited out the surge of panic, remembering his breathing, closing his eyes and going to his calm place: a brightly lit back-yard, warm from the summer sun, brittle grass underfoot, and the sound of an excited boy splashing around in the new pool. Drops of water glittered in the air, arcing gracefully up, stretch-ing and breaking and shattering on the stone surround.

He was OK. He could do this.

He trotted down the steps, down and across the red sand to the remaining buggy. He slid the life support ahead of him and climbed up, wedging the box between his legs and the seat. He started the fuel cell. No sign of Declan. That was fine. Neither he nor Zero needed to know where Frank was going.

The buggy pulled away, and Frank pointed the front wheels at the distant spire of the ship, just about visible through the surface haze. A trail of dust plumed up behind him, and the wind dragged out what didn't settle.

It took only a few minutes to cover the distance that would otherwise take an hour to walk.

He pulled to a halt outside the ship. There were empty cylin-ders, from the things they'd towed there and unpacked right at the start of the mission. But there was no second buggy. Brack wasn't at the base. He wasn't at the ship. Frank stood up on the seat and searched the distance for the telltale ribbon of pale dust, but there was nothing.

He got down and walked around the ship, expecting to find the raised cairns of his dead colleagues at any moment, but again, there was no sign. If there was anything that was going to be obvious on the flat landscape of the Heights, it was going to be a cemetery. Maybe, for some reason, it was further away.

He went back for the life support, and climbed the stairs to the ship's airlock. He'd wait for Brack inside.

25

[Private diary of Bruno Tiller, entry under 9/2/2041, transcribed from paper-only copy]

Sometimes I wonder how we got to this point. We are so far below our budget, we've had to set up shell companies to bid us for non-existent work, just so that I can keep the numbers up.

Project Sparta are right: we can build another Mars base for what we've saved. An XO Mars base. This is an extraordinary achievement. Paul is going to be so proud of me.

Frank hadn't been back inside the ship since they'd inflated the crew quarters. The internal layout hadn't changed—how had he ever thought it possible that it could?—but it had become extraordinarily dirty. The first floor was strewn with used food packets, torn foil, empty bags and dust. So much dust.

He propped up the spare life support against the airlock door and opened up his suit. There was an obvious, odd smell to the ship. When it had been eight of them in close quarters, the filters had managed to keep the odors at bay; it looked like they'd been finally overwhelmed. He pushed his head out into the thin, cold air. That smell really wasn't good. Sort of a teenager's bedroom smell. His own teenager's, for that matter.

He slipped out of the rest of the suit, and shuffled through the debris. What didn't get kicked aside, crunched underfoot. Every surface was coated with a thick film of red, oddly both oily and gritty to the touch. He ran his finger across one of the screens, and sniffed at the residue. It was sharp and sweet at the same time.

Something caught his eye in among the litter, and he crouched down. It was a blister pack. He picked it up. Every tiny blister was empty and crushed. He turned it over and read the contents: oxycodone hydrochloride, thirty milligrams.

That wasn't a good sign.

He dropped it back onto the floor, and swept his foot around. There were several more he could see, and probably more that he couldn't.

He climbed up to the next level. Brack's bedroll was there, and his sleeping bag, unzipped and rucked up, lay mostly on top of it. He'd thought that Brack slept in the base, in the examination room off the med bay. He probably did, but it looked like he slept in the ship too. There was more litter around the sleeping bag: more food pouches, more pill packs, other trash Frank couldn't readily identify.

The place was … a garbage dump. There wasn't any other way to put it. Brack was living in what could only be described as squalor.

Frank slowly turned, taking in the whole scene, and knew he was missing something.

Apart from the first few days, Brack had been pretty hands-off. He'd come over to inspect the works, making sure they—minus Alice and Marcy—were getting on with it. Then he'd go away again. And they had got on with it. They'd built the habs, fitted them out, powered them up, installed the comms, and even come up with new solutions to overcome the shortages XO had imposed on them. They'd worked relentlessly, as long as their suits had allowed them, and then when the jobs had moved inside, they'd worked until they'd dropped. Rinse and repeat. Sol after sol.

They hadn't needed Brack at all. They all knew what had needed to be done. They'd done it, by themselves, for themselves, because otherwise they would have starved to death. The ship-brought supplies would have run out before they'd finished building the base: that's what Alice had told him, and he had no reason to doubt her, even now.

They'd even made a priority of setting up the greenhouse because there'd been nowhere near enough calories to feed them. Zero, whatever else he might be, had taken to hydroponics like a pro. And yes, fish for protein and all those greens was starting to get monotonous, but the cereals were beginning to ripen, as were the beans and groundnuts and roots. They already had an abundance: an abundance that Brack hadn't so much as touched, not even a single leaf.

He gathered up a handful of empty sachets, reading the typed names on the outside of each one, and letting them fall to the ground afterwards. The same meals, over and over again. At some point, Brack was going to run out.

Frank started rummaging through the storage bins, trying to work out exactly how many days' food was left. There wasn't much: maybe a dozen packets, a few energy bars. Probably no more than a week's worth. There was a drawer in the kitchen area of the crew hab that had sachets of instant porridge they kept for emergencies, when they needed a quick hit of carbs, but there weren't many of those, either. Call it two weeks on short rations.

Then what?

Then Brack would have no choice but to eat produce grown in the greenhouse, even if he was going to prepare it himself. And as limited as the menu was, Frank had to concede that not only was it fresh and of good quality, it actually tasted of something, which he couldn't say of prison food which was mainly salty slurry. No wonder life expectancy in jail was so low: if the other cons didn't kill you, the diet eventually would.

So what did Brack expect to happen in just over a week that'd make it safe for him to suddenly start eating the greenhouse produce? Had he thought that far ahead? Frank forced himself to look at all the empty foil packs, really look at them. It was the detritus of an addict.

Brack wasn't thinking about much beyond the next pill.

What a mess. What a goddamn mess. He had two people at the base, at least one of whom was going to try to kill him, if he hadn't already tried and Frank had just not noticed because the attempt had been unsuccessful. And the man who was supposed to be the one who kept order, the one who was supposed to be on hand to sort this all out—the one he was relying on to get him back home—was reduced to this. Eating pap and scarfing down opiates.

Did XO know? Had they realized that their man had gone rogue? That the fate of Mars Base One was out of their hands, and had fallen, by virtue of being the last sane one standing, to Franklin Kittridge, construction worker and murderer?

He had to talk to Brack. Brack remained Frank's only hope of seeing his son again. So of course, he was going to have to do something. After all, he was really very good at that, wasn't he? All his previous attempts at intervention had led, failure by abject failure, to shooting his son's dealer dead in front of a crowd of witnesses.

Goddammit, Alice. She would have been able to do this. She had the right and the duty to intervene and overrule in medical matters. Instead, she was dead.

He looked up through the floor towards the top of the ship. Then he put his hands on the ladder and climbed up to where the sleep tanks were, arranged in pairs against the walls.

Four were open. Four were closed, and their controls were glowing.

He stood in front of the tank with the number one decal. Alice had been One. Dee had been Five. Marcy and Zeus, Six and Seven. Those were the tanks that were closed, and active.

He knew he shouldn't be opening them. He knew he shouldn't, but he knew he was going to try anyway, and he might as well get on with it. He knelt awkwardly down and looked at the controls. There didn't seem to be anything to press, though, and he realized they were probably all controlled by the ship's computer.

He fetched his tablet, and it automatically logged on to the ship's network. It had before, when he was looking for the cylinder containing the buggies, so why not now? He worked his way through various menus until he thought he might have found the right one, and then drilled down into it. Eventually, a schematic of eight boxes appeared, each with a status bar above it. It was the same: one, five, six and seven were working, while two through four—and eight—were offline.

He pressed box one. The information presented to him was confusing—he didn't know what much of it meant, but he could make out that the temperature inside the tank was just above freezing, and it was in something called preserve mode.

He took it out of preserve, and the drop-down gave him the option to open.

He needed to see it with his own eyes. He dabbed at Open, and immediately the lights on the tank began to blink. They blinked for a while, and then there was an audible click through the thin air of the ship.

He opened the lid, enough that he could be sure, and then pushed it down again.

He tried not to think about anything before returning the tank to preserve mode, and the lights returned to steady.

Alice was in the tank, white-skinned, cold.

He'd thought that Brack had buried her. Buried them all. Why had he thought that? Had Brack actually told them that, or had he just let them think it? Marcy, choked and smeared with her own vomit, Zeus—whatever state he was in, with ruptured lungs and eyes and ears, skin purple with bruising and desiccated as the water had simultaneously boiled and frozen inside him, Dee, scarlet and asphyxiated.

They were all there, back in their tanks, as if this was a morgue. So who the hell chose to sleep in a morgue?

Frank wiped his tablet screen and climbed back down to the first floor.

He'd talk to Brack, try and get him to stop. If that didn't work, he'd have to talk to XO: explain the situation, and get some help. Some advice at least, because help was a hundred million miles away and the distance still didn't seem real.

Wherever Brack was, though, he wasn't coming back in a hurry. Maybe he was just driving around in the crater, trying to avoid spending time in the ship.

If there was a locator on Brack's suit, all he had to do was tab up the map and find it. Which he did.

Nothing. If there was a signal, he was blocked from seeing it. Brack could literally be anywhere. Untrackable, untraceable. Almost ... as if this was deliberate.

He closed up his tablet and with a last, almost embarrassed, look around, he swapped out his life support and climbed back into his suit. Once outside, he decided that the best he could do was drive to the edge of the Heights so he could look down into the crater, and see if he could spot Brack.

The view hadn't changed for, Frank was guessing, thousands of years. Then in a few short months, humans had put their marks all over it. Tire tracks, repeatedly driven routes that subtly altered the landscape and made a track, a path, and eventually a road across the pristine wilderness.

There was such a road down from the Heights to Sunset Boulevard below, a worn, compacted trail down the red ocher slope. And at the bottom, three white cargo cylinders that had no right to be there at all.

For a moment, he thought that they might be the same ones that he'd hauled to the vicinity of the ship, with Dee, what felt like a lifetime ago. But he'd just seen those. These were new: ones that had been missed from earlier.

But Frank hadn't missed any from earlier. He'd collected—with enormous difficulty and considerable risk—every last one that had been marked on his map. If they weren't on his map, though, if they had damaged transponders, he'd never have found them on the plains. It had been hard enough finding the ones he did have co-ordinates for.

His letters. His books. They might be down there. Why hadn't Brack said anything, though? And if these weren't part of their consignment, whose were they? Having warned them off "space piracy", had Brack done exactly that? Except the cylinders, pale and pink in the evening light, looked just like XO deliveries.

There was no sign of the second buggy, no telltale ground-level cloud of dust. Frank had the time to go and check the cylinders for himself. Part of him still feared discovery. He felt he had to be good, to earn his jailer's trust and confidence, to prove himself worthy of that seat home.

But the feral part of his mind, the part that was stirred up and buzzing with wild, incoherent thoughts, was still telling him he was going to die here. Maybe not today, perhaps not tomorrow, but one day. He would die on Mars and that would be that. No homecoming. No parole board. No feeling the raw, unfiltered sun on his face and the warmth in his bones. No tentative walk up an unfamiliar driveway to a screen door and a hesitant press of the bell push.

He pointed the buggy down the slope and drove all the way to the bottom, parking up next to the nearest of the three cylinders. He ran his hand over the casing, checking to see how much dust had accumulated on the white, plasticky paint. Some, but not much. It didn't appear to have been sitting out in the desert for that long. The XO logo was still clearly visible on the side.

He undid the hatches manually, the tool for that being back at the base. It was awkward for one person to do it, but he did it in stages, and managed to pop one half of it open. He had to fight through the usual layers of insulation and packaging to get to the drums inside, but he was eventually able to see what the labels said.

NASA. Each one was stickered and sealed with vinyl labels with the NASA logo, a QR code, several serial numbers and a brief description of the contents. Science Experiment (Biology) 4B Part 2 of 7. Technical Equipment (Geology) 2F Part 1 of 3. Environmental Equipment (Atmosphere) 36G Part 1 of 1

This was a regular delivery. At least some of the descents he'd seen, and heard, had been these. So why hadn't he been dispatched to bring it back? Was it because it was deemed he was too busy working on the base, or because Brack was bored?

Brack had contributed nothing to the building or the running of the base. Why start now? Why go out, on his own, three—four, because that was surely what he was doing now—times, to collect cargo drops that weren't logged on the system?

Because the cons weren't supposed to know about them? Why would that be? There was nothing in the delivery Frank had opened to indicate any sort of contraband or dangerous chemicals or equipment that they might use to turn on each other. Certainly no more dangerous than the well-stocked pharmacy they already had.

Frank's hand went to the pouch of patches, where the surgical instruments he'd taken sat. He patted them.

If XO were sending NASA packages, it could only mean that the astronauts were coming soon. Highly trained scientists and explorers and pilots would be stepping into an environment where there was almost certainly a murderer, and potentially two. Was that why Brack hadn't told them, why Brack had kept all this secret? Why he was taking pills and sleeping in the ship? He didn't know which of them was the killer. He'd seen his crew whittled down from seven to three, and XO were going to be riding his tail, demanding he take charge and find the culprits out.

They had billions of dollars riding on being able to provide a safe working environment for the NASA people. That had to bring its own, almost unimaginable, pressures.

Frank pushed the insulation back into place, and hauled down on the hatch to close it. He retightened the restraining bolts, and as an afterthought threw a double-handful of dust high over the cylinder to obscure his hand-marks. He wasn't quite sure why he did that. He wasn't really snooping: he was helping.

He drove back up to the Heights still not knowing what to do. If Declan and Zero had conspired together, or even if they hadn't and were acting independently of each other, then they both needed to be stopped.

Stopped. There was only one way to stop them. Brack knew that, and it was about time Frank accepted it too. His buggy passed the ship, and began to close the distance to the base. Brack was still nowhere to be seen, but sunset was due in about two hours. There was going to be a confrontation, whatever time he showed up. Would Declan try and blame Zero, and vice versa, or would they gang up on Frank and pin everything on him?

Frank was pretty sure of his ground—he knew he wasn't responsible—and he couldn't have played any part in the deaths of either Zeus or Dee. Or Marcy or Alice, no matter what Declan said. Those were nothing to do with him. He didn't want any of them dead. Even if that was what was going to happen in the end.

He saw the base in the distance, the white habs reflecting a paler pink from the red ground. Someone was outside, suit lights visible as glowing colored bars where the suit itself merged into the background.

Frank slowed to a stop, and took out the surgical pack from the pouch.

It was designed to be ripped open by fingers in latex gloves, not spacesuit gloves, but the clear plastic covering over the sterile instruments could be pierced by the pointier of the tools. He used the forceps to break a hole in the package, and widened it by flexing them back and forth until it had torn through half the width.

He pushed the scalpel, still with its plastic guard, along the backing foil and into his hand.

283

It had a tiny blade, no more than an inch long, but it was wickedly sharp. The handle was slim and ridged, but designed for downward pressure, not for stabbing. He took a slap-patch from the pouch and held it up against the knife. It would do. He carefully tore off the backing—something that was purposely made to be handled with spacesuit gloves—and adhered the handle to one end of the patch.

He rolled it up tightly, making a fat, flexible grip which wouldn't slip through his hand, but which left the blade naked. It'd get blunt quickly, but he only needed it, if he did actually need it, to stay keen for a short while. He knew how to work a shank, in and out, fast and repeatedly, like a sewing machine needle.

The other two would have access to the kitchen knives and the medical supplies as well as the gardening snips and shears. He supposed that by now they were both armed. They'd probably guess he was too.

He made sure the blade guard was clipped on before he returned his knife to the bag. The rest of the surgical tools went in tucked underneath it, so he could just reach in and grab it.

He wasn't a killer. He kept on telling himself that. He was just defending himself. He just wanted to stay alive long enough to go home.

Frank tabbed his suit controls and reactivated his microphone. "Declan? Zero? I'm coming in. I think we need to talk."

26

[Private diary of Bruno Tiller, entry under 3/22/2047, transcribed from paper-only copy]

Do you know what they're calling them? Chimps. It's extraordinary the way people will treat each other when they're given permission.

And I have given them permission. It makes it easier. It always makes it easier.

They met around the kitchen table in the crew quarters. Declan was standing at one end, Zero in the middle on the far side, so that when Frank stepped into the hab, he had a natural place at the other end of the table.

He took the chair, pulled it slowly out, eyeing up the others. "I'll sit if you will."

"Sure, why not?" Declan nodded. "All we're going to do is talk, right?"

Frank reached into his pocket, and saw where the others touched their overalls. They were all tooled up, for certain. Frank's knife was in his other pocket: he could feel the hard mass of it through the fabric. He pulled out the blue latex glove and tossed it onto the table in front of him. It landed like a stranded jellyfish, limp and shapeless.

Then he sat, perched on the edge of his seat, ready to spring up at a moment's notice. Declan and Zero did the same.

"So who's going first?" asked Frank.

"Why not you?" said Declan. "You're the one playing cop. Isn't that right?"

Zero's gaze darted between the two older men. "What's going on? What d'you mean, cop?"

"It's a fair question, Frank. Why don't you answer him?"

"Zeus ... died. I thought it was my fault, something I had or hadn't done. Some structural problem with the workshop. I had to check it out. That's when I realized that the hab was perfectly sound. No leaks, no way that it could leak. Nothing that would have depressurized the whole thing quickly enough to catch Zeus out."

"So you went worrying at it like a dog with a bone, right? Trying to prove you weren't at fault."

"And I discovered that there were a couple of ways you could do it, but both of them were deliberate sabotage. You had to really want to do it. Someone really wanted to kill Zeus."

Declan placed both hands on the table between them. "You told Brack, of course."

"I told him."

"And what did you tell him, Frank?"

Zero bounced nervously in his seat. "Yeah, tell us, Frank. What did you say?"

Frank scratched at his chin. "I told him we had a murderer on the base."

"Why didn't you tell us too, Frank?" Declan's voice went very quiet. "Didn't you think we had a right to know?"

"Brack told me not to say anything. He didn't want to tip you off."

"Me?" Declan put his hand to his chest. "You thought it was me? Or did you think it was Zero here? Or maybe it was Dee?"

"It wasn't me, so it had to be one of you." Frank glared at the men alternately. "It still does. It's one of you. Or both of you. I don't know which."

"It wasn't me," said Declan. "Zero?"

286

"Not me. I'm not like that." Zero gripped the edge of the table and stared back at Frank. "You are, though. You killed someone, right?"

"That was—"

"Different? So let's look at this rationally." Declan counted off the corpses on his fingers. "Marcy run a couple of dozen people over after switching off her truck's autodrive. Alice euthanized God knows how many. Zeus sucker-punched someone in a bar."

"How the hell do you know all that?"

"I talk to people, Frank! And you shot someone; from our point of view, you're the only murderer left. To us, that looks like someone's taking out the opposition, the ones who might take you on."

"That's not what's happened."

Declan carried on regardless. "Then Dee, whose only crime is to hack various company computers and try and divert some cash his way—"

Zero shrugged. "I don't know: it was a lot of green, man. Maybe he was boasting, but what he was saying was more money than I ever made."

"Point is, Dee wasn't a killer. He was squeamish, for pity's sake." Declan folded down his thumb. "So who's next on the list, Frank? Me, or Zero? A white-collar pervert, or a gangbanging drug dealer. Who do you think's more dangerous?"

Frank clenched his jaw. "I've done nothing."

"You opened the door on Zeus, Frank."

"He was already dead. I wouldn't have been able to get that door open if the airlock had been pressurized."

"You can manually vent the airlock to the outside, just by pulling the lever. Come on, Frank, we did the same training as you did."

"But I didn't do that. And you were outside with me when Dee died. You saw me with your own eyes. I couldn't have been by the buggy at the same time as holding the Comms door shut. Could I?"

Declan screwed his face up. "Yeah. Well. Maybe that one was Zero."

Zero jerked back. "Fuck you, man. I didn't kill Dee."

"You didn't get on."

"Didn't mean I wanted to kill him."

"So who did?" Declan pointed at the other two. "Because, from where I'm sitting, I'm in the clear."

Several seconds of silence followed.

Frank cleared his throat. He should have brought his water bottle with him. "What if I'm wrong? What if they were both accidents?"

"But you don't believe that," said Declan. "You started all this because you didn't want to be responsible for killing Zeus. So which is it? Did the workshop depressurize because you installed something wrong, or not? What would you rather it was? A mistake, a catastrophic, fatal mistake that you made, or that one of us killed him?"

Frank pressed his palms against his legs. The scalpel blade's guard poked his thigh. "I checked the hab. It was sound."

"So it wasn't an accident. Someone killed Zeus."

"Someone killed Zeus," echoed Frank. "One of you two. And then killed Dee."

Zero pushed himself back from the table. "I've had enough of this, man. I killed no one. You two want to fight it out, go ahead. Tell me when you're done."

"You can say that," said Declan. "And we can say, you could have got to Zeus, and you're the only one who could have done for Dee."

"I don't leave the base!"

"I was outside with Declan," said Frank. "You were the only one inside with Dee. And you've got an airlock at the far end of the greenhouse. No one would ever see you go out, or come back."

Zero stood up, and his chair bounced away behind him, against the soft wall of the hab and clattered to the floor. He pulled out a short curved knife and held it in a shaking hand out in front of him.

"I've done nothing. You're not going to pin this on me. I'll tell Brack who really did it."

"You got any evidence to back that up?" Declan remained impassive. "No, you don't. So sit down and shut up."

Zero hesitated. Then he picked up his chair, put it back on its legs and sat down again, well away from the table.

Frank rubbed at his face. "This is crazy. We all know that. If one of us killed Zeus and Dee, we're never going to admit it because of what Brack will do to us. That just leaves us sitting here, wondering who's going to get it next."

"None of us want to get spaced," conceded Declan, "any more than we wanted to go in the Hole. Which is pretty much why we're all here. We got tricked into this, and we have to make the best of it. But living like this? This isn't what I'd call living. We're all at the point where we're terrified to even close our eyes. Our suits might kill us, the air might kill us, there's all kinds of shit out there that'll kill us, and then there's the radiation giving us cancer and the reduced gravity thinning our bones."

"We've done a good thing, though," said Frank. "We built this. We had our problems but we came together and built this. We've done something we can be proud of. That'll make other people be proud of us."

"Which is why what's happening to us now makes no sense." Declan took a deep breath of the rarefied atmosphere. He reached into his own pocket and tossed a long, thin screwdriver on the table in front of him. "I'm tired of this shit. I'm betting you are, too."

"What are we going to do?" asked Zero, passing his knife from hand to hand. "It can't be none of us."

Frank pulled out his own blade and carefully laid it on the table. He knew what he had to do, but knew that if he wasn't very, very careful, he'd never get home. That he might never

289

get home was something that had been preying on his mind ever since waking up on that first morning on Mars.

"Do you think XO can listen to what we're saying?" he asked.

Declan glanced at Zero, and his knife. "When I plugged in the controls, I didn't put any mics in. Just the fire-control cameras."

They all looked up at the ceiling.

"There's these, too." Zero used his free hand to touch his sternum. "I don't know. I guess I just forget about it most days."

"Can we turn the comms off?" Frank felt his own chest, and the hard lump under his skin. "Dee said they were pretty much on automatic."

"The tracking is," said Declan. "But I can trip the fuse to the dish controls so that it stops. Doesn't mean that a satellite won't pick up a signal as it goes overhead."

"Can we point the dish at the volcano first?"

"I reckon. But why do we want to, Frank? Why do we want to cut ourselves off?"

"Because we've got things to talk about. I've got things to talk about. I don't want anyone outside this room hearing me."

"I'll go and do it," said Declan. "OK with you, Zero?"

"Whatever. We can't get into any more shit than we are, right?"

Declan's hand hovered over the screwdriver on the table. In the end, he picked it up and pocketed it before heading towards Comms/Control. "Back in a minute."

Frank and Zero sat there, impatiently tapping and scratching and shifting while they waited for Declan to return. It wasn't long, but it felt like an age. He came back, sat in his chair, and put the screwdriver in front of him again.

"We're offline until we power up the dish again," he said. "What did you want to say that you don't want XO to know?"

Frank pressed his hands together. They were slippery with sweat.

"I went over to the ship. I wanted to talk to Brack—about you two. I know I didn't kill Zeus, or Dee, or Marcy or Alice. I was certain it had to be one or both of you. Declan, you killed Zeus. Zero, you killed Dee. I was going to tell Brack he had to space both of you, to save the mission, save the base."

"Well fuck you, Frank. Fuck you very much." Declan swept up his screwdriver and examined the point. Zero just stared, mouth open.

"He wasn't there. He'd taken a buggy, out on to the plain. To bring back a cylinder."

"What cylinder?" Zero rocked forward. "What are you talking about? We got all the cargo."

"Some of that shit falling from the sky was NASA stuff," said Frank. "He's storing three of them down at the bottom of the Heights. I opened one of them up. I also checked out the ship. It's … he's put all the bodies in the tanks. The floor's covered with empty Oxycontin packs." He took a moment's pause and looked down at his lap. "Before we left Earth, we—me and Brack—had a conversation. He said …"

A silence deepened.

"What did he say, Frank?" asked Declan.

"He said that if I watched his back for him, I'd get a seat on the NASA ship home. And if I told anyone about that, the deal was off."

"Shit."

"Fuck."

"I told him I'd find out who the killer was. Told him I'd find the evidence."

"Me too," said Declan.

Frank went cold. He could feel a knot tighten inside his guts and everything went very still.

"What?"

"Exactly what he told me. Watch his back, free trip home. And I'm guessing Zero's the same. Am I right?"

Zero gripped his knife hard and stabbed down at the tabletop. The curved point dug in and scored a line in the plastic.

"I'll take that as a yes." Declan spun the screwdriver, and

291

watched it whirl around on the table. The blade rotated until it came to a rest, aiming back at him. He picked it up and pushed it back into his pocket. "So what have we got?"

"What have we got? We've got jack," said Zero. "He's not going to get us all home, is he? He lied to us. And one of us is still a fucking murderer!"

"Yeah. About that," said Declan. "Anyone else joined the dots yet?"

Frank stood up. "I'm going to suit up. I suggest everyone else does the same."

Zero stabbed at the table again. "Will someone tell me what the fuck is going on?"

"It's Brack," said Frank. "He's gone postal."

"You're kidding me, right?"

"No."

Declan headed towards the cross-hab. "Maybe the freezing process messed with his mind. Maybe it's the drugs, the lone-liness, the stress. Maybe he's just fucking nuts. But I'm putting my spacesuit on, right now, before I do anything else."

Frank was left with Zero. "Come on," he said. "We'll think of something."

A muscle in Zero's lean face was jumping, right along the jaw-line. "I'm never going to get home, am I?"

"There's three of us, and only one of him. Maybe we can put him back in his tank, refreeze him, until help gets here. The NASA astronauts can't be far behind: all their kit's turned up. We'll be OK. Now, suit."

Zero looked at the curved edge of the gardening knife. "I trusted the Man. How else was this going to go down?"

"We've got to play this cool. We'll call up XO, we'll tell them we've got a problem, and we'll wait for instructions."

"We don't even know for sure! How do I know anything any more? This could be you and Declan doing the dirty on me. And where's Brack now?"

"We can't know: he's off the grid. He's always been off the

grid." Frank picked up the scalpel. "We've got to get into our suits, Zero. We'll be at least a little bit safer in them than not."

Zero started to cry. "What are we going to do?"

"We're going to do what we've done for the last few months, and when we were in training. Look out for each other and stay together." Frank was about to tell Zero to put the knife down, but he was holding his, and they might still need them after all. "You're not going to get left behind. All right? I won't let you. Forget what we promised Brack: we'll stick together, make them take us all home."

"Does that mean he killed Marcy? Alice?"

"I don't know. Yes, maybe."

Declan's voice cut through their conversation. "You are not leaving me to face Brack on my own. Get your goddamn asses in here and get your suits on."

Frank felt light, trembly, even inexplicably hungry. "He's right. We'll talk again in a minute. Now, come on."

He stood back when Zero walked by on his way to the door. The kid was still as twitchy as a cornered dog, and likely to lash out at anything. He was right—they didn't know anything—but none of this felt right any more.

This was their home: they'd built it, lived in it, died for it.

The main lights abruptly failed.

They were replaced a moment later by the emergency lighting, a hard blue wash over everything that left everything either black or glowing.

"Jesus, give me a break," he heard Declan say.

Frank went to put his suit on.

There was enough space for the three of them to dress simultaneously. Frank pulled his suit off the hanger, turned it around, grabbed a life support from the rack—no time to see whether it was full or still recharging—pushed it into place, turned it on, and without taking his overalls off, got his left leg in, his right leg in, hauled the suit up to his waist, pushed his left arm in, his right arm in, ducked down and squeezed his head through the

293

neck seal. He worked his fingers into the gloves and checked that nothing was pinched or tight by bouncing up and down on the spot. He opened the suit controls, thumbed the back-hatch closed and felt the reassuring deadening of sound as it sealed and locked in place.

The suit whispered air into his face, and he turned the suit lights on full. A blue-white glow diffused into the cross-hab. Declan was almost as fast as he was, but Zero wasn't as practiced. It took him longer, and by the time his suit was sealed, he was breathing hard.

Frank put his helmet against Zero's.

"In, and hold it. Hold, hold, hold. And out, nice and slow. In again. Hold, hold, hold. And out."

He looked inside, and Zero nodded.

"I'm Ok. I'm fine."

Frank bent awkwardly down, and picked up the scalpel. As well as the tablet and nut runner attached to his suit's utility belt, he still had the pouch of patches. He eased the blade back in. "Let's get the lights back on, and then phone home. We'll be OK. Hang in there."

27

[Transcript of private phone call between Bruno Tiller and (unidentified XO employee 1) 8/13/2047 1550MT.]

BT: No, we collect their personal effects and we incinerate them at Gold Hill. Nothing leaves the facility.
XO1: OK. Whatever works for you.
BT: At eighty kilobucks (80000) a pound, I've not budgeted spending over a million (1000000) dollars on shipping their shit with them. They don't need it, and won't need it.
XO1: Do I tell them that?
BT: No, you don't tell them that.
[transcript ends]

They got the power back on, and clustered around the comms console.

"How far away is Earth now?" asked Frank.

"I don't actually know. Eight, ten minutes? It could be at least half an hour before we get a reply." Declan typed in the commands for the dish to seek out the orbiting satellite and let it run. As ever, he kept an eye on the power meter, watching it crawl down. The sun was setting, and they were on batteries until dawn.

"We could be dead by then," said Zero.

"No one is going to die. We're staying together."

"Actual astronauts have something like five years' training." Declan watched the numbers. "We got barely six months. What the hell were we thinking?"

"We got enough to do the job," said Frank.

"Just."

"Are we on yet?" Zero pushed forward. "What do we do when we are? What do we say? Is there anyone going to be listening to us?"

"Just give it a few more seconds," Declan eased Zero back. "It's got to find the signal, lock on, then we can transmit."

"Why's it taking so long?"

"It always takes this long." Declan pointed to the screen. "It's doing it now."

A square on the screen went from red to green.

Frank opened up his tablet, and looked again for the second buggy. Still nothing.

"We have no idea where he is." He turned it so that the others could see. "He could be miles away. He could be outside."

Zero turned and looked behind him. "He could be here. He could be here right now."

"Maybe," said Frank. "But we don't want to get into a fight with him. He's sick: we need to find a way to make him better."

"Frank, he's killed at least two people, and maybe four," said Declan, "and you want to find a way to make him better? Good luck with that, because if he comes at me, I'm not going to be messing around. Anyway, if he thinks he can just disappear, we can all play at that game. Switch your transmitters off."

"Wait, we can do that?" said Frank. "I thought it was just the mics."

"Jesus, Frank, get up to speed. It's always been the case. Just that we chose not to, so that XO wouldn't know we were having private conversations." Declan pushed the chair out of the way of the console. "Go and stand watch by the door. I'll type out a message."

Frank and Zero tabbed through their suits' menus and turned their suit comms off. When they'd done, Frank looked through the door that led into the yard, then went a little further and stood in the big, open space. There should have been gym equipment, but there'd been nothing in the supplies they'd got so far.

Perhaps it was down in the new cylinders, ready to install when NASA got here. Frank walked a little further, towards the kitchen. He could see the table through the open doors, and something had caught his eye.

"Where you going, man?" asked Zero.

Frank waved him back. "Just ... wait there."

He stood in the doorway, checked as best he could there was no one there, and came back carrying the blue glove. He held it out, and Zero took it from him.

"Are we losing air?" He gave the glove a squeeze. It did seem plumper than before.

Frank opened his suit controls and checked the external pressure. It should have been five psi. It was four point three.

"We're depressurizing."

"Fuck. He's outside, isn't he?"

"And we're inside, in our suits. We're fine."

"But the greenhouse."

"The greenhouse is on a separate system. It'll be fine, too. Brack, even crazy Brack, won't touch that."

"I need to go check."

"No, you don't. If you're going to check, we all go and check." Frank held Zero by the shoulders. "We don't split up. Got that?"

"What's going on?" called Declan.

"We're losing pressure."

"Deliberately?"

"What do you think?"

"OK, give me a minute. Typing is hard in these gloves."

Zero tore himself away and leaned into Comms. "Just speak it. Use the mic."

"It's not that easy. We got bandwidth and compression issues. Text is certain, like sending a phone message when you've got no data signal. Almost there. And ... send."

297

Declan pushed Zero ahead of him.

"So what did you say?"

"Help, mostly. Explained we were four crew down, Brack chowing down on opioids like they're popping candy, and that he's working his way through the rest of us like virgin teens in a slasher movie. I don't know what they're going to suggest. We were, and are, always going to be on our own." Declan looked up at Frank. "You know what it means."

Frank had tried. He'd tried everything. And now, for the second time in his life, he was going to have to solve his problems the hard way. "I know what it means. That we're going to have to find him and stop him before he damages the base."

"Fuck no," said Zero. "We're not doing that. You said we weren't going to have to fight."

"That was before he started depressurizing the habs. He could sabotage the water, the power, anything. He could just cut through the greenhouse wall and bang." Frank pulled out his knife, and slid off the plastic guard. "It's starve or suffocate. Declan's right: Brack's left us no choice."

"Just ... stop, OK?" Zero backed away from them both, holding the sides of his helmet. "Brack said to all of us that we could go home with him. What if, what if, one of you is making that happen. That you know if you're the last man, you get that ride."

"Who the hell is depressurizing the hab, Zero?" Declan pointed to the slowly inflating glove that Zero still held.

"It could have been Frank, before he came in. It's Frank. It's you, isn't it? You're killing us off so that you get to go home." Zero threw the glove on the floor. It bounced rather than flopped. He looked for his knife, but couldn't remember what he'd done with it. He backed away further, then ran for the cross-hab. "Shit. Where's my shank?"

"It's not me," said Frank.

"It's what a killer would say," said Declan. His voice was thinner now the air was leaking away. "Just kidding. We should go after him, make sure he's OK."

"After you."

"Well, thanks."

But when they got to the cross-hab, Zero wasn't there. And the gardening knife, if he'd dropped it, wasn't there either.

"Zero? Zero?"

"Where did he go? Greenhouse?" Frank inspected the airlock, and tried to cycle it. "That's ... not working." He tried it again, and peered at the telltales. "Inner door not closed. He's chocked it open so we can't get in."

Declan hammered his fist on the outer door. "Zero?" Then he turned to Frank. "The only way we're getting in this lock is if I pull the fuses. Jesus, why does everything have to be so complicated?"

"He's just a kid. He's scared."

"And now he's scared and alone. At least, I hope he's alone."

"He doesn't trust us. Me." Frank lent his own hand to pummeling the airlock door. "This isn't working. And we can't vent this anyway without trashing the plants."

"No shit. It's not like we can slide a note through, either. And we still have to find Brack."

"Inside or outside?"

"I don't know. It's not like I've ever done this before."

Frank looked along the cross-hab at the medical bay. "Start down there, work our way back to here, I guess."

Everything that once looked used and familiar, now looked empty and strange: the stacked boxes, the rattling of the floor, the ladders down to the first floor, the bright overhead lights. They walked the length of the top floor, and back along underneath. It was growing gradually more and more silent.

"Where's the leak?" asked Declan.

"It'll be one of the airlocks. We should check them all." Frank cycled the nearest, and checked inside. The manual vents were all shut.

But when they went back down to the other, the controls had obviously been forced. Frank pushed the levers back up and stopped the flow. He nudged the last panel shut with his knee.

"We still need to check the others," said Declan.

"Sure. How long's it been since you sent the message?"

"Five, ten minutes."

"How can we be so far away that it takes ten minutes just for a text to get there?"

Declan stopped mid-stride. "Frank? You say some really stupid shit sometimes."

"We went to sleep on Earth. We woke up on Mars. If we'd actually traveled the distance, I might understand it better." Frank checked the external pressure. "Three point nine. We might have stopped it in time."

"Crew hab?"

They checked downstairs in the cross-hab, just a storage area, but congested with boxes. Upstairs, the airlock was fine, so they went back into the kitchen, and through to the crew quarters. The curtained-off rooms were still and silent.

"I'll do these, you do the cans," said Frank.

The toilets were at the far end. Declan brandished his screwdriver and moved swiftly down the corridor, leaving Frank to flick each curtain aside and peer around. Nothing, and no one.

"Clear," said Declan, and turned round to look at the airlock. "OK, this one's been tampered with." He moved the first lever, and pulled open the door to set the second.

"While we're doing this, he could be at the other side of the base, opening them again." Frank clenched his jaw. "We're going to have to go out and find him. Aren't we?"

"A base, made for people who want to live on Mars, not die on Mars: who would have thought it? We're going to have to go out, yes. Be easier with Zero, though."

"Try him again?"

"What's the point? We'll just have to do it without him."

"We'll go out through the lock at the end of the yard. Circle around."

"That's a terrible plan, Frank. We've got a buggy. The

buggy's got lights. We climb up and turn it round. Then we light this sucker up from a distance. How does that sound?"

"I like yours better."

They moved swiftly through the kitchen into the yard, and into the airlock at the far end. It was a squeeze, but they could just about both fit. It was only after Declan had closed the door behind him and the airlock was cycling through, that Frank realized if Declan did want to stick him with the screwdriver, there was very little he could do about it until the pressure equalized. The hard torso and helmet would stand up to some force, but his arms were in range.

It was an exercise in trust, being in such a confined space.

The airlock lights winked green. Frank opened the door and shuffled out onto the platform. There was the buggy—one of them—over by the workshop. He couldn't see the other one, but he couldn't see much at all. While they were inside, the sun had set, and it was those few minutes of dusk before pitch-black night.

With their suit lights off, they ran directly away from the base, using their fastest skipping gait, then angled towards the buggy. They both arrived and ducked down behind one of the wheels.

With touching helmets, Declan said, "You drive. You're better at it. I'll spot."

"OK. Go."

Frank climbed up, hand over hand, and turned on the fuel cell. The console came alive, and he quickly tabbed up the lights. A wash of bright white light spilled out across the landscape. The shadows were long and dark, and moving dust glittered in the beams. He took hold of the controls and started to squeeze them, when he realized that Declan wasn't on the back of the buggy.

It was impossible to turn round, so he stood up and twisted, holding on to the top of the roll cage.

Something tugged at his arm. He looked at it, and smoke was drifting from a sudden hole in the external covering just up by

301

his biceps. He registered a twinge of cold, and he put his other hand over the rent.

He'd been shot.

He leaped from the seat, and didn't care much where he was going to land. He was silhouetted against the still-glowing horizon and literally a sitting target. He landed on his feet, but he kept on falling, forwards and down. He rolled his shoulder under him, and skidded to a halt in the hard-packed dirt. His carapace had crunched down on several rocks, but he'd managed to turn his faceplate away.

Alarms were sounding inside his helmet. He was losing pressure. He might be losing blood, too, but there was no way of knowing. He sat up, and clapped his hand hard over where he presumed the hole to be.

He had to stop the leak in his suit. He had a scalpel. He had patches. Without taking his hand away, he managed to empty the contents of the pouch on the sand. He picked up the knife, moved his hand, cut the cloth into a larger rent, then chose the smallest patch he had.

Calm. Cold, calculating calm. There'd be time for panic later. Peel the backing. Slap it into place. Feel the suit reinflate around him.

Frank fleetingly remembered that locked flight case Brack had brought with him when he installed himself in the consultation room in the med bay. He'd brought a gun to Mars.

At least the alarms had stopped, and he could breathe again.

Who the hell brought a gun to Mars?

Someone tasked with overseeing a bunch of convicted criminals doing a complex, dangerous job and maybe not getting on so well with each other when things went wrong, that's who.

Where was Declan? It was almost full dark, and the suit lights that would have helped Frank find him would also have made them an easy target. The buggy's headlights were shining out across the Heights, catching the edge of Comms/Control and the yard in the beam, with little spillover.

There he was, exactly in the shadow cast by the big plated wheel. Frank scurried over, keeping a low, ungainly crawl like a beetle. Declan was face down in the dirt, and he wasn't moving. Frank leaned in and touched helmets. "Declan? You in there?"

All he could hear was the same jangle of alarms that he'd just endured.

He dragged him over, the bulky suit losing against necessity and effort.

Declan's faceplate had gone. Just ragged shards around the edge, framing the still-smoking ruin inside. All the emergency lights were flashing, and moisture was boiling and freezing and boiling again in spirals and jets.

"Goddammit."

There'd been at least two shots, and he'd heard neither. Brack could be shooting at him now, and he probably wouldn't realize.

He pushed up against the disc of the wheel and looked around the side, under the latticework of the buggy. Brack had to be somewhere close by the base.

Zero was inside. Frank was outside. Brack … there? The figure emerged from the gap between Comms/Control and the med bay, arm extended ahead of it, something flat, black and mean in the glove. One step. Two steps. Perhaps he thought he'd got them both, but he clearly wasn't sure. He couldn't see either of them.

Frank's scalpel was somewhere in the sand, with the rest of the patches. He had the nut runner, which was heavy but wasn't weighted right. It was the only weapon he had, though, and he filled his hand with it.

Then the figure retreated back towards the main airlock, quickly disappearing from sight.

Frank panted for a few breaths. He had to come up with something, and quick. Brack—he assumed it was Brack—had gone full-on psycho. There was no help coming. They were alone on Mars. He had, and he checked, six and a half hours of air left: that was less than he'd anticipated, but he'd been using

303

it up faster, what with all the fear and running and jumping at shadows.

He didn't even know if Zero was still alive. It could be just him against Brack. So much for the promised trip home, a trip that apparently had been promised to all of them, a promise that could never have been fulfilled.

It was there, crouched behind the pitted wheel of a buggy he'd helped put together, on the surface of Mars, while the body of one of his colleagues froze into the red soil in the Martian night, that he suddenly and finally realized the utter depth of his betrayal.

It wasn't that none of them were ever meant to go home. It was that none of them were ever meant to survive.

Well. Frank was going to have to see about that.

28

[transcript of audio file #145816 10/16/2047 0930MT XO Mission Control, White Sands Missile Range NM]

PL: What you've done is nothing short of incredible, Bruno. I'm thrilled, and amazed, and deeply, deeply grateful. XO couldn't have done this without you.

BT: I wanted to hear you say that. I wanted to hear your approval. It means so much to me.

PL: He's on his way, our glorious, noble astronaut. Ready to tend and nurture our investment, and ensure our successful completion of our contract. Lance Brack, I salute you, and your lonely months on Mars.

BT: He's undergone years of rigorous training and psychological evaluations. He is literally the best man for the job. He'll get it done, don't you worry.

PL: What would you like to do now, Bruno? In the next few months, while we're waiting for him to arrive.

BT: I'm not going to stop, Paul. Why would I stop? We have everything in place: the people, the plant, the production. We just keep launching.

PL: [pause] I know we were under budget, but ...

BT: We have the money. Mars is within our reach, if only we're bold enough to reach out and take it.

PL: I don't understand, Bruno. We need to clear this with the board.

BT: I have cleared it with the board. They're all onside. Are you?
[transcript ends]

Frank couldn't hear anything except his own heartbeat in his ears and the hoarseness of his own breath. The gloves, the suit, the boots, the helmet, isolated him from anything in the environment that might give him clues as to what was going on around him. He was relying completely on one sense: sight. And even his peripheral vision was non-existent.

He kept watch on the base, and opened up his tablet. No signal. It couldn't sync, and it was because his own suit transmitter was off. That might be why Brack had retreated inside—Frank's suit wouldn't give away his location, and he wasn't close enough for the telltale hidden in his chest to broadcast either.

As soon as he approached the base, the system would automatically pick him up, and even if it didn't light him up on the map, it'd push his vital signs into the medical monitor. It would tell Brack he was both alive and close, rather than as he currently was, in limbo.

Of course, Brack could afford to wait him out. He had the base. He could do pretty much anything he wanted now. He knew that Frank would have to come to him, and he'd know when that happened.

So, in order: Marcy. That could have been an accident. They were at full stretch that day, and they both knew they were low on air. But the scrubber in Marcy's life support had failed first, and it could absorb waste gases for much longer than there was air. That was suspicious.

Then Alice. Alice was the smartest one on board. She was professional and knowledgeable and didn't take shit from anyone. Yet once they were all defrosted, her work was over. In fact, she became a liability because she knew so much. She'd have spotted Brack's painkiller addiction simply by counting the pills.

It left them short-handed to build the base, but there were no more deaths until it was done. Being two people down eased the food situation hugely. It would have been tight, starvation-tight, with eight mouths to feed, and it was no coincidence that they'd just squeaked it with six. Marcy and Alice had been culled, taking out enough of the crew to make the food go around. That the first two they lost were the two women? That, surely, wasn't going to be a coincidence either.

Goddammit, Brack.

Zeus was next. Zeus was both physically strong and knew how to fight. He was also someone who would have felt it his duty to protect the others. He'd already done his job, and more, with the installation of the central heating. His dream of a steam engine had died with him, but maybe there were more panels in the stuff XO was sending later. They didn't need his generator, and they didn't need him.

Dee. Dee was just a perpetual victim. He'd set up all the control systems, and maybe he'd seen things he shouldn't have in the tech manuals. XO probably knew what he'd been reading. Maybe he was a threat after all. So they'd got Brack to kill him next.

And how? It had been all too easy because no one had thought that the person going through the crew and picking them off, one by one, was the same person who was supposed to be overseeing their work, and making sure there was a functioning base to invite the NASA astronauts into when they finally arrived.

It would have been Frank and Declan and Zero next, whichever order Brack or XO wanted it done in, until all the convicts had gone. Except they'd ruined the planned order of execution by working out what was going on and talking to each other about it. The simplest thing—an honest conversation—had led to this. It had led to Frank hiding out in the frozen Martian night, not daring to approach the one place that he could live in.

Not that that was true. There was still the ship.

Brack had a gun, though, and the walls of the ship were going to be as much use as the walls of the habs at protecting him. Was there anything there he could use? Were there more guns, or at least better weapons than what he had currently? Probably not, and driving there would give away his position as much as it would going closer to the base.

All it would do would be to give him a different place in which to die.

It simply had to be here and now. At night, and on territory which he was at least familiar with. He had no advantages, and lots of problems. It still had to be done.

If Brack was still watching the buggy, then he might see Frank break cover. But there was a way around that. He left the shelter of the wheel, not hesitating, moving quickly, because a shot could come at any moment and he'd never know until it hit him. He grabbed one of the headlight array and turned it so that it shone directly at the space between the habs.

He couldn't see anyone lurking there. And now, with a bright light aimed straight into their eyes, they couldn't see him either.

If Brack wasn't psychotic, and just a cold-hearted killer, it actually counted in Frank's favor. There'd be only so much that he'd be prepared to bust up—only so much that he'd be prepared to let Frank bust up—before pulling his punches. And bullet holes in the hab skin were going to be difficult to explain away.

That settled it. He had to get inside, and fast. Close with Brack.

He couldn't let go of the buggy chassis. He wasn't the kind of guy who ran towards danger. He was deep-down scared. No, he was a coward. Last time, he'd chosen the easy way, the simple way, the pull-the-trigger way, just to make it stop, so that all the complex decisions he wouldn't make collapsed into one course he couldn't alter.

Being in jail had been so straightforward. He hadn't had to do or be anything other than a prisoner. What had he been thinking to come here, dreaming he might have a future rather than only a past? He'd allowed himself to hope. Idiot. All his choices were going to end in abject, painful failure. He was going to die tonight, and the only difference he'd make was which part of Mars he'd water with his blood.

He was still going to have to try, though. If not now, in a minute, in an hour. At some point, he'd convince himself that not doing it was worse than doing it, and he'd run the short distance to the med hab, wondering if the next bounding step would be his last.

His arm ached where the bullet had cut his suit. If he was just bruised, then OK. If he was bleeding, then things would only get worse.

So why not now? Why not go now?

He forced his hand open, and he was suddenly running, passing behind the buggy, covering the distance as fast as he could, kicking up dust with his heels.

He caught hold of the corner support leg and let himself swing around with his back to the hab. All of a hundred feet, and he hadn't died yet. The base's Wi-Fi would have picked up his heartbeat by now, so he needed to keep going. He ran down the line of supports, and around the back to the airlock there. He cycled it, stepped into the chamber, and cycled it again.

The suit relaxed around him.

Another choice to make: take it off, or keep it on? The suit controls told him that the pressure had stabilized at three point nine. Twenty per cent less than normal. Like standing on the top of a mountain. Yes, he'd be free to move and run and fight, but he'd be gasping like a stranded fish the whole time. And the suit was, to some degree, armored. Keep it on for now.

He gripped the door handle, and in one swift movement pushed it down and swung it open, hard, like a punch. There was no resistance. Brack wasn't behind the door.

It didn't mean he wasn't there somewhere, though.

The consulting room was just to his left, the usually locked door uncharacteristically ajar. Frank nudged it with his foot, and it slowly opened. Another bedroll sitting amid a sea of squalid filth, and an open metal flight case. The foam was cut out in the shape of a gun, and there were empty slots for magazines.

A metal-edged case would be useful as a club. He slid in, and bent down to close the lid and click the latches.

As he did so, he heard a faint noise, even though it was muffled through his helmet. A creak in the metal that wasn't due to night-time cooling. He knew what that sounded like, a steady tick-tick of contraction. This noise was a flex, the muted groan of someone trying to be stealthy.

Frank stayed perfectly still. He could just see through the door from where he was crouching. The light outside in the med bay dimmed slightly. The floor creaked again. He was there, right outside, looking up and down the length of the hab, trying to see if anything had moved.

Frank slowly slid his hand inside the flight case handle, and waited. He barely dared to blink, in case his lids rasped against his eyeballs.

Another creak, and he could see the very edge of an XO-issue overall. No spacesuit. He tightened his grip on the handle, and tensed his arm.

Then they turned, and their eyes opened wide as they spotted him.

Frank was already launching the open flight case at their head when he realized it wasn't Brack.

It was a direct hit. The case seemed to wrap around Zero's face, and the momentum and suddenness of the impact carried him backwards off his feet. He fell through a loose curtain and against one of the examination tables, sending it spinning and clattering through the med bay.

Frank scrambled to his feet. "Crap. I thought you were him."

Zero ripped the case from his face. He was bleeding—a cut on his brow, a cut across the bridge of his nose—and he came up still holding his knife.

He lunged at Frank's chest. The outside curve of the blade skittered across the hard shell of the torso and Frank managed to turn so that the cutting edge didn't slide into his arm. He forced Zero back with a two-handed shove that sent the lighter man flying down almost the entire length of the med bay.

The knife seemed welded into Zero's hand. He bounced up again, wiping blood out of his eye with his fingers.

"It's me," said Frank. "It's Frank. Look."

"I know who it is! I know what you've done. You killed everyone. Brack explained it all."

"No. He's lying to you. He just shot Declan in the face. He shot me." Frank pointed to his ragged sleeve. "He's not what you think he is."

"I'm going home with him. Just like he promised me."

"He promised that to everyone, Zero. Remember? Where is he? Where is he right now?"

"Gone to the ship, looking for you. And he'll be back here soon."

"We've got to stop him. Me and you. He's been working his way through the crew, and we're next. Those are his orders, Zero. His orders from XO. He has to get rid of us."

"That's not it. That's not it at all. It's you we have to get rid of." Zero, hand starting to tremble, advanced back down the hab. "Then we'll be safe."

Frank backed away as far as he could, which was only as far as the airlock behind him. "You don't understand. We're not meant to still be here when NASA turns up."

Zero was close enough to strike again, and he hesitated for too long, shifting his weight from one leg to another, feinting and dodging but never following through. Frank jabbed for Zero's eyes, trusting the suit to take whatever counter-blow came.

Zero tried to fend off Frank's first attack, and left himself completely open for the second. Frank's knee jerked up, caught Zero right in the groin, and Zero started to fold, the air pushed out of him in one short grunt.

Frank doubled down. He crowded Zero, using his weight and the hard surfaces of the suit to keep him moving backwards and off-balance. He finally managed to get his hand around Zero's wrist and wrenched his arm up.

Something went pop in his biceps and a bright flash of pain blinded him. Zero was able to brace his feet and push, and Frank toppled back onto his life support, Zero on top of him. They were still locked together, neither willing to let go of the other.

The low oxygen was taking its toll on Zero. His face was slick with sweat and blood. It dripped down onto Frank's faceplate as they both grimaced and groaned, Zero trying to turn the knife towards Frank, Frank straining to keep it away.

"I'm not your enemy," said Frank. "You've got it wrong."

"He said. He said."

"He lied. Everything we've been told is a lie."

Frank got his hand between them, and the pain was so intense, so sharp, he thought he was going to cry. He forced himself to push the hand upwards, into Zero's face, fat, gauntleted fingers probing for the eyes. Zero jerked his head away, but it meant that he wasn't concentrating on his knife hand for a moment. Frank slammed it into the deck, point-first, once, twice, and the third time it came good.

Zero's unprotected hand slid down the blade and it cut deep.

He gasped and choked, and tried to grab the handle again but couldn't because he couldn't grip any more and everything was slippery with blood.

He twisted his hand, and Frank wouldn't release him. The wound just opened up more.

There was no way that Frank could get up or roll over. The most he could do was rock side to side on the broad curve of the life support, which was worse than useless. He couldn't bring his legs up to get his knees between him and Zero. He was left with trying to lever his injured arm up and into Zero's face.

They were stuck. Neither could do anything to the other.

"You've got to believe me, Zero. I don't want to hurt you. Brack's the real enemy. Brack and XO."

"No, no, no. Brack wouldn't do that. Brack said he'd take me home." Zero tried to break out of Frank's grasp again, and squealed with pain. Not just pain. Anguish. Loss.

"You're doing his dirty work for him. You've got to understand that. I don't want to die here, so I'm only going to let you go if you tell me you believe me, and you're not going to try and hurt me. We can still work together. We can still beat him."

Zero's head slipped away from Frank's fingers and he brought his forehead down on Frank's faceplate. Hard.

The blow was shocking, surprising, stunning. It left smears of blood and bubbles across the major portion of Frank's view.

"Don't, Zero. Don't do this."

He did it again, just as hard. The impact jolted Frank. More blood. Frank was almost blind, his vision coated in a red, liquid film.

Again. He couldn't see. He couldn't see anything.

He let go of Zero's wrist and pushed as hard as he could. The weight on him, on his legs, left abruptly, and he brought his good hand up to scrape five lines through the gore.

Zero was all but unrecognizable. His face, his fine features, were mashed, broken, swollen, bruised. His hand was not just dripping but oozing, a continuous dribble of hot red liquid streaming off his fingertips.

Frank pushed himself to sitting, and awkwardly got a knee under his body.

The knife was on the floor, next to Frank. He saw Zero squint for it, trying to see through slits where it was. Frank reached for it, to push it away behind him, and Zero jumped him, howling.

Then he made a gagging sound. He pawed at Frank's helmet, patting at it with increasingly gentle taps, before falling still.

Frank heaved him off, and Zero slipped gracelessly to one side, his own knife buried between his ribs.

"I'm sorry. I'm sorry." He laid his hand on Zero's head. "I'm so sorry. I tried. God knows I tried, but you just wouldn't listen. I'm sorry."

And there was still Brack. He couldn't rest. Brack would know he was still alive. He'd still come for him. He wouldn't stop.

The inside of the med hab looked like an abattoir. There

was blood everywhere. Ceiling, walls, the furnishings, the floor. Especially the floor.

Frank knew what he was going to do. He hated himself. He hated that he couldn't just curl up and go to sleep for a hundred years, and wake up to find everything was fine again. He hated that he'd been forced into such extremes, and even then it might not be enough.

He opened his suit controls, and opened up the back-hatch. He took his last few breaths of good air, and dipped his head out into the cool thin atmosphere of the base. It smelled of copper. Sharp and sweet and metallic on his tongue.

His left arm came out OK. His right arm stuck, and there was nothing left to do but pull, slowly and surely, until it came free.

It was like tearing something off: that feeling of fear and trepidation as to just how much pain pulling that loose tooth, peeling back that Band-Aid, was going to deliver before the glorious moment that the task was over and it could stop now.

It left him weak and breathing hard. There was blood on his overall sleeve, a hole through it, but there wasn't as much as he'd anticipated. Perhaps the suit had helped, pressing against his skin, holding it all in.

He touched it, the jelly-like plug of blood in his arm, and he could feel the bullet as a solid mass partway into his muscle. He tried to squeeze around the area, push it out, but the flesh was just too tender and the bullet didn't seem to want to move.

He pulled his legs free, and he was standing in sticky blood.

He went to the box that he knew contained the sterile packs of medical instruments. He ripped a pack open, and wondered in which order to do things. He knew he didn't have much time, but neither did he want a bullet left in him.

He used the scissors to cut the cloth over the wound, making access easier. The hole in his arm was indented, like a crater. The skin around it was puffy and hot to the touch. The clot glistened darkly.

He loaded his undexterous left hand with the forceps. He

314

rested his arm on the shelf, braced his other elbow, and pressed the open jaws deep into the wound. He couldn't not look, and screwed his face up all the same.

Frank pulled, and the plug came sliding out, like the polyp of some sea creature. He felt cold. He couldn't faint now. He turned his head, swallowed hard, took some highly unsatisfactory breaths, and came back for the second round.

He could see it, metal washed with blood, at the very bottom. He panted. Then he lowered the forceps into his arm until the tip clinked against the bullet. He slowly opened the jaws until they slid around the circumference, and closed them again.

He gave an exploratory tug. He bit at his own lip until it bled. He panted again, clenched his teeth, and pulled.

It wasn't so much that it hurt. It was that it was coming from inside of him. He dropped the bullet onto the floor, and laid the forceps back on the shelf.

He felt strangely, inexplicably, good. High. The lack of oxygen, the pain which, perversely, made him feel so incredibly alive and abruptly nauseous. He still had something else to do.

He gagged, swallowed, steadied himself.

Unzipping the front of his overall revealed the shining scar over his sternum, no more than a glossy red circle the size of his little fingernail. The monitor was long and smooth and hard under his skin. He took up the scalpel, and wondered if he should swab before he cut.

No time. No time at all. He flicked off the cover and lined up the blade. He pushed it in, then dragged it along downwards. The monitor wasn't nearly as far down as the bullet. It almost popped out on its own. He teased it the rest of the way with the flat of the scalpel, and put it in his hand, tightly closed. He put the cover back over the scalpel and pocketed it, then hid the bloodied forceps and the opened pack of instruments back in the box.

He stood astride Zero's body and pushed his monitor into the boy's open mouth, pressing it between teeth and cheek.

"Sorry," he said again.

The wound in his arm and the wound in his chest were bleeding, but not much. Neither was going to kill him. He bundled up his spacesuit and threw it down the ladder to the floor below. Then he lay down next to Zero, turned and turned again until he was caked in blood. He was a little way into the med bay, face down, head away from the connecting corridor, with Zero between him and it. He sprawled his arms out, his legs too, in what he hoped was a natural repose for death.

It was the best he could manage. Now all he could do was wait.

29

[Private diary of Bruno Tiller, entry under 1/7/2048, transcribed from paper-only copy]

This is what it must feel like to be God. To be in total control of everything. I can tell people what to do, and they'll just do it. It's crazy. They're not even people any more: they're pawns on the board. What they want, what they think, just isn't important. I move them, they move. They don't have any choice. They can't move back. They can't decide for themselves—anything that I choose to do with them, they do.

What makes this so special is that my opponent doesn't even know they're playing. They're blind. They can't see their pieces, my pieces, or how they're arranged. They just wonder why they're losing. And if I decide it's in my strategic interests to sacrifice someone, then they get no say in that either. Slide them across the squares, and boom.

That is power, and don't I deserve it? After everything I've done for XO? My only regret—and it is my only regret—is that I couldn't share this with Paul. He was like a father to me. No, that's wrong. He was my father, my true father, the one I wanted to please and emulate and defend. Not that loser who was simply content with what life gave him. If I'd followed his advice I'd still be cutting lawns. Working for other people. Instead, they work, they live and die—and more—for me.

This company will be mine one day. One day soon. Can you imagine that, Dad? Because I don't think you can.

It took a long time. Frank drifted in and out of sleep, and every time he woke, he wondered how he could have possibly slept. He was adhered to the floor. The blood had soaked into his overalls, and dried. He was stiff and cold and uncomfortable, and still Brack didn't come.

A couple of times, he thought he needed to rethink his tactics, to get up and go on the attack, but playing dead was his one advantage: throwing that away because of impatience was stupid. So he stayed where he was, as still as he could, listening out for the telltale creak of the floor panels.

Eventually, he heard them. These weren't hesitant footsteps, made by a scared young man. These were confident, almost casual. Frank took some deep breaths and then exhaled slowly. Nothing but the shallowest of breathing from now on.

"Well, won't you look at this?"

The footsteps stopped.

"You boys been having fun?"

Silence.

"You could have died cleaner, that's for sure. You've left me a hell of a job. Should bring you back just so you can tidy up after yourselves."

Silence.

"That's not going to happen, though, is it? Deader than roadkill. Looks like I was the only one to bring a gun to a knife fight, so I guess I win. Right?"

The silence was punctuated by the sound of a meaty kick into some part of Zero.

"Ask you a question, boy. Am I right?"

The kicking carried on. Zero was still in no state to answer afterwards.

"Stupid idea, bringing criminals to do real men's work. Ain't that right, Frank?"

If Brack started on him, there was no chance of him being able to carry on with his deception. But perhaps the thought of treading more blood around the base put Brack off.

"It's all over now though, for sure. None of you chimps left. Got to make this place fit for decent human beings, and then I get off this godforsaken rock. You? I got something special planned for you. Just wait and see."

Zero received another kick.

"Better go tell Control that it's mission accomplished. Ain't no sweeter sound than that."

Brack giggled, and Frank almost surged up from the floor and attempted to strangle him there and then. But there were footsteps, going away again.

Then came back.

"You want to know how we knew what was going on? Do you want to know? We could see and hear everything you did and said. Privacy my ass. I was right there, looking over your shoulder, whenever I wanted. You never realized. Even the pervert didn't know. You never stood a chance."

The footsteps went away, and they stayed away this time.

At some point, Brack would be back to dispose of his body. Until then, Frank was presumed dead.

It looked like, despite what they'd all thought, what they'd been told, they'd been spied on, almost continuously. Unless that was exaggeration on Brack's part. The ten-minute-plus delay on information getting back to Earth was the kicker, and Dee had been certain that there was no continuous delivery of data. He'd packaged everything up, and sent it in chunks.

No hardwired microphones, according to Declan. The cameras only saw infrared, according to Dee. But there was always the medical monitors in their chests. If the devices were close enough to feel them breathing, they were close enough to hear their voices resonate through their bodies. And the cameras in the spacesuits. The cameras in the goddamn spacesuits.

And, of course, the only person who could monitor everything in real time was Brack. That was his job: to watch them, to check they hadn't got wise to what was really happening, and to kill them when they became expendable. That was what he spent his days and nights doing. Monitoring his charges, popping pills, reheating food.

He wouldn't be watching them now, though, because he thought they were all dead.

Frank had a narrow window of opportunity in which he could genuinely act without surveillance.

He peeled himself off the floor, and took a moment to try and shake some life back into his limbs. His arm ached with a dull throb, and it felt weak. There was nothing he could do about that, unless—he was, after all, in the med bay. He carefully opened one of the boxes and looked through the strips until he found the dihydrocodeine. He pushed one, then two pills into his hand, because he'd been shot and not just stubbed his toe. He dry-swallowed them down.

Then he tiptoed past the end of the corridor and slid down the ladder to retrieve his spacesuit.

As soon as Brack came back, he'd see what had happened. Or would he? Would he think that Frank had tricked him? Or would he, in his drugged-up, addicted state, think that Frank had risen from the dead and was going to enact his supernatural revenge on his tormentor?

He acknowledged that as unlikely. His son had been capable of rational thought: just not rational action. Frank climbed into his suit down on the lower level, powered it up, and climbed swiftly up and into the airlock.

Would pressing the cycle button send an alarm to Comms/Control? Possibly. He opened the hatch and worked the manual lever. The air inside the chamber bled out into the freezing Martian night, and thirty seconds later he was outside with it, on a platform slippery with ice.

Brack had turned off the buggy lights, and the sky was a brighter black than the ground. Stars and planets wheeled, and one of the moons crossed overhead in a swift and silent passage. The habs were undifferentiated blocks against the horizon, and he had to progress slowly, with only memory and touch as his guides.

But they were sure guides. He'd built this base with his own hands, laid it out and ordered its construction. He'd maintained it and modified it. He knew it like the creases in the palm of his hand, and he didn't stumble once.

The satellite dish was pointing almost straight up. He could see its shape against the stars as it tracked the orbit of the relay station above. He climbed the pylon and felt for the smaller microwave transmitter that connected the base to the ship. He pushed it out of alignment, then climbed down again to open up the little control panel on the side of the dish. The row of green lights burned steady.

He risked a quick dial-up of his suit lights so that he could see what he was attempting to sabotage. They were just trip switches; undoing the damage would take only a moment, but he needed Brack as isolated as he'd been. XO was going to be out of the loop from now on, until he decided what to do. Or he died.

Whichever, XO were going to lose contact with their man, and their Mars base. Their multi-billion dollar investment. Let them worry.

He flicked the switches from green to red, one after another, then closed the panel and killed his lights.

From there, he walked along the side of the yard, past the kitchen and the crew quarters, round the back of the base to the only part of it that was protected by two airlocks: the greenhouse. He manually vented the chamber, entered it and equalized the pressure with the inside.

The bright lights and the sound of running water, the banks of green leaves and the smell of freshness, of organic life, was a welcome change over the reek of stale sweat and dried blood. Zero would never see this again. Frank guessed it would be up to whoever lived to keep it running from now on.

He exited his suit, and splashed some of the nutrient-rich water dripping off the end of the trays onto his face and across the back of his neck. It was lukewarm, and it still felt cold on his skin. Everything was hyperreal, the lights stronger, the noises louder, the scents more pungent. It was like when he was being put to sleep in Building Two: it might be the last time he ever felt anything.

He knew he was never going to beat Brack in a straight-up fist fight. Especially not now he was injured and exhausted. Brack? He was well-rested, and even without the gun could whop his ass six ways to Sunday. He had to be military-trained, probably Special Forces at some point, and no one, least of all Frank, was expecting him to fight fair.

So he'd probably only get one chance, and he had to take it without hesitating. No mercy, which was as much mercy as he'd been shown. He'd killed two people now. This was surely the point where it got easier.

He needed a weapon. All he had was a scalpel covered in his own blood, but there wasn't really anything else. The gardening tools were all small: snips and shears and dibbers, as befitted a high-tech hydroponic set-up. No shovels or long-handled rakes, which would have been so very useful.

The scalpel would have to do.

He looked through the little airlock window into the cross-hab area. There was movement, and he ducked back. If he'd been seen, it'd be over. But it was unlikely, and he risked another glance.

That pale shape bobbing around in his eyeline had to be the back of Brack's spacesuit. He was going out to see what was wrong with the transmitter.

It would mean he'd be deaf and blind to everything happening behind him. Frank knew what that was like. Now. Do it now.

He vented the inner chamber into the greenhouse, and opened the door. He kept his eye on what was happening through the window. Brack was also cycling the airlock, but it took longer to pump down than using the manual releases. He'd beat him to it. Beat him to the punch.

Frank closed the door behind him, vented the main hab air into the chamber. Mere seconds later the outer door was free, since the pressure was already almost identical. He opened the door just as Brack stepped forward into the open airlock in front of him.

He was fifteen feet away. Enough distance to pick up some speed. Frank slammed into Brack's back and catapulted him through the open door and down the length of the airlock, into the door at the far end. He hit it hard and the confined space boomed. Before he could turn, before he could do anything, Frank was in with him, grabbing his ankles and jerking them backwards.

Brack went down, face-first, sprawling, and Frank went to work with the scalpel. He'd seen it done before, several times, and had subconsciously absorbed the how.

Remembering to keep his thumb on the top of the short handle, he stabbed down, hard, repeatedly, into the back of Brack's thighs, puncturing the cloth and the airtight membrane and the skin and muscle beneath, not wasting time slicing, just in-out, in-out. The shock, the pain, the speed of the attack, was deliberately excessive, disorientating, vicious, and savage. Both legs, up and down between knee and buttock.

He could hear Brack roaring. He could see him try to reach up and slap the airlock cycle button in order to free the outer door and the only possible direction of escape, but since the inner door was still open, it wouldn't function.

Frank clenched the bloody handle between his teeth and, taking Brack's ankles again, pulled him half-into the cross-hab. His legs and lower torso were outside the airlock. His shoulders and head were still inside. He still had no idea who or what was attacking him.

Frank cut into Brack's calves with the same rapid movement, pressing hard to force the blade deeper. Brack's only response was to slap the floor and flail his arms and scream in a high-pitched keening wail. His legs would only twitch and spasm. He seemed to have lost control of them completely.

Had Frank done enough? His hands were slick with sweat and blood, and he was panting in the rarefied atmosphere. But the iron rule of prison fighting was to put the other guy down and make sure he stayed down. If you let him up, you lost.

The life-support rack was behind him. The spare oxygen cylinders were plugged in next to them. Frank snatched one up and went back to slam it repeatedly into Brack's back and shoulders. The casing to the rear hatch starred, then broke. He drove the cylinder against the crack and kept on going like he was piledriving a fence post. Now that was honest, solid labor, not this butcher's work.

He could hear the alarms sounding inside Brack's suit as he pounded away. He was destroying the life support, damaging the control systems, crushing the filters and the valves. Brack was still trying to rise on his hands, and every blow knocked him back down. At least the screaming had stopped, and had been replaced by a grunt each time the cylinder descended.

Brack went limp. Now he'd done enough.

Frank pulled Brack all the way out into the cross-hab and heaved him over onto his back. Perhaps he was dead. Frank knew better than to trust that.

He smashed the faceplate in with repeated blows, and knocked the edges of the plastic away. As the fresh air blew in, Brack's face twisted into a grimace.

So, not dead yet.

Frank took him by the ankles again and pulled him through the habs: the kitchen, the yard, and into Comms. There was the gun, resting next to the console.

Frank sat in the chair and picked it up. It had been modified so that it didn't have a trigger guard, so that Brack could fire it while wearing a spacesuit. It also made it laughably simple to accidentally discharge.

He aimed the gun downwards at the floor, between his knees, and kept his fingers well away from the mechanism. It was strange, after so long, to be holding the reason why he was even on Mars. A gun. They made killing so easy. Not like knives. You really had to mean it with knives. Just look at how much effort he'd put into killing Zero, and now Brack.

And he was tired, too. Even more than before. The thin, cold air was taking its toll. Better end this now, then, and get some rest.

He stretched his leg out and kicked the sole of Brack's boot.

"Hey. Hey, Brack. Wake up. It's over."

Was it over? Not really. It never would be. But this part of it was.

Brack blinked and stared at the ceiling. The top half of him hadn't really suffered at all. Asphyxiation, severe bruising, but nothing was broken, nothing was ruined. Not like his legs. The heroic quantities of opioids in his system were probably keeping him alive as well as dulling the pain, too, just like they were for Frank at a lesser degree.

Brack fumbled for his suit controls, but when he tried to open the back hatch, nothing would move.

"It's not going to happen, Brack. You're stuck in that suit. I could get some tools from the workshop and try and cut you out. But I'm not going to risk the spark."

Brack let his hands fall to his sides.

"You."

"Me. Good old Frank. Frank the murderer. Three times over now. It looks like, in all this, neither of us quite realized how much I wanted to live, how much I wanted to go home, and the things I'd do to make that happen. I surprised myself. Sure

325

as hell surprised you. Maybe you should have killed me first, instead of Marcy."

"They'll get you."

"Will they? Will they really? It's a very long way to come, just for one old lag."

"Your wife. Your son."

Frank looked at the gun in his hand, tested the weight of it. Because it was Mars, it was less heavy than it ought to be. How was it that something so light could cause so much damage?

Of course, he was never going to fire it inside the hab. Not only would the fire extinguishers trigger, he'd end up putting a round through the wall. It felt right to be holding it, though. The most powerful man in the room needed to be holding the gun.

"Now that's a difficult one, isn't it? What do you suggest? What's the best way of protecting them now, given that all the promises you gave me about going home in return for watching your back were just bullshit. You made the same promise to every single one of us, didn't you? It kept us all in line. It kept us from challenging you. It kept us hoping. That's the bit that really sucks, especially when you, and XO, had planned to kill us off all along."

"You can save me."

"Alice could have saved you. But you killed her." Frank scratched at his chin. "Me? I'm pretty certain I can't. You didn't train me for that. Didn't train me for a lot of things. Just enough to be useful, not enough to realize how vulnerable we were." He leaned forward, resting his elbows on his knees. "One thing I have learned: I've been denying that I'm a killer for ten years. There's not been a day that's passed when I haven't said that to myself. 'Frank, you're not a killer.' Turns out that I was wrong. I've got something inside me that says it's OK to kill if I have to. That puts me much closer to you than I'm comfortable with, because I really don't want to be like you."

"I'll tell XO to …"

Brack stopped mid-sentence with a gasp, and Frank kicked his foot again.

"What? What will you tell XO to do? Come and rescue us? Not kill my ex-wife and my kid? Do you think they care about anyone but themselves? Look at us. Goddammit, Brack, just look at the state of us. Look what they've done to us. This is what happens when you fuck up as badly as we have. We are in Hell."

Brack shook his head, as if trying to shake something from his ears. Perhaps he was just trying to dislodge fragments of broken faceplate. He rallied.

"You can still go home. Just keep me alive."

"You have to understand something. You were right. The others. They weren't my friends. I wasn't theirs. We got on, and that's the best I can say about it. You gave us a job, and we did it, and we did it well, despite everything. Despite the crappy planning and the missing supplies and whatever happened to our personal effects. So we did everything you asked us to." Frank looked at the gun in his hands. "And this is how you were always going to repay us. You were always going to kill us. Maybe you were leaving me till last because you knew I actually trusted you and believed you when you told me you were going to take me home, no matter how badly you'd treated me in the meantime: but you were going to kill me in the end. I don't understand why. I don't understand why XO would have done any of this. But they have. And you agreed to it all."

Brack was reduced to panting, and Frank carefully put the gun back down on the console. He got up out of his chair, walked around the spreading pool of blood, and knelt down beside Brack's head.

"The others didn't deserve this. But I do. I know you brought me here to kill me. But I allowed myself to be brought. I am my own worst enemy. I get it now. I finally get it."

Brack stared up at him, past him, his eyes unable to focus and skittering about in their orbits.

"You'll never see your son again."

"Fine words," said Frank. He patted Brack's shoulder. "Words to remember you by. All your hate and bitterness and poison, summed up in one sentence. You're probably right: I never will. But I'm still not going to let you die alone, because no one deserves that. Not even you."

He forced his hand into Brack's, and felt a grip tighten against his. For a while, it was just the sound of their breathing. Frank's, patient and steady. Brack's, shallow and with increasing spaces between each exhale.

Then Frank found himself listening for a breath that never came. He gave Brack's hand one last squeeze, and extricated his fingers. He went to sit back in the chair, and waited, in silence, alone.

Coda

[Message sent 11/12/2048 MBO Rahe to MBO Mission Control]

This is Franklin Kittridge. From the start, let's get one thing absolutely straight. I will destroy this base and everything in it if you try anything. Any hostile act, anything that looks like sabotage, against me or the base's systems, and I'll tear this place apart. No clean-up. Nothing. I'll just leave it all for the next people to find, and you can explain everything to them.

I know what you did. I know about the robots. I know about bringing us here in place of them, and I know about killing us all off. If you try and deny any of this, you might just make me mad enough to want to trash the base anyway. So don't. I've got all the Phase 3 docs.

I'm prepared, despite everything, to cut a deal with you. I have something you want—your billion-dollar base, and your secrets. You have something I want—my freedom and a lift home. I think that's more than fair, since you'll be getting more out of this than I will. If this goes south, a lot of you reading this message will end up on death row. And you know it.

So this is what I'm willing to do for you. I'm willing to carry out your Phase 3. I'll clean up the base, look after it like you were expecting Brack to, and wait for the NASA people to arrive. When they do, I'll pretend to be Brack, and keep things running smoothly. I'm not looking to rock the boat.

329

I don't know what you promised Brack, but I'm guessing it's a suitcase full of dollar bills and a lifetime of silence. I'll take that, and a commutation: time served will do. I'm not looking for parole, or early release on license. I want to be done with it. A clean start. Obviously, I get Brack's place for the flight home. I'll play along with the deception as long as you do. When I get back to Earth, you give me my money and my paperwork, and that's it: that's the only contact I want or need from you. You leave me alone after that.

One last thing. If you threaten, attempt to threaten, or in any way mention, my family in these negotiations, I will burn this base to the ground, without hesitation or thought about myself. I hope that's really clear, because I'll do it, and I need you to know that. This deal is between you and me and it doesn't involve anyone else.

Take your time. I'm not going anywhere in a hurry, no thanks to you. But don't take too long, because I'm not lifting a finger to help you until we come to an agreement we can both stick to.

The story continues in...

NO WAY

Coming in February 2019!

extras

orbit

meet the author

DR. S. J. MORDEN has won the Philip K. Dick Award and been a judge on the Arthur C. Clarke award committee. He is a bona fide rocket scientist with degrees in geology and planetary geophysics. *One Way* is the perfect fusion of his incredible breadth of knowledge and ability to write award-winning, razor-sharp science fiction.

if you enjoyed
ONE WAY

look out for

THE CORPORATION WARS: DISSIDENCE

by

Ken MacLeod

Sentient machines work, fight, and die in interstellar exploration and conflict for the benefit of their owners—the competing mining corporations of Earth. But sent over hundreds of light-years, commands are late to arrive and often hard to enforce. The machines must make their own decisions, and make them stick.

With this new-found autonomy come new questions about their masters. The robots want answers. The companies would rather see them dead.

337

extras

*They've died for the companies more times
than they can remember. Now they must fight to
live for themselves.*

CHAPTER ONE

Back in the Day

Carlos the Terrorist did not expect to die that day. The bombing was heavy now, and close, but he thought his location safe. Leaky pipework dripping with obscure post-industrial feedstock products riddled the ruined nanofacturing plant at Tilbury. Watchdog machines roved its basement corridors, pouncing on anything that moved—a fallen polystyrene tile, a draught-blown paper cone from a dried-out water-cooler—with the mindless malice of kittens chasing flies. Ten metres of rock, steel and concrete lay between the ceiling above his head and the sunlight where the rubble bounced.

He lolled on a reclining chair and with closed eyes watched the battle. His viewpoint was a thousand metres above where he lay. With empty hands he marshalled his forces and struck his blows.

Incoming—

Something he glimpsed as a black stone hurtled towards him. With a fist-clench faster than reflex he hurled a handful of smart munitions at it.

The tiny missiles missed.

Carlos twisted, and threw again. On target this time. The black incoming object became a flare of white that faded as his camera drones stepped down their inputs, correcting for the flash like irises contracting. The small missiles that had missed a moment earlier now showered mid-air sparks and puffs of smoke a kilometre away.

From his virtual vantage Carlos felt and saw like a monster in a Japanese disaster movie, straddling the Thames and punching out. Smoke rose from a score of points on the London skyline. Drone swarms darkened the day. Carlos's combat drones engaged the enemy's in buzzing dogfights. Ionised air crackled around his imagined monstrous body in sudden searing beams along which, milliseconds later, lightning bolts fizzed and struck. Tactical updates flickered across his sight.

Higher above, the heavy hardware—helicopters, fighter jets and hovering aerial drone platforms—loitered on station and now and then called down their ordnance with casual precision. Higher still, in low Earth orbit, fleets of tumbling battle-sats jockeyed and jousted, spearing with laser bursts that left their batteries drained and their signals dead.

Swarms of camera drones blipped fragmented views to millimetre-scale camouflaged receiver beads littered in thousands across the contested ground. From these, through proxies, firewalls, relays and feints the images and messages flashed, converging to an onsite router whose radio waves tickled the spike, a metal stud in the back of Carlos's skull. That occipital implant's tip feathered to a fractal array of neural interfaces that worked their molecular magic to integrate the view straight to his visual cortex, and to process and transmit the motor impulses that flickered from fingers sheathed in skin-soft plastic gloves veined with feedback sensors to the fighter drones and malware servers. It was the new way of war, back in the day.

extras

*   *   *

The closest hot skirmish was down on Carlos's right. In Dagenham, tank units of the London Metropolitan Police battled robotic land-crawlers suborned by one or more of the enemy's basement warriors. Like a thundercloud on the horizon tensing the air, an awareness of the strategic situation loomed at the back of Carlos's mind.

Executive summary: looking good for his side, bad for the enemy.

But only for the moment.

The enemy—the Reaction, the Rack, the Rax—had at last provoked a response from the serious players. Government forces on three continents were now smacking down hard. Carlos's side—the Acceleration, the Axle, the Ax—had taken this turn of circumstance as an oblique invitation to collaborate with these governments against the common foe. Certain state forces had reciprocated. The arrangement was less an alliance than a mutual offer with a known expiry date. There were no illusions. Everyone who mattered had studied the same insurgency and counter-insurgency textbooks.

In today's fight Carlos had a designated handler, a deep-state operative who called him-, her- or itself Innovator, and who (to personalise it, as Carlos did, for politeness and the sake of argument) now and then murmured suggestions that made their way to Carlos's hearing via a warily accepted hack in the spike that someday soon he really would have to do something about.

Carlos stood above Greenhithe. He sighted along a virtual outstretched arm and upraised thumb at a Rax hellfire drone above Purfleet, and made his throw. An air-to-air missile streaked from behind his POV towards the enemy fighter. It left a corkscrew trail of evasive manoeuvres and delivered a viscerally satisfying flash and a shower of blazing debris when it hit.

"Nice one," said Innovator, in an admiring tone and feminine voice.

Somebody in GCHQ had been fine-tuning the psychology, Carlos reckoned.

"Uh-huh," he grunted, looking around in a frenzy of target acquisition and not needing the distraction. He sighted again, this time at a tracked vehicle clambering from the river into the Rainham marshes, and threw again. Flash and splash.

"Very neat," said Innovator, still admiring but with a grudging undertone. "But...we have a bigger job for you. Urgent. Upriver."

"Oh yes?"

"Jaunt your POV ten klicks forward, now!"

The sudden sharper tone jolted Carlos into compliance. With a convulsive twitch of the cheek and a kick of his right leg he shifted his viewpoint to a camera drone array, 9.7 kilometres to the west. What felt like a single stride of his gigantic body image took him to the stubby runways of London City Airport, face-to-face with Docklands. A gleaming cluster of spires of glass. From emergency exits, office workers streamed like black and white ants. Anyone left in the towers would be hardcore Rax. The place was notorious.

"What now?" Carlos asked.

"That plane on approach," said Innovator. It flagged up a dot above central London. "Take it down."

Carlos read off the flight number. "Shanghai Airlines Cargo? That's civilian!"

"It's chartered to the Kong, bringing in aid to the Rax. We've cleared the hit with Beijing through back-channels, they're cheering us on. Take it down."

Carlos had one high-value asset not yet in play, a stealthed drone platform with a heavy-duty air-to-air missile. A quick survey showed him three others like it in the sky, all RAF.

"Do it yourselves," he said.

"No time. Nothing available."

This was a lie. Carlos suspected Innovator knew he knew.

It was all about diplomacy and deniability: shooting down a Chinese civilian jet, even a cargo one and suborned to China's version of the Rax, was unlikely to sit well in Beijing. The Chinese government might have given a covert go-ahead, but in public their response would have to be stern. How convenient for the crime to be committed by a non-state actor! Especially as the Axle was the next on every government's list to suppress...

The plane's descent continued, fast and steep. Carlos ran calculations.

"The only way I can take the shot is right over Docklands. The collateral will be fucking atrocious."

"That," said Innovator grimly, "is the general idea."

Carlos prepped the platform, then balked again. "No."

"You must!" Innovator's voice became a shrill gabble in his head. "This is ethically acceptable on all parameters utilitarian consequential deontological just war theoretical and..."

So Innovator was an AI after all. That figured.

Shells were falling directly above him now, blasting the ruined refinery yet further and sending shockwaves through its underground levels. Carlos could feel the thuds of the incoming fire through his own real body, in that buried basement miles back behind his POV. He could vividly imagine some pasty-faced banker running military code through a screen of financials, directing the artillery from one of the towers right in front of him. The aircraft was now more than a dot. Flaps dug in to screaming air. The undercarriage lowered. If he'd zoomed, Carlos could have seen the faces in the cockpit.

"No," he said.

"You must," Innovator insisted.

"Do your own dirty work."

"Like yours hasn't been?" The machine's voice was now sardonic. "Well, not to worry. We can do our own dirty work if we have to."

From behind Carlos's virtual shoulder a rocket streaked. His gaze followed it all the way to the jet.

It was as if Docklands had blown up in his face. Carlos reeled back, jaunting his POV sharply to the east. The aircraft hadn't just been blown up. Its cargo had blown up too. One tower was already down. A dozen others were on fire. The smoke blocked his view of the rest of London. He'd expected collateral damage, reckoned it in the balance, but this weight of destruction was off the scale. If there was any glass or skin unbroken in Docklands, Carlos hadn't the time or the heart to look for it.

"You didn't tell me the aid was *ordnance!*" His protest sounded feeble even to himself.

"We took your understanding of that for granted," said Innovator. "You have permission to stand down now."

"I'll stand down when I want," said Carlos. "I'm not one of *your* soldiers."

"Damn right you're not one of our soldiers. You're a terrorist under investigation for a war crime. I would advise you to surrender to the nearest available—"

"What!"

"Sorry," said Innovator, sounding genuinely regretful. "We're pulling the plug on you now. Bye, and all that."

"You can't fucking *do* that."

343

Carlos didn't mean he thought them incapable of such perfidy. He meant he didn't think they had the software capability to pull it off.

They did.

The next thing he knew his POV was right back behind his eyes, back in the refinery basement. He blinked hard. The spike was still active, but no longer pulling down remote data. He clenched a fist. The spike wasn't sending anything either. He was out of the battle and *hors de combat*.

Oh well. He sighed, opened his eyes with some difficulty—his long-closed eyelids were sticky—and sat up. His mouth was parched. He reached for the can of cola on the floor beside the recliner, and gulped. His hand shook as he put the drained can down on the frayed sisal matting. A shell exploded on the ground directly above him, the closest yet. Carlos guessed the army or police artillery were adding their more precise targeting to the ongoing bombardment from the Rax. Another deep breath brought a faint trace of his own sour stink on the stuffy air. He'd been in this small room for days—how many he couldn't be sure without checking, but he guessed almost a week. Not all the invisible toil of his clothes' molecular machinery could keep unwashed skin clean that long.

Another thump overhead. The whole room shook. Sinister cracking noises followed, then a hiss. Carlos began to think of fleeing to a deeper level. He reached for his emergency backpack of kit and supplies. The ceiling fell on him. Carlos struggled under an I-beam and a shower of fractured concrete. He couldn't move any of it. The hiss became a torrential roar. White vapour filled the room, freezing all it touched. Carlos's eyes frosted over. His last breath was so unbearably cold it cracked his throat. He choked on frothing blood. After a few seconds of convulsive reflex thrashing, he lost consciousness. Brain death followed within minutes.

if you enjoyed
ONE WAY
look out for

ANNEX
The Violet Wars

by

Rich Larson

At first it is a nightmare. When the invaders arrive, the world as they know it is destroyed. Their friends are kidnapped. Their families are changed.

Then it is a dream. With no adults left to run things, Violet and the others who have escaped capture are truly free for the first time. They can do whatever they want to do. They can be whoever they want to be.

But the invaders won't leave them alone for long....

1

The pharmacy's sign was burnt out and the windows all smashed in—Violet had done one herself—but there were still three customers standing gamely in line. She stepped around them, shoes squealing on the broken glass, and headed for the counter. None of the three wasters noticed her butting in. They didn't notice much of anything, not their torn clothes or singed hair or bloody feet. The slick black clamp at the base of their skulls saw to that. Violet tried not to look too closely at wasters. Peripherals only, was her rule. If she looked too closely, she was liable to see someone she recognized.

Of course, she made an exception for the pharmacist. "Oh, hi!" she said, feigning surprise. "I think you helped me last week, right?"

The pharmacist said nothing, moving his hands in the air a foot over from the register, his glazed-over eyes trained on something that wasn't there. His beard was hugely overgrown, but Violet had sort of a thing for the mountain man look. He was still tall and muscly, though in a wiry way now, because wasters forgot to eat more often than not. Still handsome.

"Well, if I'm an addict, you're my dealer, jerk," Violet said, cocking her hips and trying to flutter her eyelashes without looking like she'd detached a retina. She was getting better at it. Maybe she would try it on Wyatt soon.

The pharmacist said nothing, now pulling imaginary pill bottles out of an empty metal cupboard Violet had already ransacked. His vacant half smile didn't seem as charming today. Violet gave a sour shrug and tossed her duffel bag over the counter, then nimbly followed.

"That's our problem...Dennis," she said, leaning in to read the red plastic name tag stuck through his shirt. "You're a shitty communicator. We're not going to last."

Violet gave the pharmacist a consoling pat on the arm, then unzipped her duffel and set to work. Wyatt had told her to get antibiotics and painkillers, and since Violet knew her way around from last time, it didn't take her long to fill the duffel with Tylenol-4s, ibuprofen, three rattling canisters of Cipro, and a bottle of liquid codeine. Wyatt was strict about who got the medicine ever since one of the younger Lost Boys made himself sick chugging cough syrup, and he never used it himself, never took a single pill, even though Violet knew the scar along his hips made him wince sometimes.

Violet wasn't interested in painkillers. She had more important drugs to look for. She rifled through the birth control until she found her estradiol—Estrofem this time—then emptied the tablets into her own private ziplock stash. She hunted for more Aldactone but didn't find any. The spiro would have to wait.

She rattled the plastic baggie, eyeing the candy-shop assortment of pills and counting days, then pincered a pale green Estrofem and swallowed it dry. Her Parasite rippled in response, whether with pleasure or revulsion, Violet never knew. She folded the baggie carefully into the bottom of her duffel bag with the other meds and dragged the zipper shut.

"Well, I *might* be free for coffee this weekend," Violet told the pharmacist, slinging the duffel over her bony shoulder.

"But I can't give you my number because, you know, an alien invasion fried all the phones. No, I swear to God. Maybe next time, handsome."

She scooted across the counter and dropped down on the other side, brushing a slice of dark hair out of her face. The wasters ignored her on her way out, all of them still standing patiently in line.

Violet kept them in her peripherals.

2

Bo was hiding behind a powerjack, only meters from the fire door and the emergency exit sign glowing above it through the gloom. The Parasite in his stomach wriggled madly. He held his hand to the icy concrete floor; when the flesh of his palm was stinging cold, he pressed it against his stomach. That helped soothe it a bit.

The electricity had gone out earlier that day, dropping the grimy corridors and sleeping rooms into darkness, and Bo wasn't going to waste his chance. He'd snuck out of his bed while a boy named James was wailing and weeping loud enough to make the whirlybird drift over to him with its sleep-inducing syringe. A few of the other kids had watched Bo slip away, but he'd put a fierce finger to his lips and none of them had seemed particularly interested anyways. Most of them drank the water.

His older sister, Lia, was the one who'd realized that they put something in the water that made you feel dull and happy, and that it was better to collect drips off pipes in the bathroom. She was thirteen to Bo's eleven and she usually did the thinking. But she was gone now.

So Bo had found his way through the dark corridor alone, running one hand along the pitted concrete wall and its retrofitted wires, making his way toward the emergency exit that led outside. Now he was waiting for the last group of kids to go from supper to bed, trying to breathe slowly and keep the Parasite in check.

A familiar whine filled the air, then a whirlybird emerged from the corridor. It was as big around the middle as Bo and drifted along at head height, like a balloon, except made of slick rubbery flesh and gleaming black metal and other things he couldn't guess at. A tangle of spidery multi-jointed arms dangled down from its underbelly, flexing slowly in the air, and there was a bright acid-yellow lantern set into the top of its carapace that illuminated the kids plodding behind it.

As always, Bo scanned their faces. Everyone's eyes were turned to deep dark shadows by the sickly yellow glow, and everyone was stepping slow and dreamy-like. For a moment he fooled himself into thinking he saw Lia near the back of the file, faking the effects of the water, because there was no way she'd started drinking it, but it was a different black girl. Shorter, and lighter-skinned.

He knew Lia was in some other facility. They'd been split up weeks ago. But it didn't stop him from looking.

The whirlybird floated past and Bo imagined himself springing at it, seizing one of its trailing limbs, smashing it against the floor, and stomping until it cracked open. The Parasite in his stomach stirred at the thought. But his wrists and hands were still crisscrossed with feather-white scars from the first and last time he'd tried that.

Instead, he waited until the glow of the whirlybird receded into the dark and the last of the kids got swallowed up in the shadows.

Bo was alone. His heart hammered his ribs and the Parasite gave another twitch. He levered himself upright, crept out from behind the powerjack. Three surreal strides and he was at the door, hands gripping the bar.

A girl named Ferris had tried to open it before, and the wailing of the alarm had drawn the whirlybirds in an instant. But with the electricity out, there would be no alarm and no fifteen-second delay on the crash bar. Bo still made himself pause for an instant to listen, to be sure there wasn't a whirlybird drifting on the other side of the paint-flaking metal. He heard nothing except the toddlers who'd been crying ever since the lights went out. With a tight feeling in his throat, Bo pushed.

The door swung open with a clunk and a screech, and cold clean air rushed into his lungs like the first breath after a storm. He'd been in the chemical-smelling warehouse for so long he'd forgotten how fresh air tasted. Bo gasped at it.

He took a shaky step forward, only just remembering to catch the door before it slammed behind him. He tried to focus. He was in a long narrow alley, garbage whipping around his feet and graffiti marching along the soot-stained walls. Bo knew, dimly, that the warehouses they'd been put in were near the docks. The briny sea-smell confirmed that much. He was far, far from their old neighborhood, and he didn't know if it even existed anymore.

Bo looked up. The dusk sky seemed impossibly wide after months of fluorescent-lit ceilings, but it wasn't empty. Unfurling over the city like an enormous black umbrella, all moving spars and flanges, was the ship. It didn't look like a spaceship to Bo, not how he'd seen them in movies. It didn't look like it should even be able to fly.

But it drifted there overhead, light as air. Bo remembered it spitting a rain of sizzling blue bombs down on the city, burning the park behind their house to white ash, toppling the skyscrapers downtown. And up there with the ship, wheeling slow circles, Bo saw the mechanical whale-like things that had snatched up him and his sister and all the other kids and taken them to the warehouses. Remembering it put a shock of sweat in his armpits, and his stomach gave a fearful churn. The Parasite churned with it.

Bo started down the alley at a trot before the panic could paralyze him. He didn't know where to go, but he knew he needed to put distance between himself and the warehouse. As much distance as possible. Then he would find somewhere to hide. Find something to eat—real food, not the gray glue they ate in the warehouses. He had been fantasizing about pepperoni pizza lately, or, even better, his mom's cooking, the things she made for special occasions: *shinkafa da wake*, with oily onions and the spicy *yaji* powder that made Lia's eyes water so bad, and fried plantains.

That made him think of his mom again, so he buried the memory, how he had for months now, and picked up his pace to a jog. The Parasite throbbed in his stomach and he felt a static charge under his skin, making the hairs stand up from the nape of his neck. That happened more often lately, and always when Bo was angry or frightened or excited. He imagined himself smashing a whirlybird out of the air right as it went to jab his sister with the syringe, and her thanking him, and admitting that if he had his shoes on he was faster than her now. He pictured himself opening the doors and all the other kids streaming out of the warehouse.

A harsh yellow light froze him to the spot. Shielding his watering eyes, Bo looked up and saw the silhouette of a whale-thing descending through the dark sky. He took an experimental step to the left. The beam of light tracked him. The whale-thing was close enough that he could hear its awful chugging sound, half like an engine, half like a dying animal trying to breathe. Bo was never going inside one again.

He ran.

After four months in the warehouse, four months of plodding slowly behind the whirlybird because anything quicker than a walk agitated them, Bo felt slow. His breath hitched early behind his chest and he had an unfamiliar ache in his shoulder. But as the whale-thing dropped lower, its chugging sound loud in his ears, adrenaline plowed through all of that and he found his rhythm, flying across the pavement, pumping hard.

Fastest in his grade, faster than Lia. He said it in his head like a chant. Faster than anybody.

Bo tore down the alley with a wild shout, halfway between a laugh and a scream. His battered Lottos, tread long gone, slapped hard to the ground. He could feel his heart shooting through his throat, and the Parasite was writhing and crackling in his belly. The static again, putting his hair on end. He could feel the huge shape of the whale-thing surging over him. Its acid-yellow light strobed the alley, slapping his shadows on each wall of it, moving their blurry black limbs in sync with his. Bo raced them.

Faster than his own shadow.

He blew out the end of the alley and across the cracked tarmac of a parking lot, seeing the yellow-stenciled lines and trying to take one space with each stride. Impossibly, he could feel the whale-thing falling back, slowing down. Its hot air was no longer pounding on his back. Bo didn't let himself slow down, because Lia said you were always meant to pick a spot beyond the finish line and make that your finish line.

The fence seemed to erupt from nowhere. Bo's eyes widened, but it was too late to stop. He hurtled toward it, more certain with each footfall that he wasn't going to be able to scale it. It wasn't the chain-link that he used to scramble up and down gecko-quick. It wasn't metal at all, more like a woven tangle of vines, or maybe veins, every part of it pulsing. A few of the tendrils stretched out toward him, sensing him. Ready to snatch him and hold him and give him back to the warehouse.

He couldn't stop. The whale-thing was still chugging along behind him, hemming him in. Bo had to get out. Bo had to get out, he had to get help. He had to come back for his sister and for the others, even the ones who cried too much. His throat was clenched around a sob as he hurled himself at the fence, remembering Ferris being dragged away by the whirlybirds. His limbs were shaking; the Parasite was vibrating him, like a battery in his stomach. He squeezed his eyes shut.

There was a shiver, a ripple, a strange pulse that passed through every inch of him, and he didn't feel the fence's tentacles wrapping him tight. He didn't feel anything until he collapsed onto the tarmac on the other side, scraping his left elbow raw. Bo's eyes flew open. He spun around, still on the ground, and stared at the fence. In the dead center of it was a jagged hole, punched straight through. The fence wriggled around it, fingering the hole like a wound.

Bo clambered to his feet, panting. He wiped the ooze of blood off his elbow, nearly relishing the sting of it—he hadn't been properly scraped up for months. Then he put his hand on his stomach. The static was gone, like it had never been at all, and the Parasite felt suddenly heavy, no longer twitching or moving. Had he done that? Had he made the hole?

The whale-thing was stopped on the other side of it, and it didn't have a face but he got the sense it was as surprised as he was. Bo gave an instinctive glance around for grown-ups, even though he knew he wouldn't see any, then flipped it the bird. The whale-thing didn't respond, still hovering in place. Then a strange moaning noise came from inside of it. Bo watched as the whale-thing's underbelly peeled open. Something slimey and dark started unfolding itself, then dropped to the paving with a thick wet slap. It was human-shaped.

Bo felt a tiny trickle of piss finally squeeze out down his leg. The human shape moaned again, and that was enough to give Bo his second wind. He turned and ran again, the cut on his elbow singing in the cold night air, the Parasite sitting like lead in his gut. But he was out of the warehouse, and he wasn't going to let them take him again, not ever. When he came back, it would be to get Lia, and the others, and to smash every last whirlybird in the place.

It was the only way to be sure he got the one that had pinned him down that first day and injected the Parasite right through his belly button.

Bo made it his new pact as he jogged, deeper and deeper, into the dark and ruined city.

Violet was heading to Safeway to pick up some groceries, walking down a silent street under a cloudy gray sky. Gray as the day the ship came down, scorching the city with the electric blue pulses Wyatt said were exhaust from its engines. There'd been no sun since. Just gray, a hazy emulsion that looked close to rain but never gave it up. Violet didn't mind the new weather. Sun burned her and rain made everything too wet.

She walked down the middle of the street instead of the sidewalk, weaving through the stalled-out cars. Some had wasters sitting inside, imagining themselves driving off to work, but most of the cars didn't work anyway. Their chips were fried. The ones that did work were useless, what with the roads so clogged and nobody really knowing how to drive besides.

The intersection ahead was stoppered up with the splintered

geometry of a crash, a three-car pile-up that had happened during the big panic when the ship came down. Violet didn't want to walk around it, so she clambered up onto the accordion-scrunched hood of an SUV. The soles of her Skechers popped little dents in the aluminum. She tried to ignore the dead-thing smell that wafted from the backseat.

On the other side of the wreck, she faced a corner liquor store, half of it black and crumbled from an electrical fire, and then beyond it her destination: the Safeway where she'd shopped with her mom four months and a lifetime ago. The parking lot was strewn with garbage, picked at by a flock of dirty gulls, and wasters shuffled slowly around it with grocery bags that Violet knew were sometimes full, sometimes empty. Some of them were pushing squeaky shopping carts across the ruptured tarmac.

But one of the carts wasn't being pushed by a waster. Violet narrowed her eyes. It was a boy, maybe ten or eleven, skinny frame swallowed in an oversize hoodie. She watched him roll his sleeves up to his elbows, one of which was swatched with Technicolor Band-Aids, and start wrestling with the cart again. He'd picked one with sticky wheels, but it had alright stuff in it: a sleeping bag, a trussed-up Styrofoam mattress, canned food, and bottled water. Usually kids fresh out of the warehouse were too dopey to do much more than wander around all shell-shocked.

Violet swapped the duffel to her other shoulder and cut across the culvert of yellowed grass to the parking lot pavement. By the time she was close to him, the boy had snatched an empty cart from one of the wasters and was dumping everything from his own into the replacement.

"Hey," Violet said. "Those Winnie the Pooh Band-Aids?"

The boy looked up, startled. The hood fell back off his head and Violet could see his face still had a bit of chub to it, the kid-

die kind, but his eyes were sharp. A little bloodshot from crying, but focused. His black hair reminded her of a ball of steel
wool, and she could see a comb mostly buried in the tangle. He
yanked his sleeve down over the yellow patchwork on his elbow
and stared back at her for a moment, mouth working for words.

"You're not a zombie," he finally said, in a voice that was a
little closer to cracking than she'd expected from someone his
size. It made her extra conscious of her own.

"Nobody's a zombie," Violet said, as the waster he'd swapped
carts with stumbled past. "They don't eat brains or anything.
Just wander around being useless. We call them wasters."

"Where'd you come from?" the boy asked.

Violet peeled the stretchy fabric of her shirt up off her stomach, showing him the rust-red Parasite under her pale skin.
The boy immediately stuck his hand to his own belly. His face
twitched.

"Same as you, Pooh Bear," Violet said, tugging her shirt
back down. "You thought you were the only one who got out?"

The boy frowned. "Is everyone else…Is all the grown-ups…"
He tapped the back of his head, where the clamps went in.

"Everyone over sixteen," Violet said. "Or around there." She
reached over and yanked the sleeping bag and a single bottle of
water out from the cart. "What's your name?" she asked.

"Bo," the boy said. "Bo Rabiu."

"Violet." She stuffed the sleeping bag into his arms and
tossed the bottle on top with a slosh. Getting groceries could
wait. "Alright, Bo, time to get out of the streets," she said. "The
othermothers are going to start coming through soon."

"What?"

"The o-ther mo-thers," Violet enunciated. "You'll see one
soon enough. For now, we're going to a safe spot, alright? A
hideout. So you can meet Wyatt."

Bo tucked the sleeping bag under his arm and tossed the water bottle up and down with his other hand. "Who's he?" he asked suspiciously.

"He's a jerk," Violet said. "Let's go."

She set off back out of the parking lot, mapping the way back to the theater in her mind's eye. She didn't bother to check if Bo was following. They always did.

Follow us:

f /orbitbooksUS

🐦 /orbitbooks

▶ /orbitbooks

Join our mailing list
to receive alerts on our
latest releases and deals.

orbitbooks.net

Enter our monthly
giveaway for the chance
to win some epic prizes.

orbitloot.com